Undeniably Wrong

A Phoebe Braddock Fiction

L. STARLA

To request permission, contact the author:
laelia@starlaarts.com

Graphics & book design by L. Starla
Cover art purchased under licence from Adobe Stock
Editing by J. Wake

First edition 2022.

ISBN-13: (paperback) 978-0-6452783-3-0
ISBN-13: (eBook) 978-0-6452783-2-3

Self-published.

Note from the Author

22 chestnuts were roasted in the making of this novel.

This is a prequel to *Crystal's Crucible (The Phoebe Braddock Books #3)* and will feature some Book 2 characters. While you can read *The Phoebe Braddock Books* in any order, I suggest reading *From Prying Eyes* prior to this one to avoid spoilers.

Trigger Warnings: Cheating, sexual violence, domestic abuse, miscarriage, and sex scenes, including f/f.

Dedication

- This one goes out to anyone who has ever been demonised for falling out of love.

Epigraph

"What kills a relationship between two people is precisely the lack of challenge, the feeling that nothing is new anymore. We need to continue to be a surprise for each other."
— Paulo Coelho (Adultery)

Playlist

"Crush" by Jennifer Paige
"Pony" by Ginuwine
"Music" by Madonna
"One More Time" by Daft Punk
"It's Alright" by East 17
"Case of the Ex (Watcha Gonna Do)" by Mýa
"Can't Get You out of My Head" by Kylie Minogue
"Till The Sky Falls Down" by Dash Berlin
"Like I Love You" by Justin Timberlake
"Toxic" by Britney Spears
"Another Chance" by Roger Sanchez
"Diving" by 4 Strings
"Silence" by Delerium
"Angel" by Sarah McLachlan
"Is It Love?" by iio
"Ooh La La" by Goldfrapp
"My My My" by Armand Van Helden
"Right in the Night" by Jam & Spoon
"Set You Free" by N-Trance
"Embrace" by PNAU

Playlist available on Spotify.

Part 1

Something Old, Something New

Chapter One

Lucinda

Innocence is such a fleeting phase, yet even now society prizes a woman's virtue as a treasured commodity. Lucinda once valued the ideal of saving herself for marriage, but in the blink of an eye, she let a stranger pluck the precious pearl from her oyster. She never even knew his name. Looking back on the deed, she questioned her reasons and came up with a plethora of excuses: the guy's sex appeal, peer pressure, alcohol, hormones, growing tired of behaving. They all seemed valid, but one truth shone brighter than the rest: she wanted *him*. Undeniably. It all started with a stupid game at a ski resort....

'Let's play truth *and* dare,' Erin Higgins declared from on high, perched precariously on her pillow throne.

Lucinda groaned, exchanging a look with Nicole who offered a sympathetic simper, but neither of them spoke up to protest. Defying Erin was top on the social suicide list, right next to double denim and listening to Aqua. The other four girls giggled, passing a French Champagne between them. *How do they not see the irony of drinking their "classy" beverage straight from the bottle?* Shivering, she wrapped herself in the sleeping bag on her bunk.

Wicked intent gleamed like sapphires in Erin's eyes. 'For that show of enthusiasm, Lucy should go first. Does anyone have a question for her?'

'I do!' Sally waved her hand in the air, and Lucinda narrowed her eyes on the daft girl. 'Last I heard, you were a virgin. Is that still true?'

A sigh slipped out as Lucinda's shoulders deflated. 'Yeah, still true. I told you I'm saving myself.'

Zoe Bristow—Erin's cousin—giggled. 'That's like *so* archaic. No one *really* waits for marriage anymore, do they? I mean, who's gonna check?'

'But God knows all,' Erin mocked, impersonating their religious studies teacher, Sister Josephine, with hands held in a sign of prayer. Everyone except Lucinda and Nicole sniggered. The

2

Queen Bee returned her attention to Lucinda. 'I dare you to get off with someone tomorrow. Find a hot single guy on the slopes and flirt with him, then in the evening, make your move.'

Lucinda gaped at Erin. 'I… I can't.'

'For Christ's sake, girl, I'm not insisting you have sex with the guy, unless you *want to*.' Erin's lips curled in a lopsided grin. 'You only need to get as far as second base, bonus points if you do so in his bed.'

'I'm still not sure.' Lucinda bit her lip, debating the consequences of forcing the issue with the most self-important girl she knew.

'Refuse the dare, and I'll let the records show you slept with Terrance Bristow.'

Bile climbed her throat at the thought of such a horrid rumour spreading. Zany Zoe's brother was one of the vilest men to walk the Earth, and he would embrace Erin's claims, especially given their history. She shuddered as the memories pushed their way out of the locked recesses of her mind. Gulping down the bitter taste, she nodded. 'Okay. It's only second base, right?'

Erin smiled wide enough to show her sparkling teeth. 'Right.'

Zoning out as the girls continued, her mind reeled with the prospect of intimacy. Aside from the

French kiss she had shared with Erin's other cousin Michael during another party game, the only guy she had done things with was Terrance, and those were times she would rather forget. The trauma had been enough to put her off dating anyone else. Boarding school had been a convenient excuse, 'sheltering her from the corrupting influence of the male species' as her mother had put it. She still had another six months of seclusion to savour, although holidays were a different matter. There was no avoiding the school's requirement to return home during the term breaks.

'Are you seriously daring us all to make out with a guy?' Nicole's voice brought Lucinda back to the moment.

Erin laughed. 'Damn straight! Need I remind you we are free of the parentals? We've got to make the most of mid-year break, bitches. I'm making it my personal mission to find a hottie to keep me warm for the next five nights. I suggest you all do the same.'

Ick! On the bright side, I won't have to share a room with her again if she's busy shacking up with a winter fling. She held her tongue despite the urge to voice her thoughts.

'Please don't bring any hook-ups back here,' Nicole begged. 'I don't need to see that shit. I'll carry through with my dare, but I can't promise to get lucky every night, so when I am sleeping in this room, I want a dick-free zone.'

'Of course,' Erin agreed. 'This is our safe space. No guys allowed. Now let's get our beauty sleep. We all need it for tomorrow… some of us more than others.'

℘℘℘

Crisp snow sparkled in the morning light, the sun ducking between wispy white clouds. The slopes of Mount Hotham glowed with the same pristine purity Lucinda brandished. *But for how much longer?* Leaving her novice friends behind, she headed straight for Brockhoff, one of the longer black trails down Heavenly Valley. While there was less snow than on most of the other resorts her family had taken her to around the world, Hotham still boasted the best powder Australia had to offer.

She paced herself on the first run, learning the terrain. On her third descent, she noticed someone in a camo print tracksuit watching her from the trees. The man was still there on her fourth go, so she carved across the snow in a tight turn to approach him.

Pushing green goggles up onto his head, he revealed dark eyes set deep in his hooded gaze. 'I'm impressed. Where'd you learn to ski so well?'

Feeling her face flush, she silently thanked her mother for the full coverage her pink balaclava provided. 'Switzerland.'

He whistled his approval. 'Is that where you're from?'

'No, I'm local, but I travelled lots with my parents.'

'Nice. When you say local….' His voice trailed off as he inched closer, stepping out from the shade of the eucalypt he had been leaning against.

She sucked in a breath as she took in his sculpted face. In the light, his eyes were more of a deep reddish-brown like chestnuts, and stubble lined his chiselled jaw. *What had he asked? Oh right, he hadn't phrased it as a question.* 'I'm Victorian. Grew up in Barwon Heads.'

A cheeky smile lit up his features. 'You're a beach girl too?' His eyes scanned her body, and she wondered what he was thinking.

'Yes, of course. I *live* at the beach in summer.'

Licking his lips, he stared shamelessly, lust blazing in his eyes. 'Fancy a race? Loser buys the winner a drink at the bar tonight.'

The suggestion caught her by surprise, and she laughed. 'Um, sure. Sounds like fun.'

'Indeed.'

They waddled to the summit together and the gorgeous guy counted down from five. On 'Go!' he pushed off at break-neck speed, gaining the lead by a considerable margin. She pushed herself but failed to gain on him. He waited for her at the base, clutching his skis in one arm and grinning as she reached him. After catching her breath, she extended her hand. 'Congratulations. I'm glad you didn't hold back. I hate it when guys let me win.'

He shook her hand, smirking. 'Trust me sweetheart, I'm all for gender equality, but you have to earn your wins. There's only one activity where I *let* a woman come first and then I pretty much guarantee it.'

Her cheeks burned and it took several seconds for her to realise he had not released her. She glanced at their joined hands, drawing her bottom lip between her teeth as her eyes returned to his heated stare. 'I—'

A hulking oaf charged into the back of her sexy stranger and slapped him on the back. 'Come on man, let's grab some grub!'

'Be right there, Russ.' He kept his eyes fixed on her while dismissing his friend. When the giant stomped off, Mystery Man leaned in to press his lips to her ear. 'You owe me a victory drink, so what do you say to meeting at The Tavern tonight? Say around nine?'

Instinctively, she attempted to tuck a strand of hair behind her opposite ear, forgetting it was all tied back in her ski mask, so her fingers hovered awkwardly against her face. 'It's a date.'

'I wasn't game to make any such presumptions, but if you insist.' He winked and strode away, leaving her heart in a flutter.

Wow! That was easier than I expected. She had succeeded with the first half of her dare without even trying. Then again, she never had difficulty attracting attention from the opposite sex, unwanted as it often was. The next stage of her challenge would be the true test.

ఈఴ

The girls drew every eye as they entered the bar at quarter past nine. 'Fashionably late,' according to Erin, who paused to survey the room while Lucinda sought one man in particular. And… bingo! The unmistakable smile greeted her. He sat alone at a table near the front windows wearing jeans and a grey knit sweater.

Erin nudged her. 'Is he here?'

'Yes, there he is.' She nodded toward her date whose grin widened.

'Hubba hubba!' Erin patted Lucinda's back. 'Good choice. Go get him, tiger.'

Golden waves of coiffured hair bounced around Lucinda as she sauntered toward the man of the hour. Accustomed to the attention she attracted, along with her group of friends, she ignored the wolf whistles and crass remarks other guys directed her way as she passed them.

He rose to meet her, planting a chaste kiss on her cheek and filling her senses with his spicy cologne. 'Hey. It's so good to see you again.'

'Likewise,' she beamed.

'I've got to ask though, what's with the entourage?' He glanced over her shoulder.

'Don't worry about my friends, they won't bother us. They're here to find their own fun.'

'I hope so, because the redhead is wigging me out.'

She giggled. 'Yeah, Erin freaks everyone out. Seriously, forget her.'

He placed his hand against the small of her back, touching her ever so lightly, yet sparking something deep and sensual within her. 'Okay. What can I get you to drink?'

Blinking, she tried to break the magnetic pull between them. 'I believe the first round is on me. That was the deal, right?'

'Hmm, no.'

She gaped at him. 'But—'

'You changed the rules when you said those three magic words.'

'What words?' She felt her brow creasing as she thought back to her previous encounter with him.

'It's. A. Date. What sort of gentleman would I be if I let you pay for anything here tonight?'

'Ha! So much for gender equality.' Not that she was complaining.

'Some old school values are worth keeping, don't you think?'

She nodded, relieved she would not need to take her fake ID on a test drive.

'Good. Now that's settled, what would you like to drink?'

Beverage choice was the furthest thing from her mind. 'Surprise me. Anything but gin,' she quickly added.

With eyes bugging out he chortled. 'Brave woman. Have a seat, and I'll be right back.' Tugging a chair out, he helped her into it and brushed his fingers over her shoulder before walking away. Tingles trailed down her back from the contact.

After taking a deep breath, she looked around the room. Erin and the other girls caught her attention, grinning maniacally and offering thumbs up. Lucinda smiled as she shook her head before turning her attention back to her *date*. She admired the firm form of his backside while he stood at the counter and chuckled to herself when 'Crush' by Jennifer Paige started playing over the sound system.

With drinks in hand, he turned and caught her perving on him, a knowing smirk lighting up his face. The rest of the room faded from view as he approached, filling her vision with his radiance. A tall glass appeared in front of her and after glimpsing what she assumed to be soft drink, she cocked her head. 'Cola?'

Taking the seat opposite, he offered her a lopsided grin. 'Try it.'

Sucking through her straw, she almost choked on the burning sensation. 'Woah! It's… strong. What is this?'

'A Long Island iced tea. Five different shots topped with cola. Although I got them to double up on the triple sec in place of the gin.'

She laughed. 'Are you trying to get me drunk, sir?'

Mischief glimmered in his beautiful brown eyes. 'You wanted a surprise.' He chugged down a mouthful of his own deadly concoction without any trouble. 'Do you like it?'

With the advantage of hindsight, she took another taste, enjoying the tang on her tastebuds. 'Yes, actually.' A few more sips and a buzz began to set in. 'So, what do you occupy your time with?'

'Aside from skiing and surfing, you mean?' He waited for her nod of acknowledgement. 'I also love camping and travelling the world, searching for *daring adventure*.' Lowering his voice to add emphasis, he sounded like the narrator of a nature documentary.

She cracked up laughing and they enjoyed a moment of mirth before she clutched at her sore ribs. 'Sounds awesome. Do you work?'

'Not yet. I'm still studying at uni, finishing up my degree in business management.'

'Business? Really? That sounds so… dry for a thrill-seeker like you.'

He snorted. 'It's not so bad, plus I'm also majoring in tourism. I have ambitions to open my own outdoor adventures company. The sort where the tour guides can also offer instruction, whether it be abseiling, bungee jumping, kayaking, scuba diving, you name it.'

Her eyes grew wider with every death-defying activity that rolled off his tongue. 'Have you done all those things?'

'Of course.'

'What about skydiving?'

'That too. How about you? Have you jumped out of a plane?'

'Not yet, but I'd love to.'

'Then you should,' he insisted. 'It's a huge rush.'

'There are so many things I want to try,' she replied.

'What's stopping you?'

She shrugged. 'Study.'

'That's a lame excuse. I'm still at uni, remember. What's your major?'

'I'm working toward architecture,' she boasted.

'Sounds intense, but still, you need to make the most of your holidays.' The husky quality of his voice betrayed another layer of meaning and her heart skipped a beat.

Clearing her throat, she steered the conversation to safer territory, 'What's your favourite outdoor activity?'

His lips quirked at her attempt, and his fingers started walking across the table. 'Skiing. Yours?'

Watching the journey his digits took, she gulped when they slipped between her own. 'Same, with sailing a close second. What is it you love about skiing?'

'Well for starters, it's how I met you.' He stroked tiny circles along the back of her hand.

Her eyes popped from their sockets. 'You must have other reasons?' The high-pitched upward inflection made her statement sound more like a question.

'Sure I do. I love the sense of freedom I get as I glide down the slopes. Not to mention the beauty of a snow-covered landscape.'

'That's what I love most about skiing and sailing—the vast, exquisite views. Nature at her finest. What about indoor activities?'

He gave her a lopsided smile. 'There is one that comes to mind.'

Damn! I walked straight into that one. With her cheeks burning, she lowered her gaze and glimpsed the delicate dance of his index finger along her knuckles. Snatching her hand back, she wrapped it around her glass and swallowed a large mouthful of liquid fire. There was no denying his intentions.

She needed time to work up the courage to give him what he so clearly wanted. *What I want*, a dormant part of her subconscious pointed out. 'Tell me about your adventures, perhaps you'll inspire me to get out there more.'

As the night wore on, he regaled her with tales of his exploits. Halfway through listening to his account of hiking along the Inca Trail, she realised she had no idea what his name was. Blushing, she bit her lip.

His gaze lowered to her mouth. 'What?'

Too embarrassed to ask so late into their conversation, she wondered how she could find out. 'Nothing.'

'Sorry, I've been talking your ear off, I must be boring you by now.'

She shook her head adamantly. 'No, not at all. I just….' Searching for a way to dig herself out, she spotted the bathrooms. 'Need to use the ladies' room.'

'Oh right.' Springing to his feet, he helped her rise from her chair. His arm snaked around her waist, and he led her to the amenities. She did not need the support to walk even though she felt tipsy, but there was no way in hell she was letting go of him until they reached the threshold he should not pass.

Erin burst through the door a moment later. 'You better not be chickening out. I swear to God if you waste this opportunity—'

She giggled. 'Hell no. I'm all in.'

If brows could fly, Erin's would have made it halfway across the world. 'Like all the way?'

'Maybe. He is amazing and so… yummy.'

Squealing, Erin attempted to hug Lucinda who ducked into a cubicle. 'Sorry hun, I'm busting to pee.'

Erin huffed. 'Okay, fine. Take these. I bet you'll need them.' A box of condoms slid under the door and Lucinda shoved it into her clutch bag. 'I'll leave you to it. I want a full report in the morning.'

The outer door closed, leaving her in peace.

When she returned to her mystery man, he led her onto the dancefloor. Grooving to the first few R&B tunes, he held her at arm's reach, maintaining a polite distance between them. But then "Pony" by Ginuwine started and his lascivious grin invited her to sample sin. She stepped closer, bringing their bodies together and conceding to the music. Letting herself go felt liberating and she relished the freedom. No one stood around judging her, no one told her what to do, and no one stopped her claiming the man's lips in a deep, passionate kiss. He tasted like memories of winter: drinking chai beside a wood fire; smoke, spice, and sensuality. Hot blood coursed through her veins, and she mewled into his mouth.

Reciprocating her sentiments with a grunt, he spoke gruffly in her ear. 'You want to get out of here? My room's not far.'

'Yes,' slipped out in a breathless, needy voice. She followed him outside and down the path to her purgatory, the road to her ruin.

Chapter Two

Lucinda

Festive spirit and the scent of pine filled the air. Lucinda admired the angelic ice sculptures near the ballroom's entrance, shivering in her strapless red gown. Hugging her red shawl around her shoulders, she approached the buffet.

Nicole greeted her with a warm embrace, pecking each cheek with a quick kiss. 'Merry Christmas in July.'

'Thanks, and likewise. You look amazing.'

Her best friend wore a shimmering gold number and her hair shone like polished mahogany. 'Speak for yourself, Lucy. I fear I might be competing with you for Michael's attention tonight.'

Shaking her head, she refrained from vocalising her argument and cast her eyes across the room. 'You guys have gone all out. I noticed you literally decked the halls with boughs of holly and everything.'

Nicole chuckled. 'Yes well, Mum couldn't help herself. Look, she even roasted chestnuts.' Nicole's mother, Annette, grew up in New York, and brought many of her family's holiday traditions with her.

Plucking one of the nuts from the crystal bowl, Lucinda studied it. The shell reminded her of a pair of deep brown orbs burning with desire, and she lost herself in the memory.

Fingers snapped in her ear. 'Hello? Earth to Lucy?'

Simpering, she glanced up at Nicole. 'Sorry, I was thinking how much they remind me of *him*.' Unable to eat the chestnut, she dropped it in her bag.

'Good Lord, girl! It's been two years. You need to get over him.'

'Who's getting over whom?' Michael Higgins asked, drawing near with Terrance Bristow in tow. Both men sported tousled hair, a contrast to their usual gel slicked styles. Terrance even appeared dishevelled with his shirt half untucked.

Nicole huffed. 'Lucy ought to move on from her obsession over Ski Resort Guy before all the food in the world reminds her of him and she starves to death.'

Terrance crunched into a candy cane and grinned. 'You know what they say? Best way to get over a guy is to get under another.'

'Ugh, you're disgusting, Terry. I'd volunteer for a lobotomy before jumping into bed with you.' Lucinda glared at him.

He scowled. 'I'm growing tired of your innocent act, Saint Lucy. Quit pretending like you haven't been sleeping your way across campus doing exactly that. How's it working out for you, hmm?'

Michael punched Terrance in the arm. 'Stop being such a douchebag. Slut shaming is for chumps and it's not like you can talk.' He grinned. 'Now apologise to Lucy.'

Hanging his head in shame, Terrance mumbled an apology.

'What was that?' Lucinda asked.

'I said I'm sorry, okay?'

'Whatever. For the record, you can't even hold a candle to Ski Resort Guy.'

Jaw wagging, he almost spat a retort, but shut his trap and kept his thoughts to himself. He smirked at Michael. 'I guess I need a pair of chestnut contact lenses and a blond dye job, then she might drop her panties for me.' Turning on his heel, he strode away.

'Such a pig,' Nicole hissed in his wake. 'Don't listen to him, Lucy. He's a bitter old man in a young arsehole's body.'

Lucinda laughed. 'Trust me, I'd sooner pay attention to pond scum.'

'Lucy, I'm sorry I haven't been able to talk sense—' Michael began.

But she cut him off. 'Forget it, Mike. I know he's your best mate, but he's not your responsibility. Let's grab a drink.'

The three of them each took a glass of Champagne from one of the waiters and headed out onto the deck.

'I love your parents' new house, Nicki,' Michael mused as he took in the view of the sprawling back garden. 'I'm impressed they snatched up such prime real estate in Toorak.'

'Thank you, Mike.' Nicole fluttered her lashes at him.

Feeling like the third wheel, Lucinda left them alone, making her way back inside to mingle. Nicole's parents—who had virtually adopted her—introduced several of their new neighbours and the hours passed in pleasantries. Feeling the urge to explore, she excused herself from a 'riveting' conversation about local politics with Mr. and Mrs. Vianello. Taking the stairs to the first floor, she followed the corridor until she found an empty sitting room with a burning wood fire. The warmth and fragrant smoke beckoned her to the fireplace, where she stood mesmerised by the flickering flames.

'Well, isn't this cosy?' The voice chilled her to the bone despite the blazing furnace in front of her.

She spun around to face Terrance, who let the door close behind him. 'Leave me alone, Terry.'

'Why? Are you waiting for someone else? Newsflash, princess: there is no one else. I'm the only man at this shindig who has spared you a glance. Even Michael is otherwise occupied. So, if you want to get lucky tonight, I'm your best option.' He swaggered toward her.

The contents of her stomach protested, and she swallowed hard against the reflux. 'Not true. I still have my vibrator, which has much less to prove than your laughable length.'

'You never used to complain about my dick when swallowing it whole.' As he closed in on her, she stepped aside, needing to put as much space between them as possible. Terrance growled before leaping forward and grabbing her. She screamed as he shoved her back. Falling to the floor, her head smacked against the hard timber, blurring her vision.

'I'm staking my claim on you, *right now.*' Climbing on top of her, he muffled her cries with his hand, so she bit into his leathery skin until she tasted his blood. The bastard did not even wince. 'Feisty, aren't you princess? You never used to struggle this much.'

As he tugged her dress up and reached between her thighs, she flailed her legs, forcing him to release his grip on her mouth. 'Get off me, you creep!' she cried with all the air in her lungs.

'Oh, I plan to get off.' He grinned maliciously, reminding her of every villain she had ever seen in a movie. The face of pure evil. With knees pinning her legs apart, he cupped her mound in his palm. 'You don't get to give *this* to complete strangers yet deny *me* the pleasure. You know how much I've wanted you all these years. I was prepared to wait when you told me you were saving yourself for marriage because I had a plan to make you mine. But you threw your virtue away for that arsehole and still won't give it up to me.' He ripped her underwear apart, exposing her to his hungry gaze.

Squirming under his bulk, she tried to push him off. He would not budge. 'Please stop!' she cried between sobs. As his head dove between her legs and she felt his putrid panting tickle her entrance, she closed her eyes.

A second later, Terrance disappeared. No more hot breath against her bare skin, no more weight pushing her into the hardwood floor. Her eyes flicked open, and she looked up into a pair of burning chestnut orbs.

ೞಆ

He knelt beside her like a mirage. Reaching up for his face, Lucinda expected her hand to pass straight through, but it landed on a firm bristled jaw. She blinked. Twice. Her mystery guy remained, solid and very much in the flesh. 'It's you,' she whispered.

'It's okay love, that bastard won't touch you again. My sister is calling the police.'

She ran her hand along his chiselled jaw. 'You came back for me.'

'Greg, I think she bumped her head, or he struck her. She seems dazed and her eyes aren't focusing. Tell Becky to request an ambulance too.'

'Sure thing.' Another man's voice drifted across the room. He sounded older than her guy, but she did not shift her gaze to confirm. 'What do you want me to do with this bastard?' Greg asked.

'Keep him unconscious until the police get here. If he stirs, knock him out again.' He helped her sit up and wrapped a blanket around her shoulders.

As the reality of what transpired kicked in, she shuddered and collapsed against his chest, bawling her eyes out. Terrance had come within seconds of defiling her. *If Ski Resort Guy hadn't….* Bile churned in her gut as she contemplated the possibility until her survival instinct pushed to the forefront, shoving the what ifs aside. *Don't go there Lucy. He* did *show up in time. My first. My hero.* 'Please,' she begged, 'tell me your name. I never caught it before.'

He smiled. 'Adam. Adam Fairfax. What's your name, beautiful?'

'Lucinda Seymour. Although you can call me Lucy. Thank you, Adam. You saved me from….' She choked on another sob.

'Hey, shh. It's over. I'm glad I heard your cries in time.'

Several uniformed officers shuffled into the room, along with two paramedics. They all talked at her with voices blunt enough to wield as weapons. Words like rape kit, statement, and testify bombarded her. She hated them all—the words, not the boys in blue who were simply doing their jobs. After a few deep breaths, she cooperated, knowing it was the best way to see justice served.

'Oh my gosh! Lucy, darling what happened?' Annette charged forward, swatting at the men surrounding Lucinda.

'Please calm down, madame,' one of the officers insisted.

'Don't ma'am me!' She shrieked like a banshee. 'This is my house! Show some respect and tell me what is going on here!'

Adam stepped forward. 'Sorry Mrs. Parker. I caught a man about to sexually assault her. My friend and I pulled him off her and clobbered him before he could... have his way with her.'

Annette gasped. 'Oh my sweet girl!'

'Are you her mother?' A paramedic asked.

'No, but I'm the next best thing since her own mom lives out of town.'

'Lucinda has a mild concussion, but is otherwise unharmed, physically that is. Are you okay to keep an eye on her for the next two days? I also recommend seeking trauma counselling.'

'Of course. Yes, I'll look after my Lucy,' Annette agreed. With dramatic gestures that would have served her well on Broadway, she ushered her guests out of the house, insisting her girl needed some peace and quiet.

Lucinda clung to Adam's hand despite Annette's polite request.

He laughed softly, caressing Lucinda's nerves with silk. 'I promise to visit you tomorrow, but you need to rest now, okay?'

Nodding, she eased her grip, frowning as his hand slipped from hers.

৪০০৪

Shrouded in shadows, Lucinda curled up on the leather sofa with a packet of chips and *another* home magazine, reading by the light of a single crystal lamp. Following strict orders from the medical professionals (according to Annette), she felt as though she was under house arrest. *Why is God punishing me for Terry's crimes?* The three ladies had spent the morning doing facials, mani-pedis, and makeovers. During the afternoon, they exhausted their repertoire of card games, growing more restless by the hour.

When she had reached for the television remote, Annette snatched it away. 'Screen time is a big no-no for your concussion recovery, no matter how mild.'

'Can I at least have one of my novels?' she had asked.

Annette shook her head. 'Light reading only. I'll get you some magazines.'

Lucinda was learning about the rising popularity of open floor plans when Nikita Patel, the estate manager, entered the room. 'Excuse me Miss Seymour, there is a Mr. Fairfax here to see you.'

Her heart thumped hard against her ribs. 'Thank you, Ms. Patel. Please let him in.' She rose to brush the crumbs from her lap before he stepped through the door. Annette and Nicole vacated promptly, although Lucinda knew they would not stray far. The older woman was likely eavesdropping from an adjacent room.

The air evacuated her lungs when Adam approached. Muscular thighs filled out his navy dress pants, and an equally toned torso stretched the seams of his designer polo shirt. He appeared shorter than she remembered but the same chestnut eyes smiled back at her, as warm and inviting as ever.

UNDENIABLY WRONG

Embracing like long-lost lovers, he planted a chaste kiss on her cheek. 'How are you feeling today, Lucy?'

Hearing her name spoken by his velvety voice heated her to the core. 'Bored out of my brain.'

He tickled her ear with a light chuckle before pressing his hand to the small of her back and guiding her back to the couch. 'I've suffered a few concussions in my time, so I know they aren't much fun. Have you had any pain or nausea?'

'A little.' She shrugged. 'Nothing major.'

'You look amazing, especially considering the ordeal you have been through.'

A blanket of silence fell over them and the air thickened as they stared into each other's eyes. Studying his face, she compared his features with her mental image of the man who had taken her virginity yet given her so much more in return. There were subtle differences: the shape of his nose, the breadth of his smile, the height of his cheekbones. Nothing significant and she could hardly trust her photo recall after three years, but there was something she could not put her finger on.

'I—'

'Th—' She started at the same time as Adam. They laughed together. 'You go first.'

He grinned. 'I have a confession to make. I recognised you the moment I caught a glimpse of you at the party.'

Taking a deep breath, she tried to steady her erratic pulse.

'When I saw you disappear upstairs, I seized the opportunity to approach you. Several other people waylaid me on my way out the ballroom. I… I'm sorry I took so long to reach you.'

Her heart skipped a beat. 'Oh gosh, Adam. It's not your fault. If anything, you arrived in the nick of time. You were my literal hero last night. Thank you for coming to my rescue.'

Adam leaned in, lowering his voice to a husky whisper. 'My intentions were less than honourable when I came looking for you, although I would never do anything so vile as that monster.' He cupped her cheek with his palm and her eyes widened. 'I've been meaning to ask you out since I first laid eyes on you in our math class at uni.'

What? She blinked. Twice. 'Excuse me?' she asked in a soft whisper. 'Did you say you're in my math class?'

Sitting back, he straightened. 'That's right. I thought you knew; that you recognised me too.'

Shit! If we are in the same year at uni, he can't be Ski Resort Guy. The other notable difference struck her. His fragrance was much fresher and crisper than the smoky spice she remembered. Even if he had changed cologne, there would be no masking the natural scent of her first love. 'Oh right! Of course,' she bluffed. 'I knew I recognised you from uni somewhere, but I couldn't work out which class it was.'

His eyes lit up with renewed joy, reeling her back with their hypnotic hold. 'Would you like to go on a date with me, Lucy?'

She nodded. Adam may not be the man she had obsessed over, but he was equally charming, just as gorgeous, and he had saved her from…. 'I would love to go out with you, Adam.'

ℰℭ

A perfect gentleman, Adam treated Lucinda by the book. From opening doors and holding chairs, to listening to every word she spoke over dinner. Even his choice of restaurant impressed her. The riverside venue offered fine dining with an exquisite view from their window seat, although she barely noticed the vista. Her date captivated her attention.

After swallowing a small bite of food, he rested his cutlery on the edges of his plate, dabbed his mouth with a napkin and smiled. 'Aside from math, what else are you studying?'

She washed her mouthful of duck confit down with a sip of Pinot Gris. 'Statics, three-D modelling, and drawing. I'm majoring in architecture.'

'Wow, that's awesome. Do you enjoy it?'

She nodded. 'I hope to run my own firm one day, so I'll need to take some business management courses too.'

'It would certainly help. What are your favourite architectural styles?'

Failing to suppress her giggle, she let a small snort slip out.

'What?' His own eyes crinkled in mirth.

'Everyone asks me that when they learn about my plans.'

Holding his hand to his chest, he feigned insult. 'Are you implying I am dull and predictable?'

Shaking her head, she laughed again. 'Of course not. You are anything but dull, Adam. I don't know you well enough to comment on your predictability, but would it matter if you were?'

'Hmm.' He stroked the stubble on his chin with comical emphasis as he pondered her question. 'They say most ladies prefer exciting, spontaneous men, so it might.'

'I don't know what your sources are, but speaking for myself, I can assure you that while the dangerous bad boys are great for one-night stands, I'd much rather a steadfast partner in the long run. Someone who can provide comfort and security.'

Flecks of gold twinkled in his chestnut eyes as he kept his thoughts to himself.

'So which kind of guy are you?'

He tasted his own wine and licked his lips, adding to the agony of his delay by stirring her primal desires. Returning his glass to the table, he narrowed his eyes. 'What are you looking for, Lucy? Do you want some no-strings fun, or a long-term relationship? Because I've heard you prefer the former, but your words suggest otherwise.'

A red haze started clouding her vision as her muscles tensed. 'Are you implying that you asked me out because you want to sleep with me?' She knew it was not an unreasonable expectation given her reputation, but something about Adam's forward manner rubbed her the wrong way. *Is it because he was such a gentleman to begin with, or due to his... uncanny resemblance to Ski Resort Guy?*

'Is that an offer?' He waggled his brows, an unnatural gesture on his handsome face.

Gaping, she shot to her feet. 'How dare you take me for an easy lay because of campus gossip!' She grabbed her purse and headed for the door.

'Lucinda, wait!'

Every eye in the place turned to watch the drama unfold as Adam chased after her. She reached the parking lot before he caught up to her because he stopped to cover the bill first. He snatched her hand, turning her to face his pleading eyes. 'I'm sorry. I didn't mean to offend, I put my foot in my mouth sometimes. I don't care what anyone else says about you regardless of the truth.'

'What do you want with me, Adam?' she asked in a resigned tone.

'I want *you*, Lucy. In whatever capacity you are willing to give.' He closed the remaining distance between them, bringing their bodies flush. 'You are an extraordinary woman with unparalleled beauty. I'd like to get to know you better, to be your boyfriend if you'll have me.'

'Adam I....' She stared into his hopeful puppy dog eyes and felt her willpower crumble. 'Truth is, I struggle with commitment, in all things. I'm amazed I've stuck it out with uni this long. I'm worse when it comes to men. I don't know, I guess I get restless or something, but I'm also very picky about who I'll date, especially after sleeping with someone.'

He sucked in a breath. 'I appreciate your honesty, and I'd still like a chance to prove myself.' Lowering his gaze to her mouth, he brushed her bottom lip with his thumb.

His bold confidence broke through the last of her restraint and she crashed against his lips with the tidal wave of all kisses. They devoured each other, her fingers combing through his dirty blond locks, destroying all his styling work, his digits digging into her waist. When his hand ventured down to her backside, she moaned into his mouth and hooked a leg around his thigh. The heat of their passion draped a blanket around them, protecting her from the winter night's chill. Coming up for air, she heard the honking car horns from onlookers.

'Get a room!' heckled a man as he strode out from the restaurant, chuckling as he approached his late model sportscar.

A smirk tugged at Adam's mouth. 'So, did I pass the first round of auditions?'

Her eyes bugged out and she smacked his arm. 'That wasn't a test.'

'No? I can't help but think you'll be judging me after what you admitted. It's enough to give a guy performance anxiety.' He winked. 'I don't know about you, but I'm starting to feel the cold. Let's go.' With his hand pressed against the small of her back, he led her to his sedan. Once again, he opened the door for her, ensuring she sat within the confines of the vehicle before closing it.

Taking a deep breath, she inhaled the fresh scent of Adam's cologne within the upholstery. At the click of his seatbelt, she glanced at him, meeting his hooded gaze.

'Are you still staying at the Parkers' house, or should I take you home?'

'I actually live with the Parkers now. Annette kindly invited me to board there when my recent rental lease expired. I was sharing with Nicole before her parents moved to town, so it made sense.'

'So back to Toorak?'

Toying with a strand of her golden waves, she considered her options. She clenched her thighs together and realised the tingles between them were not about to diminish of their own accord. 'Unless you have a more private abode.'

His eyes widened a moment before burning with lust. 'Are you sure? I'm a patient man, so I can wait for you to take all the time you need.'

She let out a short laugh. 'Yeah, but I'm *not* patient and after our kiss I'm dying to explore more of your body.'

Adam exhaled through pursed lips, whistling as he did. 'My place it is then.'

Chapter Three

Six Months Later

Lucinda

January had been Lucinda's favourite month—sun, sand, and surf, along with the excitement of new beginnings—until the acrid smell of chlorine, the sour taste of gin, and a strong urge to gag had tainted her summer memories five years ago. The funny thing about trauma is how the mind locks away those dark moments in the depths of the subconscious, yet a single sensory trigger can bring them crashing back to shore. She avoided swimming pools, and anything made from juniper berries, but there was no hiding from the first month of the calendar year. The word *January* jumped out at her from the whiteboard as she entered the meeting room. Gulping back the bile rising in her throat, she averted her eyes and forced a smile toward the woman at the head of the table.

Michelle Fairfax rose to greet Lucinda and Nicole with hugs, kisses, and a warmth usually reserved for family. Considering Lucinda had been dating her son for the last six months, she practically was, and Michelle had dropped several hints implying her desire to formally welcome Lucinda into the clan. Naturally, Nicole was part of the package. The girls were sisters in all but blood and name. Michelle returned to her seat. 'So, what's new, ladies?'

Rounding the table, Lucinda chose a chair with its back to the board. 'The court case finally resolved, so I can breathe again. For the next five years, anyway.'

Nicole scowled. 'I can't believe the fiend got off so lightly.'

'I assume you're talking about Terry.' Michael sauntered in, bee-lining for Nicole who jumped into his embrace. They kissed briefly, although Lucinda knew Nicole wanted nothing more than to climb all over him like a monkey, and up the thermostat with their passion.

'Sorry babe.' Nicole spoke in a breathless voice. 'I know he was your friend, but what he did to Lucy was unforgivable.'

He nodded. 'The man is an idiot.'

The rest of the fundraising committee drifted in while Lucinda caught up with her friends.

'How are your studies going?' Michelle asked the room at large, although only a few of them went to university.

'Great actually,' replied Lucinda. 'I'm excited to be working on a collaborative project with Nicki because architecture students are pairing up with interior design.'

'We're working on a post-modern house together,' Nicole explained.

'Sounds lovely,' Michelle agreed.

'Pfft.' Brooke Aquila huffed, puffing out her chest as she sashayed through the doorway. 'It sounds like a waste of time and money. Proper ladies don't need to work, so why bother attending uni?'

'Enhancing the mind and developing our talents is never a waste,' asserted Michelle. 'Now we are all here, I would like to open the meeting at…,' she glanced at her gold watch, 'seven twelve. The previous minutes have been distributed and I motion to approve them as correct. All in favour?'

Everyone except Brooke raised their hand.

Michelle sighed. 'What is it this time, Miss Aquila?'

'Wendy failed to note my uncle Paolo's generous sponsorship offer for the Easter Show.'

'Firstly, he missed the sponsorship submission deadline,' Wendy, the secretary explained. 'Secondly, we can't accept sponsorship deals from state parliamentary candidates. I told you this before, Brooke.'

'I know,' Brooke huffed. 'But the fact that he made an offer should have gone on record, along with your *rejection.*'

Michelle was massaging her temples by this point. 'Just add the corrections, Wendy. Brooke, please tell Mr. Vianello that if he wants to support our cause, he can make a private donation instead. Can we please move on to more important matters? With the summer fair around the corner, we need to finalise arrangements.'

Lucinda felt a wave of sympathy for the woman, along with admiration. Michelle Fairfax devoted her time to numerous charitable causes and sat on the board of a few not-for-profits. She did all this, not out of a sense of duty like most of the group, nor to look good in the public eye like Brooke, but because her compassionate heart *wanted* to help people.

The rest of the meeting followed smoother rails. As the older committee members left to attend various family commitments, Rebecca Fairfax, Adam's sister, approached her. 'Hi Lucy. I know it's six months away, but I wanted to ask if you had plans in mind for your twenty-first?'

Brooke's ears pricked up at the prospect of a party and she drew closer to the conversation, not bothering to hide her obvious eavesdropping.

'I hadn't thought about it to be honest,' Lucinda admitted.

Rebecca beamed. 'I figured, and I was wondering if Mum and I could organise and host something for you; so you and Nicki can focus on your studies.'

'Wow, that's a very generous offer.' Lucinda glanced at Michelle.

'It was Rebecca's idea,' Michelle explained, 'and I'm delighted to help in any way I can.'

'Gosh, thank you. Both of you.'

Brooke sidled up to Rebecca and draped an arm over her shoulder. 'You're such a sweetie pie, Becky. Let me know if there is anything I can do to assist.'

Blushing, Rebecca smiled at Brooke and mumbled her thanks.

Lucinda never understood how the kind-hearted Rebecca ended up becoming best friends with a bitch like Brooke, but she assumed it had something to do with growing up in the same circles and going to school together. It was unfortunate because the two were inseparable and maintaining any kind of sisterly relationship with Rebecca meant including Brooke in all social gatherings. Lucinda hugged Rebecca. 'Okay, hun, I'd be grateful if you put on a shindig for me. I better get going. I have a hot date with your brother tonight.'

'Ick.' Rebecca shuddered. 'TMI.'

Laughing, she patted Rebecca on the shoulder before leaving with Nicole and Michael.

'That girl is too cute,' observed Nicole as they stepped out into the carpark. 'And pretty. I'm surprised she is still single. She must have men lining up around the block dying to ask her out.'

Michael laughed. 'Maybe Mr. Fairfax beats them off with a stick.'

Lucinda shook her head. 'No, violence isn't his style. He probably pays them large sums of money to stay away. But you're right. Rebecca is nearly twenty and as far as I know, she hasn't ever dated, let alone had a boyfriend.'

'We should set her up,' Nicole suggested. 'Michael, who do you think would be suitable?'

'Hmm, maybe Troy Ellis. He's a decent bloke with good breeding.'

Lucinda rolled her eyes. 'I'll leave you both to play Cupid without me but watch where you aim those arrows. They can be more dangerous than bullets.' She hugged them both and climbed into her convertible sportscar. A rush of excitement surged through her as she started the ignition. She had not been kidding about the hot date. Adam had invited her over for another pizza and movie night. In keeping with true to form, they were unlikely to see much of the film, and the pizza would be cold by the time they ate it.

૭ᏏᏇ

'Oof!' A red balloon smacked Lucinda in the face as a giggling girl dashed past.

Stopping in her tracks, the little blonde in a daisy-print dress turned and simpered when she realised what she had done. 'I'm sorry, miss. Are you okay?'

Lucinda smiled. 'I'm fine. A little startled is all.'

With a nod, the girl reeled in the string of her improvised weapon and took off, two boys hot on her heels.

'She reminds me of you at that age,' mused Lucinda's father as he placed a hand on her shoulder.

'Right down to the unwanted male attention,' her mother agreed.

Noticing Lucinda's shudder, Dad frowned. 'Tiffany, please. It's best if we put that horrid business behind us. Lucy dear, why don't you introduce us to your gentleman friend we've been hearing so much about?'

The sound of laughter and squealing amplified as she led her parents across the parklands, especially as they passed the sideshows. 'Not that I'm complaining, but how did you find room in your summer schedules to come to the city and attend a fair with me?'

'We were in the neighbourhood,' Dad admitted.

'Your father is schmoozing a local politician interested in purchasing one of our yachts,' Mum explained.

'He suggested meeting here. His niece is on the planning committee, so I guess you know her.'

Lucinda sighed. 'Is Mr. Vianello the name of your politician, perchance?'

'Yes. Do you know him?'

She nodded. 'We've crossed paths a few times.' She reserved her judgement of Vianello himself. She barely knew him, although he did ooze the sleaze vibe. What was it her parents used to say? *'If you don't have anything nice to say about someone, don't say anything at all.'*

'Hurry up and ask her already!' Rebecca's pleading voice drifted out of the small staff marquee, halting Lucinda. 'Mum wants grandchildren, and we all know you're her best hope. There's no way James will ever settle down.'

Signalling to her parents to stay quiet, Lucinda stood outside to eavesdrop on the banter between the Fairfax siblings.

Adam laughed. 'Knowing James, he has kids scattered across the globe.'

Lucinda had not yet met their elusive older brother and she wondered if she ever would. Wanderlust consumed him about as much as the regular kind, and last Adam reported, the man was sleeping his way through Europe.

'I wouldn't be surprised either,' Rebecca scoffed. 'But they don't count as far as Mum's concerned.'

'Even if I do marry Lucy, there's no guarantee we'll have children. Maybe we just want a lifetime of hot sex, unhindered by a bunch of rugrats.'

Rebecca's gagging noises made Adam laugh.

Feeling beyond awkward with her parents beside her, Lucinda pushed aside a STAFF ONLY sign and marched up to Adam. 'Hi honey.'

The mischievous glint in his eye turned lascivious and he rose from his seat to pull her into his arms. He leaned in to kiss her, stopping when movement behind her caught his attention.

'You must be Adam,' her father surmised with a furrowed brow. The man was big on first impressions, and he clearly disliked the way Adam had spoken about his baby girl, even though it had likely been in jest.

Tucking her into his side, Adam stepped forward offering a free hand. 'That's me. Sorry Sir, I didn't catch your name.'

'Harry Seymour.' He took Adam's hand in a vice grip and Lucinda prayed he did not crush it.

Adam's face paled, but he did not back down or wince as they shook. 'Lucy's father?'

'The very same,' he confirmed.

'Well, it is great to meet you at last, Mr. Seymour.'

As Lucinda completed the round of introductions, Brooke burst into the tent, screeching, 'Oh my gosh Becky! You'll never guess who's here!' A moment later her eyes surveyed the group, landing on the older man in the room and darkening with a sickening hunger. 'Oh, I did not realise you had company, Becky. I am so sorry to interrupt.' She directed her apology at Lucinda's father.

Rebecca smiled. 'It's okay. Lucy was introducing us to her parents, Harry and Tiffany.'

Brooke sidled up to Harry, batting her lashes as she offered her hand. 'Such a pleasure,' she purred.

To his credit, Dad merely shook her hand, then wrapped an arm around Mum's waist.

'What is your exciting news?' asked Rebecca.

'Oh right! Casper Van der Berg is here. You know the TV actor from *The Dark Matter Between Our Hearts*?'

'The one who plays Grayson?' Lucinda piped up.

Brooke nodded. 'My uncle texted me to say Casper and his *boyfriend* are both talking to him in the VIP tent. You guys should come meet him.'

They followed Brooke out of the marquee, although Lucinda doubted her parents cared much for the television show in question, let alone the actors from it. She trailed behind, linking arms with

Adam and keeping pace with her father. 'Brooke is Mr. Vianello's niece, so I guess this will give you a chance to catch up with the man.'

Her dad kept his hands in his pockets as he walked. 'I figured.'

'I can't believe Grayson is gay!' Brooke complained.

'Could explain his reaction to Danika's advances,' Rebecca offered.

'No way!' Lucinda countered. 'It's as clear as day how much Grayson wants Danni. He already explained his reasons for waiting.'

Adam gaped at Lucinda as though she had grown a second head.

'What?' she shrugged. 'I'm a fan of the show.'

He shook his head. 'Don't you girls understand that an actor's sexual persuasion has nothing to do with the characters they portray?'

'*Of course we do!*' all three of them snapped in unison.

Raising his hands in surrender, Adam laughed. 'Right then, carry on.' His steps faltered a second later and he spun on his heels to confront Lucinda. 'Wait! Is Grayson one of those shirtless guys I see you drooling over?'

Biting her lip, she lowered her gaze and mumbled, 'Maybe.'

He chuckled. 'I guess it's a good thing this Casper dude is gay then, huh?'

Blushing, she glared at him. 'Thanks for putting that image in my head! Now I'm going to recall all the times I've seen Casper half-naked while trying to carry polite conversation with the man.'

'Me too!' Rebecca added. 'Not cool *Brother*!'

'As if my little sister drools over anyone.' He bumped Rebecca's shoulder with his fist, prompting her to scowl at him.

The scent of hot cinnamon doughnuts teased Lucinda's empty stomach as they passed the food trucks.

Adam glanced at her belly when it rumbled. 'You're hungry. Go on ahead and meet your celebrity heartthrob. I'll get us something for lunch.'

She smiled at him. 'Thanks.'

'No probs.' He pecked her temple with a chaste kiss before disappearing into the crowd.

Her dad drew close and whispered, 'I had my doubts at first, but Adam seems like a nice fellow with a good sense of humour. You should bring him home for dinner.' He patted her on the back. 'Well done, buttercup.'

Her eyes brimmed with happy tears. 'Thank you, Dad.' When they reached the VIP tent behind the stage, she flashed the staff pass on her lanyard at the security guard. 'And these are my parents.'

The guard gave his silent assent, unhooking the red rope from the stanchion to let them enter the large pavilion. Mr. Vianello sat at a table near the bar, chatting to a familiar blond man and his *much* older partner with grey hair still showing a few patches of honey brown.

'Hello Uncle Paolo.' Leaning in, Brooke kissed Mr. Vianello on the cheek.

Vianello beamed. 'Hi princess. I see you bought your friends and… Mr. Seymour?' He reached out to shake Harry's hand.

'Yes, hello sir. I was catching up with my daughter. Such a happy coincidence that we both have family on the planning committee.'

'Indeed. Allow me to introduce you all to Casper Van der Berg and Drew Webster. They recently moved into the area.'

'Becky and I are huge fans,' gushed Brooke as she clasped Casper's hand.

'Is that so?' Casper cocked a brow and glanced at Lucinda. 'And what about you?'

'Oh, I'm sure Lucy is,' Brooke replied.

Drew's glasses slid down his nose as he peered at Brooke. 'I'm sure Lucy has her own voice with which to answer.'

Lucinda was not so sure. The image of sculpted muscles beneath Casper's polo shirt were wreaking havoc with her senses. Her cheeks burned when her gaze met Casper's and she cleared her throat. 'I enjoy the show,' she admitted.

Clapping his hands, Casper grinned. 'Fabulous! Can I get you all a drink?'

Dad raised a protesting hand. 'Please allow me.' He took their orders and headed for the bar.

'Harry's company makes the best yachts in Australia,' explained Mr. Vianello. 'I'm thinking of buying one of his luxury models.'

'Sounds marvellous,' Casper replied. 'What's with the indecision? If they are the best, I mean?'

'It's a big investment.'

'But a sound one. Think of all the amazing parties you could host for your niece on it.'

Brooke's eyes lit up at Casper's suggestion. 'Oh yes! Please get the boat, Uncle Paolo.'

'Nice one,' Lucinda murmured near Casper's ear as she watched Brooke talk her uncle around to the idea.

'What can I say? I'm a perceptive guy.' Casper winked at her.

Drew's arm slid across Casper's shoulders. 'You mean nosy. Casper is the biggest gossip queen under the sun.'

Casper nudged Drew. 'There's nothing wrong with showing an interest in people's lives.'

'Do you ever get sick of people showing an interest in *your* life? Like with the paparazzi?' Rebecca asked.

'Not at all,' Casper admitted.

'He *thrives* on the attention,' Drew drawled, tensing slightly as he did.

Lucinda wondered if he was less comfortable with all the reporters sniffing around. 'What do you do for a living, Drew?'

'I'm a philosophy professor at Melbourne University.'

'Really? I'm studying architecture at Melbourne U. Perhaps I'll see you around campus?'

'Maybe.'

The fresh scent of Adam's expensive cologne enveloped her a moment later, his arms caging her in as he placed a white pastry bag and a bucket of curly fries on the table in front of her. She peeked in the bag and her mouth watered at the Dagwood dog[1], a treat she loved indulging in at carnivals. Tilting her head back, she grinned up at Adam. 'You're the best.'

'I try.' He covered her lips with his own in an upside-down kiss.

છ૭ઝ

Rebecca

As soon as Casper and Drew took their leave an hour later, Brooke turned to Rebecca. 'Let's go get ice cream.'

Rebecca glanced at her brother and Lucinda who spoke to each other in hushed voices, then at Mr. Vianello who carried on with his own private conversation about boats with Mr. Seymour. *Everyone else looks preoccupied.*

Brooke's breath tickled Rebecca's ear as she whispered, 'I meant just us.'

'Oh, okay.' Possibilities lurked in the undercurrents, and her cheeks flushed before she could stop them. 'Ice cream sounds lovely, but—'

---

[1] Dagwood dogs, also known as Corndogs, are deep fried sausages on a stick.

Her conscience tapped on the forefront of her mind, reminding her she ought to get back to work soon. As volunteer staff they did not have set break times, but she did not want to let things slip.

'Relax sugar.' Brooke spoke with a soothing voice, like silk caressing skin. 'Everything is running smoothly, and people can contact us over the radio if they need to. We've worked hard toward this weekend, so we deserve a decent break. Come on.' Springing to her feet, she grabbed Rebecca's hand and propelled her forward. Brooke linked arms with her, a typical gesture for her best friend, yet it covered Rebecca in tingles from head to toe.

As they entered a laneway with walls of stuffed animals, a large plush St. Bernard puppy attracted her eye. 'Oh gosh, he's so cute!' She had always wanted a real pet, but her parents denied every request, insisting animals were too much work for busy people.

'He would look great in your collection,' added Brooke. 'Want me to win it for you?'

'Oh, um….' Heat rose from her chest and set her skin ablaze. *Isn't that the sort of thing guys do for their girlfriends? Why is she behaving so… inappropriately?*

Brooke laughed. 'It's just a sideshow game, Becky. You can play too. If you want.' She handed some cash to the man behind the counter in exchange for five small balls.

The carnival merchant approached her. 'G'day Miss Fairfax. You wanna play too?'

She glanced at Brooke who smiled and gave her an encouraging nod. 'Yes please.' She reached for her purse, but the man waved dismissively.

'This one's on me, Miss. You've been such a great help this year.' He grinned, showing a set of crooked teeth, some missing and the rest yellow.

'Thank you so much Mister….'

'Call me Roger.' He handed her a set of balls and directed her to one of the gaping clowns. They were meant to be laughing according to the sign above the stall, but she always thought they were gasping in surprise. *Like, are you really going to shove those things down my gob?*

'Let's take it in turns,' Brooke suggested. 'You can go first.'

Concentrating on the clown's rotating head, she lined up her shot, popping the ball in its mouth and watching as it dropped into one of the slots marked with a 4.

'Not bad,' Roger mused.

Brooke ensnared Rebecca's attention with her warm, coffee-coloured eyes and directed their gazes to the white plastic ball in her manicured hand. Bright red nail polish sparkled in the sunlight as she brushed the ball across the clown's lips, as if teasing it. Rebecca imagined the clown was no longer surprised, but ravenous for whatever Brooke offered. She released the ball, plucking at the clown's bottom lip, and Rebecca bet it would have groaned had it been sentient.

Good God, how can she turn a simple act into such an erotic display? Looking up at Roger, she caught him leering at Brooke and bile rose in her throat. *Surely Brooke isn't intentionally seducing this creep?* Picking up her second ball, she cleared her throat. 'My turn.' She let it go without bothering to wait and hummed when it scored six points. The game continued in much the same way, with Brooke's fingers making love to the clown's mouth while Rebecca's discomfort grew. Eventually they each won their pick of the high-end toys, both of which filled her arms.

After putting the plush prizes away and purchasing their ice cream, she followed Brooke to the outskirts of the fairgrounds. Finding a bench beneath an old tree with a leafy canopy, they sat close together.

Brooke tucked a strand of Rebecca's strawberry blonde hair behind her ear. 'What's wrong Becky? You've disappeared inside your head again.'

'Why did you flirt with Roger?

Brooke's eyes widened a moment before she cracked up. 'I'm sorry,' she rasped as her mirth settled. 'I wasn't flirting with him.'

'Good because that was gross.' Rebecca swallowed a mouthful of her dairy whip.

'You are so precious sometimes.' Mischief twinkled in Brooke's eyes as they trailed down Rebecca's face. Leaning in, she licked the corner of Rebecca's mouth, stopping her heart in the process. 'You missed a bit.'

Giggling, Rebecca shoved her away. 'You are so strange!' Turning away to hide her embarrassment, she spotted Adam and Lucy walking nearby and tensed. *Oh no! I hope they didn't see Brooke's rather intimate behaviour.* Arousing Adam's suspicions would spell the beginning of the end. Her brother pushed Lucy against a tree and shoved his tongue down her throat. *Ick!* She decided it was safer to give her undivided attention to the melting iced confection in her hands, especially since it was about to drip on her brand-new summer dress.

Brooke's hand rested on Rebecca's knee. 'Don't worry, the sight of Adam and Lucinda together sickens me too.'

Gulping back a mouthful of ice cream, she braced herself as the brain freeze kicked in. 'I don't mind them being together. They make a cute couple and it's good to see my brother happy, but their public displays are a bit much at times.'

'Ha! You are such an innocent prude,' Brooke teased.

'I am not a prude!' she retorted. 'I just can't bear to think of my brothers… doing it.'

'Oh yeah? If you aren't bothered by sex, why don't you ever talk about it?'

Flames filled her face.

Brooke stroked a finger along one of those burning cheeks. 'See, you're even blushing at the prospect. In all the years I've known you, you've never shown any interest in sex. You even clam up when I talk about screwing guys.'

'I *am* interested, it's just….' Rebecca did not know how to broach the subject, not even with her best friend. *Especially* not with her best friend.

Drawing closer, Brooke presses her lips to Rebecca's ear. 'It's okay, Becky. I know.'

Gulping, she lowered her gaze, too scared to see Brooke's disgust. 'But how? I've never told *anyone.*'

'I'm not blind, sugar. I've seen the way you look at other women. The way you look at *me.*'

The heat emanating from her face could have melted the polar ice caps. 'Does anyone else know?'

'I don't think so. No one else knows you like I do.'

This explains the weird behaviour today. She was trying to coax a confession out of me. Red hot anger surged through her blood, and she sprang to her feet. 'Stop toying with people, Brooke. You can be so horrid sometimes.' Tossing her ice cream in the bin, she took off at a sprint toward the market stalls, refusing to halt when she heard Brooke calling out. Her initial instinct had been to run home and lock herself away, but she was not about to shirk her responsibilities, so she distracted herself with work instead.

Chapter Four

Adam

Groaning, Adam sat up in bed and wiped the sleep from his eyes. His blurry vision cleared, giving him a glimpse of the angel resting beside him, her golden hair forming a halo on the pillow. As he shifted, the quilt dipped below her breasts and images of their wild night flooded his mind. *How did I get so lucky with Lucy?* She had warned him about her commitment issues, yet here she was—six months later and still returning to his bed. The doorbell rang again, reminding him of the disturbance that had plucked him from his slumber.

He rose, dressing quickly in a pair of grey trackpants and plain white t-shirt. Crossing his apartment in a few long strides, he threw the door open and shivered despite the warm summer air.

Brooke stood beyond the security screen. 'About friggin time! What took you so long?'

'Not that it's any of your business, but I was asleep,' he replied through a yawn.

Her brows arched. 'Seriously? It's nearly noon! Don't you have study or something?'

His temper shot from zero to almost snapping in an instant. 'It's uni holidays. What the hell do you want?'

'Can I come in?' she asked in a demanding tone.

'No. I have company.'

She sobbed. '*Please?* It—It's about Becky. I can't reach her.'

Damnit! Rebecca was his Achilles heel and Brooke knew it. So help him God, but he could not deny such a request. He unlocked the screen door and ushered her inside.

Licking her lips, Brooke let her eyes roam across his body. She stepped closer and placed her hands on his chest. 'You're looking exceptionally fit these days. I hope Lucy appreciates your stamina.'

He pushed Brooke away with a gentle shove and glared at her. 'What's going on with Becky?'

Slumping into his favourite armchair, she groaned. 'I may have said something to upset her at the fair the other day, and now she won't talk to me. I need your help contacting her so I can apologise and make it up to her.'

He pinched the bridge of his nose to combat the impending headache. 'From your panicked tone earlier, I thought she was in trouble.' He sat in the chair opposite Brooke. 'If the pair of you are fighting, I'm one-hundred percent on Becky's side.'

As she crossed her legs, the hem of her dress rose halfway up her thighs. 'Oh, it's nothing like that. We didn't have an argument per se. I kind of put my foot in my mouth. I'm not asking you to take sides or anything, I want you to arrange a meeting where she can't flee at the sight of me.'

Drawing a line in the plush white carpet with his big toe, he considered the situation. 'I don't know. I'd rather not get caught up in your drama, and if Becky is avoiding you, she probably has good reason.'

'I'll make it worth your while,' she countered.

He huffed. 'What could you possibly have to offer me? I don't need your money, and I most definitely don't want anything else from you.'

Brooke's expression darkened as she laced her fingers together and rested them on her bare knee. 'I won't tell your girlfriend about our sordid past.'

Clenching his fingers into fists, he scowled. 'Blackmail? Really?'

'Yes really. Trust me sugar, you don't want me whispering in Lucy's ear, not if you want a future with her.'

Throbbing pain filled his head, and he massaged his temples. He hated to admit it, but Brooke was right. Hooking up with the conniving cow had been the worst decision of his life thus far, and she was not about to let him forget it. 'I assume you've already concocted a plan. What do you want me to do?'

Brooke grinned. 'I knew you'd see reason. I'm hosting a party on my uncle's new yacht, and I want you to bring Becky.'

He could already feel the sand chafing his bare skin. 'Are you trying to torture me?' One side of her lip curled up and he cut in before she could speak, 'On second thought, don't answer that. How am I supposed to get Becky to your party if she doesn't want to see you?'

'Easy. Don't tell her I'll be there. Make her think it's something else.'

'You want me to lie to my sister?'

Brooke shrugged. 'It's only a little white lie. You've told worse.'

Lucinda shuffled into the living room a moment later with dishevelled hair, wearing nothing more than a sleek satin nightgown, and he thanked God there were no other men present. 'Oh, hi Brooke.' She perched on the arm of his chair and leaned in to peck him on the lips. 'What's going on? I heard something about lying to Becky.'

'I'm putting on a surprise party for Becky, and I need you both to bring her,' Brooke replied with the most saccharine smile.

'Is this for her birthday?' Lucy asked excitedly.

Brooke smirked at Adam. 'Of course it is.'

'I was wondering what she intended to do,' mused Lucinda. 'Becky has put more thought into my twenty-first in six months than her own birthday which is just around the corner. What's the plan?'

'Indeed,' agreed Brooke. 'She is far too selfless sometimes. I'm planning a yacht party.'

Lucinda's eyes lit up as she turned to look at him. 'This will be fun. Dad's yachts are amazing. You'll love it.'

A guttural noise slipped from his throat and Brooke snickered.

'What's wrong?' Lucy asked.

'Adam detests the beach,' Brooke replied with a sinister sheen to her eyes.

Lucinda's brow furrowed. 'How could you hate the beach?'

'I don't like the sand,' he stated, refusing to reveal the regrettable memories he associated with shorelines.

She gave him a sidelong glance. 'Lame. Well, there won't be much sand to worry about once we are on the boat, and there is no way I'm letting you miss your sister's birthday party because you're afraid of a little sand getting in your shoes.'

He gaped at her before exhaling with defeat. 'Fine. I'll do it.'

Lucinda clapped her hands together. 'Excellent. Email me the details, Brooke. I'm going to shower.'

As the bathroom lock clicked into place, Brooke impersonated the sound and motion of cracking a whip and tittered. 'I'm beginning to respect her. It's a pity I'll never be able to like her.'

'Not that I care what you think, but what do you have against Lucy?'

Brooke studied her glossy red nails as if the sight of him bored her. 'Is that a rhetorical question, or are you really so clueless?'

Schooling an impassive expression, he remained silent until she met his gaze. 'Humour me.' Making eye contact was a mistake because the depths of her hungry eyes were like a black hole drawing him in and threatening to rip him apart.

She smiled. 'I could never like a woman who has the man I want.'

෯෬

Lucinda

Lucinda noticed Adam squirming the moment his feet left the carpark at St. Kilda Beach. She figured there had to be more to it than he was letting on, and it hurt to think he was keeping secrets from her. Ignoring the nagging feeling in her gut, she linked arms with Rebecca and led her towards the marina.

'Gosh this place brings back memories.' Rebecca beamed as her thoughts appeared to travel back in time. 'Brooke's family used to host some of the most spectacular parties down here during our high school years, didn't they Adam?'

Adam shrugged, avoiding eye contact. 'They were okay.'

A light sea breeze fluttered the ruffles of Rebecca's pastel yellow dress, and she shivered as goosebumps rose on her bare arms. Lucinda dropped her pashmina scarf around the birthday girl's shoulders. 'Here, you need this more than me. I'm used to coastal climates.' Her own dress—a white asymmetrical slip—revealed more skin than Rebecca's conservative outfit, yet she did not feel the chill.

'Thanks.' Rebecca glanced at Adam. 'What's up with you, grumpy bum?'

'He doesn't like the beach,' Lucinda replied.

Rebecca's eyes widened. 'Since when?'

'Since forever.' Picking up his pace, he strode on ahead. 'I'm taking our bag to our room.'

'Odd,' mused Rebecca. 'He used to love coming down here. I wonder what changed.'

So do I. She would get the truth out of him one way or another. They took their time, treading carefully with their stilettos, and giving Adam time to warn the party goers that their guest of honour was arriving. As they reached the berth, she recognised her father's branding on the boat Mr. Vianello had named *Merry Majesty*, a luxury superyacht with four decks.

Running her hands along the gilded railing, Rebecca whistled. 'Your dad made this?'

'Yes. He engineered the boat and his company built it.'

As soon as Lucinda opened the door to the saloon and flicked on the light, Rebecca's friends and family sprang forward shouting, 'surprise.'

Rebecca gasped. 'Oh gosh! I can't believe you guys. This is so cliché, but I love it. Thank you.'

Scanning the room, Lucinda noticed a conspicuous lack of Brooke. *Shouldn't she be at her best friend's party, especially since she organised it?* Then her eyes landed on Adam who sat by the bar with a rocks glass in his hand. Leaving Rebecca to mingle, she beelined for her boyfriend and took the stool beside him. 'You didn't waste any time.'

Adam stared into his drink as he spoke, 'I needed something to take the edge off.'

'Right because there is so much sand on this boat. What's really upsetting you?'

'I don't want to talk about it.'

Summoning a waiter, she grabbed a Champagne and took a sip while considering the best way to tackle the topic. 'Do you want a future with me, Adam?'

His head whipped up, and he stared at her with wide eyes. 'W—'

The yacht's engines roared to life, and a deep voice boomed through the PA, 'This is Captain Roger Hayes speaking. Happy birthday to our special guest, Rebecca Fairfax!' Cheers erupted until the captain's voice spoke up again, 'We are about to head out for a cruise around Port Phillip Bay, but before we do, I'd like you to watch a short video explaining the safety equipment and protocols on this boat. Please turn your attention to the screen on the aft-most wall.'

They watched the safety briefing in relative silence and as it finished, Adam staggered out of the room.

She followed him. 'Where are you going?'

'Bathroom.' He stumbled a few more paces.

She rushed forward to catch him as he teetered, guiding him toward the handrail along the wall for additional support. 'Good God! How much have you drunk? You can barely stand!'

'Not much. I'm having trouble finding my sea legs.' The slur of his speech told her otherwise. He must have been on the boat for all of fifteen minutes.

Has he been chugging down shots?

Swinging her around, he pushed her against the wall and caged her between his arms. 'You know, our cabin isn't far.' He dropped his head into the crook of her neck and sucked in a breath. 'Let's go christen the bed.' His nose trailed from her pulse point up to her ear, eliciting a moan as her core heated.

'Adam,' she pleaded breathlessly. 'I want answers first.'

He nipped her earlobe. 'Make love to me now, then I'll tell you everything you want to know.'

'I thought you needed to use the facilities.' She was grasping at straws, but if she didn't escape his seduction attempt soon, she would lose this battle.

'The urge passed. Something stronger took its place.' One of his hands cupped her backside. 'Do you want me inside you, Lucy?'

Arching her back, she felt his growing desire pushing against her. 'Yes, but—'

His lips clamped over hers, sending the last of her willpower overboard. Propping herself up with the railing, she wrapped her legs around Adam's waist, grinding her needy core against his belt buckle, letting her lust trickle into the threads of his suit.

Gasping, he drew back slightly. 'Bedroom. Now!' When he tried to carry her along the passageway, he lost his balance and they both hit the deck in a fit of laughter.

'Maybe you should take me here,' she suggested, only half joking.

Adam hovered over her and held her gaze for an intense moment before springing to his feet and sprinting towards the cabins. Reaching one of the doors, he bent over a large ceramic pot and emptied his guts into the base of a palm tree.

Sighing with resignation, she helped him through the door. Relief washed over her when she spotted their overnight bag on the bed. *At least he found the right cabin.* She cleaned him up in the ensuite and tucked him into bed. When his head hit the pillow, he blacked out. Rolling him onto his side, she left a bin beside the bed in case he got sick again, then returned to the party.

The Champagne she abandoned had disappeared, so she grabbed a fresh drink and joined Rebecca who was talking to Casper Van der Berg and Drew Webster.

෴

Rebecca

Rebecca smiled at Lucinda. 'Where's Adam?'

Lucinda's countenance drooped. 'Not feeling well, so he called it a night.'

'Oh.' Schooling her expression, she tried to hide her disappointment. 'Lucy, you remember Casper and Drew?'

'Of course.' Lucinda shook each of their hands. 'I didn't realise we had A-list celebrities coming.'

Casper chuckled. 'We simply couldn't turn down Brooke's invitation after the part I played in convincing her uncle to buy this yacht. Not to mention present company.' He winked at Rebecca.

'Wait! Are you telling me this is Mr. Vianello's boat?'

'Of course,' Lucinda replied. 'Brooke planned the whole thing for you.'

Her jaw hit the deck. 'I thought you and Adam—'

An arm snaked around her shoulders and the fruity fragrance of a designer perfume— Brooke's latest favourite—filled her nose. 'Happy birthday, sugar.'

Where the hell did she come from? She slinked out of Brooke's clutches and glared at her.

Brooke threw her hands up in supplication. 'Before you say anything, I want you to know I'm truly sorry for everything I said and did last weekend. Forgive me?' She batted her luscious lashes.

Taking a deep breath, she conceded. 'Fine. Thank you for the party.'

Casper clicked his tongue. 'As far as bitch fights go, that was quite disappointing.'

Drew smacked him upside the back of his head. 'I'm glad the pair of you resolved your differences, whatever they were.'

The issue was far from settled, but she did not want to make a scene.

Stunning as always, Brooke wore a glittering black slip with her hair in an updo and diamond droplets dangling from her ears. 'I'm sorry we could not get James to return home for your party.'

Rebecca shrugged. 'It's okay. I doubt he'll even return for Adam's twenty-first in June. He never put much stock in birthdays. I'm sure he'll show up when Adam and Lucy get married.'

Spluttering, Lucinda spat her mouthful of bubbles back into her glass. 'Um. We aren't even engaged.'

'Not yet.' She tapped her nose conspiratorially and giggled. 'I'm sure it's only a matter of time.' She already loved Lucinda like a sister and looked forward to welcoming her into the family.

'It will be good to finally meet the elusive James,' Lucinda remarked. 'I still have no idea what he looks like.'

She nodded, missing her raffish brother. 'James looks a lot like Adam, but older and taller.'

'And more rugged,' added Brooke. 'It's a good thing Adam met you first Lucinda; else he might have lost his chance. James is a real ladies' man.'

Rebecca huffed. 'Fortunate for Lucy more like. James breaks hearts wherever he goes. Monogamy is a dirty word to him.'

'Maybe he hasn't met the right woman yet,' suggested Lucinda.

'Or man?' added Casper with a wicked grin.

A loud laugh burst from Rebecca's belly. 'No offence guys, but there isn't a gay bone in James' body.'

'What if…,' Brooke captured Rebecca's gaze before she continued, 'he let the right woman slip between his fingers and has lived with regret ever since, numbing the pain as best as he can.'

Rebecca bit her bottom lip, and Lucinda gasped beside her.

Casper said something about the stuff romances and tragedies are made of, but she tuned out as Brooke's meaning sank in. 'Excuse me.' She turned and dashed out of the saloon, finding herself in a long, narrow passageway.

'We need to talk,' Brooke announced behind her.

'Not here,' she protested. 'There's too many eyes and ears around.'

Tugging at her arm, Brooke led her into a cabin with a queen-size bed.

She took in the spacious suite. 'Whose room is this?'

'Ours.' Brooke locked the door and stalked toward her. 'I never toyed with you, sugar.'

Shaking her head, she backed away until she bumped into a porthole. A chill crept through the back of her dress, providing a stark contrast to the blazing inferno within her chest.

Closing the distance between them, Brooke placed her hands on Rebecca's shoulders, then slid one down to her hips and the other cupped her cheek. 'I genuinely want you.'

'We can't. My family will never accept or approve.'

'They don't need to know. I promise to keep your secret. Our secret.' Without further preamble, Brooke kissed her deeply.

Chapter Five

6 Months Later

Lucinda

The limousine pulled up to the curb beside Fairfax Manor, and Lucinda spotted the red carpet. 'Becky has gone all out.'

'I suspect Brooke had a hand in the additional pageantry,' remarked Nicole. 'Are you ready to lose your glass slipper, Cinderella?' She glanced at the silver stilettos on Lucinda's feet.

'I better not,' she huffed. 'These things cost a small fortune.'

Nicole got out of the car, along with Michael, and they both stood beside the chauffeur as he opened Lucinda's door. The attractive couple had dressed as Belle and her beast.

A hint of mischief glimmered in Michael's eyes. 'I heard the glass slipper is a metaphor for virginity.'

Lucinda let out a short, sardonic laugh. 'We all know that ship sailed years ago. Luckily, Prince Charming doesn't mind.'

'Speaking of your prince, where is Adam? Shouldn't he be meeting you out here to make your grand entrance together?' asked Nicole.

'He had some uni work to finish, so he'll be along later.'

Nicole shook her head but held her tongue.

Another two Disney princesses greeted them at the gate. Bouncing on her toes, Rebecca squealed and clapped her hands. 'You look gorgeous!' The energetic Sleeping Beauty embraced her. 'Happy birthday, hun. Here, I couldn't wait to give you this.' She handed Lucinda a pink gift bag.

Inspecting the contents, she found a large bottle of perfume.

'I know it's your favourite, so I figure you can always use more,' Rebecca added with a wide grin.

'How very thoughtful. Thank you.'

Brooke stepped forward and handed her a blue gift bag. It came as no surprise that she pulled off the Jasmine costume. She never took half-measures when it came to coordinating a theme. When Lucinda held up the anti-ageing cream she retrieved from the bag, Brooke smirked. 'At least you don't have to *appear* old.'

Laughing away the thinly veiled insult, she thanked Brooke for the offering.

Ushering them inside, Rebecca handed her a Champagne.

Glancing at the bubbles in her glass, she felt her stomach flip. 'Could I please have juice instead? I'm feeling a little queasy.'

Creasing her forehead, Rebecca swapped the drink. 'Are you okay? Can I get you anything else?'

The sisterly concern warmed her heart. 'I'm sure I'll be fine.' Nearing a familiar redhead, she nudged Michael and whispered, 'Who invited your cousin?'

He simpered. 'Brooke asked us who your school friends were, so I put her in touch with Erin.'

Naturally, the rest of Erin's cohort had tagged along too. A horde of fake smiles gleamed at her, filling the air with the stench of melted plastic.

'Hello ladies.' Lucinda kept her own expression neutral as she accepted their half-hearted hugs.

Erin wore Ariel's teal princess dress. 'No date tonight? Don't tell me you are still pining after Ski Resort Guy?'

'I have a boyfriend,' Lucinda assured her. 'Adam will be here soon.'

'Who's Ski Resort Guy?' Brooke asked.

Zoe grinned. 'The guy who popped her cherry.'

'Oh?' Brooke's brows arched. 'When did this happen?'

'Year Twelve,' Lucinda deadpanned. This was the last thing she wanted to discuss, and Brooke's curiosity unnerved her.

'Adam's here,' Rebecca announced, gesturing to the door.

Lucinda's prince scanned the room, his eyes lighting up when they landed on her.

'What on Earth are those things on his shoulders?' queried Michael. 'He looks ridiculous.'

Nicole tittered. 'At least he wore the costume. I heard it was a struggle talking him around to the idea.'

'I think he looks quite… Charming.' Rebecca barely contained her own laughter.

Slinging an arm over Lucinda, Erin studied Adam as he approached. 'You know, he looks a lot like Ski Resort Guy. I can see why you fell for him.'

Brooke gave her a sidelong glance before dialling up the charisma. 'Oh Adam, you look dashing this evening.'

He cocked an eyebrow at her before enveloping Lucinda in his arms. Their lips met in a chaste kiss, and he whispered, 'happy birthday,' in her ear. 'I have a surprise for you later.'

Her toes curled at the possibilities. Stepping out of the embrace, she looked into Greg's leering eyes and shivered.

Adam's best mate took her gloved hand and pressed his lips to it. 'Happy birthday, love. Sorry I kept your man away from you for so long tonight, but deadlines wait for no one, am I right?'

She never understood their friendship. Quite aside from the age-gap, they were vastly different people. Yet they clicked the moment they got paired together for a project in first year university. Forcing a smile, she nodded. 'It's okay. Is your wife here this evening? You still haven't introduced us.'

''Fraid not. Louise isn't one for big social dos. She did insist I give you this.' Greg handed her a pink organza bag.

Her jaw gaped open as she retrieved the string of ivory pearls. She removed the glove from her right hand to feel them. They were cold at first, warming as she inspected the slight irregularities in the otherwise spherical beads. She detected a glimmering hint of a translucent pink sheen covering the surface of each pearl. At first glance, she guessed they were real. Not wanting to appear rude, she resisted the urge to rub them against her teeth. 'They're beautiful, thank you.'

'Of course they are,' Greg snorted. 'They're natural pearls from the Mediterranean Sea.'

Gasping in unison, Adam exchanged a wide-eyed look with her. 'This is too much Greg; Lucy can't accept them from you.'

The back of her neck prickled as she glared at Adam. 'Excuse me? How is this any of your business, Adam?' She had been on the verge of refusing the gift when Adam triggered her defiant edge.

'Greg's not exactly made of money, Lucy.' He turned to his friend. 'How the hell did you afford these?'

'Don't fret man. I didn't spend a cent,' Greg explained. 'They were an old relic Louise inherited and she didn't want to keep 'em. We figured they'd suit the glamorous Lucinda more. Louise is a bit superstitious about the darn things.'

'Do you know how much natural pearls are worth these days?' Adam asked. 'You could sell them and make a fortune.'

He patted Adam on the back. 'Nah. I'd rather see 'em on a pretty gal. Don't you think they'll suit Lucy?' Plucking the pearls from her fingers, Greg moved behind her. 'Please, allow me.' He released the blue ribbon around her throat, letting it fall into her cleavage, before fastening the pearls in place. His fingers lingered a moment on the nape of her neck, sending a chill down her spine. 'There we go.' Turning her to face him, he gave her a toothy grin. 'Perfect.'

Retrieving the discarded ribbon, she clutched the pearls against her chest. 'Thank you, Greg. Please let Louise know how grateful I am.' After tucking the ribbon in her purse, she slipped her hand back in the white evening glove.

'Will do, love.'

Adam yanked her arm with more force than necessary, making her stumble. 'Let's get a drink.' He led her to the bar.

Her friends and acquaintances followed. She figured at least half of them were sticking their nosy beaks into her conversation, hoping for more drama to unfold.

'Oh my gosh!' exclaimed Zoe. 'Is that Casper Van der Berg?'

All eyes shot toward the door where the man entered wearing a black cape and horns. After flapping his cape in a flourish, he bowed to the applauding room. Spotting Lucinda, he sashayed toward her. His boyfriend, Drew, followed close behind in a Jafar costume. Casper opened his arms wide. 'Hello darling. You look magnificent!'

Accepting the hug, Lucinda giggled. 'And you look Maleficent.'

He beamed. 'Oh good! I'm glad you know your villains.'

Brooke stifled a laugh. 'That remains to be seen.'

Taking two champagne flutes from the bar, Adam handed her one.

Shaking her head, she turned to the bartender. 'Can I have an orange juice, please?'

Handing the spare glass to Rebecca, Adam lifted his in the air. 'I'd like to propose a toast to the lovely Lucinda.' He directed his passive poker face at her. 'Have a wonderful birthday and many happy returns.'

A chorus of cheers and birthday wishes rang out.

Casper pointed at Lucinda's drink. 'I see you're drinking your mimosas without the Champagne. Don't tell me you're pregnant,' he jested with a glint in his eye.

Her cheeks flushed as she met Adam's gaze, his eyes growing wider with each second of silence passing between them.

෪෬

Adam

'Can we talk in private?' Adam tugged at the long white glove on Lucinda's arm.

'Yes, of course.' She followed him up the sweeping staircase into his old bedroom.

As soon as the door clicked behind her, he dropped the social façade in favour of a frown. 'Are you pregnant?'

She nodded. 'I—'

'Why didn't you tell me before? Or am I not the father?' Images of Greg's hands all over her twisted his gut into knots.

Her own brow furrowed. 'Of course you are!' she snapped in a defensive tone. 'I haven't slept with anyone else for the past year.' She inhaled a deep breath and softened as she released it. 'The test results came today. I didn't get a chance to tell you earlier because this is the first opportunity we have had to talk since finding out.'

He sighed. 'I'm sorry about the accusation, but Greg was acting awfully familiar. Not to mention the absurdly expensive gift.'

She huffed. 'Puh-lease. Give me some credit. Greg is the second to last man on Earth I'd sleep with.'

He did not need to ask who out-ranked Greg in that department. He had rescued her from the creep, after all. 'I'm sorry.' He wrapped his arms around her and kissed her forehead. 'Forgive me?'

Tears pooled in her eyes as she nodded. 'Damn hormones,' she quaked.

'I know it's your body and your choice, but I want you to know I'm keen for you to keep the baby. I want to raise him… or her with you. What do you plan to—'

'I'm definitely keeping it. I've already fallen head over heels for this baby.'

He heaved a sigh of relief. 'I'm glad. I know we are still young, but I'm sure we can work it out.' He claimed her lips in a passionate kiss, hoping it conveyed the depth of his love for her better than his crappy words. 'So about that surprise….' Trembling, he pulled her down onto his bed.

Letting out an exaggerated gasp, she pressed a palm across her chest. 'Adam Fairfax! You don't seriously want a quickie in the middle of my party?'

He chuckled at her antics and gripped her thigh. 'Hm, now you mention it.'

Her hazel eyes smouldered, turning a vibrant gold.

'Before we get to that, I have something *else* for you.'

'Hell no. You don't go working a pregnant lady up like that and not deliver. Everything else can wait.' Lucinda climbed into his lap, billowing her skirts out around them. She tore her gloves off with teeth and unzipped his fly. Her warm hand brought his dick to life the moment she grasped it.

The way she took him from zero to scorching amazed him. He would never need Viagra so long as he had his angel. 'You're incredible, Lucy,' he rasped, finding the thin thread covering her core. 'And so wet for me already.'

'Fuck me, Adam,' she demanded in a fierce growl. Her filthy, assertive mouth drove him wild.

Groaning, he eased into her. *So soft and snug.*

'Harder,' she pleaded, rocking back and forth.

'Give me a moment to savour this feeling.' He gazed into her soul, seeking some form of reassurance, but her eyes drooped shut. Lust possessed every inch of her body. Her other emotions would not resurface before she reached her climax. *Time to let go.* He thrust deep, pulled out to the tip, and rammed back into her.

'Oh God yes!' she cried.

Clamping a hand over her mouth, he hushed her. 'Do you want your party guests to hear us?'

Mischief twinkled in her eyes.

'Forget I asked. Still, I'd prefer to spare my parents the embarrassment.'

Her lips pouted, begging for punishment. Biting them provoked her to moan against his mouth and clamp onto his dick. His breath hitched and he upped the pace. One of her glass slippers dropped to the floor with a thud, so she kicked the other free and rode him even harder. As soon as her jaw dropped, he swallowed her scream with a kiss, and emptied himself inside her. Both panting, they collapsed across the mattress.

'I want to make you come like that for the rest of our lives, Lucy.' After slipping back into his pants, he slid his hand under a pillow and retrieved the small box he had stowed there earlier. 'You should know I planned this before finding out about the baby.' Rolling onto his side, he gazed upon her glistening face. He wiped a few stray tears away with the pad of his thumb and opened the box. 'Will you marry me, my sweet angel?'

Awe sparkled in her eyes, reflecting the round, glittering diamond she stared at.

His heart skipped a beat waiting for her reply. 'Lucy?'

'Yes! Absolutely yes!' A squeal burst from her lungs, and she embraced him. She claimed his lips in a frantic kiss, not pulling away until someone knocked on the door.

'Everything okay in there?' Nicole's voice carried a hint of worry.

'Yes!' Lucinda held out her left hand for him. It shook almost as much as his as he slid the ring onto her finger. She shrieked again, ran to the door, and threw it open. 'We're getting married! Adam proposed and I said yes!' She shoved the ring in Nicole's face.

Cocking a brow, Nicole glared at him. 'Did you propose because you knocked her up?'

'Do you think I keep diamond rings lying around just in case?' he countered.

Nicole smiled. 'I guess congratulations are in order then.' She hugged Lucinda, who bounced up and down on her bare feet.

'I can't wait to show everyone else.' Lucinda started toward the stairs, when Nicole caught her.

'Don't forget your shoes.' She shot him another look. 'You might want to change your pants, too.'

He glimpsed the aftermath of sex on his thighs. 'Good point. Thanks Nicole.'

'You're welcome.' Nicole left them to clean up.

Grinning with smug satisfaction, he grabbed a pair of black suit pants from his old wardrobe. 'At least we didn't ruin your Cinderella gown. It's too early for pumpkin time.'

ॐ

Him

Finding Brooke alone in the Fairfax wine cellar, He seized His opportunity. 'You look ravishing in this costume. With all your charms, how are you still single?'

A dainty finger trailed through a film of dust on one of the shelves. Turning to face Him, she smirked. 'Are you trying to fill a supposed void?'

He whispered in her ear, 'In a more private setting, I'd feel tempted to fill all your openings.'

After gaping at Him a moment, her eyes darkened with lust. 'What about your other lover?'

Shrugging, He curled one side of His mouth. 'Does your lack of relationship have anything to do with Adam?'

Brooke gasped. 'How—'

Running His hand along her bare shoulder, He grinned as goosebumps appeared. 'I've seen the green-eyed daggers you shoot at Lucinda when you think no one is looking, especially tonight. I bet you'd love to sabotage their relationship, am I right?'

A small whimper escaped her lips as His fingers brushed her midriff and she nodded.

'We both have reasons for messing with Lucy, so we should work together for mutual gain.'

Her eyes narrowed on Him. 'What do your motives stem from?'

'Does it matter?'

'Yes, it does. If we are going to work together, I need to know as much as possible about my co-conspirator.'

He sighed. 'Fine. Much like you, I'm seeking vengeance for unrequited love.'

A scowl marred her otherwise perfect features. 'You want Lucy?'

'I never said that.'

'But—'

'That's enough about me. Let's focus on our mutual enemy.' He handed her a stack of cropped photos.

Brooke's eyes bugged out as she glanced at the first few. 'Holy cow! These would ruin her. We must show Adam!'

'No, not yet. I have a plan, one that will break Lucy bit by filthy bit. You in?'

'Yes, of course.' Flicking through the rest of the pictures, she froze on one image. 'Is this who I think it is?'

'One and the same.'

Chapter Six

1 Month Later

Lucinda

A gust of wind brought black storm clouds overhead. Seconds later, the rain pelted down. Lucinda shrieked and ducked for cover beneath the gazebo.

Laughing, Adam strolled after her and dropped their picnic basket on the table. 'You're such a drama queen,' he jested. Caging her in his sopping arms, he kissed her against the baluster.

'Adam!' she protested, pushing him back. 'You're getting me all wet.'

He grinned. 'Kind of the point.'

She rolled her eyes at his innuendo. 'You picked the worst kind of weather for a picnic in the park.'

'Where's your sense of adventure? You're the one who's always harping on about wanting to try new things.'

'I meant things like skydiving and travelling the world, all while wearing the appropriate clothes. This is *not* skirt weather. Ugh. I can feel water trickling down my thighs.' She squirmed as the moisture continued to tickle her skin.

Adam's gaze perused her damp dress. 'You sound like my brother. Not that I'd ever want to see him in a skirt, let alone do the things I planned—' His eyes widened the moment they reached her legs.

'What?'

'That's not water you can feel, Lucy.'

'Huh?' She looked down and gaped at the blood. People often describe the moment before death as a flashback reel. Only this was not such a moment. It was not *her* death. How does one see a life flash before them if they haven't yet lived? Tears streamed down her cheeks as she looked up at Adam and whispered, 'The baby.'

'He might still be okay. We should get you to a hospital though.'

She did not need a doctor to tell her what she already knew. She shook her head. 'He's gone. I can feel it.'

When he grabbed her arm, she froze. 'Lucy, *please*. I need to make sure *you're* okay.'

With legs turning to jelly, she fell limp in his arms. Adam carried her to the car, easing her into the front seat. The seatbelt clicked into place, and he sprinted to the driver's side. Wipers whooshed across the windscreen as the car jerked into reverse. Once they reached the road, she rested her head against the side window and watched the beading drizzle. *Is God mourning the loss of an innocent child*, she mused. *Or is He welcoming my baby into His arms?*

Mayhem reigned through the emergency department. Something about the weather was bringing out people's crazy. One of the triage nurses gave her a pad and a bunch of towels to contain the mess before showing them into a private waiting bay.

Adam helped Lucinda onto a stretcher and tucked a warm blanket around her. 'Are you okay? Do you feel any pain?'

Why did he have to ask? She doubled over as the most intense cramp clamped her insides like a vice. Her reply came out as a whimper.

He began rubbing her back. 'I'm so sorry, angel.'

They waited for an eternity while the cacophony of chaos clattered around them.

'Lucinda Seymour?' A woman in blue scrubs peeked through the curtain.

'Yes, that's me,' she groaned.

'I'm Doctor Whitmore and I specialise in obstetrics.' Stepping up beside her, the doctor checked her wristband. 'I'm going to take you through for an ultrasound to check on your baby, okay?'

Unable to talk through the lump in her throat, she nodded. Adam stayed by her side and squeezed her hand.

Doctor Whitmore applied the frigid gel to her belly. 'How far along is your pregnancy?'

'Ten weeks,' she replied with a croaky voice.

'When was your last ultrasound?'

'Last week.'

The room fell silent as the obstetrician slid the probe across her abdomen. 'Hm. Were you able to hear the baby's heartbeat last week?'

Fresh tears pooled in her eyes. 'Y-yes.'

'I'm sorry, Lucinda, but I cannot detect a heartbeat anymore. Also… it looks like the placenta is breaking away from your uterus and your cervix is dilating.'

A garbled sob erupted from deep inside her. *My poor little peanut.*

'The miscarriage will likely take several days. I would like to see you again in a week to check on you….' The doctor's voice grew distant, droning like a swarm of bees as reality kicked in.

She was no longer carrying Adam's child. *What will he think of me? Will he still want to marry me?*

After prescribing some pain medication and booking a follow up appointment, Doctor Whitmore released her to the harsh light of day.

Adam pushed her to the car in a wheelchair he borrowed from the hospital. 'Do you want to go home, or…?'

Shit! Does this mean he doesn't want me anymore? 'I-I'm not ready to tell anyone else yet.' *To break their hearts.* Nicole and Annette had been so excited for them. And Adam's parents. *Oh God!* Michelle had started buying nursery furniture for when they stayed over.

'I'll take you back to my place then.' Adam kissed the crown of her head before lifting her into the car. He took her straight to bed as soon as they reached his apartment.

Curling into the crook of his arm, she opened the floodgates. 'I-I'm s-sorry,' she sputtered between sobs.

He combed his fingers through her tangled hair. 'What are you apologising for, my love?'

'I c-couldn't b-bring our b-baby to term.'

'That's hardly your fault. You heard the doctor; you are healthy enough. It was probably a chromosomal defect at the time of conception,' he assured her.

'W-what if my womb isn't cut out for childbearing?'

He kissed her temple. 'Hush, my love. This isn't the time to worry about such things. Neither of us were expecting this baby. Yes, I'm sad we never got to meet him, but you must admit the timing wasn't ideal. Let's finish university and get married first. Then we can prepare for a family. Worst case scenario, we investigate surrogacy.'

'You still want to marry me?' she asked in a squeaky whisper.

'Of course I do. I love you with all my heart, Lucinda.'

℘Ϫ

The black and white marble of Fairfax Manor glittered under a canopy of fairy lights. Once again, Rebecca and Michelle had insisted on hosting a soiree and they had gone all out. Pink floral arrangements and votive candles lined the buffet table. The hint of a smile touched Lucinda's lips as she approached her future in-laws. She walked hand-in-hand with Adam, and he refused to release his grip until the last second, and only because his mother pulled him into her arms.

'There's the bride-to-be!' Michelle held her at arm's length, studying her long, carnation sheath dress. Her eyes travelled from the lace bodice, past the thigh-high split along her left leg, and down to the sweep train wafting around her crystal studded shoes. 'You look stunning tonight, my dear. Congratulations.' She embraced Lucinda. Stepping back, she studied the couple with a radiant grin. 'You make me so proud.' The way she glowed, anyone would think it were *her* engagement party.

Adam wore an indigo tuxedo with a shirt and pocket square to match Lucinda's dress. He scanned the small crowd of early arrivals, most of whom were family from out of town. 'Where's James?'

Daniel—Adam's father—huffed. 'You ought to know by now that your brother does things in his own time. He'll be down when he's good and ready.'

With a gentle squeeze of her hand, Adam led Lucinda toward his extended family. 'Come on. Let's meet my relatives before yours arrive.'

Adopting her high society mask, she drifted through the sea of faces with her best airs and graces.

'I hear you've bought yourself a new house?' queried one of the uncles.

'That's right,' Adam agreed. 'Settlement just went through, so Lucy and I are moving in next weekend.'

'Where abouts?' asked the aunt.

'Brighton. It wasn't my first pick, but Lucy fell head over heels for the place the moment we put one foot inside.' He met her gaze with warmth and adoration. 'Isn't that right, my love?'

'Actually, it was more like love at first sight when I stepped out of the car, but yes, I felt drawn to the art deco masterpiece.'

'I couldn't very well deny her something that made her so happy,' Adam explained.

'Good lad.' His uncle patted him on the arm. 'You're learning fast. A happy wife makes a happy life.'

Resisting the urge to roll her eyes, she glanced toward the entrance. 'Oh look, my parents are here.' Harry and Tiffany Seymour strode through the door with Nicole Parker and her parents close behind.

Excusing them from the current conversation, Adam linked arms with Lucinda and joined her for the next round of greetings. More hugs, kisses, and well wishes.

'How are you feeling, Lucy dear?' Tiffany inquired. 'You know after the....' her voice trailed off as her eyes lowered to Lucinda's stomach.

'I'm fine,' she insisted, swallowing the lump of emotion in her throat. Two months had passed since her miscarriage; enough to mourn, but never enough to forget the sorrow.

Her mother's left brow arched. 'Are you really? You never talk about what happened and—'

'I said I'm fine!' she snapped.

Mum's jaw hit the floor and Annette drew closer, wrapping an arm around Lucinda. 'Hey, it's okay, sweetie. Your mom worries about you because she loves you. We all do.'

Heaving out a sigh, she stared at the crystals on her pink designer pumps. 'I want to put it all behind me and move on, but it's hard when you all keep reminding me.'

'Okay fine! If that's how you want it.' Mum stormed off towards the bar.

With a simper, Dad followed her.

Nicole traced a finger along the lace on Lucinda's shoulder. 'I love your dress. Is this the one you were telling me about?'

'Yes, it is. I could not believe my luck when I found it and—'

Nicole's attention climbed the staircase and her eyes widened.

Peeking over her shoulder, Lucinda gasped. A familiar pair of chestnut eyes locked onto hers. Too familiar. They sizzled a moment, flicked to the arm she wrapped around Adam's, then frosted over.

'What?' Adam spun them around—to see what she was gawking at—and grunted.

The man in a cream tuxedo stirred a barrage of memories. A whirlwind of emotions spiralled through her chest. He was her Ski Resort Guy. Undeniably. *No wonder I mistook Adam for….* 'Is he your brother?' The question came out dry and cracked through her parched throat.

'The typical showstopper that he is? Yes, he is James,' Adam scoffed.

James descended the black and white carpet-lined steps with a swagger.

'Hot damn!' Casper appeared beside her. 'That man knows how to fill out a suit.'

Casper was not wrong. The years had been kind to James' body. He made his way through the room, shaking hands with distant relatives who crossed his path. Reaching them at last, he focused his gaze on Adam. 'Hey there little brother. Congrats on getting hitched.' James pulled Adam into a side-ways hug and slapped him on the back. 'You're looking good.'

'Thanks, so are you,' Adam admitted with a hint of bitterness lacing his tone.

James shrugged. 'I do my best.'

'James, this is Lucy, my fiancé.' Adam drew his brother's attention back to her.

Peering down his nose, James scrutinised her. When his eyes reached her legs, his Adam's apple bobbed. She doubted anyone else would have caught the subtle movement unless they were ogling him as much as she was.

Schooling his expression and tone, James thrust his hand forward. 'It's a pleasure to meet you, *Lucy*.'

'Likewise.' She shook his hand, ignoring the current zapping through their connection. 'I hear you've been travelling abroad?'

'Indeed, I have.' James returned his gaze to Adam. 'So, how'd you two meet?'

Adam stiffened. 'At a party. Through mutual friends. Speaking of whom, I ought to introduce you to the Parkers.' He tied his brother up in a string of introductions, giving her a chance to escape to the bar.

With a champagne flute in hand, she watched the Fairfax brothers laughing together. James ruffled Adam's hair, earning a playful punch in the arm. Their displays of affection brought a new wave of emotion crashing through her chest. Unable to watch them any longer, she turned back to the bar and asked for a refill.

Nicole joined her five minutes later. 'Is James who I think he is?'

Swallowing a mouthful, she nodded.

'Yikes!' Silence filled the air between them for a few seconds. 'What are you going to do?'

'There you are!' Adam's arms snaked around her waist, and he tucked his chin into the crook of her neck. His fresh fragrance replaced the smoky spice lingering in her senses. 'Are you okay?'

'Yes. I felt a little thirsty. Sorry for disappearing on you.'

'It's all good.' His lips pressed against her ear. 'So, what do you think of my brother? Do you like him?'

Bubbles stuck in her throat and fizzed up into her nose. She coughed and wheezed to clear her airways. 'Sorry. My drink went down the wrong way.'

Adam's eyes narrowed before he grabbed a glass of water for her.

Accepting his offering, she sipped a couple of mouthfuls. Spinning on her heels, she looked at the man in question. 'James seems okay, I guess. A bit abrupt and attention seeking, but I can tell he cares for you. Why?'

'I'd like to ask him to be a groomsman, but only if I have your blessing. Don't worry, I won't give him the best man duties. He isn't reliable enough. We've drifted apart a little in the last few years, but James is still one of my closest friends.'

She had finished swallowing her water when Adam dropped that bombshell. *Thank God for small mercies.* Inviting James onto the bridal party would mean spending more time with him. Lots more time. If James felt even a trace of the initial spark that had ignited between them over three years ago, they were both in for a rough, torturous road. *But is it reason enough to deny Adam the opportunity to bond more with his brother?* 'If you want James to be one of your groomsmen, by all means, ask him.'

Beaming, Adam gave her a chaste kiss on the lips before beelining for James.

Nicole sighed beside her. 'This is not going to end well.'

෧෬

James

The one who got away. It was his own stupid fault of course. Still, he never should've let his fears get in the way. Bile shot up his throat as he watched Adam wrap himself around the only woman James had ever connected with. Nasty, itchy feelings prickled his insides.

'Hello James,' Brooke purred.

He looked at her for half a second before returning his attention to Lucinda. *Why did it never occur to me Adam was referring to the same girl when he told me about her?* 'Oh hey, Brooke.' *I guess I never knew her as Lucy, so….* The happy couple turned around and stared at him. *Fuck!* He averted his gaze, catching a glimpse of Lucinda's long, silky leg poking through the slit in her dress. Vivid images of those legs wrapping around his neck intruded on his thoughts.

'You okay there?' Brooke inquired. 'You look like you've seen a ghost.'

Close enough. He forced a smile. 'Yeah, I'm good. How've you been? I can't imagine it's easy for you to see Adam engaged to another woman.'

'Pfft.' Brooke waved her hand in a dismissive gesture. 'I got over my crush years ago.'

One of the men loitering nearby chuckled.

'Michael, wasn't it?' When the guy nodded, James recalled something about Michael dating Lucinda's friend. 'Have we met before?'

'I doubt it man. I'm not from around here. I grew up in Lucy's hometown—Barwon Heads. I moved to Melbourne for university two-and-a-half years ago.'

'I guess you have one of those familiar faces,' he mused.

'Guess so,' agreed Michael.

Having detached himself from Lucinda, Adam approached James. 'Hey bro, can I have a word with you?'

His chest tightened. *Did she tell him?* 'Sure thing. Lead the way.' He followed Adam into the back garden. *At least the surveillance cameras have us in their sights, so he isn't likely to murder me here.*

'Do you like her?' Adam asked in a neutral tone. Even his expression hid any signs of a tempest brewing within.

James peeked at the camera. *What if he turned them off? Best to play it safe.* 'Who?'

'Lucy, you daft dolt.' Humour rumbled through Adam's chest.

He shrugged. 'Attractive enough I suppose. It's a bit early for me to form much of an impression. I heard you knocked her up. Why isn't she showing more?'

Adam's brow furrowed. 'She miscarried at ten weeks.'

'Ah shit! I'm sorry. Honestly, I'm surprised you're still marrying her.'

Adam's visage mimicked beetroots. 'This isn't a shotgun wedding, James.' His tone turned lethal. 'I'm madly in love with Lucy. I planned to propose even before I knew she was pregnant.'

Hearing Adam's declaration of love tapped another nail in the coffin. *There's no way I can act on my feelings for her now, not without breaking my little brother.* Throwing up his hands, he showed his white flag. 'Woah, chill bro. I didn't realise how serious your relationship was. If she means that much, I'm happy for you.'

Adam took a deep breath and the tension vanished from his muscles. 'Thank you. I hope you grow to like her because she is going to become a member of our family. Also….'

Tap, tap, coffin. *Future family functions are going to suck.*

'It would mean a lot to me if you'd stand by my side as a groomsman.'

James gaped at him. *Oh hell no!* 'Um, don't get me wrong. I'm flattered you asked, but surely you have plenty of other mates who deserve the honour more than I do?'

'Few of them know me like you do, brother. Don't fret, I'm not asking you to organise anything. I've got Greg on board as best man. You just need to stand around looking pretty and we all know you can pull that off.' He gestured toward James' tuxedo. 'What on Earth are you wearing by the way? Did you intend to outshine me at my own engagement party?'

He snorted. 'Not my fault if you can't keep up.'

'So, will you do it?' Adam's eyes pleaded with him.

'I dunno. I've got a lot on my plate at the moment.' It was the best excuse he could think of.

'*Please?*' Adam turned on the puppy eyes. Damn things worked every time.

'Fine,' he huffed.

Adam smirked. 'Thanks, man.' After sharing a bro hug, he ushered James inside. 'It's speech time.'

Throughout the formalities, he watched his brother's fiancé. He did not realise what he was doing until Lucinda's eyes met his. Caught in the act, he scowled at her and jerked his head back toward whomever was harping on about love and whatnot. An invisible thread kept drawing his gaze back to her glossy hair, her plump lips, her soulful eyes. *Crap! Not again. This woman will be the death of me.* He glared at her and looked away. Despite himself, he continued the game of cat and mouse. At one point, Adam announced each of his groomsmen, pointing to James as he did so and summoning him up to join them in a toast.

The atmosphere became stuffier as the night wore on, and he sought refuge in the crisp outdoors as soon as he could. A series of neat green shrubs caught his attention and he soon realised they formed a hedge maze. 'Huh. That's new.'

'Your father wanted to keep up with the Vianellos. When they built a hedge maze, he decided to make one bigger and better.' Lucinda's voice put him on high alert, and he spun around to frown at her. She came alone.

Stupid girl. 'What are you doing out here? People might get the wrong idea if they see us alone together.'

Her brow furrowed. 'Why would they think anything at all?'

He shoved his hands in his pockets to keep them from reaching out and touching her. 'Don't play dumb, sweetheart. I know you recognise me.' He choked back a sardonic laugh. 'I'm not sure if I should feel flattered or creeped out by your choice of husband.'

Moisture pooled in her eyes, but she suppressed the tears. 'What are you talking about?'

'Do you expect me to think you hooked up with *my* brother by pure chance?' Seeing the jibe pain her twisted his guts into knots. Unable to bear the sight, he turned and started walking into the maze.

Her footsteps shadowed him. 'James, please! I need to know —'

'You don't need anything from me. You have Adam.'

She grabbed his arm and forced him to look into her shimmering eyes. 'I need to know if you told him, or anyone, about us.'

His heart sank with lead weights keeping it beneath the surface. *Lucy isn't here to chase after me. She wants to keep her secret safe.* 'No,' he scoffed. 'I'm not suicidal. He'd gut me like a fish if he knew what I did to you. I assume this means you'll keep your mouth shut?' Wrenching his arm free of her burning touch, he continued strolling through the labyrinth.

Lucinda continued to trail him. 'You've changed over the years. You're meaner now.'

'No Lucy. I kept this side of myself hidden until I got what I wanted from you.' Her garbled sob pierced his very soul. Still, it was better to make her hate him. She fled. *Let her think what she likes so long as she remains a safe distance from me.*

Chapter Seven

1 Month Later

Lucinda

The television droned on in the background as Lucinda's vision blurred. She had already flicked through all the channels numerous times and lost interest in the options. At this point, she doubted her favourite rom coms would hold her attention. Too many memories threatened to resurface from the dark recesses of her mind. *Why does Adam have to take night classes? Would he come home if I asked?*

Slapping her hands on her thighs, she swallowed a proverbial spoonful of concrete and sprang to her feet. *There's nothing to fear anymore. The bastard is in prison.* Crippling Adam's career in its infancy because of her insecurities would be selfish. He was already working hard to finish his double degree early for her sake, so they could get married at the end of next year with university behind them both. Turning off the television, she pushed her feet into the kitchen to make some tea.

The kettle crackled and sizzled, heating the water as she opened the china cabinet. Choices presented themselves thanks to their recent housewarming. Settling on the art deco-themed set, she pre-warmed the teapot before adding the Earl Grey leaves. The sweet, floral aroma of bergamot infused the air and soothed her frail nerves. She sank into a stool at the breakfast bar and sipped her brew.

Eerie quiet blanketed the house and a chill crept into her bones. Lucinda hated silence. Her imagination sought ways to fill the void. Nightmares were one thing, but waking dreams were the worst. Wind rattled glass panes, startling her. Knocking the cup over in its saucer, she spilled half the contents. *Damnit!* Reaching the sink, she switched on the radio. Pop music held her ghosts at bay. Grabbing some cloths, she mopped up her mess and poured another drink from the pot.

After another two sips of tea, Madonna began singing 'Music' over the airwaves. Lucinda dashed into the living room and cranked the tune through the main sound system. She twirled, jiggled her shoulders, and shimmied her hips along with the rhythm. Dancing was the perfect distraction. She did not even care if she was acting like a dork. Losing herself in the music helped the minutes tick by.

Bang! Her heart skipped a beat and her senses sharpened. *What the hell was that?* The crashing noise had been close, but she could not tell what direction it came from. Her pulse thundered in her ears and icicles stabbed the back of her neck. Something moved in her peripheral vision, and she spun around to face the window. Sheer curtains covered them, providing ample vision of the street and vice-versa. *Oops! I should have closed the roller shutters.* Stepping closer, she spotted an unfamiliar black SUV parked up against the opposite curb. She knew it had not been there earlier in the evening because she had watched the sunset through the same window. *Is someone watching me from that car?* She shuddered and lowered the blinds.

Thump! That definitely came from the back garden. *A trespasser?* Lucinda retrieved a sharp carving knife from the block on the kitchen bench. She tiptoed down the hall, wincing as the floorboards creaked beneath her feet. Opening one of the rear patio doors a crack, she peered out through the security screen.

Yeeooowl! A pair of cats circled each other near the fence. Laughing at herself, Lucinda eased her grip on the knife. Then she remembered the SUV. It might have belonged to someone visiting neighbours, but her gut told her otherwise. Their surveillance system did not monitor across the street, so she snatched up her camera and strode to the front door. Standing behind the safety of steel scrollwork and wire mesh, she aimed the lens. Before she got a chance to snap the photo, an engine roared to life and the SUV sailed down the road. *Bugger!*

Sighing, she glanced around the front porch. The doormat lay at an odd angle. *Blasted cats.* Something white peeked out from beneath the rug. *Then again.* Switching out the camera for the knife, she unlocked the screen and inched it open. When no one jumped out of the bushes, she snatched the hidden envelope and slammed the door.

She triple-checked the deadbolts before returning to the kitchen. Someone had printed LUCINDA in a simple serif font on the DL envelope. Holding it up to the light and giving it a gentle shake ruled out any suspicious substances. Inhaling a deep breath, she opened her mail. A single sheet of paper sat inside. Perching on a stool, she unfolded the page and read the printed text:

Lucinda,
You are a shameless tramp. Your
very existence poisons the people
around you. You will never be good
enough for Adam. If you love him, you
will set him free.

A mix of rage and trepidation coiled around her chest, cinching her lungs so tight she struggled to breathe. *Who would have the audacity to use emotional blackmail like this? Does Adam have a jealous ex I don't know about?* Lucinda had been so worried about her own history, she never stopped to consider Adam's.

෧෬

Rebecca

Rebecca waved a cloud of nicotine out of her face and rolled over to face Brooke. 'Why do you always smoke after sex?'

Forming an O with her lips, she exhaled a white ring. 'It keeps me in the zone longer.'

'The zone?'

'Yeah. The post-orgasmic afterglow feeling.' She sucked on the cigarette and blew the smoke in Rebecca's face.

Coughing, Rebecca turned onto her back. 'I find the smell a turn-off.'

Brooke shrugged. 'If you don't like it, you can always sleep in your own bed.'

Tears welled in Rebecca's eyes, and she choked back a wave of emotion. 'You know that bed is only for show. I belong here, with you.'

'Of course you do, sugar.' After stubbing out the cigarette in a crystal ashtray, she kissed Rebecca on the cheek. 'I've been thinking.'

'O-oh,' she jibed, suppressing the stammer in her voice.

Brooke climbed on top of Rebecca, pinning her arms against the mattress. 'This is no joking matter.'

Heat pooled in Rebecca's core, and she blushed. *This probably isn't a sexual matter either*. She could not help it though. Her body reacted to Brooke's touch like tinder sparking under a naked flame.

'I'm worried our parents are starting to suspect something,' Brooke explained.

Her eyes widened, and her already crazy fast heart thumped out of control. 'H-how?'

'Something Mum said about my dry spell lasting too long. She worries about how much time we spend together rather than finding prospective husbands. I blame your brother for getting engaged two months ago.' Stroking the pulse point in Rebecca's wrist with her thumb prompted a guttural moan, and she grinned. 'I love how responsive you are. Anyway, I have an idea, a way to get our families off our backs... so you can spend more time on yours,' she added with a sly smile.

'What do you suggest?'

'We should both find ourselves some beards.'

Did she say beards? She stared blankly at Brooke. 'Some what?' Images of donning fake Santa beards came to mind; yet somehow, she doubted this was what Brooke meant.

'Beards. Someone who makes you look straight. If we both get fake boyfriends, no one will question our relationship or housing arrangement anymore.'

'That's actually a good idea.'

Smirking, Brooke shuffled down and sucked Rebecca's nipple. As the bud hardened in her mouth, she bit into it gently.

Rebecca bucked against her and groaned.

'You thought I was about to break things off, didn't you?'

'Maybe,' Rebecca rasped.

'Admit it!' Brooke clamped harder on Rebecca's tender nipple.

The pain outweighed the pleasure this time, and tears trickled down her cheeks. 'Yes, okay. I admit it. I thought you were going to dump me.'

Brooke released the abused flesh and stared at her with eyes the colour of dark, roasted coffee. 'I love you, Becky. I will never leave you. *Never*. You understand?'

She nodded.

'Tell me what you understand,' Brooke demanded, cupping the other breast.

'Y-you love me. You'll n-never leave me,' Rebecca replied.

'Good girl.'

ৡ৻ঽ

Lucinda

A floral plume of steam swirled around Lucinda's head. Sinking into the bathtub, she sighed. She still struggled spending time alone at home, but at least

Adam's summer school had nearly finished. Studying honours in architecture would keep her too busy to notice Adam's absence in the coming months. *I just need to get through these last few weeks.*

Closing her eyes, she began to visualise her goals, what she wanted to see in her future. The strategy had helped her cope with Adam's absence. This time, she focused on the wedding that would take place in the Yarra Valley:

> *I'm wearing a classic A-line dress with a chapel-length train and full veil, designer to be decided. Linking arms with Dad, I walk down the aisle alongside vineyards, gumtrees filtering the sunlight overhead, and a river flowing off to the side. Reaching Adam, I take his hands and bask in his infectious smile. We promise each other a lifetime of love and exchange gold rings. As he lifts the veil, preparing to kiss me, I lose myself in his chestnut gaze. My skin tingles and Adam morphs into James before my very eyes. His mouth crashes into mine and with a twirl, we find ourselves in the honeymoon suite. A scattering of blue*

*rose petals top the silver bedspread. In
nothing more than my white bridal
corset, I hold onto the bed posts and let
him worship every inch of my body
with his luscious lips.*

Shit! Water sloshed all over the floor as she
jerked upright in the tub. 'Bad girl,' she chided
herself. Putting a name to the face of her Ski Resort
Guy had not ceased her fantasies about him; rather
they had turned more vivid and ramped up in heat.
They might have been dangerous if James did not
show such bitter contempt for her.

Thoughts of James had left her core
throbbing despite the knot forming in her gut. *What
harm is there to finishing what my subconscious started?*
She reached between her thighs and brushed a
finger over her clit, imagining a certain tongue in its
place. Writhing against the feather-light touch, she
spilled more fragrant water onto the tiles. 'I need it
harder, James,' she rasped. He answered her plea,
increasing the pressure inside and out.

She reached her climax as a door slammed
downstairs. *What the hell?* Stepping out of the bath
on unsteady legs, she waded through the puddles
and wrapped a towel around her torso. Deafening
silence greeted her when she reached the top of the

winding staircase. Each step represented a slow descent toward danger, escalating the pace of her racing heart. *If someone is inside the house, I ought to arm myself.* Grabbing her favourite carving knife from its block, she tiptoed into the front living room. To her left, she noticed the library door stood shut. Certain she had left it open after picking out her next romance read, she crept across the floorboards. She threw the door open and scanned the library. Empty. As she spun on her heels to face the open plan living area, a strong breeze slammed the door behind her. She snapped her attention to the window, curtains billowing in the breeze. *Didn't I close the shutters and lock the window?* Doubts trickled through the blanks in her memory. Assuming anxiety had caused her lapse, she lowered the knife. Then she spotted it. The same black SUV had parked across the street. *Does that mean—*

She ran to the front door, flinging it open. In the rush, her towel dropped around her ankles. Blushing, she watched the car drive away. In the panic, she had forgotten about her lack of clothing. *Stupid girl. If they had been a stalker or rapist—*

Shuddering, she picked up her towel and secured it. Glancing at the doormat, she froze. Another envelope. She sprinted up to her room, threw on some trackpants and one of Adam's t-shirts, then barrelled down the stairs. Snatching the envelope from the front step, she took it into the kitchen. Once again, she checked it for suspicious substances before retrieving the single sheet of folded paper. The bitch had typed the message in the same font:

Adam deserves a woman who can bear his children.

She knows about the miscarriage. Not that obtaining such information would be difficult. Tears dripped from her eyes, falling in fat blobs on the note. Scrunching the damn thing into a ball, she threw it in the bin and slid down the counter. With knees up, she hugged her legs and bawled her heart out.

Adam found her weeping on the kitchen floor when he arrived an hour or so later. 'Oh Lucy! What's wrong?' His arms encircled her.

'The baby,' she sobbed. 'I miss our little peanut.'

෴

Clutching Rebecca's birthday gift in her lap, Lucinda stared at the passing traffic, the blur of lights hypnotising her.

'How did the dress shopping go?' Adam asked from the driver's seat.

'Huh? What?'

'I asked how you and Nicole went with looking at wedding dresses today?' he repeated in a patient tone.

'Great, actually. I found the perfect gown.' It really had been. Champagne coloured tulle with ivory beaded lace. 'I'm getting quite excited now things are becoming tangible.'

'Same here,' he agreed. 'Did you still want to go to the wedding expo?'

'Absolutely. There's still plenty of research to do.'

'Would you like to invite the bridal party along?' He stopped at a busy intersection, waiting to turn right. 'It'd be a way to include them in our planning. I know Greg's keen to help out more.'

'Good idea, although I doubt James will join us. I don't think he likes me very much.'

'James needs time to get to know you better,' Adam assured her. 'I'm sure he'll love you once he does.'

She stifled a dry laugh.

'I'll have a word with him,' Adam promised. 'With a little encouragement, I'm sure he'll agree to spending more time with you. Your natural charisma will do the rest.' He winked at her before returning his attention to the road. 'Did you hear? Rebecca invited Troy to her birthday soiree.'

Thanking God for the change of subject, she shrugged. 'So? Troy attends most of our social functions.'

'You're missing the point, my love. She personally invited him *as her date.*'

'Really?' She perked up at the news. 'That's awesome.' She wondered if pairing the two of them in the bridal party had something to do with it, or if Nicole had been playing cupid. Possibly both.

Arriving at Fairfax Manor, Adam pulled into the enormous garage right alongside a black SUV.

Her brow furrowed as she studied the familiar car. 'Who owns that?'

'Pretty swish, isn't it? It's James' new set of wheels.'

The garage opened into the family room at the rear of the house where James lounged on a couch, playing a gritty video game. The sight of him sprawled out—wearing black slacks and a half-buttoned shirt—made her blood boil. *He's not even ready for his sister's twenty-first.*

126

James gave them a fleeting glance. 'Oh hey guys.' His focus returned to the screen.

'Adam, can you please give me a moment alone with James?' she asked, handing Adam the gift bag.

'Um, sure. I'll let Becky know you are on your way.' He pecked her on the cheek and left her alone with his cocky brother.

James paid her no heed, so she waltzed up to him, blocking his view of the television, clenching her fists by her sides. 'I know you hate me James, but to sink so low? You make me sick!'

'Woah! Chill chickadee. What's got your panties in a bunch?' Tossing the controller aside, his eyes glazed over as he looked at her.

She narrowed her eyes at him. 'Don't play dumb, you bastard. If you don't quit the late-night visits, I'll tell Adam what you did to me.' She watched his tanned complexion pale with each word. 'Then I'll show him the letters you've been leaving at my doorstep.'

The colour rushed back into his cheeks as he straightened. 'Hold on a second. What letters?'

'Are you seriously going to deny this? I have seen you in that creepy arse SUV of yours.' She waved toward the garage. 'Adam confirmed it belongs to you.'

His eyes darted around the room, looking at anything but her. 'I may have stopped by a few times… on my way home from the office. When I realised… um because Adam wasn't home, I took off.'

'That's bullshit, and you know it. You waited until I opened the door before leaving. Were you waiting to make sure I found the letters before Adam?'

This time James stared straight into her eyes. Foreign emotions swirled in those deep chestnuts. 'I swear I never left any letters. Did they threaten you in any way? Did you show the police?'

She shook her head. 'They were more taunting than threatening. Harassing me to call off the wedding. At first, I figured they were from an old, jealous flame of his. It didn't occur to me that the sender might simply hate me and want to keep me away from Adam for other reasons, not until tonight when I realised you were driving that car.'

He sighed and rose to his feet. 'I don't hate you, Lucy, and I would never send such horrible messages. I happen to think you will make my brother a very happy man. You ought to take those notes to Adam and the police.'

'What's the point? It's not like they threatened me, or anyone else for that matter. I've already trashed them anyway. With everything else going on, I don't want to worry Adam about a petty bully.'

A hint of concern marred his roguish features. 'I suppose you're right. If they escalate though—'

'Any hint of threat and I will definitely go to the police,' she agreed. 'I don't suppose you saw who dropped them at my doorstep?'

'I didn't, sorry.' He inched closer, invading her personal space with the scent of pine forests, smoke, and spice. 'Don't you have surveillance on the house?'

She stepped back, putting much needed distance between them. 'I already thought of that. No one showed up on any of the camera feeds.'

'Hm.' He rubbed his chin, drawing attention to his rugged stubble. 'They're good. Either they know how to stick to the blind spots, or they've hacked the security system.'

'Puzzling.' *Not to mention disturbing.* 'Do you know if Adam has any ex-girlfriends who might harbour amorous feelings for him and animosity for me?'

'Not really. I've been out of the loop too long. I could do some digging though.'

Her eyes widened. 'You'd do that for me?'

'On one condition,' he demanded in a gravelly voice.

'Name it.'

'Don't give into that arsehole's demands. You and Adam deserve a life of wedded bliss.'

Nodding, she turned to hide the emotion welling in her eyes. 'Thank you.' Moving toward the hall, she halted with a hand on the doorframe and glanced over her shoulder. 'Why did you park outside my house like a creeper?'

James smirked. 'Momentary lapses in judgement.'

Chapter Eight

7 Months Later

Lucinda

Reaching the corner of her street, Lucinda slowed her run to a brisk walk. She stopped beside a large tree and cooled down with a few leg-stretches. A gentle breeze trailed after her, carrying the scent of brine. The sun had vanished below the horizon, and the yellow-orange glow of sodium lamps flickered overhead. Going on high alert, she hushed the Planet Funk song on her iPod and scanned the path ahead for signs of danger. Then she spotted it. The familiar black SUV. Common sense took a couple of seconds to calm her hind brain, to quell the initial fight-or-flight response. She knew who sat in that vehicle. *What the hell is James doing here?*

She wanted answers. Getting them would be the challenge. If James saw her approaching, he would likely drive away. Dashing across the road, she darted from tree-to-tree, using the big old trunks as cover. At the last one, she inhaled a deep breath. *Okay, this is it.* Marching up to the passenger side, she tapped on the window.

Jumping in his seat, James stared at her as he lowered the window. 'Oh hey, Lucy.'

'What are you doing here? Adam isn't home.'

His teeth ground together. 'I know. When I found out he was working late at uni, I decided to swing past and check you are okay. That no psychos are dropping by with unfriendly mail and such.'

She gaped at him, ignoring the flutter in her chest. 'I'm surprised you care.'

'Of course I care, Lucy. You're marrying my brother in two months. We're going to be family. You'll be like my sister.'

The word 'sister' felt wrong. It sounded gritty in her ears. Pushing those disturbing thoughts aside, she focused on the positive progress she was making with James. 'Adam will be out for a while, so you may as well come and play bodyguard inside.'

'Nah. I'm good,' he insisted.

She frowned at him. 'Nonsense. It's cold and boring out here. Please, come inside. I'll heat up some left-overs, and we can watch a movie.'

'What sort of left-overs?'

'Chinese. We ordered way too much takeout last night, so—'

'Fine. You've twisted my arm.' Leaving his car, James joined her inside. He hovered in the kitchen, drumming his fingers on the marble counter.

If she did not know better, she would have guessed James felt nervous. But she had never known him to do awkward or anxious. She retrieved four plastic containers and put two in each microwave. Leaving the food to reheat, she ushered James into the home cinema. 'What sort of film do you fancy watching?'

James shrugged. 'Whatever. Nothing too soppy though.'

Rules out most of my DVDs. She flicked through Adam's collection until the title *Wild Things* caught her attention. The blurb suggested a crime thriller. *Might be a little scary, but I'm sure I can handle it with James here.*

As soon as the menu loaded on the sixty-inch plasma screen, James cursed the Lord under his breath.

'What's wrong? Is this one no good?'

'No, the movie is fine. I'm not sure it's appropriate though.'

'I'm not a prude,' she scoffed. 'Besides, it's only MA fifteen plus. I'm sure I can handle it. Make yourself comfortable while I fetch dinner.' A cacophony of beeps greeted her in the kitchen. She stacked the containers on a serving tray, along with side plates, linen napkins, and cutlery. Returning to the media room, she found James on a couch at the back of the tiered seating. 'Help yourself.' She placed the tray on a coffee table in front of James and grabbed a bottle of Riesling from the wine fridge.

He accepted the glass she offered with a smile. 'Thanks.' Something glimmered in his eyes, and he turned his gaze to the plate of food in his lap.

Hitting PLAY on the remote, she settled in beside him. They watched in relative silence for the first fifty minutes, concentrating on eating their food and following the plot. Tangible tension grew in the inches between their bodies, especially after they emptied their plates. With a furtive glance, she spied his clenched fists and white knuckles. *Is the suspense keeping him on edge, or is something else going on in his gorgeous head?*

Meanwhile, the heat had ramped up in the movie. The Lombardo character started removing Kelly's clothes in between passionate kisses.

Clenching her thighs, she tried to stifle the ache in her core. She stole another glimpse of James and froze. Desire had erected a tent in his lap.

'I warned you.' His raspy voice drew her eyes up to a pair of smouldering chestnuts.

God help me! Biting her lip, she turned her attention back to the television. It did not help though. Lombardo was drinking Champagne off Kelly's bare breasts. The scenes both on and off screen made her heart drum wildly. Keeping her gaze fixed on the movie, she asked, 'Do you ever think about that night?'

James sucked in a breath. 'No more than any other one-night stand.'

The dismissal stung more than she expected. She had no claim over James. *And I'm about to marry Adam. I should not be having sinful thoughts about another man, let alone his brother. Maybe the author of those horrid letters had a point.* She stiffened. *Ugh!* Lending any credence to those nasty words left a bitter taste in her mouth.

'Hey, are you okay?' James asked in a soft, gentle tone, stirring the pot of mixed emotions in her chest.

'Yeah,' she replied through gritted teeth. A few seconds later she looked at his intense gaze.

'Why are you lying to me?' he demanded.

'Did you know I was a virgin?' She blurted the question out before she could stop herself.

His eyes bugged out and he turned away. 'Not at first, but I guessed as much as the night wore on.'

She laughed nervously. 'Was I so obvious?'

'There were tells,' he admitted.

'Like what?'

Closing his eyes, James reclined his head against the cushioned backrest of the couch. He counted the reasons on his fingers. 'For starters, there was your shy hesitation, your anxious tremble, your lack of initiative, and willingness to let me lead. Not to mention your innocent doe eyes and how….'

'How what? Was I a lousy lay?' she spat.

His eyes flicked open, betraying the inferno blazing deep inside. 'Not at all. You should drop this line of questioning, Lucy.'

'No. Tell me what you were going to say.'

An animalistic growl rumbled up from his diaphragm. 'You felt incredibly tight.'

A smug grin tugged at her lips. 'So, I wasn't bad then?'

'You're playing with fire, Lucy. I suggest a change of subject before I betray my brother and fuck you on this sofa.'

She smirked. 'You're assuming I'd even consent to such an act.'

His eyes narrowed, turning darker than she thought possible. 'Oh, I know you would. I can see you're as turned on as I am.'

Squirming, she poured herself another wine and sculled half the glass. 'You wouldn't do that to Adam,' she asserted.

He snickered, his voice rough, yet the sound glided over her skin like silk. 'Wouldn't I? The fact I've kept my hands off you thus far is testament to my love for Adam. Nothing more. It's why I've eluded you, to avoid temptation. I'm not a good guy, Lucy. I've broken hearts and wrecked homes. When I want a woman, I don't usually hold back, consequences be damned.'

She gasped at his confession. 'If you've been *avoiding temptation*, why swing past here on nights when I'm home alone? Don't tell me you worried for my safety because you started doing this before I told you about Bitchy Letter Writer.'

'There were times when my inner demon took the driver's seat, literally and figuratively, and I exercised immense willpower to put him in check. On such nights, I drove here without thinking and sat outside, struggling with my urges until I won the battle and headed home. Either that, or you opened the door, and I took off before you caught me.'

Staring into her riesling, she processed his words. 'There's no shortage of women in this city—'

He cut her off with a snort. 'Believe me, I know. I've probably slept with half of them by now, but that's not the point. It's like you have your own gravitational field pulling me back, drawing me in.' Leaning in, he spoke gruffly in her ear, 'You're a delectable dessert, Lucy. I know how good you taste, and I want more, but I also know how bad you are for my health.'

She whimpered as he sat back.

'Don't throw away your future happiness for me. I can't give you what Adam can. I don't do commitment or monogamy, and I don't believe in marriage.'

'Lucy?' Adam called from the doorway, putting an end to the risky conversation. 'Ah, there you are.' Rounding the couch, he planted a kiss on her lips. He glanced at James and smiled. 'Well, this is a pleasant surprise. It's good to see the two of you getting along at last.' Sitting between her and James, he separated his fiancée from the man who had ruined her, the man who could destroy everything they held dear.

ഌഝ

James

Did I really offer Crystal a lift to work? What the hell was I thinking? After returning his phone to its James lined up with the rowdy guys who had followed the buck's party from the Casino to the strip club. In addition to the groomsmen, Adam had invited Michael and a few other mates from uni. He studied the unassuming terrace building with a grey stone frontage. He'd walked past the place countless times in his life without knowing what went on inside. Trance music blared through the open door, and on any other night he could've mistaken the venue for an ordinary nightclub.

Troy chuckled and elbowed him. 'I can't believe Greg is a member at one of the most exclusive gentlemen's clubs in Melbourne.'

James cocked a brow. 'Really? I can believe it. The dirty bastard probably joined *all* of them.'

Glancing over his shoulder, Greg smirked. 'Nah, just the good ones. Call me a connoisseur of the female form. I'm sure you can relate, right Jimmy[2]?'

'Of course I can, old man.' He returned the smug grin. 'Although I don't need to pay to see naked hotties, *and* I get to fuck them.' Sighing wistfully, he rubbed his chest. 'Ah! The perks of being single. I don't understand the appeal of tying a ball-and-chain around oneself.' He patted Adam on the shoulder, adding, 'No offense, brother.'

Adam's shoulders shook with laughter. 'None taken. Why would I care to chase all the tail in Melbourne, when I'm about to marry the most gorgeous woman on Earth?'

The retort coiled around his chest like barbwire. *Damn kid has no idea how right he is.* Since returning home for Adam's engagement, he had not been able to shake Lucinda from his thoughts.

---

[2] Jimmy is a common nickname for guys named James.

Images of her flooded his mind. He'd come so close to giving in to his urges on so many occasions. That night one month ago in the media room where her body glistened with perspiration from jogging, crop top and track pants clinging to her curves. The time she flashed him from the front door, all flushed cheeks, and buoyant breasts. He'd watched her dance around her living room on numerous occasions, shaking her booty like it was no one's business. All the family gatherings where he could have pulled her aside or led her up to his room at Fairfax Manor. Resisting his brother's girl was becoming more difficult as the months wore on. With any luck he could spend the rest of the night drowning his perverted arse in booze and sleaze.

'I've booked us a private room,' Greg explained. 'And I'll be shouting our stag a lap dance with all the extras.' He winked and lowered his voice. 'The ladies here let you touch 'em if you tip high enough.'

Adam winced. 'I could never betray Lucy by touching another woman.'

'That's fine. You don't have to get gropey, but you ought to treat yourself to a lap dance at least once in your life,' insisted Greg.

'I dunno. If Lucy finds out....'

James slapped him on the back. 'Lighten up bro. Tonight is the one night when you can get away with shit like this. If it makes you feel better, we'll all get one at the same time. That way you won't have an audience.'

'A man after my own heart,' Greg gurgled. 'Adam gets first dibs though.'

'Of course,' agreed James.

Once inside, a topless waitress showed them to a room where red velvet couches surrounded a stage with two poles. She took their drink orders and handed Greg a folder. 'We have a great selection of girls on tonight. Will our guest of honour partake in a lap dance?' She fluttered her fake lashes at Adam.

'We all will,' replied Greg, returning the folder. 'Send us eight of your sexiest ladies.'

'Certainly sir.'

Eight buxom babes filed into the room: four brunettes, three blondes, and a redhead. Their waitress introduced them by their stage names, explained the rules, and pointed out the security guard in the corner. The ladies paired up, and each duo performed a short pole dance, stripping down to pasties and G-strings[3].

---

[3] G-Strings are known as thongs in the USA.

'So Adam, who will it be?' Greg asked.

Adam scanned the group and settled on the redhead. 'Elektra.'

'This was your marvellous idea, James, so you get second pick.' Greg gestured toward the remaining girls.

Fixing his sights on a pair of hazel eyes that reminded him of Lucinda, he crooked his finger and summoned Arabella. Golden waves of hair bounced around the stripper as she sashayed toward him.

'I'm surprised Adam didn't ask for Arabella, given her remarkable resemblance to Lucy,' Michael observed as he pulled one of the other blondes into his lap.

James sat back and let Arabella do her thing for a bit. He'd always preferred a slow-burn seduction. 'I'm not. Adam used to have a thing for redheads before meeting Lucy.'

Adam grunted. 'It was never about the hair colour. I'm attracted to women with fire in their souls, women who challenge me. Lucy has these qualities in spades.'

'That she does,' Michael agreed.

Lucinda's look-alike began to grind hard against the bulge growing in James' lap. Throwing his head back, he cussed under his breath. *That feels so good, Lucy.*

She whispered in his ear, 'My name is Arabella, darling.'

Fuck! He shot Adam a look, but Elektra's show had distracted him from that slip of the tongue.

'Don't worry. Your brother didn't hear you,' Arabella assured him with a soft purr. 'I'll keep your secret safe if you promise to book one night with me.'

Is she blackmailing me?

Placing his hands on her bare breasts, she lowered her voice, both in volume and in pitch. 'I can pretend to be Lucy, and I'll wear whatever you like.'

Brushing his thumbs across Arabella's hard nipples, he considered her offer. *She could be the perfect distraction to keep my willpower in check.* 'Hourly rate?'

'Flat rate and you get me *all* night.'

'Yeah okay. I'll bite.'

She giggled. 'Oh, I hope you do. Ask for my card at the cloak room.'

ುೞ

Brooke

While the boys are away, this girl will play. She giggled as she opened the live camera feed, flicking from one room to the next until she found Lucinda curled up with a book in the library. *Ugh! She is such a drag.* Brooke did not understand what Adam saw in her. Sure, the whore had killer legs and perfect tits, *but so do I.* Lucinda was the definition of boring, much like her hen's party. Where the guys had planned a night of gambling and strippers, Little Miss Lucy had celebrated with high tea and silly games.

Another sweep of the property confirmed that Lucinda did not have any company. *No chance of James barging in tonight either*. Although the last time had come close to giving her some real entertainment. *Not to mention blackmail material.*

Opening the list of available wi-fi connections, she scrolled past the ones from the apartment building and clicked on FAIRFOX. The weak signal would prove useless for downloads, but it gave her the access she needed. She entered the passwords, for the wi-fi, then for the security system. Good thing her partner in crime had shown her how to hack like a pro before heading out to play with his "friends." She set the front door camera feed to loop, grabbed her letter, and locked up. The mild, spring night, overcast and dimly lit by a crescent moon, made perfect conditions for skulking in the shadows. She knew most of the blind spots for the camera, sticking to them to be on the safe side. She deposited the letter beneath the doormat, then crept back to the building next door. Within the safety of her partner's flat, she opened the north facing window and lobbed a tennis ball at the fence. The *bang* set off the neighbourhood dogs, and, more importantly, it alerted Lucinda.

Watching through her hidden camera feed, she laughed as Lucinda plucked a knife from the block in the kitchen. *So predictable. What does she hope to achieve with that thing anyway?* A serious attacker could disarm her and use the weapon against her. This time, Lucinda went to the computer room and opened the surveillance footage. After switching between the cameras, she relaxed for a moment. A frown marred her features as she opened the front door, filling Brooke with glee. Lucinda snatched the letter and took it to the kitchen where she inspected the contents against the light.

At last, the moment of truth. Lucinda opened the letter and read the latest masterpiece:

*Hey slut! Not long until the big
day. Word of advice: end it now before
you ruin Adam's life.*

'Screw you bitch!' Lucinda's cheeks
resembled tomatoes as she scrunched up the letter
and tossed it in the trash.

Seeing the bad mood she had incited in
Lucinda turned her hot under the collar. Not quite
as much as the time she made the stupid cow cry,
but enough. *Time to return home to Becky.*

Chapter Nine

James

Everything was too damn perfect. Soft white clouds filtered the sunlight without threatening a single drop of rain. Standing between Greg and Troy, James helped Adam greet his wedding guests with sweaty palms. At least Lucinda had convinced Adam to have a civil ceremony, so they weren't standing in a stuffy church. The choice had disappointed both sets of parents, but it wasn't like the bride, nor the groom, had attended mass in years.

During a lull, Greg turned to Adam. 'I hear Lucy plans to wear those pearls I gave her.'

'Indeed. When I asked Becky what sort of jewellery would suit Lucy's dress, she told me to go with pearls. I suggested Lucy use the necklace as *something old* and gave her a set of matching earrings for *something new*.'

'I'm glad she's getting some use out of 'em.'

Something about the whole exchange did not sit right with James. 'Um Greg, when and why did you give Lucy a pearl necklace?' Wincing, he realised how inappropriate that sounded.

Greg snickered. 'I gave Lucy a strand of pearls for her twenty-first. My superstitious missus didn't want them anymore. Something about pearls symbolising tears. It's all bollocks if you ask me. When I researched their meaning, most sources claimed they represent purity and loyalty.'

A new wave of guests arrived, demanding their attention until the celebrant asked everyone to find their places. Savage Garden started singing 'Truly Madly Deeply' and Rebecca strolled down the aisle in a long, dark red gown. Hearing Troy's breath hitch, James made a mental note to ask for an update on their situation. Lucinda's cousin Heather entered next, followed by Nicole. Then the crowd gushed as the cutest little flower girl with blonde curls strolled down the aisle, tossing cream rose petals across the red carpet. *If Lucinda ever has a daughter, she'll look like that.*

The music changed to 'This I Promise You' by NSYNC.

Seated guests stood and their collective gasp mirrored his sentiments. The most stunning woman he had ever seen paused at the end of the aisle. Lucinda had outdone herself in the beauty department. A veil sat atop her mass of golden waves without masking her beaming face. She took a moment to survey the sea of happy faces. When her eyes locked with his, her countenance flickered and she snapped her gaze to Adam, focusing on him as she strode forward with the confidence of a catwalk model.

Layers of champagne tulle billowed around her hips and the plunging neckline kept drawing his eye. *What I would give for another chance to touch her silky skin. To inhale her sweet, floral scent while tasting her. To hear those cries of ecstasy.* Indulging his fantasies with Arabella, the stripper/prostitute, over the last month had backfired. Rather than quell his thirst, the escort had stoked the flames of his desire for Lucinda.

Reaching Adam, she took his hands, and James basked in her infectious smile. As they promised each other a lifetime of love, he imagined what he would do with Lucinda if he were the one taking her to bed. *Christ! I need my head checked. I can't be lusting after my brother's bride on his wedding day!* A more disturbing thought wiggled its way out of the depths of his mind. *Is it only lust?* He needed to get out of town before he did something reckless.

Timing wasn't great for his fledgling business, but he'd find a way to make it work.

The celebrant presented the newlyweds, announcing that they had tied the knot, one that cinched around his chest.

Photo time sucked harder than a hoover giving head. Forcing fake smiles that felt more like grimaces. Watching Adam put his hands all over Lucinda like it was his God-given right. *Technically it is now. Argh.* When the newlyweds disappeared for some 'couple shots', he wandered over to Troy. The man was lining up at the bar, ogling Rebecca who was giggling with Brooke. He clamped a hand on Troy's shoulder. 'Are you banging my sister?'

Troy spluttered. 'Ah, no. We've had like two dates and haven't even kissed yet.'

Wow okay. Not what he had expected given the fire in Troy's eyes. 'You want her though, don't you? Becky's a sensitive soul—'

'Listen man, I understand your alpha brother concern. I really do. I have two of my own little sisters. But you don't need to worry. Not about me at least. I care for her a lot. Too much to rush in and put pressure on her.'

'Good to hear.' He slapped Troy on the back. 'What are you drinking?'

He shook his head, partly bemused, partly amused. 'I'll start with a pale ale.'

With beers in hand, James proposed a toast: 'Here's to the women who drive us crazy.'

೫೦೧

Lucinda

Lucinda emerged from the changeroom and watched Adam's jaw drop. 'See something you like?' she rasped, grinning from ear to ear. The burgundy ballroom gown she wore produced the intended effect.

'Dear God, Lucy! That dress.' Adam pulled her flush against his body, alerting her to his growing desire. 'Can we skip the reception and go straight to our room? Please?' His palms slid along the sleek bodice and stopped at the cut-out on her left side. He toyed with the tantalising cords criss-crossing each other over the opening. 'I love these, and this.' His hand slid down to the split in her skirt that started at the top of her thigh.

'Let's go eat first. We'll need the energy.' She winked, eliciting a guttural noise and provoking a playful pinch on her arse. Entwining her fingers in Adam's, she led him toward the dining hall.

The rest of the bridal party waited in the foyer, preparing for their grand entrance. All eyes widened as they landed on her. Greg even wolf-whistled. Laughing it off, she avoided James' heated gaze burning into her soul. Awareness of his attention had tingled across her skin all through the ceremony, and the intensity ramped up tenfold at this point. She hoped pretending to ignore him would save them from Adam's scrutiny.

Michael tapped the microphone. 'Ladies and gentlemen, can I have your attention please?' The din hushed. 'Emcee Mike is on the mic tonight!' The crowd applauded, a few laughed, and some even groaned. 'Thank you, thank you. I'll be here all night. Well, until midnight at least. On behalf of the Fairfax and Seymour families, I would like to thank you all for your presence and your presents. Now… I have a few special people waiting in the wings, so without further ado, let's get this party started. First up we have everyone's favourite sister, Rebecca Fairfax, escorted by the dapper Troy Ellis.' Everyone cheered as the pair waltzed into the room. 'Next up we have the bubbly Heather Seymour accompanied by the adventurous James Fairfax.'

She breathed a sigh of relief as James disappeared around the corner.

'Are you okay?' Adam asked.

'I'm a bit nervous about our first dance.' Lies rolled off her tongue so easily by this point, she wondered if it were forked.

He squeezed her hand. 'Me too. Remember to breathe. I can't have you fainting on me.'

She nodded. 'I know.'

Michael had just introduced the maid of honour and the best man who were taking their seats at the bridal table. 'Call me biased, but Nicki looks especially lovely tonight.'

Nicole probably rolled her eyes at her boyfriend's remark.

'Now the moment you've all been waiting for. Ladies and Gentlemen, I present Melbourne's most marvellous married couple to date: Adam and Lucinda Fairfax.'

The room roared as they entered. The next hour or so flashed by like the constant click of the cameras capturing the occasion. Cake. Toast. Greetings. First course. More greetings. Then the speeches started. She laughed at all the jokes, whether they were funny or not. She even teared up through some of the more sentimental bits.

Michael took the microphone at the end of the best man's speech. 'Most enlightening, thank you Greg. Now—'

'Hold up.' James staggered to his feet.

Oh crap! How much has he drunk?

'I'd like to say a few words.'

Glancing at Adam, Michael waited for a nod before handing James the microphone.

James fixed his gaze on Adam as he spoke. 'I'd like to congratulate my little brother on finding such a beautiful woman *and* convincing her to marry him.' The comment earned him a few chuckles.

While Adam schooled his expression, Lucinda drummed her fingers on her thighs.

'I know I'm the least qualified person here to offer relationship advice,' continued James. 'But I've learnt a few things from the many women I've had the pleasure of… meeting over the years. To say there are many fish in the sea is to assume luck will be on our side, where often it is not. If by chance they are even biting, and we don't have to throw them back because they are too young, many of us struggle to hold onto the perfect catch. Adam, what I'm trying to say is: don't let Lucy slip through your fingers. Always cherish and protect her. Never, and I mean *never* take her for granted.'

Her eyes welled with emotion. *Is James implying he made that mistake with me?*

'You recently mentioned that one of the things you love about Lucinda is the way she challenges you. I'm glad to hear it, because challenging each other will help keep your relationship alive, along with surprises, spontaneity, and frequent reminders of your love for one another. Don't let Lucinda be the one who got away… from you.' Clearing his throat, James lifted his champagne flute. 'Ladies and gentlemen, I'd like to propose a toast. To Adam and Lucy.'

'To Adam and Lucy!'

෪෨෬

Rebecca

Watching Adam and Lucinda tango to Debelah Morgan's 'Dance with Me' was like watching a scene out of *Dirty Dancing*. Romantic and hot as hell. Rebecca could not peel her eyes from Lucinda's erotic movements. Good thing her sister-in-law was too straight to tempt her.

'Christ! Not you too,' Brooke complained from where she stood beside Rebecca. 'Is there a single Fairfax Lucinda hasn't enthralled?'

'What are you talking about?'

Brooke directed her gaze toward James who watched Lucinda with hot, glimmering lust in his eyes. 'I'd keep an eye on him if I were you. Given his history with seducing married women….'

She gasped. 'He wouldn't! Not to Adam.'

'I wouldn't be so sure. That speech of his? Sounded more like a threat than words of advice if you ask me.'

The dance ended and Rebecca joined the round of applause.

'Wow! Weren't they spectacular?' Michael asked the room at large from the microphone. 'Now it's time for the bridal party to join our star performers on stage.'

'Go work your magic on Troy.' Brooke nudged her.

'I wish I could dance with you instead,' she whispered in Brooke's ear before strolling onto the stage and taking Troy's hands.

Troy led her through twirls and turns, their bodies flowing together. Despite what she told Brooke, she enjoyed dancing with him. After several songs, she leaned in to ask, 'Can we talk somewhere more private?'

Grinning, he nodded and followed her outside.

Shivering in the brisk night air, she accepted the blazer he placed over her shoulders. 'Thank you.'

'You are most welcome, Becky.' Drawing close, he coiled a ringlet of her hair around his finger. 'You look beautiful tonight. This shade of red suits you. It brings out the copper highlights in your hair almost as much as when you wear blue.'

Her cheeks flushed. 'Um, thanks. Listen Troy, I need to know if I can trust you with a secret?'

His brow furrowed. 'Of course. Is everything okay?'

'Yes. I'm fine. Please promise not to tell a soul,' she pleaded.

'I promise not to tell anyone any of your secrets,' he assured her.

She took a deep breath. 'I like you a lot, Troy.' Watching his eyes widen, she prayed she wasn't about to break his heart. 'If I were different, I could see myself falling for you. As it is, we could only ever be friends. Is that enough for you?'

'Different how?'

'Please answer my question, Troy.'

Sighing, he combed a hand through his blond hair. 'I'll admit I had hoped for more, but I care about you, so I will learn to live in the friend zone.'

She bit into her quivering lower lip. 'I-I'm sorry.' A tear slid down her cheek.

'Hey, it's okay.' Retrieving his pocket square, he dabbed her guilt away. 'May I ask why?'

'I'm a lesbian,' she whispered.

A pregnant pause filled the silence as he stared at her with a blank expression. 'Oh. That makes a lot of sense, actually.'

'What do you mean?'

'To begin with, I've been sending you overt signals all year. Even after two dates you made no move toward anything physical. You always seem much friendlier with Brooke… is she also—'

She clamped a hand over Troy's mouth and nodded. 'Shh. No one else can know about either of us.'

Closing his hand over hers, he lowered it from his lips. 'You have my word, Becky. I'm curious though. Given your persuasion, why ask me on dates?'

She lowered her gaze, studying the shimmering gold straps on her shoes. 'A few people were getting suspicious. I needed to put them off the scent. I'm sorry for using you, and I swear—'

'Don't sweat it sunshine. I'm flattered you picked *me* to cover for you.' He winked at her. 'Do you still need my help? I could be your fake boyfriend if you like.'

She gaped at him. 'Would you really do that for me?'

'I'd be happy to, on one condition.'

'What's that?'

'I get to kiss you in public. To make it believable.'

Her eyes bugged out. 'Y-you still want to kiss me even though I….'

Troy chuckled. 'You have a lot to learn about men. Short answer is *hell yes*.'

Kissing him can't be so bad, right? It's not like he is asking for sex. 'Okay. It's a deal.'

One side of his mouth quirked.

'What?'

'No time like the present to practise kissing me.'

Oh.

He cupped her face in his palm and brought his mouth down to hers. Champagne tang mixed with fruity burgundy as their tongues danced together. Heat coursed through her body, and she mewled into his mouth. Stepping back, he grinned. 'See you round, lover.' Troy waltzed back inside, leaving her breathless and stuck for words.

'Wow! My sister has turned into a master manipulator.' James emerged from the shadows holding a cigarette. 'And she bats for the other team. I never saw either of those bombshells coming.'

She jumped. 'Holy cow! You scared me to death. Were you listening to *all* of that?'

'Yep.' He stubbed out the cigarette in the top of a metal bin.

She slammed into him, scrunching his shirt in her hand. 'Please don't tell anyone. Especially not Mum and Dad.'

He wrapped his arms around her. 'I've never tattled on you, and I'm not about to start. I'm a little hurt that you didn't share your big news with me. You ought to know I'd never judge you.'

'Thank you, James.' She breathed in the warmth and security he offered for a moment.

He snorted. 'I bet you didn't expect him to kiss you. I'd call that a win for Troy.'

'Shut up!' She pushed against him as she stepped back.

Hooking an arm around her shoulder, he guided her back inside. 'Come on. I have some news of my own to discuss with the fam.' They found Adam and Lucinda mingling with extended family from interstate. Their parents had joined the conversation too. James glanced at Dad. 'Oh good. Everyone's here. Saves me repeating myself.'

'Don't tell me we are in for another one of your rousing speeches, bro,' scoffed Adam with wine-stained teeth.

'Hardly,' James countered. 'I limit myself to one a night with those. Speaking of limits, you might want to slow down on the drinking. I'd hate to hear you disappointed Lucy on her wedding night.'

'James!' chided Mum.

'What's your news, James?' Rebecca asked, ever the mediator.

'I need to get back to my field work, so I'll be leaving Melbourne tomorrow.'

She watched the joy fall from Lucinda's face as her own heart sank. *Hm. Maybe there was something to what Brooke mentioned earlier.*

'You're heading overseas again?' Lucinda asked.

'I am,' James replied. 'The perks of running my own tourism company. I get to travel the world and call it research.'

Adam laughed. 'And call it a tax write-off. Seriously though, I'll miss you bro. It's been good having you around this past year.' They hugged each other.

'I'll miss you all,' James admitted. 'Adam, you'll need to keep an eye on Becky for me. I sense romance on her horizon.'

Blushing, she smacked him on the arm.

'Oh?' Mum inquired.

'Troy and I have made things official.'

Mum's face lit up. 'Oh honey, I'm so happy to hear that. Troy is a lovely gentleman.' She embraced Rebecca, as did the rest of the family. All except James who had snuck off amidst the excitement.

Spotting James slinking out through the door, she peeked at Lucinda. The way she watched him walk out of her life, you'd think someone killed her puppy. *I guess it's for the best. If he ever returns for an extended stay, he'll bring bucket loads of trouble with him.*

Part 2

Something Borrowed

Chapter Ten

2 Years Later

James

A golden bird lit up the digital display outside Alicanto Adventures, flapping her wings and circling the logo. James smiled at the mascot he had named Cindy until she exploded in a shower of sparks, giving way to a list of the current special deals. He sauntered inside, taking in the store's bright signage and colourful décor.

The only travel agent who wasn't busy with a client approached in his safari suit sans hat. 'Good morning, sir. My name is Max. Would you like some information on a specific destination, or are you still deciding where you'd like to go?'

He snorted. 'I'll be staying in Melbourne for a while.'

'Ah, well in that case, we have some great deals for local adventures,' Max enthused.

'What would you recommend for wayward proprietors who are recovering from the travel bug?'

Max's eyes widened as deep-bellied laughter emerged from the back office.

'Stop teasing the new guy,' chided Russell in his Aussie drawl. The bear of a man pulled him into a sideways hug, slapping his back. 'It's good to have ya home, partner.' He turned to the eager consultant. 'Max, this is James Fairfax, ya other boss.'

'I'm so sorry, sir. I didn't realise—'

He waved off Max's apology. 'It's all good. I haven't exactly made my existence known around here. You did well and I'm thinking of trying out some of those local adventures you mentioned. Anything to take the edge off.'

Max cocked a brow. 'Surely you've done everything Melbourne has to offer?'

'You'd be surprised how little time I spend in my own city. Grab me some pamphlets and I'll mull over them tonight.'

'Absolutely.' Max hurried over to the brochure carousel.

'Let's go grab a coffee. I'll introduce the others at lunch.' Russell gestured toward the door.

They walked through the bustling mall and Russell led him into a café. 'My shout this time. What are you having?'

He scanned the cake assortment and spotted his favourite. 'Citrus tart and a macchiato. Thanks man.' Grabbing a newspaper, he beelined for a booth in the back. He flicked through the tabloid, skimming over the headlines, and skipping the details.

'There're better ways to catch up on current events.' Russell sat opposite, sliding James' tasty treat across the table.

'Have I missed anything?' he scoffed. 'On the face of it, not much has changed. We've even had the same Prime Minister for eight years now.'

'True,' Russell admitted. 'But business is boomin', which is why I need ya back on deck.'

He sighed. 'I know. Give me a day to ease back in, then we can talk about expanding.'

A tiny waitress with silky black hair delivered their coffees, and Russell grinned at her. 'Cheers, Lisa.'

'You're welcome,' she replied, blushing.

Russell's eyes followed her trek across the room.

'Still single, I take it?' He shovelled a forkful of lemony goodness into his gob and washed it down with a bitter brew.

'Work hasn't exactly given me time for much of a social life,' Russel huffed. 'At least I've been able to indulge in a little stress relief lately.' He gestured toward Lisa.

'Here I thought you chose this place for the coffee,' he laughed. His gaze returned to the paper as he reached the entertainment news. Familiar faces stared back at him from a photo. One particular likeness drew his eye and stole his breath. He read the caption:

> *Casper Van der Berg celebrates*
> *the launch of his latest blockbuster with*
> *partner Drew Webster, and friends:*
> *Lucinda Fairfax, Nicole Parker ....*

'You 'kay, mate?' Russell asked. 'You look a little flushed.'

'Not really,' he admitted.

Russell snatched the distressing page and studied the photo. 'This Lucinda bird any relation of yours? She looks kinda familiar.'

'Sister-in-law.'

'Hm, okay. So where—' His eyes bugged out and he scrutinised the article. 'Oh shit!'

James jumped, already anxious from a long flight, frayed nerves, and too much caffeine. 'What?'

'I know this chick.'

'Lucinda?' he gulped.

'No. Her brunette friend, Nicole. I hooked up with her at Hotham. Must be where I'd seen Lucinda before. Hang on a minute, didn't ya….' Russell looked up and gaped at him. 'Cindy?'

Slumping forward, he pinched the bridge of his nose. 'Guilty as fucking charged.'

'How did she end up with ya brother and why the hell did ya let such a gorgeous woman go?'

'Adam met Lucinda through Melbourne's microcosm of the rich and famous. As for me: I made a huge mistake. Waking up beside her the next day, I realised I still didn't know her name, so I peeked in her wallet. I found her *high school* student ID which included her date of birth. She was only seventeen; underage and three years my junior. I thought she was studying at uni, Russ. I didn't think she was so young. Panicking, I packed in a hurry and checked out of the hotel before she even opened her eyes. Despite all that, I couldn't stop thinking about her. Lucinda was the first and only woman I ever connected with both inside and outside of the bedroom.' Seeing Russell shaking his head, he asked, 'What?'

'Ya didn't break the law, dude. Age o' consent in this state's sixteen, and you weren't in a position of authority over her.'

'I know,' he exhaled. 'I discovered that after the fact. Even so, the intensity of my feelings for her were freaking me out. After spending one night with her, she had turned into my obsession. Granted, we had tons of fun... and the sex... fuck! I still fantasise about her, Russ. Being around her again... I don't know if I'll be able to resist her much longer.'

'Is this why you ran away two years ago and left me to manage the store?'

He nodded. 'What should I do? It's not like I can avoid her. She will be at every function my family drags me to.'

'Take me with ya,' Russell suggested. 'Whenever ya go to one of ya fancy soirees or galas, invite me as ya plus one and I'll keep ya outta trouble.'

He gave Russell a sidelong glance. 'Why do I get the feeling you have an ulterior motive?'

'Because I do,' Russell snickered. 'Don't worry, you can count on me. I'm a stickler to the bros before hoes code.'

'Yeah okay. You'll need to tone down the colourful language and invest in a quality suit or two. I'd lend you mine, but I doubt they'd stretch over your ridiculous arms and shoulders.'

'Fear not, friend. I'll scrub up alright.'

৪০৫৪

Lucinda

The universe must be mocking me, Lucinda thought. In the same conversation where Adam had apologised for needing to work late, he mentioned James returning home for business. Staring at her phone, she considered inviting temptation. The foundations of the house creaked, startling her out of her reverie. She grabbed her mobile and dialled Nicole.

'Hi Lucy. What's up?' Nicole chimed.

'Not much. I was wondering if you were free tonight. Adam is working late and I'm at a loose end.'

'I'm flying solo too. Michael has a business meeting, so Mom's cooking dinner for me. Why don't you join us?'

'Sounds great. I'll meet you there.' She ended the call and put her phone in her handbag. Assessing herself in the mirror, she touched up her makeup, and spritzed a light mist of her favourite floral perfume. Twenty minutes later, a servant greeted her outside the Toorak mansion.

Annette beamed. 'It is so good to see you again. How have you been? And how is that handsome husband of yours?'

'We have been well, although I wish he didn't have to work so many nights. I miss him.'

'Oh sweetie, I'm sorry.' Annette led her into the family dining room.

Rising from her seat, Nicole pulled Lucinda into her arms. 'Hi hun. How are you holding up?'

She shrugged. 'I've been lonely. This pharmaceutical company that recently hired Adam is pushing the overtime. He keeps taking it because he wants to make a good impression and climb the ranks, but I doubt it's worth it.'

'I'm sure it will be in the long run,' Annette assured her. 'I used to feel the same way with Roger, but I adapted. There's no way we could have afforded this house or the luxuries we have without two sizable incomes. These days, I love having time to myself: I get so much done when he isn't around. When he is: we make the most of it.'

Lucinda sighed as servants laid out taco platters and poured glasses of grenache. Luxuries were just that. She did not think they were worth sacrificing a marriage over. 'The food looks delicious. Thank you, Annette.'

'You are most welcome. Please join me in saying grace.' Lowering her gaze, she closed her palms together. 'Bless us O Lord, and these Thy gifts, which we are about to receive, from Thy bounty, through Christ our Lord. Amen.'

'Amen,' Lucinda echoed along with Nicole.

Silence prevailed while they filled their plates and nibbled on their Tex-Mex. Unfortunately, this gave her an opportunity to think about her circumstances: nights alone with James back in town. She had hoped time apart would have extinguished her longing, yet his absence fanned the flames. *Knowing he is a phone call away, that he'll likely give me what I crave.* A tear trickled down her face.

'Oh no! What's wrong, my sweet girl?' Annette shuffled closer. 'You know you can talk to me about anything, right?'

Sniffling, she dabbed her eyes with her napkin and nodded. 'I-I don't know what to do. I love Adam, I really do. But with all the late nights… I have feelings for another man.'

Annette gasped. 'Have you acted on these feelings?'

'N-no. Not in the time I've been with Adam. I met this man first, we hooked up, then he disappeared for years. When he returned, I was engaged. The last time he left, he told me it was for work, but I know he was putting distance between us… to avoid betraying Adam.' She focused her attention on Nicole. 'He's back.'

Nicole's eyes widened. 'Have you spoken to him? Did he say how long he is staying this time?'

She shook her head. 'Adam told me on the phone today. It was the first I've heard of his return.'

'I gather Adam knows this man?' Annette asked.

'The man in question is James Fairfax.'

Annette spluttered, choking on a mouthful of wine. Nicole patted her back until she was able to sip her glass of water. 'Oh dear. This is an unfortunate situation. Does Adam know about your history, or how you feel about his brother?'

'No, he doesn't. I'm afraid of how he might react if I tell him. I don't want to create a rift between brothers who care a great deal for each other.'

'That's exactly what you'll do if you give into your urges, Lucy,' Annette advised. 'You need to find a way to move on from James. I'd suggest prayer, but I don't know if you find comfort in it anymore. Is there an activity you enjoy that could distract you from thoughts of James?'

'I don't know.' The thought of letting go, of releasing James from his special place in her heart, stung like a piercing blade. The pain sucked the air from her lungs, and she sprang to her feet. 'Excuse me a moment.' She dashed upstairs to a bathroom and let the grief gush from her in ugly sobs. *This is ridiculous. Adam is the man I love, the one I exchanged vows with. He is a good man.* Breathing deeply, she calmed her emotions and freshened up at the sink.

Leaving the bathroom, she peered down the hallway toward *the* room. She had not since plucked up the courage to return to the place where Terrance had almost stolen the last skerrick of her soul. Her psychologist had suggested facing this fear to help recover from the trauma, but only when she felt able. *Am I ready?* She inhaled a deep lungful of courage and inched toward the sitting room. *It's just a room. Terry is behind bars. There's nothing to be afraid of.* Standing before the door, she reached out for the handle….

Scritch! Footsteps followed the sound of something scraping over the floorboards.

Her pulse thumped loudly in her ear. Jerking back her trembling hand, she sprinted back up the hall. *I'm so not ready.*

Chapter Eleven

6 Weeks Later

Lucinda

Sitting at her dressing table, Lucinda scrutinised the hazel eyes in the mirror. There used to be a time when the gold flecks dominated like the fire in her soul. Over the years, the spark had withered, leaving a muted green. She applied violet eyeshadow up to the brow bone and cut the crease with shimmering gold, hoping to bring the dormant colour out of hiding.

Adam approached her when she was finishing up. His reflection smiled at her. 'You look gorgeous, my love.' Standing beside her, he adjusted his tie. 'Are you ready?'

'Almost. I still need to put on some jewellery. I'll meet you downstairs shortly.'

'Okay.' He kissed the back of her head and strolled out the door.

The moment she opened her jewellery cabinet, beads spilled out and bounced along the floorboards. 'What the…?' Kneeling, she picked one up and examined it. 'Oh shit!' They were the natural pearls from the necklace Greg had given her. She gathered up as many of the precious gems as she could find and deposited them in a small zip-lock bag. *How did they break?* Thinking about the possibilities sent a chill down her spine. Shoving the baggie in a drawer, she side-boarded the mystery for another day. There was a party to get to, so she picked out a ruby pendant and earrings to match her glittering red cocktail gown.

During the drive, she buzzed with nervous energy. New Year's Eve at Fairfax Manor was always a grand affair, and she looked forward to catching up with everyone. Well, almost everyone. There were a couple of people on the guest list she would prefer to avoid, both for very different reasons. Brooke was… well… Brooke, and James…. Annette's distraction strategy had worked thus far, keeping her too busy to see James since his return. She had resumed sailing, joined a women's golf league, and picked up painting lessons at the local art school.

Casper and Drew cornered her as soon as she arrived, greeting her with grins and hugs. 'Ooh, I love what you've done with your makeup,' Casper marvelled. 'You've made the gold in your eyes po*p*.' He popped the 'P' for emphasis.

'Really?'

'Oh yes, darling. You look simply radiant tonight. I wonder if it has something to do with a certain gentleman.' He winked and cast a casual glance out toward Adam.

She laughed. 'I don't know *what* you're talking about.'

'Puh-lease.' He patted her shoulder. 'There's nothing wrong with a healthy sex life.'

There is if it involves the wrong man.

Drew rolled his eyes. 'Embarrassing the girl won't win you any favours, honey.'

'You're right. I'm sorry, Lucy.'

She shrugged. 'Nothing to apologise for.'

'So anyway, Drew and I would like to ask you something.' Casper bounced on the balls of his feet.

'Oh, okay. What's up?'

'Would you do us the honour of designing our new house?'

Her heart lit up, and tears of joy brimmed her eyes. 'Absolutely! Yes! Oh my God! Thank you for thinking of me.' Creating a home for an A-list celebrity would lift her career off the ground; her own ticket to fame and fortune.

'Of course! Who else would we trust with such a big investment? We'll visit your office early in the new year to discuss the details.'

Beaming, she grabbed Casper's hand and dragged him across the room. 'Come on, I want to share the news.'

Adam was talking to his parents, his brow furrowing when he looked at her. 'Where did you disappear to? You haven't even spoken to Mum and Dad yet.'

Taken aback by his icy demeanour, the excitement evaporated from her own. 'Sorry, I—'

'It was my fault,' Casper cut in. 'I couldn't wait to speak to her.'

She noticed her in-laws cringing. They only tolerated Casper for his status. 'That's right. Casper and Drew ambushed me because they asked me to design their new house.'

Adam's scowl deepened. 'You were talking business at a social gathering?'

'It wasn't like we discussed the details.' She brushed past him to greet Michelle and Daniel, then excused herself. Seeing Nicole and Michael arrive, she approached them, knowing they would elevate her mood.

Casper followed her. 'Talk about proverbial wet blankets.'

While inclined to agree, she bit her lip.

Nicole embraced her. 'Hey hun, why so glum?'

'*Some people* don't know how to celebrate another's success,' huffed Casper. 'I asked Lucy to design a house for me and Drew. When she shared the news with Mr. Prim and Proper Fairfax, he was like "Oh my God, I can't believe you would talk about business on such an occasion." Honestly darl, if he wasn't such a dreamboat, I'd question your choice of husband.'

'Adam has a lot of good qualities, give the guy a break.' She may not always agree with her husband, but she still loved him.

'I'm sure he does, but none of it matters if he isn't making *you* happy,' Casper countered.

'So, you have an exciting new project ahead of you,' Nicole interjected. 'We should toast to that.' She beckoned a nearby waiter who carried a tray of champagne flutes. Once the four of them held a glass, she continued, 'Congratulations Lucy. Here's to a profitable business in a prosperous new year.'

'Cheers,' Lucy replied with a smile returning to her face. It sank the moment she spotted James entering with a burly, bearded friend in tow. She could not quite place his whiskered face.

Nicole followed her gaze and paled. She whispered in Lucinda's ear, 'Things are about to get awkward.'

'Why do I get the impression you aren't referring to my situation with James?'

'Because I'm not,' replied Nicole. 'That man with him? His name is Russell, and he was like my James. Same night, same place.'

'Holy cow! Really?'

Nicole nodded.

James sauntered up to them; the fire in his eyes betraying the casual air he tried to convey. He looked divine in his red, Italian jacquard blazer. 'Evening ladies and gents. This is Russell, my good mate and business partner.' He introduced Lucinda and her three friends.

'No grand entrance on the staircase to show off your flashy suit tonight?' She hoped an attempt at humour would disguise her blatant perving.

He smirked at her. 'I could still arrange it if you like.'

Fanning himself, Casper piped up, 'Yes please.'

A deep, husky chuckle slipped out. 'Sorry to disappoint but living with the folks got a little old, so I moved into a rental.'

'You got your own place?' This was news, and she wondered why Adam had failed to mention it.

'Sure did.' His eyes narrowed on her. 'Although, I still have my own bedroom here.'

Her cheeks flushed as she heard what he did not say aloud: *In case you would like to join me there later*. Lifting her mind back out of the gutter, she shifted her focus to the storm brewing beside her.

Russell engrossed Nicole in an animated discussion while Michael stared daggers at him and clutched his girlfriend's arm in a vice grip.

Curious. Does Michael know their history? Most of the conversation washed over her as she stole furtive glances at James.

Some of Russell's words eventually filtered through and registered. '… it's good to have James back on a more permanent basis, so I can finally have some of me own fun again.'

She shot James a wide-eyed look. 'You're staying in Melbourne for good this time?'

'I am. It's hard to say "No" to Russ and escape unscathed. I mean, have you seen the muscles on this man?' James squeezed one of Russell's biceps and Nicole blushed.

Casper cleared his throat. 'If you are looking to buy a residential property, I recommend building.' He clamped a hand on Lucinda's shoulder. 'I know a great architect, although you'll have to wait for her to finish designing my dream home.'

'You landed a job with Van der Berg?' James grinned when she nodded. 'That's awesome! Well done.' Grabbing a drink from a passing waiter, he clinked it against her glass. 'Cheers.' His magnetic chestnuts held her gaze for an inappropriate length of time.

She let happiness creep back into her visage. 'Thank you. Please excuse me a moment, I need to use the facilities.' *And to escape a riptide named James Fairfax.* Tingling awareness told her he was watching her crossing the room. Once inside the safety of the ground floor bathroom, she took a few deep breaths before relieving herself. Turning off the gilded tap, she reached for a hand towel when the door burst open. She spun around to gape at James. 'What are you doing here?'

He locked the door behind him and stalked toward her. 'Are you trying to get me killed, Lucy?'

'Ah, no?'

Closing the distance, he caged her within his muscular arms: one hand on the vanity, the other on her mid-thigh-length hem. 'Do you have any idea how fuckable you look in this dress?' he rasped as his nose trailed along her neck.

Goosebumps invaded her flesh. 'James, you should go.' She referred to the room. Although leaving the party, or even the city would not be such a bad idea.

'I know what I *should* do,' he growled. 'And this isn't it.' He began inching her dress up, his calloused fingers sliding closer to her core. 'Why did you have to wear red?'

'Excuse me?' she squeaked. 'What's wrong with red?'

'Don't tell me you've forgotten. I never did. Every detail from that night haunts me. Right down to the colour of your dress and the lingerie you wore underneath. Are you wearing the same set tonight, or something similar?' He tugged the chiffon slip above her hips and gawked at her panties. 'Fuck!'

Indeed. She had not chosen red for his benefit, but she wondered if a sick part of her subconscious had. Because she had not forgotten a single detail from that night either.

His gaze met hers. 'I can see the lust blazing in your eyes like an inferno, one consuming us both. Tell me to stop and I will.' Stepping back, he unbuckled his belt, drawing her attention to the pressure building in his pants. She licked her lips as he released the clasp and lowered the zip.

The S word lingered on the tip of her tongue, but she struggled to spit it out.

A knock at the door halted progress with his pants. Frozen, he locked his startled eyes with hers.

'Just a minute,' she called out. *Shit! How do we explain this?*

'It's Russell. I know ya in there, man. Sorry I took my eyes off ya for a split second. Coast is clear out here, but you gotta leave *now*, before doing something you both regret.'

'You told Russell about us?' she asked in an angry whisper.

'As if you haven't confided in anyone,' he huffed. 'My money's on Nicole.' James glared at her as he fastened everything in place. 'You should've stopped me. We got lucky this time. Don't count on it again.' Turning on his heels, he stormed out of the bathroom.

She stared at his retreating form. *Why is the burden of responsibility on* my *shoulders?*

L. STARLA

Rebecca

Surveying the ballroom of Fairfax Manor from the mezzanine, Rebecca spotted James skulking toward the bathrooms. Something about his manner did not sit right with her, so she scanned the crowd for Lucinda. Adam was mingling with some of their Toorak neighbours, but there was no sign of his wife. Frowning, she started for the stairs, getting as far as the top landing when she saw James reappear with his friend Russell. Sighing with relief, she leaned against the black, iron lace railing.

Brooke's familiar smoky aroma—poorly masked by her latest perfume purchase—filled the air as her warm presence shuffled into the space beside her. 'Magnificent view from up here, isn't it? You can see what or *whom* everyone is doing.' Her pinkie finger tickled the back of Rebecca's hand, a subtle but loving gesture. 'Take Michael and Nicole for example. Can you see the tension between them now after the conversation they had with James' brawny friend? I don't know if you were watching their interaction, but Nicole didn't show any obvious interest in the guy, yet something about him woke up Michael's green-eyed monster. I bet Nicole has a sordid history with Beefcake.'

'I'm more concerned with what is *currently* going on between James and Lucinda. Have you noticed the way they look at each other?'

Brooke snickered. 'Oh sugar, those two have more sexual chemistry than a tinfoil cock in a microwave.'

She spun around to face Brooke. 'Do you know if they're having an affair?'

'Possibly, but I can't be sure. Would you like me to investigate it for you?'

'You'd do that for me?'

More of Brooke's fingers brushed against her hand. 'Of course I would. I'll let you know if I find anything.'

'Thanks.'

They watched as Michael dragged Nicole across the floor, away from Beefcake and… toward the stage? He picked up the microphone and tapped it. The PA speakers hissed as he adjusted the volume. 'Excuse me ladies and gentlemen. Sorry to disrupt your night, but I have a question I need answered.' He dropped to one knee and looked up at his wide-eyed girlfriend. 'Nicole Annabelle Parker, would you make me the happiest man alive by becoming *my* wife?'

Nicole smiled when Michael handed her the microphone. 'Yes. I will marry you.' The room erupted with thunderous applause as she kissed her fiancé.

'Huh. I didn't see that coming,' Brooke mused. 'I thought for sure Beefcake would steal her out from under him. I guess there's still time. You know what this means?'

'What?'

Brooke faced her head on. 'My folks will start nagging me about marriage again. The guys I've been dating have provided a good cover, but I need to find a more permanent arrangement.'

She gasped. 'Are you suggesting we can't live together anymore?'

'It only needs to be for show. With the right setup, we could *visit* each other all the time. You should whisper in Troy's ear; see how he feels about a fake marriage. Speaking of whom, you ought to return to his side before anyone gets suspicious.' Brooke gestured toward the Ellis family who chatted with the Pacinis.

'Yeah, okay,' she sighed, ambling away from Brooke.

'There you are sunshine.' Troy tucked her into his side. 'Mr. Pacini was telling us how both of his kids graduated from high school this year.'

She smiled at the middle-aged Italian man who only had a few strands of grey in his thick, espresso hair. 'You must be very proud, sir.'

'We both are,' Mrs. Pacini responded. 'Sofia has her debut next year too.'

'That's exciting. I hope to see the twins at some social functions soon.' She squeezed Troy's hand, signalling her need to talk privately.

Troy excused them from the conversation and led her onto the dancefloor. 'Can we talk while dancing? The music is loud enough to cover our conversation.'

She nodded. 'A good idea.'

He entwined his fingers in her right hand while sliding his other arm across her shoulder blades. Holding her close, he spoke softly in her ear. 'Your dress looks beautiful tonight. Did you know turquoise was my favourite colour?'

'Is it? I had no idea.'

His arm drifted down her back, settling around her waist as they moved to gentle jazz. 'It's also my birthstone. My grandma has given me a piece of turquoise for my birthday every year since I was born.'

'Such a sweet tradition. Explains your affinity for the colour.'

One side of Troy's mouth quirked. 'I love it even more now.' Releasing her hand, he brushed her blushing cheek with his thumb. 'This shade of pink suits you too. What did you want to discuss, Becky?'

'Brooke thinks we should get married.' When his eyes widened, she added, 'You and I, that is. Because—'

'I know what you mean, sunshine.' Sighing, he halted their steps. 'Dating is one thing, but a fake marriage? It's a big deal. We'd need to live together, entertain friends and family, not to mention….'

'What?' she squeaked; afraid she had already overstepped the bounds of their friendship.

'What happens when people start asking us about kids?'

'I- I hadn't thought about children. It's not something Brooke and I have talked about either.'

'You should.' He resumed swaying them to the syncopated rhythm. 'If you are going to make long-term plans, you both need to be across each other's aspirations and expectations. This includes any arrangements you make with men.'

'Are you saying you don't want to do it?' she asked.

'I'm not saying that at all.' He led her through a spin and pulled her flush against him.

She gasped at the bodily contact and heat rose in her face again.

'I need time to think about such a commitment. Can we talk about this later? After you've had a good chat with your other half?'

'Yes of course. I didn't expect an answer tonight. I wanted to let you know what Brooke has in mind.'

Troy nodded. 'I understand. Let's have some fun for now, okay?' He spun her out and back in, making her giggle. They danced away the hours and when the countdown started, his eyes smouldered. 'Not long until I get another Becky kiss.'

During their two-year fake relationship, there had not been many occasions calling for public displays of affection, so when they did arise, Troy made the most of the opportunities. She did not mind; in fact, she had grown to enjoy the contrast of his kiss compared to Brooke's.

The clock struck midnight, and shouts of 'Happy New Year!' joined the chorus of party poppers. Troy's fingers threaded through her hair as he claimed his kiss. Their lips sparked when they touched, and she fell into the moment. His tongue massaged her mouth with expert finesse, sending a rush of blood zipping down to her core. *Dear God!*

This man is actually turning me on. The distant *Boom* echoed her heart as awareness crackled through her nerves.

Chapter Twelve

Lucinda

'That ought to cover it for now.' Lucinda arranged the papers covering her desk in a neat stack and slid them inside a document case. 'I love the vision you both have for a mansion to harmonise with your neighbours', and the examples you brought will definitely help me. The next step is a site visit together, then we can finalise the contract so I can start designing your home.'

Casper clapped his hands together. 'Yay! I'm so excited!'

She opened the client booking calendar on her computer. 'When are you available to meet next?'

Drew retrieved his BlackBerry, and they scheduled a time. 'I assume we'll see you at Nicole and Michael's engagement party tonight?'

'Of course.' Rising from her desk, she led her friends through the bright, open studio to the entrance of Ambience Architecture. A few other architects glanced up from their workspaces and smiled as they passed.

'I know it's Valentine's Day, but Monday night is still a strange time for an engagement party,' mused Drew.

'The date is significant for them, although they won't tell me why,' she explained.

Casper's eyes lit up. 'I bet I can guess.'

She giggled when Drew rolled his eyes. 'On that note, I better let you guys go. Enjoy the rest of your day, and I'll see you both tonight.' She watched the doors close behind them before returning to her cubicle.

As she sat in her gas-lift chair, she spotted a red apple beside her keyboard. *Huh. Odd.* The fruit did not belong to her, and she did not recall Casper or Drew putting it there. She attempted to progress with some sketches, but the mystery plagued her thoughts, making it impossible to concentrate. Annoyed with herself, she snatched the blasted thing and sprang to her feet. 'Excuse me everyone. Did any of you leave an apple on my desk?'

Several colleagues popped furrowed faces over their partitions and shook their heads, while others murmured 'No.'

Not knowing where it came from, she played it safe and tossed the apple in the bin under her desk. It landed with a thud the moment her phone buzzed, and she jumped. Chiding her own stupidity, she read the text from Adam: WORK IS HECTIC TODAY AND I NEED TO WORK LATE. I'LL MEET YOU AT THE PARTY. 'Typical,' she huffed, dropping her phone in her handbag.

Melody, the receptionist, approached with a large, colourful bouquet of flowers. 'A courier delivered these for you. I must say, your husband chose an odd assortment, especially the monkshood.'

Accepting the bunch, Lucinda inspected the mix of purple flower stalks, yellow roses, pink and white blossoms, and red orchids. 'What do you mean? What's monkshood?'

'The violet ones are poisonous, symbolising danger and disdain, while the yellow roses often mean infidelity or betrayal. Is everything okay at home dear?'

'As far as I know. I'm sure he didn't understand what they meant, but I'll ask him. Would you mind fetching me a vase of water?'

'Certainly.' Melody strode away, leaving her to open the attached envelope.

The words HAPPY VALENTINE'S DAY embellished the front of the card in an elegant cursive. She smiled at the sentiment, realising this was the first time Adam had ever sent her flowers, or even recognised the holiday. Several cropped photos dropped out of the card, littering her desk. Gasping, she looked at one of the indecent images, then another. Her gut twisted in knots, threatening to spill its contents as she studied the collection of four-by-four-inch photos. Each depicted her being intimate with a different man—some of her dates in the years between James and Adam—and all showed a pattern she feared revealing. Hearing footsteps approaching, she swept the photos into her top drawer before Melody rounded the corner.

'Here you go, dear. They *are* quite a lovely bunch, just be careful of the monkshood,' Melody cautioned.

'Thank you.' She dumped them in the water without removing the plastic and tissue paper. Alone again, she opened the card. A chill prickled her spine as she read the familiar font on an adhesive label:

Lucinda,

A slut like you doesn't deserve Adam.

Her heart sank as she realised Adam had forgotten yet another Valentine's Day. *Even Bitchy Letter Writer remembered.* This was the first creepy note she had received in over two years. *And what a doozy!* She shuddered to think how someone took those photos. Feeling parched, she guzzled the last of her vitamin juice and sank into her chair. *Why would they contact me again after so long? Were they biding their time for a reason?*

₭‑

Annette Parker's decorating prowess could have rivalled Michelle Fairfax's. Her mansion sparkled under a golden hue of fairy lights. Everywhere Lucinda looked, she glimpsed pink hearts and roses against white linens. The guests of honour looked stunning in their matching pink and white outfits. *No risk of Nicki's old flames outshining Michael on his special night.*

After a round of obligatory formalities, she grabbed a glass of Champagne and found a quiet corner to sit in. Mulling over the explicit photo issue, she debated telling Adam. There was no doubt in her mind, whoever sent them had copies of their own. She recognised the veiled threat implicit in the message. *If I don't tell Adam about my past, they will.* Rubbing her temples, she tried to fight back the start of a tension headache when she spotted James weaving through the crowd toward her. 'What are you doing here? I thought you were avoiding me?'

He shrugged. 'Nicole invited me, and I didn't think there would be a risk of temptation here. Are you okay?'

'Not really. I've had a shitty day.'

James glanced around the room and sat beside her. 'I see Adam isn't here. Is there trouble in paradise?'

'Among other things,' she huffed.

He stiffened. 'I swear to God, if my brother is mistreating you—'

'No! It's nothing like that. Although he has been neglecting me a little.'

'Some men don't know how good they've got it. Do you want to vent?'

'I shouldn't complain. I know he is working hard to support me and our future family, but our big empty house gets lonely and….' She bit her lip, realising how close she came to admitting one of her biggest fears to another man when her own husband did not even know.

'And what?' The genuine concern in his warm chestnut eyes weakened her resolve.

'I'm afraid of being alone, especially at night.'

He sucked in a breath. 'Is this because of the psycho sending you creepy letters, or something else?'

'Bitchy Letter Writer isn't helping matters. They sent me a disturbing message today—first one in years. But my anxieties go way back to adolescence.'

James snatched a drink from a passing waiter and gestured for her to continue. 'I'm all ears.'

'During my fifteenth summer, my parents left me to my own devices for a whole month while they took their second honeymoon in Europe after renewing their marriage vows.' Pausing, she noticed how his breathing had quickened in time with her own. 'My friend Zoe's older brother, Terrance Bristow, learned I was home alone, likely from his sister who didn't know how to keep her trap shut. At the time, I didn't mind Terry's company, and like most girls who knew him, I harboured a minor crush on him. That all changed the night he invited himself over, bringing a bottle of expensive gin:

'Hey Lucy, I thought you might enjoy some company since your parents left you all alone.' Grinning, Terrance held up the bottle. 'I come bearing gifts.'

'I don't know, Terry. They told me not to host any parties.'

'One guest hardly constitutes a party.' He barged inside and beelined for the crystalware in the back room. 'Shall I pour, or would you like the honours?'

She let out a sigh of resignation. 'You can.'

He served the drinks and handed her a glass. 'I swiped this from my folks' liquor cabinet. They have so many bottles of the stuff, I doubt they'll miss it.' His gaze shifted to the shimmering ripples of water in the swimming pool outside. 'You know, it's such a warm night, we should cool off in the pool, don't you think?'

Excitement surged through her veins thinking about the possibilities. 'Sounds good. Do you want to borrow a pair of Dad's bathers?'

Shaking his head, he snapped the waistband of his boardshorts. 'I came prepared.'

'Right, of course. Give me a sec to change.' She sprinted up to her room and slipped into the skimpiest bikini she owned. When she returned to Terrance, his eyes bugged out and her stupid, naïve heart performed somersaults. Sculling a glass of liquid courage, she felt a buzz kick in. She had no idea how many standards he had given her in the first round, but it was more than two. Giggling, she held it out for a top-up.

He obliged before taking her hand and leading her outside. Setting the drinks beside the pool, he walked her into the water. 'Pace yourself with the alcohol, babe. I don't want you drowning on me.' Pressing her against the edge, he brushed his fingers along her cheek. 'I've grown quite fond of this face, and I couldn't live with myself if I let such a devastating fate befall you.'

The moment she blushed; his lips slammed into hers. She returned the kiss with equal vigour, and they made out for what could have been hours. As soon as his hand slid between her legs, she startled and pushed him back. 'W-what are you doing?'

Closing the distance again, he hugged her. 'I'm sorry. I didn't mean to freak you out. I want to make you feel good. You mean the world to me, Lucy, and I want to be your boyfriend. Would you like that? To be my girlfriend?'

'Yes, I would.'

'So what's wrong with touching each other?' His fingers inched closer to her core. 'Do you ever pleasure yourself?' When she nodded, he groaned, invading her with his rough digits. 'This will be much the same, only better.' As soon as she came, he removed his hand and lowered his shorts.

A wave of panic crashed through her. 'Terry, stop! I don't want to go all the way.'

He frowned. 'Why not? I know you enjoyed my fingers inside you. This will feel better still.'

'I'm saving myself for marriage.'

He gaped for a moment, then smiled. 'I didn't realise you were such a good little Christian. I can respect your decision to wait.'

She exhaled her relief as he tugged his shorts up.

'There are plenty of other ways to have fun in the meantime. Come on.' Dragging her out of the pool, he collapsed on a deck chair and whipped his dick out. 'Suck it.'

'What? No!'

'Please princess,' he begged. 'It's the least you can do after getting me so turned on. Tell you what, I'll sweeten the deal. Do this for me, and I'll buy you anything you want as a thank you gift. I know how much you want to upgrade the stereo in your room.'

He was right. She'd had her eye on a Bose sound system for a while, but her parents had refused to replace something when it still worked fine.

She took a long sip of her drink before continuing. 'I gave in to his demands, hating every minute of it. Anyway, long story short, Terry announced that we were going steady despite my protests. When I told him I didn't want to be his girlfriend, he laughed before turning stone faced and insisting I continue to date him otherwise he'd tell the world I accepted gifts and money in exchange for sexual favours. Then he made me go down on him again. In fact, for the following year, whenever he discovered I was home alone, he would break into my house and force his dick down my throat, leaving a wad of cash behind as my *payment*. I eventually plucked up the courage to publicly end our relationship, but not before collecting enough of my own blackmail material with Nicki's help. I also told my parents what he had been doing to me. They were irate and wanted to take the matter to the police, but I needed to forget it all, so I convinced them to let it go on the condition they upgrade the home security system.'

James had grown an unhealthy shade of red while clenching his fists. 'Shit. I'm so sorry you had to endure such vile treatment.'

A single tear slid down her cheek. 'I haven't even gotten to the worst part yet.' His jaw lowered as she told him about Terrance attempting to assault her at Nicole's party. 'Thankfully, Adam was there to rescue me in time. He was my hero that night, and I was enamoured with him as a result.'

Adam found her sobbing in James' arms a few minutes later. 'What's going on?' he demanded.

'She told me about what Terrance Bristow did to her,' James explained.

'Why? What brought this on?' Adam's tone softened, losing its accusatory edge.

Springing to his feet, he glared at Adam. 'You left her in a vulnerable position, brother. I suggest taking better care of your wife.' He strode away, leaving Adam gaping in his wake.

Dropping into the seat James had vacated, Adam embraced her. 'What happened, my love?'

෴

Excusing herself early from the engagement party under the pretence of coming down with something, Lucinda followed Adam to his car.

'You were crying on my brother's shoulder but clam up with me. What's going on, Lucy?' asked Adam as they reached the open road.

'Please drive. I'll explain when we get home.' Resting her head against the window, she closed her eyes and practised some deep breathing. It was all she could do to survive the suffocating tension in the air. She jumped as Adam slammed the car door, storming off toward the house. *Shit! So much for staying calm.* Trailing after him, she found him pacing the loungeroom floor. 'Please sit down.'

Tossing his suit jacket on an adjacent armchair, he collapsed onto the couch and stared up at her.

'Before we get into this, I want you to know James has not seen the photos. He doesn't even know about them. When you found me crying tonight, it was because I told him about Terrance and my resulting fears.'

'What photos?' Adam ground out.

Time to pull the band-aid off. She grabbed her work bag from the hallway and sat beside him. 'I received a series of bitchy letters in the lead up to our wedding. I didn't want to add to your stresses, and I didn't think much of them at the time. They did not threaten me or anyone else. They just said nasty things about me not deserving you. I assumed they came from a jealous ex-girlfriend of yours. Until today. Once we married, they stopped. Until today.' Reaching into her bag, she handed him the card first.

His eyes widened as he read the message. 'When and where did you get this?'

'At work. It came in a creepy bunch of flowers that are still sitting on my desk. There were also a series of photos inside the card. I promise they are all from before we started dating. I'm not going to lie, though. They will be hard for you to digest, so brace yourself.' She handed him the pictures.

After glancing at the first two, he flung them on the coffee table as though they burned his hands. 'Dear God! I can't look at any more of them. I know you had a past but seeing it like this….'

Gathering up the photos, she tucked them back into her bag. 'I'm sorry, but I felt it best to show you before someone else did. It feels like whoever is sending these notes is trying to break us apart.'

Turning to face her, he held her hands, caressing the crook of her thumbs. 'Listen my love, I may find it hard to stomach the visuals, but I accepted your past a long time ago. To be honest, knowing you had a lot of sexual partners before me did not bother me then and it still doesn't. It will take a hell of a lot more than this to drive us apart, and I swear I will fight for us every step of the way. We won't let this bastard get to us, okay?'

Tears trickled from her eyes as she nodded. She let him pull her into his lap and snuggled against his chest.

'I'll give you a few minutes, but we should contact the police. Whoever took those photos broke the law and I worry about things escalating.'

Wiping her eyes on the back of her hand, she sat up. 'What do you mean?'

'This looks like classic stalker behaviour, Lucy. A guy who wants you for himself. Can you think of any men who have displayed an unhealthy obsession for you?'

Terrance came to mind at first, but she dismissed him. 'Only Terry, but he is still in prison.' One other man occurred to her, one whose photo did not appear in the mix. *No way! Surely the timing is a coincidence.* Besides, if James wanted to break her marriage, there were more direct ways of doing it. She sure as hell was not mentioning this to Adam.

'If I call the police, will you talk to them?'

'Okay,' she agreed.

Two male officers arrived in a patrol car an hour later. They took her statement along with the evidence she gave them.

'I'll be honest with you,' the taller of the two explained. 'There is not a lot to go on here. We will process the evidence and keep it on file in case anything else happens. But without a clear threat to anyone's safety, we can't justify a surveillance team.'

Adam turned bright red. 'So you're going to stand by while some pervert harasses my wife? What if he plans to sexually assault her?' He tucked her into his side as she shuddered and kissed the crown of her head.

'I'm sorry, Mr. Fairfax, but until we have evidence of an obvious motive, there is little we can do,' Tall Cop reiterated.

A frustrated sigh escaped Adam as he closed and locked the door behind the officers. A frown marred his expression when he turned to look at her. 'I'm sorry, my love. I had hoped for a better result.'

'Me too,' she murmured. 'I'm feeling quite spooked. Would you mind coming home early tomorrow, so I don't have to spend the night alone?'

He hugged her tight. 'No promises, but I'll see what I can do.'

Chapter Thirteen

Lucinda

Melancholy seeped into Lucinda's bones as she ate her leftover bolognese. She was developing a strong dislike for pasta thanks to its association with lonely nights. Then again, if she tried something new, she would come to hate it as much. Adam had pandered to her request and stayed home the night before, but they were back to the painful routine. *May as well suck it up*, she thought, doing exactly that to a strand of spaghetti.

Smash! The sound of glass breaking upstairs blew her newfound determination right out the window. *What the hell was that?* Springing to her feet, she grabbed the carving knife and tiptoed up the steps. Each turn of the spiral tied a fresh knot in her stomach, and she cursed the architect who designed such dreadful stairs.

A gentle sea breeze greeted her at the top of the landing, and she shivered. *I don't recall leaving anything open up here.* Creeping along the hallway, she checked each room until she reached her own. Her skin prickled all over as she surveyed the damage. One of the sheer curtains billowed out from a broken windowpane, and the culprit sat dead centre on her marital bed. Strands of jute twine fastened an envelope to the offending brick. Taking care to avoid shards of glass, she approached the window. Given the size of the hole, she doubted the psycho had entered the house. Snipping the twine with her blade, she removed the envelope, leaving the rest of the scene untouched. She should not have disturbed as much as she did, but she needed to see the message before reporting the crime.

She took the envelope to her study and checked the contents against her halogen lamp. It felt thicker than a single sheet of paper, but not as bulky as the Valentine's note. Satisfied there were no harmful substances inside, she opened the envelope. A single cropped photo slipped out from the folded page. *Oh shoot!* The picture showed her in the throes of passion with James on the night she lost her virginity. She opened the letter:

Lucinda,
Does Adam know you fucked his
brother?

'No!' she gasped. While she had already shared much of her sordid past with Adam, she did not want to dredge up details that would only drive a wedge between him and James. *Is Bitchy Letter Writer forcing my hand? Surely this rules James out as a suspect. He never wanted to tell.* She needed to apprise him of the situation before informing Adam.

Picking up her phone, she noticed a missed call from a private number and a new voicemail. Dialling her inbox, she listened to the recording:

'Hi Mrs. Fairfax. This is Police Sergeant Wilkins,' the woman's voice started. Lucinda recalled the officer who had helped her four-and-a-half years ago. 'I wanted to let you know Terrance Bristow finished his prison sentence early today. Conditions of his release include a lifelong Personal Safety Intervention Order requiring him to maintain distance from you and avoid all forms of contact. If you have any queries or concerns, feel free to call me on....'

Bile climbed her throat as she hung up. *Is Terry behind the letters after all?* Scrolling through her contacts list with trembling hands, she called James.

214

'Hey Lucy, what's up?' His voice sounded a little distant, as though he had put her on loudspeaker.

'C-can you c-come over p-please?' she faltered. 'I'm feeling s-spooked.'

'Woah!' He came through louder this time. 'What happened?'

'Terrance got out of gaol today and someone threw a brick through my bedroom window.'

'Fuck! Where's Adam?'

'Where else,' she scoffed. 'He's at work.'

'You should call him,' James advised. 'I'm sure he'll come home early for this.'

'I need to talk to you first and you should be here when he gets home.'

'Why?'

'The brick delivered a message and… a photo of us.'

࿇

James

James rushed out of his office and charged into Russell's. 'Hey man I gotta go. Can you lock up tonight?'

'Wait up! Where are you going?' Russell narrowed his eyes.

'Family emergency. I'll update you later.' Flying out the door, he sprinted through the mall toward the staff exit. Apologies rolled off his tongue as he bumped into people. Racing out of the carpark, he weaved through traffic and thanked God for his curb-mounting SUV.

Seconds after he rang her bell, Lucinda inched the door open. Perceiving her visitor's identity, she exhaled and let him in.

Following her down the hall, he could not help but notice how her thin workout clothes showcased her perfect curves. When they reached the living room, he spotted the knife she clung to with a vice grip. Approaching her face-on, he eased the weapon from her hand. 'You don't need this now.' When she relented the blade, he placed it on the coffee table. Embracing her shaking body, he soothed her with further reassurances.

'Thank you.' She stepped out of his hold and sat on the sofa, patting the space beside her.

Accepting her invitation, he kept a good half-metre between them, but she shuffled closer. 'Lucy—'

Ignoring his warning, she plucked an envelope from the coffee table and handed it to him. 'We need to tell Adam before this arsehole does.'

Retrieving the letter, he read the message first. Memories flooded in as he studied the image. The photographer had captured them both facing the mirror as he took her from behind. Groaning, he returned it, along with the note to Lucinda, and adjusted himself.

She slumped against the back of the couch. 'I'm worried about how he'll react, especially after the last lot of photos.'

James sat upright, every muscle in his body tensing. 'What photos?'

Her cheeks flushed, and she closed her eyes as if she could hide from her embarrassment. 'On Valentine's Day I received a note with a bunch of explicit pics. Each one depicted me sleeping with a different guy during my early uni years; before I met Adam. Every one of those men….' Biting her lip, she opened her eyes and looked at him.

'Go on.' He snorted. 'I don't throw stones in glass houses.'

She sucked in a breath. 'They all resembled you, James.'

His eyes grew as wide as saucers. 'What are you trying to say?'

'When Adam learns about us, I fear he'll suspect the truth: I never got over you.'

'Yikes!' Curling over with elbows on thighs, he braced his head. 'I'm sorry, Cindy.'

'What for? And why did you call me Cindy?'

Leaning back, he fixed her gaze with his. 'Ever since Hotham, I knew you as Lucinda. In my mind I shortened your name to Cindy, and it was how I remembered you.'

'How did you know my name?' she whispered.

'The morning after we…,' he gestured toward the photo. 'I realised we hadn't introduced ourselves properly; so I checked your wallet for some I.D. When I discovered you were underage, I panicked. I felt so stupid after,' he huffed. 'You were old enough to consent, and I'm only three years and a few months your senior. I couldn't stop thinking about you afterwards. Not just about the amazing sex, but all the other fun we had, and the conversations…. I've never connected like that with anyone else.'

She gasped at his confession. 'Why didn't you tell me this before I married Adam? You even lied when I asked if you thought about that night.'

He laughed drily. 'I spent the next couple of years looking for you, intending to tell you. I scoured Barwon Heads every chance I got, and I even returned to Hotham the following July. By the time I found you, you were celebrating your engagement to my brother, and I didn't want to interfere. I couldn't bring myself to destroy Adam's happiness, or yours for that matter.'

A single tear escaped her glistening eyes and plopped on her lower lip. Leaning forward, she reached out for his face.

Grabbing her arm, he halted her progress. 'I meant it when I told you I'm not a good guy. I'll ruin you, Cindy.'

'You already have.' She held his stare with equal intensity.

Years of yearning propelled him forward and he pinned her to the chocolate suede upholstery. Their lips merged in passion, and he tasted the salty residue of her rogue tear. She mewled as his fingers skimmed along her bare arm; the sound of her arousal stoking his own. Taking advantage of her open mouth, he swept his tongue along her teeth, enticing hers to come out and play.

Snaking a hand around the back of his neck, she took control: sucking, licking, and nipping his flesh. Her other hand slid down his back and cupped his arse. Trailing kisses along his jaw and down his neck, she bit his earlobe and rasped, 'You feel better than I remember and smell just as good.'

Dear God! Lucinda had grown so bold, a far cry from the innocent girl he had deflowered. He smirked at her. 'We haven't even gotten to the best part yet. I'll make you come so hard; you'll forget every other man you've had since the last time I was inside you.'

She whimpered as his fingers dipped between her thighs and pressed against her nub. 'Wait!'

Jolting, he snatched his hand away. 'What's wrong?'

'We can't do this here. Adam could arrive home any minute. Seeing us together would destroy him, and I hate to imagine what he'd do to you.'

Collapsing beside her, he sighed. 'You're right. We shouldn't be doing this at all. Not while you're still married to him. This is why we can't be alone together, Cindy. I don't trust myself around you, not after so many years of craving another taste, another touch of the best woman I've ever known.'

She hissed. 'You want me to divorce him?'

'No!' He leapt to his feet and combed his fingers through his hair. 'Well kind of, but not for my sake. If you are happy together, stay together. If not, then I'll gladly swoop in and steal you away from him. Just… don't let *me* become the reason your marriage crumbles.'

'I- I don't know what to say to that,' she admitted. 'My relationship with Adam is far from perfect, but….'

'You still love him?'

Lucinda nodded, tears welling in her eyes.

Kneeling at her feet, he placed his palms on her knees. 'It's okay, sweetheart. I want to see you both happy. Promise you'll give Adam a chance?'

'Promise.'

His hands crept a few inches up her thighs. 'And if he screws up and breaks your heart?'

She dropped her forehead to his. 'You'll be the first to know.'

His lips quirked into a crooked smile. *I shouldn't pray for that to happen, right?* 'Don't expect me to hold back next time.'

Panting, she sat back and stared at his hands.

Following her gaze, he realised they had almost reached her apex. He lurched back, stumbling into a cross-legged pose on the floor. 'Shit! Sorry.'

'We should sit at the dining table. Less chance of misbehaving there.'

He followed her to the adjacent room. 'Don't count on it.' Visions of bending her over the table filled his filthy mind. While it might have been smarter to sit across from Lucinda, he chose the chair next to her. 'Have you reported the broken window incident to the cops?'

'Not yet. I guess I should, although I doubt they'll be able to do much this time either.' She left the room, returning a moment later with her phone. 'Will you help me through this?'

He hooked his arm over her shoulders. 'Of course.'

හ⃝ශ

Adam

Turning onto his street, Adam spotted two police cars and a CSI van beside his house. The pulse in his ear hammered, drowning out the music on the radio. When he reached the wrought iron gate, he fumbled with the keypad, failing twice before entering the correct code. *Dear God, please let Lucy be okay.* Rolling along the drive, he pressed the button on the garage key. He tapped his left foot during the excruciating seconds, waiting for the door to rise. 'Come on, come on.' Stomping on the accelerator, he almost rammed into the wall as he came to a screeching halt. Not bothering to grab his briefcase, he dashed inside.

He found Lucinda in the living room, sitting on the middle of the couch as she talked to a pair of officers. James was there too, draping an arm over her shoulders. Relief washed over him like a warm shower on a cold morning. *She is safe.*

A man with a crew cut in plain clothes stopped him at the door. 'Excuse me, sir. Can I see some ID please?'

Furrowing his brow, he plucked his wallet from his back pocket and retrieved his licence.

As Crew Cut studied the card, his eyes lit with recognition. 'You live here?'

'Of course I live here. I'm Lucy's husband,' he snapped.

'Apologies Mr. Fairfax. I thought….' His voice trailed off as he glanced toward the couple on the sofa.

I guess they do look rather cosy. 'James is my brother. What's going on?'

'I'm not at liberty to say. I suggest asking your wife once she finishes her statement.'

Hovering at the edge of the room, he watched the law enforcement team wrap up and leave. The moment they cleared out, he approached Lucinda. 'What happened?'

Shivering, she sank deeper into James' embrace. 'I received another letter. This one came via a brick through the bedroom window.'

'Good Lord!' He sank into the spare seat next to her. 'Are you okay?'

'Physically, yes, but I'm still freaking out.'

'Understandably.' Placing his hand on her thigh, he offered a comforting squeeze. 'Can I see it? The note I mean?'

She shook her head. 'The police took it as evidence.'

'Did you read it? What did it say?'

When she bit her lip, his stomach sank. He knew it contained another secret from her past he would not like. Tears brimmed her eyes as she looked at him. 'There was a photo of me losing my virginity.'

He wanted to kill the creep who thought he had any right to invade Lucy's privacy, especially when she was still a teenager. 'Wait, you told me that happened at Mt. Hotham when you were seventeen. What am I missing here? What's the big secret?'

'The who.'

He noticed James stiffen as he removed his arm from Lucinda. 'Oh heck! Are you for real? *You're* Ski Resort Guy?'

James winced. 'I'm sorry, man.'

'Neither of you thought it worth mentioning at any point in the last…,' he did a quick mental sum, 'four-and-a-half years?' A new sense of dread twisted his stomach in knots, and he clenched his teeth. 'Are you still sleeping together?'

'What? No!' Lucinda insisted. 'It was a one-night-stand, and we didn't see each other again until the engagement party. There is nothing going on between us, I swear.'

He wanted to believe her, but his brother's averted gaze did little to reassure him. *Is James harbouring feelings for Lucy? Is that why he took off after the wedding and stayed away for so long?*

Lucinda reached out and grabbed his hand. 'I'm sorry I didn't tell you before, but I didn't want to upset you over something that happened before I even knew you when it meant nothing to me or James.' She held eye contact the whole time she spoke to him.

While Adam believed her, James still refused to look him in the eye. *It may have meant nothing to Lucy, but I bet James feels differently.* 'Yeah, okay. I'm sorry for jumping to conclusions. Getting back to the letter; did the police find anything?'

Lucinda shuddered. 'This house was crawling with bugs and hidden cameras. Unfortunately, the culprit didn't leave any trace. No prints, nothing. Also… someone tampered with our own surveillance footage. The police suggested switching to a monitored security system. They gave me this.' She handed him a brochure with a list of reputable companies.

'Good idea. I'll get something organised ASAP.' After tucking a strand of her blonde hair behind her ear, he moved in to kiss her cheek and lowered his voice to a whisper. 'Who could have done this?'

'Terrance Bristow got out of gaol[4] today.'

A red haze blurred his vision. 'Fffudge.'

Frowning and balling his hands in fists, James mirrored the rage he felt. 'How is the bastard out already?'

Lucinda took a deep breath. 'I don't know. They placed a restraining order on him as a condition of parole.'

---

[4] British English spelling of Jail

'Hang on,' James scratched his head. 'If this jerk was in the big house until earlier today, he couldn't have sent the previous letter, right?'

'Not directly, Lucinda agreed. 'But he could've orchestrated the whole thing as part of some twisted revenge scheme.'

Images of the time Adam caught Terrance attacking her came flooding back. 'Or worse. What if revenge isn't his motivation? What if he wants to finish what he started?'

Chapter Fourteen

Lucinda

Tossing her shirt in the laundry hamper, Lucinda reached for her bra hooks. *Squeak!* She startled, dropping her hands. *What* — The floorboards creaked again, and she froze. Since the brick incident and Terrance getting out, she had spent the last fortnight in perpetual panic. A familiar crisp citrus scent wafted around her, and she heaved a sigh of relief.

Adam's warm hands gripped her shoulders as he pressed his body against her back. 'Hi there, angel.' He trailed kisses down her neck and along her shoulder, eliciting goosebumps. His fingers slid down to her bra strap, unclasping it and freeing her breasts.

Arching her back, she tilted her head up against his chest and closed her eyes.

A deep groan rumbled through him as he cupped her in both hands. 'Are you ready to expand our family? I'm keen to get started right away.'

She spun around to face him. 'You'll need to stay home a lot more if we have children. I'm not raising them on my own.'

He sighed. 'You know I've been working hard to secure our family's future. When the kids arrive, I promise to ease up on the office hours.'

Embracing him, she peered up into his hooded eyes. 'Good. Would be nice to have you home more beforehand too. Babies don't make themselves. Plus, with my income contributing more to the household than your own, you don't need to push yourself so hard at work.'

'Why do you think I'm here now?' Smirking, he unzipped her skirt, letting it fall to the floor. His hands tugged at the waistband of her panties, stripping her bare. Stroking her sensitive nub, he spoke gruffly in her ear, 'Besides, I'm not taking on the overtime for the extra savings. I'm doing it to prove I am the best candidate for promotion when a management position opens. That way I can support our family when you are too focussed on motherhood to earn a stable income.'

Talk about instant mood killer! Smacking his chest, she pushed away from him. 'How dare you presume I want to be a stay-at-home mum! Yes, I intend to take a few months of maternity leave, but I will not give up my lifelong dream of being a successful architect.' She crossed her arms over her chest and glared at him.

'Jeepers, love. I wasn't assuming you'd quit your job, and I don't expect you to, either.' Drawing close, he pulled her arms down and hugged her tight. 'I meant during the times you take leave, or when the kids are sick etc.'

Exhaling, she relaxed her arms and wrapped them around his waist. 'I'm sorry for overreacting. I've been so stressed lately. I keep expecting Terry to jump out at me any second.'

Adam stroked her back. 'I know. I can feel how tight your muscles are. Would you like a massage?'

When he pressed a knot in her shoulder blade, she rasped, 'Yes please.'

'Hop on the bed then.'

Pulling back the quilt, she lay face down on the middle of the mattress. The clinking of Adam's belt buckle filled her with anticipation, and she listened to him undress. Each garment dropping to the floor sent another rush of blood through her veins.

Sitting beside her, he swung a leg over and straddled her backside. His arousal prodded against her as he leaned forward, kneading and rubbing the tension away.

'God, that feels so-o good!'

'Try not to worry about Terry when you're at home. There's no way he can bypass the improved security measures. You hear me?'

'Yes,' she croaked.

'I'm the only man who will take you in this bed.' Dropping a knee between her legs, he spread her thighs apart. 'Will you stop taking the pill tomorrow?' He continued to work at her knots, delivering a delicious mix of pleasure and pain.

She bucked against his erection. 'If you promise to come home early and ravish me every night until I'm pregnant.'

'You drive a *hard* bargain.' He thrust against her opening for emphasis. 'You have yourself a deal.'

Rising on all fours, she grinned into the pillow. 'I guess it's a good thing I stopped taking the pill a few weeks ago.'

'Why you...,' digging his nails into her hips, he crowned her entrance and chuckled, 'cheeky minx.' Adam buried himself inside her, putting a lid on her immediate fears.

ഇറ

Rebecca

A buzz echoed through Rebecca's apartment. Hurrying over to the intercom, she glimpsed Troy through the camera. He waited at the door to the building, hands in jacket pockets as he bounced on his feet. Unlocking the door, she leaned into the speaker. 'Hi Troy. Come on up.'

Brooke sauntered across the open-plan living area in one of her power suits. 'I didn't know you were expecting company tonight.'

'I wasn't.' She returned to her spot on the leather sofa, closing her Austen novel. Emma's amusing antics would have to wait for another time.

Kneeling before her, Brooke smirked. She grabbed Rebecca's thighs and hiked up her dress.

Wide-eyed, she gasped at her girlfriend. 'What are you doing?'

'Showing you how much I love you.' Brooke spread Rebecca's legs and tugged her white lace panties down around her ankles.

'Troy is on his way up,' she rasped as Brooke's thumb found her bundle of nerves. There was a time and place for intimate moments like this, and greeting guests was not one of them.

'Let him watch. It's not like he doesn't know about us.' Brooke's tongue slid along Rebecca's slit.

'I don't think—' Teeth nipping at her bud stole the words from her mouth and breath from her lungs. She threw her head back and let the pleasure consume her. A knock at the door startled her seconds later. She attempted to move, but Brooke pinned her in place and continued to feast on her.

Upon the second knock, Brooke came up for air and shouted, 'It's open.'

If you haven't yet forsaken me, please help me dear Lord. A thrilling mix of spine tingles and a throbbing core brought her close to the edge.

Troy stepped inside and froze. His eyes surveyed the scene before finding hers. The door clicked as he leaned back into it, still holding her gaze. His expression gave nothing away.

She would have given up her trust fund to know what was going through his mind. *Are we grossing him out, or…?* Glancing at his groin, her cheeks heated when she noticed the bulge. *Okay, so not repulsed then.* Closing her eyes, she focussed on the soft lips caressing her skin, the velvet tongue flirting with desire, and the teeth toying with her darkness. Pressure mounted, and an explosion shuddered through her body as she cried out, '*Aaah!*' When her eyes fluttered open, Brooke gave her a glistening grin.

'Such sweet sugar.' Brooke rose and crossed the room. 'I need to finish getting ready.'

'Where are you going?' She asked in a breathless voice.

'I have a dinner meeting with some potential gala guests.'

Troy remained glued to the door, evidence of his arousal bringing more colour to her cheeks. His eyes flicked down, and she realised her legs were still open, exposing her bare flesh.

Smacking her thighs together, she lowered her hem and turned to Brooke. 'Should I go too?' Anything to escape the sticky situation.

Brooke laughed. 'Oh hun, I don't want to scare them by taking a female date. No, I have my beard lined up for this one.' She disappeared into the bathroom, leaving Rebecca to face the awkward aftermath alone.

A throat clearing brought her attention back to Troy. He had made himself at home in one of the armchairs. 'That was um… interesting.'

'Sorry,' she squeaked. 'Brooke ambushed me. I don't know what came over her.'

'If I were to hazard a guess, I'd say she wanted to remind me who you belong to.'

Her brow furrowed. *Why would she behave in such a territorial manner? Brooke's the one who told me to date Troy. She isn't jealous of our fake relationship, is she?* Shaking her head, she focussed on her guest. 'What can I uh… do for you?'

Averting his gaze, he stared out the floor to ceiling window overlooking the city. His voice adopted a cold, distant edge as he spoke. 'I wanted to discuss our arrangement and your marriage proposal.'

Something about his tone told her she would not like what he was going to say.

Emerging from the bathroom, Brooke drew her eye. With hair slicked back in a French roll, and diamonds dangling from her ears, she portrayed pure elegance. Few knew of the wild side she hid from the world and less had witnessed it firsthand. Warmth pooled in Rebecca's core as she mapped out the curves of Brooke's body, committing them to memory. Catching her admiration, Brooke smiled. 'Come here, sugar.'

Stepping out of her discarded underwear, she stumbled into Brooke's open arms. Fresh, minty breath surrounded her as their lips merged in a languid kiss.

'Promise you'll be a good girl while I'm out,' Brooke whispered against her ear.

Her chest constricted. She would never betray the love of her life. Surely Brooke knew that. 'Promise.'

'Good. Don't wait up for me. I'll be home after midnight.' Brooke collected her designer purse and left.

Hot hands gripped her shoulders, and a firm chest pressed against her back. 'The pair of you gave me quite a show tonight.' Troy's fingers trailed down her arms and threaded between her own. He kissed the back of her neck, sending shivers through her nerves.

'Troy,' she protested. 'We're in private. You don't need to put on a performance.'

'Who said I'm acting?' he growled. 'If Brooke wanted to deter me, she failed. Seeing you in the throes of passion… I wanted nothing more than to be the one delivering such pleasure, to make you writhe and scream.'

She gasped. *Is this what Brooke meant? Did she know—*

Spinning her around to face him, Troy peered into her soul. 'I'm not sure I can keep up any of the charade much longer, let alone do the pretend marriage thing.'

'W-why?' she stammered.

He cupped her cheek. 'Because this stopped feeling fake for me a long time ago. I'm deeply in love with you, Becky.'

When his lips crashed into hers, she tried to push him away, but he clutched the back of her head and deepened the kiss. She tried to resist the sweet taste of temptation, but his fruity scent reeled her back in. Hints of apple and vanilla flirted with her senses. Relenting, she lost herself in their burning passion. Flames surrounded her soul, and there was no way out.

Hoisting her up around his waist, Troy carried her toward the spare bedroom.

The movement broke the spell. 'Wait! I can't do this.' Reaching out to brace herself against the door frame, she slid down and planted her feet on the floor. 'I love Brooke. I won't leave her, nor will I cheat on her.'

He narrowed his eyes. 'What about us? You can't tell me you don't love the feel of my lips or hands on your body. That kiss was a lot of things, but it wasn't one-sided. I'm happy to share you with her, but I need to know how you feel about me.'

'I- I don't know.' Tears welled in her eyes as she tried to make sense of everything. She had never felt attracted to men before, but there was no denying the connection with Troy or the animal magnetism between them. *Is this love? Can I share my heart with more than one person?*

Troy's shoulders hunched. 'Let me know when you decide.' He stormed out of the apartment, slamming the door in his wake.

৩০৪৩

Lucinda

Red lanterns hung above the entrance to one of the best restaurants in town. Lucinda entered hand-in-hand with Adam, finding Casper and Drew waiting beside a large bonsai fountain.

After exchanging hugs and kisses, Casper led them to the host sign[5]. 'Brooke is running a few minutes late, so we should head inside.' He cast an eye over the interior and whistled. 'Isn't this place simply divine?'

---

[5] The sign near the entrance to restaurants instructing patrons that they must "Wait to be seated."

She studied the room beyond the bamboo screen with warm ambient lighting. Glittering gold and jade embellished wood carvings along the walls. 'It looks lovely,' she agreed.

A Chinese man in an impeccable tuxedo greeted them with a wide grin. Showing them to their table, he pulled out a chair for her. 'Would you like to order some drinks while you wait for the rest of your group?'

Casper picked up the wine list. 'Do you fancy red or white, Lucy?'

'Oh, I won't be drinking alcohol tonight, so get whatever you want. I'll have a diet lemonade please.'

One of his brows rose before he returned his attention to the drink selection. 'We'll have two each of your finest Pinot Gris and Shiraz, thank you.' As the waiter disappeared, Casper narrowed his eyes on her.

'Before you ask, no I'm not pregnant, but we have started trying. I want to do everything by the book to improve our chances of a healthy baby.'

Casper's eyes lit up. 'That's fantastic news! I wish you both luck. Drew and I want kids too, but we can't agree on how to go about things, right darling?'

Drew chuckled. 'Yeah. This young stud wants to sow his seeds all over town, but I'd rather adopt. I don't want to further populate the planet when there are so many kids already looking for a decent home.'

'But we would have to move interstate to adopt,' Casper pointed out. 'I like living here, and we have our new house in the works.' He winked at her.

'I hope you work out something you are both happy with. I'm excited by the prospect of parenthood,' Adam admitted, rubbing her shoulder.

She smiled at him. 'Me too.'

Their guests filtered in, and Casper introduced his celebrity contacts: an Australian television star, a local pop idol, a ruckman for one of Melbourne's football teams, a radio news reader, and several up-and-coming actors from film and television.

She was explaining the importance of the charity gala to the woman beside her when Adam groaned. 'You have got to be kidding me.'

She followed his gaze and spotted Brooke. Recognising the man on her arm, Lucinda sucked in a lungful of air and froze. *What the hell is he doing here?*

Eyes as black as coal zeroed in on her, and the embers in his putrid soul sparked to life. With mid-length, obsidian hair in a side part, chevron moustache, and chinstrap beard, he looked like Adam's evil twin. He even wore a darker shade of the same suit. His jawline had hardened, and he looked a little older, but no one would guess he had spent the last four and a half years in prison.

Was the resemblance a coincidence, or…. Bile climbed her throat as she considered the possibilities. Glancing at Adam, she noticed his hand balling into a fist and his teeth clenching together.

'Hello ladies and gentlemen,' Brooke beamed as they reached the table. 'Thank you for joining us. I am Brooke Aquila, your liaison to the fundraising committee. Obviously, you know Casper, who handles sponsorship and donations, and his partner Drew. Lucinda is our venue coordinator, and her husband, Adam Fairfax is a good friend of mine from way back. This handsome fellow'—she stroked her date's arm and Lucinda almost gagged—'is my boyfriend, Terry Bristow.'

Did I hear right? Boyfriend? She glared at the sleaze. 'You shouldn't be here!' she snapped.

Scanning the faces around the table, Terrance chuckled and took a seat. 'Apologies all, I had no idea my ex-girlfriend would be here tonight. I don't mean to cause any trouble.'

'Yeah right,' she huffed, slamming her palms on the table as she rose. 'This man—'

'Now is not the time or place to air petty grievances, Lucinda.' Brooke cast her eyes across the gathered group to emphasise her point. 'Please sit down. There is much to discuss.'

Sitting down, Lucinda wrapped a hand around Adam's fist. She hoped he would not do anything stupid, like get himself arrested on assault charges. As much as she loved him for wanting to protect her, he could not do much from behind bars.

Crossing his arms, Terrance gave her a smug grin.

'Ooh. So much drama!' Casper clapped his hands together. 'You know I live for this stuff, right?'

Drew rolled his eyes. 'Don't you mean you make a living from it?'

Casper tutted. 'Same difference. Shall we order? I was thinking of sharing the deluxe banquet unless anyone wants to order specific dishes?'

As much as she wanted to enlighten everybody—to explain the tension as more than animosity between disgruntled ex-lovers—she held her tongue. Exposing Terrance as a sicko would bring down the mood and the Fundraising Committee needed these celebrities at the upcoming gala. So, she suffered in silence, her skin crawling every time she felt or caught his gaze on her.

Chapter Fifteen

Rebecca

Browsing the classic literature aisle, Rebecca struggled with indecision. She had narrowed her shortlist down to ten when her phone buzzed. Opening the device, she read the message from Brooke:

HI SUGAR. COME STRAIGHT HOME. I HAVE IMPORTANT NEWS ABOUT LUCY.

Running her finger along the spines of the books in her basket, she shrugged. *Screw it. I'll get them all.* Placing the stack of novels on the counter, she blushed as the clerk scanned the top title. In the last month, she had started reading more steamy romance. It was the best way she knew to explore her sexuality. In doing so, she hoped to find the answers Troy waited for. Their friendship teetered on thin ice, and he had declined most of her invitations to social functions. If she did not act soon, she feared losing him for good.

Entering the apartment, she dropped her bags on the dining table. Not seeing Brooke in the living area, she almost called out when a grunting noise drifted through the bedroom door. *Odd. That didn't sound like her....* Stopping in the doorway, she stifled a gasp with a hand over her mouth. A dark-haired man sat on the edge of the bed with Brooke kneeling between his legs, her head bobbing up and down as she took him in her mouth. Heat filled Rebecca's cheeks and pooled between her legs as she watched them, wondering what it would be like to taste a man. *To taste Troy.*

Turning his head toward her, the man grinned. 'You must be Becky.' He threaded his fingers through Brooke's hair. 'You look a lot like your brothers.'

She inched into the room. 'And you are?'

'Terry's the name.' He threw his head back and moaned. 'Hell, that feels good. I love it when women choke on me. Lucy used to do this for me when we dated during our teenage years. She never slept with me though.'

Why is he telling me this? Lucy's past personal life was none of her business.

He sought her gaze with his charcoal eyes. 'No, the lucky bastard who took her virginity was none other than your brother, and I don't mean the one she married.' He huffed. 'Lucy never even knew his name when she opened her legs to him on the slopes of Hotham. She referred to him as Ski Resort Guy, and he became her obsession—the one who got away. For years, she screwed around, only choosing guys who looked like James. I guess the resemblance was strong enough with Adam to keep him.'

Oh. The reason Brooke invited this sleaze into their home began making sense. 'Do you know if she is having an affair with James?'

'I have my suspicions,' he replied. 'But no concrete evidence, not *yet*.'

Brooke's tongue trailed along the tip of Terry's penis. She turned and smiled. 'Don't take this personally, sugar. I still love you and your delicious body, but I've missed men.' She climbed into his lap.

Removing Brooke's dress, Terry exposed her bare flesh. He ran his hands all over her breasts. 'Your girlfriend is exquisite, Becky. I hope you don't mind if I borrow her from time-to-time.' Gripping Brooke's hips, he slammed her pelvis against his own and they both cried out.

246

She watched in horror as a man offered Brooke the sort of pleasure only she should be giving her girlfriend. *What does she even see in him?* Studying Terry with an objective eye, she supposed he was handsome in a classic way, all high cheekbones and sharp jawline. The suit draping over the back of the chair in the corner of the room looked expensive, possibly even tailored, so he must be well-off. Chances are he came from money if he grew up in Lucinda's circle. Yet none of these qualities excused his brutish behaviour or loathsome language. Something was off about his essence, and she did not like him.

'Oh fuck yes!' Brooke roared. With the position she had adopted in Terry's lap, it was impossible to see her eyes at this angle. Even so, Rebecca knew they would be glazing over as the orgasm rippled through her body.

Wiping a tear from her eye, she spun on her heels and rushed out the room. She needed to be anywhere but here. *May as well go to my parents' place early.* They had organised a family dinner to celebrate James' business expansion, although she knew this was their excuse to have him over for his birthday. Grabbing her handbag, she put the dreadful scene behind her.

ॐ૭ಜ

Lucinda

'Just because you succeeded so quickly, doesn't mean you get to go back to being the absent husband!' Lucinda spat as she slammed the car door.

The immobiliser activated, beeping as Adam sighed. 'It's not like I want to spend so much time away from home. We have an audit going on, which means work is crazy right now. Things will settle down again soon, I promise.'

'For like a week before the next thing comes along. If you love your job so much, why don't you marry *it* instead of me!' Movement in her peripheral vision caught her attention, and she glimpsed something over Adam's shoulder. James hovered by the garage door with a furrowed brow. Even though the Fairfax siblings all lived in their own houses, they still had parking spaces and access to their family home to come and go as they pleased.

His gaze danced along her skin like tiny pebbles of awareness. 'Everything okay with you guys?'

Adam turned to face his brother. 'Mind your own business.' Storming inside, he let the door swing shut with a *bang*!

Stalking toward her, James closed the distance between them. He stopped a hair's breadth away and squeezed her shoulder. 'Are *you* okay?' Tears pooled in her eyes. When one escaped, he sucked in a breath and embraced her. 'I swear, if I don't start seeing the two of you happy together soon….' He did not need to finish the threat. She knew he was waiting in the wings.

She soaked in his warmth for a full minute. It took every ounce of restraint she possessed to keep her hands and lips to herself. 'We should go inside before Adam grows suspicious.'

'We're not doing anything wrong, Cindy.' His gruff voice sent shivers straight to her core.

'Not yet, but if you don't stop holding me soon….'

He peeled himself away from her. 'Go on, I'll join you all in a bit.'

Her eyes travelled down, and she bit her lip, understanding why he needed a moment. 'Okay,' she rasped.

The rest of the Fairfax clan greeted her with hugs and cheek kisses as they assembled around the massive family dining table. With chairs enough for twenty, she had never seen it full—not even when both sets of grandparents came for dinner. *Are they expecting lots of grandkids?*

When James sat opposite Lucinda, she avoided his gaze, instead fixing her attention on the display of elegant filigree fine china, shimmering silverware, sparkling crystal, and crisp linens before her. She sensed his eyes on her and prayed to God Adam did not notice.

As if in answer to her prayer, Michelle placed a wrapped parcel in front of James. 'I know you don't like to make a fuss about birthdays, but as your mother I reserve the right to celebrate the day I brought you into this world.'

He exhaled a huff of humour. 'I s'pose I'll let you get away with it this time. But no more after this.'

Something glimmered in Michelle's eyes, and Daniel chuckled. 'You say that every time, Son. I don't think she will ever take the hint.'

'Dad's right,' said Adam. 'You're two years off thirty now. Don't think for a second you'll be escaping the inevitable soiree that comes with a milestone.'

Rolling his eyes, James set to work unwrapping his gift. His eyes widened as he uncovered a sports watch.

Michelle smiled at his awe. 'I know you like your gadgets.'

'Mum, this is more than a gadget. It must have cost a fortune.'

Standing behind James, Daniel squeezed his son's shoulder. 'A trifle I assure you.' He tapped the details on the box. 'It's waterproof and it comes with an altimeter, so it should be good for mountaineering and skiing.'

'We all know how much you love skiing,' Michelle added.

Spluttering, Lucinda reached for a carafe of water. 'Sorry,' she croaked. 'Something tickled my throat.' As she took a sip, she caught James staring. The heat in his chestnut orbs promised a world of wicked pleasures. She gulped down another mouthful and averted her eyes, glimpsing Adam's in the process. His frown told her all she needed to know. *Have you already forsaken me, God?*

The household staff entered a second later, breaking the tension as they served food and sparkling wine. Daniel lifted his glass of Champagne. 'I'd like to propose a toast to James. I'll admit I worried about your wanderlust over the years, but now you've succeeded in your business endeavours, and I see your travels paid off. Alicanto Adventures is already taking the industry by storm

251

within days of expanding. Congratulations Son, you've done us all proud.'

'Cheers, Dad.' James clinked his glass against his father's before reaching across the table to Lucinda's.

The meal commenced with small talk and praises for the gourmet feast. Glancing at the medium rare steak on Adam's plate, her mouth watered. But as she bit into her duck fillet, she soon forgot the forbidden meat. Closing her eyes, she savoured the sweet juices exploding in her mouth before going back for more.

Daniel placed his silverware aside and dabbed his mouth with a white linen napkin. 'Where is Troy tonight, Becky? You know he is always welcome here.'

'We're kind of taking a break,' she admitted, lowering her gaze.

'Why? The pair of you seem perfect together?' her father inquired.

'I-I'm not sure if I'm ready for the type of commitment he wants.'

Michelle's cutlery clattered on her plate. 'Did he propose to you?'

'Not exactly, but we did talk about marriage.' Her cheeks flushed, and Lucinda felt sorry for her. Adam's parents were lovely people, but she knew their expectations were difficult to live up to, especially for Rebecca.

Taking a sip of her wine, Michelle stared at Rebecca over her glass. 'That man is head over heels for you, Becky. I can see it in the way he looks at you and everything he does. He is also one of the better choices around. Don't let him slip through your fingers.'

'Give her a break, Mum,' James cut in. 'Becky is still young. She has plenty of time to find the right partner and settle down.'

'Unlike you,' Michelle huffed. 'When are you going to make an honest woman of one of your conquests?'

James shook his head. 'Not everyone needs to get married and have kids to find fulfilment in life. Besides, I'm too busy with work for a love life.'

'Sounds familiar,' Lucinda mumbled under her breath, not loud enough for anyone but the man beside her to hear.

Adam gasped but held his tongue.

'So, Lucy,' Rebecca chirped. 'When are you going to make me an aunty?'

Nice diversion tactics, Sister. 'Well actually—'

Gaping, Rebecca clapped her hands together and squealed. 'Oh my God! That's why you turned away the steak. You're pregnant, aren't you?'

She nodded. 'Six weeks to be precise. After last time, I wanted to wait until twelve weeks before sharing the news, but you all know now.'

Rebecca and Michelle both rose from their seats and rounded the table for hugs from Lucinda and Adam.

'I guess another toast is in order,' Daniel announced as everyone settled back at their places. Glasses chimed and congratulations echoed around the dinner table.

'We'll have to turn one of the spare rooms into a nursery,' Michelle enthused. 'Oh Lucy, dear, I can't wait to take you shopping for baby stuff!'

'Sounds lovely.' She caught James' eye. His brow creased, and a pang of guilt cramped her chest. She did not like hogging his spotlight, especially for something that reminded him of everything he is missing with her and giving to Adam instead.

'Why aren't you happy for them, James?' Rebecca asked.

He glared at his sister. 'I am, I guess I'm in shock. I didn't realise they were trying for kids.'

Jesus! What's with all the friction in the room? A sinking feeling paralysed her lungs as she studied the silent exchange between Rebecca and James. *Does Becky know?*

෧෬

Rebecca

When the rest of the party moved to the games room, Rebecca followed Lucinda to the bathroom. She waited at the door with bated breath, processing the night's proceedings. *Did I imagine the heated gazes and suspicious glares?* One thing she knew for certain: Lucinda's reaction to talk of James and skiing pretty much confirmed what she had heard. The toilet flushing alerted her to the imminent confrontation.

Lucinda startled as she opened the door. Fair enough too, since line-ups were rare in this house. If Rebecca had wanted to use the facilities, she could have chosen from five other options. Regaining her composure, Lucinda smiled. 'Oh hey. Do you need something from this bathroom?'

'No. I wanted to talk to you, in private.' She sauntered forward, backing Lucinda into the restroom.

'Oh? What about?'

'My brothers.'

Lucinda's brows hiked up her perspiring forehead.

At only five-foot-five, Rebecca was hardly an intimidating person, especially compared to her sister-in-law who towered four inches above her. Something other than her presence was affecting Lucinda. *Is it guilt?* 'Are you having an affair with James?'

Gasping, Lucinda shook her head. 'Heavens no! I would never do that to Adam. There's nothing going on between me and James.'

Standing straight, she crossed her arms and narrowed her eyes. 'Really? Because he looked crestfallen when you announced your pregnancy. For your sake, that better be Adam's child you're carrying.'

Turning her head, Lucinda stared at the glittering wall tiles. 'James may have feelings for me, but they are one-sided.'

'I know the pair of you hooked up at Mt. Hotham. He was your first, wasn't he?'

Lucinda gaped at her. 'How do you know that?'

'Your old school friends are big on gossip, and word travels fast in our world.' She may not like Terry, but she was not about to reveal her source. If Lucinda deceived her, his intel could prove valuable down the track.

Lucinda sighed and held her gaze. 'Yes, James took my virginity when I was seventeen, but that was the only time we slept together, I assure you.' Her eyes lowered as she added, 'Any lingering attraction wore off by the time he came back into my life.'

While she believed the first part of Lucinda's statement, she suspected the chemistry was very much alive. 'Does Adam know?'

Her hazel gaze rose. 'Yes, Adam knows all about my history, with James and every other guy. He doesn't like the fact that I had sex with his brother, but the rest of them don't bother him. I guess it's different when you can put a name and face to your partner's past.'

'Worse still when they are your own kin, I'm sure. I don't know if you're in denial or straight up lying, but the way you lust after James is plain to see. But so is Adam's love for you. I implore you *not* to act on those feelings for James. Doing so will break Adam's heart and shatter this family. I don't think I could forgive James for hurting Adam, and I know it would destroy their relationship.'

Lucinda's lip quivered and she burst into tears. 'I'm trying so hard to resist him,' she admitted between sobs. She slumped against the vanity and Rebecca caught Lucinda in her arms. Clinging to her like a life raft, Lucinda sank into the embrace. 'I'm sorry. I don't want to come between the three of you. I love Adam, I really do, but….' She continued to cry while Rebecca hugged her.

In some ways she understood Lucinda's turmoil, the pull of opposing forces, torn between those who wanted her. It was like two people stretching a rubber band, and at some point, one side would have to let go, else it would break. Like a game of tug-of-war where only one side could hold on to her. But what would happen if the wrong person won the game? And who was the right choice?

Soft knocking preceded footfalls. 'Lucy?' Adam inquired. 'What's wrong?'

'She's feeling emotional about everything,' Rebecca answered. 'Must be the pregnancy hormones.' Easing out of Lucinda's grip, she let Adam take her place. He could provide better comfort, and she wanted a word with James. 'I'll leave you to it.'

She found James playing eight ball with their father while Mum sat by the bar and watched.

Dad looked up from his shot and grinned. 'Ah, good. Now Becky's here, we can play doubles.'

James laughed. 'You're looking to blame someone else for losing, *old man*. Hurry up and take your turn.'

Mirth rumbled through Dad's chest. 'Nonsense. I merely wanted to include the ladies.'

'Wouldn't hurt to even the playing field a little,' James admitted. 'Especially if you have Mum's skill to help you out.' He winked at Rebecca and her heart melted.

If Lucinda keeps dragging her bleeding heart through this family, drowning us all in conflict and misgivings, then I for one shall miss it.

Chapter Sixteen

Lucinda

Adding the finishing touches to Casper and Drew's dream home, Lucinda clicked SAVE and hit PRINT. Endorphins rushed through her as she strolled to the kitchenette. Few things in life compared to the feeling of satisfaction that came with completing a big project. She looked forward to celebrating with friends and family. For now, she would have to make do with a short break before getting on with the rest of her workday. Retrieving her chicken salad and vitamin juice, she returned to her desk to eat. While the doctor had prescribed pregnancy supplements, Adam had explained that the body absorbed vitamins better when consumed in their natural forms. Wanting to improve the odds of bringing a healthy baby to term, she took his advice on board, loading every meal with as many nutrients as possible.

Eager to share the good news, she picked up the phone and called her client.

'Casper Van der Berg speaking.'

'Hi. It's Lucy. How are you?'

'I'm fabulous darling, how are you? How is my house coming along?'

'Great actually. I finished it!' Sipping her juice, she watched as the printer spat out the last page of her design.

'Oh wow! That's fantastic! I can't wait to see it!' His excitement bubbled across the airwaves. 'What's next?'

'I need you to look at the blueprints and give me your feedback. When can you guys come in?'

'Drew isn't teaching any classes this afternoon, so we could pop in in about an hour or so.'

'That's great for me. See you then.' Hanging up the phone, she guzzled the last of her juice and started on her salad. Between anticipation and morning sickness, the food was harder to stomach. She forced it down anyway, knowing it would help.

The next hour whizzed by like a film in fast motion as she prepared all the paperwork necessary for approval and handover to the builders. Before she knew it, Casper and Drew sat with her in the meeting room.

Inspecting each page, Drew's smile grew as he handed them to Casper. 'This all looks great. So much attention to detail.'

Her heart somersaulted at the praise. 'Do let me know if there's anything you'd like to change. Anything at all. I want this house to be perfect for you both.'

Casper placed the last page on the table and grinned. 'It already is. We will have to get you on one of those home shows once the building is complete. I'm sure I can pull a few strings.'

Gasping, she clapped her hands together before buckling over as an agonising cramp seized her abdomen. 'Shit! The baby!'

'Baby? What baby?' Casper asked in a bemused tone.

'I'm pregnant,' she rasped, still clutching her stomach as another cramp clamped her insides.

'What? Since when? Why didn't—'

'Now's not the time!' Drew chided Casper. 'Can't you see the woman's in pain? What's wrong Lucinda? Is there anything we can do?'

Her cheeks flushed. 'Um, could you, um….'

'Go on,' Drew encouraged.

'Help me to the bathroom?' she squeaked.

'Of course. Casper, you grab her left side.' Drew moved around to her right and together, the men hoisted her to her feet.

She leaned on them heavily as she trudged across the office. A few of her colleagues gawked at the show.

When Lisa, her boss, spotted them, she hurried over. 'What's going on?'

'I'm not sure yet.' Suppressing the tears, Lucinda told herself not to jump to any conclusions. 'I'm experiencing some extremely painful cramps.' She almost collapsed as another one stabbed at her womb. Thankfully, the guys held her up. Something damp began to pool between her legs, and she swallowed a wave of emotion. 'I need to check if….' She was not sure how to broach the topic with Lisa. She had not yet told her the news.

'She's pregnant!' Casper burst out. 'Did you know? We're like her besties, and she didn't tell us.'

What a time to fixate on that fact! She had not even told Nicole yet, her actual best friend. The family only knew because Rebecca guessed.

'No, I didn't know,' admitted Lisa in a strict matron voice. 'How many weeks?'

'Eight.'

Lisa softened her tone. 'Were you waiting until twelve before announcing it?'

Lucinda nodded.

'Thank you both for helping Lucy, I'll take it from here,' Lisa insisted as she took Lucinda from them.

She heard the guys arguing in hushed voices as Lisa escorted her into the ladies' room.

'Have you lost a baby before?'

There was no holding back the tears this time. With a nod, she dashed into the cubicle and locked the door. The moment of truth arrived, and boy did it smack her in the face. There was blood. Far too much to be healthy. 'Lisa? Can you please bring me my bag?' After the last time, she had made a point of carrying supplies for this possibility.

'Of course, dear. Is there anything else I can get you?'

She almost declined the offer, but then she thought about what she would do next. 'Actually, could you grab my mobile[6] too?'

Once she had cleaned herself up and changed, she returned to the meeting room with her boss. Her friends waited for her with expectant expressions. 'Things don't look good. Adam is on his way to pick me up and take me to the hospital.'

---

[6] Cell phone

Casper's visage drooped, and he rose to hug her. 'Oh sweetie, I'm sorry.'

'If there are no design changes required, I can go through the rest of the paperwork with them,' Lisa offered.

'That would be great, thank you.' They all waited with her, taking turns to hold her as she fell apart in their arms.

The meeting room door practically flew off its hinges when Adam entered. He rushed forward like a tornado, surprising her when the papers did not scatter across the table. Adam lifted her in his arms like he had done on their wedding night. He winced at the sight of her puffy, bloodshot eyes. 'Are you still in pain?' he whispered. When she nodded, he closed his eyes and took a deep breath. As his lids fluttered open, Adam's beautiful chestnuts adopted a glassy sheen. 'Let's get you out of here.'

৪০৫৪

Rebecca

Sitting alone in her apartment and listening to her favourite pop music playlist, Rebecca toyed with the idea of inviting Troy over. *If Brooke can have her fun with Terry, why can't I enjoy a man's company?* Not once had they spoken about opening their relationship to other sexual partners. When she challenged Brooke about her behaviour, going so far as to call it cheating, she earned a slap across the cheek.

'Sex with Terry is a means to an end,' Brooke had explained. 'I'm doing this for you, sugar. To protect *your* secret while uncovering Lucinda's.'

Screw it! She picked up her phone and messaged Troy: CAN YOU COME OVER? WE NEED TO TALK.

Her phone chimed a second later with his reply: ON MY WAY.

A short laugh slipped out. *Talk about eager. At least he hasn't given up on me.* Butterflies began to swarm in her stomach as she anticipated his arrival. She was not sure how to approach things with him, or even if she was ready to go all the way. Most men turned her off. *What if the same happens with Troy?* Thinking back to their heated kiss, she dismissed the thought. He had managed to push all the right buttons back then.

Curled up on the couch, she ran her hands down her bare legs. Short hairs bristled against her touch, and she cussed under her breath. Dashing to the bathroom, she grabbed her razor and shaving foam. *If tonight is the night, I want to make a good impression.*

Thanks to the last-minute grooming, she barely had time to dress in her favourite lingerie when the intercom buzzed. Slipping on a silk robe, she raced over to the speaker box and opened the building door for him. 'Come on up.' She spotted her dirty dishes on the kitchen bench a second later. *Damn it! I should have planned this night better.* She chucked them in the dishwasher.

A gentle knock on the door sent her mind into a tailspin. She had not even had a chance to put more clothes on. Glancing down at the turquoise lace babydoll, she shrugged. *One way to tempt fate, I suppose.*

Troy's eyes almost popped from their sockets when they took in her skimpy attire. 'Jesus, Becky. Do you always greet your guests with such erotic displays?' Blond tresses he usually spiked up with wax sat in a dishevelled mess atop his head. With the five o'clock shadow forming on his face, he looked like he had just stepped out of bed. Even his jeans and t-shirt added to the sexy casual look he pulled off so well.

Her cheeks flushed as she remembered his last visit, and she giggled. 'No, only the ones I'm trying to seduce.' The words escaped before she could stop them, and she bit her lip. *May as well roll with it.*

Wrapping his arms around her waist, he backed her into the apartment, letting the door slam behind him. He brought his lips to her ear. 'And here I thought that was my job. Do you do this often?' His gruff voice sent ripples of excitement through her nerves.

'Almost never,' she admitted. 'Brooke was the last and only.'

His nose traced the lines of her neck, tickling her in the best way possible. 'You've never slept with a man?'

'No. You're the only one I've felt attracted to.'

A moan rumbled through his throat. 'Did you want to talk, or shall we skip straight to the part where I tear our clothes off?' His assertive tone made her lady parts quiver.

'I had planned on talking first.' Stepping back, she put an inch between them, immediately missing his warmth. 'To be clear, I'm not leaving Brooke.'

Closing the distance, he cupped her chin in his enormous hand. 'I don't expect you to. I won't share you with anyone else, though, and I promise to return the courtesy. That okay with you?'

She gulped. 'You have no idea how much that means to me.'

His eyes narrowed, and he placed his other hand on her hip. 'Enlighten me then.'

A single tear slid down her cheek. 'Brooke is sleeping with her beard. She assures me it means nothing, that she loves only me, but it still hurts.'

'Is she with him tonight?'

'Yes. I hate it, knowing how much she enjoys someone else touching her.'

'Then don't think about them. Let me distract you.' He pressed a gentle kiss on her lips, giving her the opportunity to pull away if she wanted. She loved his intoxicating mix of dominance and courtesy. When she reciprocated, he wrapped his arms around her and deepened the kiss. The slight graze of his stubble reminded her she was kissing a man, and she relished every second. His breath became hers, filling all the pockets in her soul she never knew existed. 'Mm, I'll never tire of your sweet mouth, Becky.' His fingers trailed along her shoulder and down her arm.

She clasped his hand when it reached her wrist and held it tight. 'Then why did you stop?'

A soft laugh tinkled over his tonsils. 'I still need air from time-to-time, sunshine.'

'Nonsense!' she joked, giving him a Cheshire grin. 'We can be each other's oxygen.'

A guttural sound slipped out as he lowered his forehead to hers. 'You are the cutest thing ever.' His mouth consumed hers with even more passion as he backed her towards the bedrooms.

The flutters in her belly grew exponentially with each step until she bumped into the couch. 'Ow, shoot!' Losing her balance, she collapsed against the armrest and erupted in a fit of laughter.

Dropping to his knees in front of her, Troy joined the chorus with short bursts of merriment. When they calmed down, he sat on the sofa and pulled her into his lap. 'Are you okay?'

She nodded. 'I'm good. No injuries to speak of unless you count my bruised ego.'

His brow arched, making him look even sexier. 'How so?'

'That was a little embarrassing and well… tonight has been a comedy of errors for me. I have no idea what I'm doing.' Her face heated with each word of her confession.

Smiling, he combed his fingers through her strawberry blonde hair. 'I'll let you in on a little secret. None of us do. There's no roadmap to love, no rules telling us how to express our feelings. Each couple is different and what works for some won't for others. But that's okay, because it can be fun exploring one another, discovering each other's on and off switches.'

Shifting her position, she straddled his lap. 'So far you've only hit my on switches.'

His lips quirked. 'So have you, sunshine.' Pinching her nipple through its turquoise lace covering, he bucked against her pelvis.

Bulging denim brushed against the thin scrap of fabric covering her sensitive flesh. She almost shattered from the friction. 'Ahh!'

'You like that huh?' he asked in a deeper than usual voice.

'Yes,' she replied breathlessly.

'Want more?' He pressed her nipple harder.

'God yes!'

Rocking his hips, he began grinding against her. The pressure sent intense shockwaves through her core. 'I want to make love to you, Becky, but only when you're ready. Physically *and* mentally.'

Good Lord, he is so damn hot! Her pleasure reached a peak and she erupted in his arms. 'I am so-o ready!'

'Hold on tight then.' As her arms and legs gripped him like a vice, he rose and carried her to the spare room.

She loved that he had paid attention to the small details, like which room she used with Brooke, and then opted to use the other. She did not need constant reminders of the woman who was breaking her heart, not while she lay with the man who promised never to do such a thing.

Easing her down, Troy planted her feet on the floor. He slid the robe from her shoulders, letting the silk pool on the carpet. Toying with the straps of her babydoll, he sighed. 'I like this so much; I can't decide whether to take it off or leave it on. Did I ever mention how much I adore turquoise on you?'

She smirked, feeling more confident after his pep talk. 'Once or twice. What if I keep it on for the first time, but take it off for the rest?'

His amber eyes darkened. 'I love the way you think, Becky. In fact, I love everything about you.' He claimed another fervent kiss, cutting it off with a groan as he plucked the t-shirt from his torso.

She gaped at the rippling landscape covering his body. She gathered he was strong by how easily he lifted her, but seeing the evidence was something else.

Reaching into one of his pockets, he retrieved a concertina bundle of foil packets and tossed them on the bed before unfastening his jeans. As she glanced at the condoms, reality began to set in again. Not once had she considered contraception. The issue had never come up before. Doubts plagued her mind. *What if I get pregnant?* She knew barrier methods weren't the most effective.

'Hey.' Cupping her chin, Troy coaxed her head back to face him. He stood before her in nothing but a pair of silk boxers. 'It's okay if you're not ready. We can have plenty of fun in the meantime.'

There he goes pushing my on switch again. 'I want to, I really do. It's just... I'm not on the pill.'

He exhaled sharply, as though relieved by the reason for her apprehension. 'I'll wear a double layer and if I notice any breaks, we can get you the morning after pill. Is that okay with you?'

'Yes, it's a good plan.' She could barely hear herself over the thumping of her heart. 'I'll get a prescription as soon as possible.'

Embracing her, Troy whispered in her ear, 'Relax sunshine. Everything will be okay. More than okay, I promise to make you feel good, tonight and always.'

She took a few deep breaths and focussed on the sensation of his arousal pressing against her. Curiosity got the better of her and she reached into his shorts. Wrapping her hand around his shaft, she blushed at the way he throbbed in her grip.

Closing his eyes, he moaned. 'That feels amazing. Squeeze it as hard as you like.'

Taking his suggestion on board, she rubbed him with her clenched palm.

A droplet formed on the tip, and he hissed. 'At this rate I'll need the double rubber to last long enough.'

Releasing him, she rounded the bed and pulled back the covers. She sat on the mattress and watched in awe as Troy rolled one, then another condom onto his large dick. Not that she had anything to compare to other than a few toys, but he looked and felt big, so….

Crawling up the bed, he grabbed her feet and tugged her down. She yelped with delight and giggled as her head hit the pillow. He grinned up at her from between her legs. 'You make the most delightful sounds with that pretty mouth of yours. What will I hear when I do this?' He buried his face in her panties, biting at her through the lace.

Playful mirth turned to raw lust, and she mewled.

'Hm, love that noise too,' he mumbled against her. Removing the final obstacle between them, he peered deep into her eyes. She felt herself sinking into his gaze. 'Last chance to back out, Becky.'

She shook her head. 'I'm not going anywhere. I want you. Now.'

Hovering above her, he inched himself inside, giving her time to adjust and stretch around him. 'You feel so damn tight, sunshine.' Pushing himself into the hilt, he touched her cervix.

She cried out as pleasure and pain merged into one incredible moment of ecstasy. Their bodies started moving together in a synchronised rhythm, as though their minds had already tuned in to each other. He increased the pace, hammering the spot that sent her over the edge.

Coming down from her climax, she heard knocking at the door. Troy's brow furrowed as he slowed. 'Don't stop!' she begged. 'It's probably a neighbour wanting to borrow a cup of sugar or something.' Very few people had keys to the building, so most guests needed to buzz the intercom.

He smirked. 'Or they're here to complain about the noise.'

'Oops,' she laughed. 'I hadn't thought about that.'

'If you're worried, I know a great way to muffle your screams.' His mouth engulfed hers in a searing kiss as he continued to move inside her.

The hammering on the door grew louder.

'Persistent bastard, aren't they?' Troy huffed, going harder as he chased his own orgasm.

'Becky, I know you're in there, I can hear the music!' Adam shouted.

'Damn it!' she whined. 'I should see what he wants. Might be a family emergency.'

Pinning her wrists to the mattress, Troy grunted. 'He can wait another minute. I won't let anyone ruin our first time.' As the pounding on the door increased, so did Troy's thrusts.

She soon forgot her brother was out there. All that mattered for the moment was within the four walls of *her* bedroom. The room may have been a ruse, yet on this night, she claimed it as her sanctuary.

Troy soon brought her to new heights, and they exploded together, his mouth swallowing her cries. He collapsed beside her, panting as though he'd sprinted across the finish line. 'I'd prefer to hold you until we are ready for round two, but you should go see what the annoying idiot wants.'

She laughed as she staggered to her feet. *Crap!* It usually took a tonne of alcohol to make her so unsteady on her feet. She threw on a nightgown and stumbled across the apartment.

𝕤𝕠𝕔𝕣

Adam

Rebecca flung the door open, glaring at Adam, although her expression softened when she glimpsed the pain haunting his countenance. Noticing her sleepwear, he hoped he had not woken her. Although it could explain the look she gave him at first. She was like a grizzly bear when people disturbed her sleep. 'A little early for bed, isn't it? Especially for a Friday night. Is everything okay?'

'I'm fine, no thanks to you. What's going on, Adam?'

'I-I need to talk. Is Brooke here?'

Her brows shot up her forehead. 'Um no, she's out on a date, why—'

'Good. I was hoping to catch you alone.' He barged into the apartment and beelined for the liquor cabinet. There were few places he felt comfortable making himself at home like this.

'Adam…,' Rebecca started as he poured himself a whiskey.

'What did your brother want?' a gruff voice asked to his right. Troy emerged from Rebecca's bedroom with the scruffiest bed hair Adam had ever seen. He wore a pair of boxer shorts and nothing else.

Oh shit! Did I interrupt… that. 'Sorry, Becky. I didn't realise you had company.'

'It's not like you asked,' she scoffed.

He swirled the amber liquid in his glass, letting the aroma soothe his nerves. 'I take it the pair of you patched things up?'

'We did.' Troy drew close to Rebecca, hugging her from behind. 'Seriously dude, you have the worst timing.'

He winced. 'TMI bro! Way too much. That's my sister you're talking about.' He crossed the room and slumped into an armchair.

Heaving out a sigh, Rebecca perched on the couch. 'Why are you here, Adam? I love you to bits, but you do have poor timing. Unless something serious happened, I—'

'Lucy lost the baby.'

They both stared aghast at him.

Folding his hands together in his lap, he stared at the lines on his palm. 'It started a week ago. Today, the doctor confirmed the miscarriage. She's not pregnant anymore. I-I'm sorry Becky. I know how much you want to be an aunty.'

'Christ, Adam! How can you worry about me at a time like this? Is Lucy okay? Why aren't you with her?'

'She's not in a critical condition if that's what you're asking.' He swallowed two large mouthfuls of liquor and glimpsed Rebecca's wide-eyed stare. 'What?'

'I meant emotionally, dumb arse! I recall how much the first time upset Lucy, and you guys weren't even planning to get pregnant back then. I can tell you're distraught too, but you can't leave her alone at a time like this, especially when….' Her voice cracked as it trailed off.

He narrowed his eyes on her. 'Especially when what?'

'Nothing.' Rebecca bit her lip and averted her gaze.

The hairs on the back of his neck bristled. Something was definitely wrong, but extracting the information from his sister would be like getting blood from a stone. 'Is there something about Lucy I should know?' he asked softly.

Turning her gaze back to him, she nodded. 'You shouldn't be leaving her alone so much. She's very fragile right now. If you're not careful, you might lose her.'

He gasped. 'Lose her how?'

Rebecca shrugged. 'What would you do if you felt depressed and neglected by your partner?'

'I-I don't know, I guess....' The answer slapped him across the face. *I'd seek comfort elsewhere*. 'Blast!' Springing to his feet, he retrieved his phone and called Lucinda.

'You've reached Lucinda Fairfax —'

'Damn it, Lucy!' Hanging up on her voicemail, he tried again. He met Rebecca's worried eyes as the automated message started again before a single ringtone. 'She's not answering.' Leaving half his drink on the coffee table, he moved toward the door. 'I need to get back to my wife. If I can find her, that is.'

'Adam, wait!' Rebecca shuffled across the floor with bare feet and threw her arms around him. Hugging him tight, she whispered, 'I'm sorry for your loss. I know how much *you* wanted this baby, so please don't give up trying. And... promise me you won't do anything rash tonight. No one's perfect and we all make mistakes.'

His heart thundered in his chest. He knew Rebecca meant well, but her words did little to ease his anxiety. 'Promise,' he croaked out.

Lead weights settled in his stomach during the walk back to his car, and the air grew thicker with every step. There must have been some merit in the expression 'Ignorance is bliss,' because in this moment he feared the truth more than anything else. Not wanting to jump to any conclusions, he headed home first. *Who am I kidding? I don't want to face reality yet.*

ೞೞ

James

As James opened the front door, Lucinda barrelled into him. He stiffened as she wrapped her arms around his waist, keeping his own like rigid pillars at his sides. Glancing out the door he spotted a taxi pulling out of his driveway. 'What's going on? Where's Adam?'

'I don't know,' she sobbed, tears trickling down her cheek. 'He wanted to clear his head.'

Shit! Knowing Adam, that means he is either pissed off or struggling to process his grief. 'What's wrong?'

'I had another miscarriage. It started a week ago and the doctor confirmed our fears today.' She buried her head in the folds of his t-shirt, right next to his racing heart. 'My baby's really gone.'

'I'm sorry, Cindy,' he rasped.

She sighed. 'I love it when you call me Cindy.' Her words surged straight to his dick like an adrenaline shot.

Fuck! This is so not the time. I need to call for backup. 'Mind if I invite a friend over? We shouldn't be alone together. Especially not here.' When she looked up at him through hooded eyes, his restraint stretched almost to breaking point. 'I don't know how much longer I can resist ravishing you.'

Molten gold shimmered in her bloodshot gaze. 'What if I'm sick of refraining from these urges?' she asked in a husky voice. Her hands slipped under his top, sliding along the ridges of his abs and up along his bare chest. 'I need to forget all this pain and heartache. Take me back in time, back to the night you ruined me.'

And snap! Hoisting her up, he welcomed the vice grip of her thighs as their mouths collided. 'If I take you to my bed, there'll be no coming back from this. I won't let you slip away this time.' She nodded, and waves of heat washed over him as he carried her down the hall. 'Do you taste as good as I remember?'

She blushed with recollection.

'Oh yes, sweetheart. You wanted a re-enactment, so it's what you'll get.'

'Not many guys I know like doing that.' Her confession floored him.

'Those guys are idiots who don't know what they're missing.' *Nothing compares to the sweetness of a woman falling apart at your touch, knowing you're the source of her pleasure.* Reaching his minimalist bedroom, he eased her down, still holding her close. His fingers found the buttons of her blouse. As much as he wanted to rip the clothes off her body, he also wanted to savour the moment, to seduce her all over again. Pastel pink chiffon fell away, revealing a white silk camisole. The hint of a lace bra peeked out from under it, curving across her heaving breasts. *Pure perfection.* His thumbs traced the edge of her delicate lingerie and she arched into his touch. 'Undress me,' he whispered.

Sliding under the hem, her hands lifted his t-shirt with more confidence than before, yet he still detected a slight tremble.

Is she anxious, or putting on an act for old time's sake? When his t-shirt hit the floor, their eyes locked together. For a moment it felt like some intangible force transported them back to Mt. Hotham. Her body quivering with anticipation while trepidation prevented her from taking in the view. He sucked in a breath as she fumbled with his belt buckle, his heart hammering against his ribs when she reached for his zip and halted. 'You okay? We don't have to do this—'

'I want to,' she assured him as she had done back then. Lucinda dropped to her knees so she could remove his jeans. She continued to hold his unwavering stare, bringing him an ounce of relief as she freed his pulsing cock from its confines. It still ached to be inside her, but he wasn't about to rush things.

When she rose to her feet, he unclasped her skirt, letting it slide away. 'Take a seat.' He glanced toward the edge of the bed.

Perching on the mattress in her matching set of white lace, she looked like a virginal goddess. Ironic how she appeared more innocent well after the fact. *Oh but it's fun to pretend, isn't it?* He straddled her lap and kissed her deep. Short, shallow breaths tickled his neck as he spoke in her ear. 'I'm going to make you come all over my tongue.' She shivered at his promise and again as he removed her undergarments. Kneeling before her, he pried her legs apart and tested the waters. *God, she's so wet for me already.* Her moans filled the air as he explored her depths. Sensing more than a physical connection, he delved deep into her soul. He craved her body but needed all of her.

Lucinda cried out her climax and mumbled, 'Feels so good.'

Grinning, he rose and rounded the bed. She shuffled up toward the pillows, golden hair sprawling out like a halo. He took great pleasure in corrupting his beautiful saint, in clipping her wings so she wouldn't fly away from him.

Their bodies writhed as they rode the waves of passion together in every position he knew. With each crest they reached, he grew more certain of something that should have terrified him. He recognised the intense feelings for what they were. Rather than run from them this time, he toppled over the edge.

Spooning her hours later, he barely registered the distant sound of the doorbell. His heart drummed louder, beating in time to Lucinda's laboured breaths. Ignoring whoever stood at his door, he whispered in the softest voice, 'I love you, Cindy.'

L. STARLA

Chapter Seventeen

Lucinda

Images of the life she had built with Adam filled Lucinda's dreams, seeping through to her waking thoughts and clouding her mind with ugly realisation. Rolling over in bed, she faced James. He slept; the quilt gathered around his waist showing off his gorgeous torso. Biting her lip, she swallowed back a wave of nausea.

'If you don't stop gawking,' James rasped, 'I'll show you how much I love feeling your eyes on me.'

A tear trickled down her cheek as she sat up, covering her nudity with the silky soft sheet. 'We made a mistake.'

His eyes shot open, drilling into her heart. 'What did you say?'

Her voice quavered in time with her hammering heart. 'L-last night was incredible, but it can't continue.'

'What the hell, Cindy? I told you there would be no coming back from this. I won't let doubts creep in and steal you away.' Reaching out, he tried to pull her into his arms, but her frozen form resisted. He frowned at her refusal. 'Not after the night we had. Not after—' James jack-knifed, his narrowing eyes piercing her soul like needles. 'You never replied when I....'

Gulping back the bile, she averted her gaze. She hated breaking his heart, but the ring on her finger reminded her she had already made her choice. 'I can't and won't do this to Adam. I love him—'

'Don't fucking remind me!' James leaped out of bed, giving her an eyeful of his sculpted body. 'I'm sick of hearing it; have been ever since your engagement party. I hate seeing the pair of you acting like the perfect little couple, parading your love around and reminding me of everything I don't have.' His bitter words left an acrid taste in the air.

Blinking a couple of times, she stared at him. 'I thought you wanted Adam and I to be happy. Don't you care about hurting your brother?'

'To hell with him! Adam ought to know complacency is a mistake in any marriage, more so when temptation knocks at your wife's door. Listen Cindy, *your* feelings are what matter most.'

She shook her head. 'That's where you're wrong. I made an oath before God—'

'Are you happy with him?' James knelt on the edge of the mattress.

'That's beside the point.'

'It's entirely the point, or have you forgotten what we talked about when I came over to your house because some stalker creep threw a brick through your window?'

'Of course not.' She remembered his words with almost as much clarity as the heart-stopping, panty-melting kiss they had shared that night. 'There's no way I'd forget any night I've spent with you.'

'I'll ask you again, and I want you to think very carefully about your response. Does Adam make you happy?' He bounced on his right knee, waiting for her reply.

She had never seen James so unsure of himself. 'For the most part,' she admitted. 'I'm alone too much, but when I do see him, we spend quality time together.'

The tremor in his limbs vanished as James crawled toward her. 'If you're so happy with Adam, why did you come to me last night?' He stopped a few inches away from her.

'I-I didn't say our relationship is perfect, not by anyone's standards. Last night… I felt lonely. Adam left me in a vulnerable place, and I needed comfort.'

'You could have found a shoulder to cry on with any number of your close friends, yet you came to me knowing where things would lead. Why?'

'Because I needed to forget my sorrows, not wallow in them. I wanted you to… fuck me senseless.' She knew how dirty she sounded, and admitting her desires stung like a bitch.

'Why didn't you ask your *husband* to service you?' He spat the word, as though it was more offensive than any of the profanities he often uttered with ease.

'I-I told you. Adam was absent last night.'

'You could have called him, begged him to come home and rip your sweet little pussy apart.'

She gasped as her cheeks flushed. 'Adam doesn't….'

'What doesn't my dear brother do?' James paled. 'I swear to God, if he doesn't even get you off—'

'No! It's not like that. I just… he….' She bit her lip, unsure how to explain the issue.

A smug grin formed on his soft, kissable lips. 'He doesn't fuck you like I do.' He sighed when she nodded. 'If you weren't his wife, I'd take immense pleasure from teasing him about it. As it stands, he still has the only woman I've ever loved.'

She gaped at him. *Surely there had been others?* James was approaching thirty, and she knew all about his womanising ways.

'Don't act so shocked. I know you heard me last night.'

'I'm not, I mean I did, but… you've been with a lot of women. Didn't you catch feelings for any of them?'

'Nope. None of them compared to you.'

This time her eyes bugged out. He never got over her either. In some ways their stories were much alike, except she had found love with another, someone who did compare to him in some ways. *But not all.* Deep down she had been craving the unbridled passion she knew only James could give her. 'It's more than the sex.' She clamped her hand over her mouth a second too late.

His eyes burned like chestnuts on an open fire: deep, dark, and sensual. 'You feel it too, don't you? The unfathomable pull between us. The deep connection giving a whole new meaning to the word euphoria.'

As much as she wanted to admit it, she feared where such a dangerous acknowledgement would lead. 'I won't leave Adam. You told me not to let *you* be the reason my marriage falls apart.'

'Hmph! I was trying to act all noble and shit,' he scoffed. 'I take those words back. I want you, Cindy, and after last night I'll do anything in my power to keep you.'

She shifted uncomfortably and the sheet slipped from her grip, exposing her breasts to his hungry gaze. Lifting the linen up to her neck, she waited for James to meet her eyes again. 'You shouldn't take them back. They were wise words. What if I grow to resent you for breaking my marriage?'

James winced. 'Is that likely?'

She shrugged. 'I don't know, but I wouldn't want to risk it.'

'Then don't leave him.' Plucking the sheet from her hand, he threw it aside and straddled her. 'You said it yourself, he leaves you alone too much.

We'll have plenty of opportunities to see each other.'

Her jaw dropped. 'What you're suggesting is adultery. I won't commit such a heinous sin.'

James snorted. 'What do you call last night? Aside from the best sex of your life, I mean.' His growing arousal rubbed against her tender flesh, reminding her of the night in question.

'I call it a mistake. A lapse in judgement and a transgression I will repent for in confession. God's not likely to forgive me if I come straight back to your bed over and over.'

A growl slipped from James. 'Are you really so concerned for your immortal soul?'

Choking back tears, she nodded. 'Among other things. Don't you worry?'

He let out a short, sardonic laugh. 'I fell from grace a long time ago, sweetheart. You're not the first married woman I've slept with. Honestly though, I'm not sure I even believe in heaven and hell.'

'Well, I do, which means we need to apply the brakes on whatever this is.' She waved her hand in the short amount of air between them.

'*Whatever this is?*' he mocked, sitting back while still pinning her legs to the bed. 'Are you afraid to admit your feelings? Too chickenshit to accept the truth; the possibility that what we have might come to mean more than your lacklustre marriage to my emotionally stunted brother?'

'Yes, I'm scared. Is that what you want to hear? I'm terrified of so many things I've lost count. Like how Becky knows about us, and she could drop the bomb on Adam's lap any day now. Not to mention I have a stalker hellbent on destroying my relationships. I'm not even sure if he is the same creep who tried to rape me, a man who is now out of prison. Or how about the fact I might never be capable of bearing a child?' *Petrified I married the wrong man.* The tears began to flow.

'Jesus, Cindy! I'm so damn sorry.' He gathered her into his arms and let her cry against his chest. After a few minutes of rubbing her back, he broke the silence, 'What exactly does Becky know about us?'

'She knows our history,' Lucinda sobbed.

'So? It's hardly news to Adam.'

Yanking a few tissues from the nightstand, she blew her nose and wiped her eyes. 'She also knows we're still hot for each other. She confronted me about it at your birthday dinner and I broke down in tears, admitting how hard I was trying to resist you.'

'Ah hell. I'm sorry to put you in this situation, sweetness. For what it's worth, I don't think Becky would go blabbing to Adam. Me and her... well we've always had each other's backs. We keep each other's secrets. I suspect Adam was jealous of the bond we shared. He was always too much of a goody two-shoes to understand. Whenever he caught wind of my misdeeds, he ran straight to our parents. But not Becky. She has a wild side of her own, far more covert than my own of course....' His voice trailed off as he stared into the realm of reminiscence.

Seeing and hearing how much Rebecca meant to James tugged at her heartstrings. 'Becky loves both of you. She warned me that should anything happen between us, it could destroy your family. I don't want that for any of you.'

His fingers travelled down the small of her back and brushed over her buttocks, leaving goosebumps in their wake. 'We can keep it under wraps. I don't mind sneaking around. I quite enjoy it, actually.'

'James!' she wheezed. 'I'm not doing this. I mean it. These things always have a way of coming out.'

'Not true. Do you have any idea how many married women I've fucked without their husbands ever finding out?'

She screwed up her face and bit back the foul taste in her mouth. 'I'd rather not know.'

'Way more than the rare few who slipped up and got caught.'

'Gross. You're disgusting.'

He chuckled. 'Glass houses, sweetheart.'

She groaned. 'You can't compare my one blunder to your premeditated adultery.'

'Christ, sweetheart! You make it sound like a serious crime on par with murder. Besides, you knew what I was like. I've told you as much before, yet it didn't stop you jumping my disgusting bones last night. One in particular.' He waggled his brows and thrust his erection against her thigh for effect.

She sat up and rolled her eyes. 'Ugh! I'm going home. To my *husband*.'

James' expression darkened. 'I don't need more salt in these wounds, Lucy.'

Shit! That name on his lips sounded so foreign and… angry. Leaving the bed and putting distance between them felt like tearing out a vital part of her, but she knew it was for the best. 'Sorry James, but you needed the reminder. This ends now.' She dressed in silence, aware of his heated stares the whole time.

'Cindy?' he called out when she reached the bedroom door.

Glancing over her shoulder, she took in his provocative pose, admiring his body a second too long before meeting his smouldering eyes.

'I'm only letting you leave now because I've got work to do. Call me the next time you're feeling lonely.'

Shaking her head, she walked out of the devil's bedroom and prepared herself to face hell on Earth.

೮೦೦೩

Rebecca

Stepping out of the ensuite bathroom, Rebecca found Brooke sitting on *her* bed. Not the one they shared, but the one she used with Troy. Jumping out of her skin, she lost her grip of the fluffy white towel. 'Yikes! You startled me. I didn't think you'd be home yet.'

Brooke studied her a moment before running her hand over the fresh bedspread. 'Why did you change the linen?'

Oh shit! I can't get anything past Brooke. 'I had a man in here last night,' she admitted in a quavering voice.

Brooke smiled. 'Really? That's awesome. I want to hear everything. Did you enjoy it?'

When she nodded, they both giggled. Their laughter transported her back to adolescence when she would blush every time Brooke related one of her conquests. This time she had her own sexcapade to share. Relief also flooded through her. She had not expected such an amicable reaction. She sat beside Brooke on the recently christened bed. 'Oh my God it felt amazing. I had no idea sex with a man could be so good. He knew all my on switches.'

'Did it hurt?' she queried. 'I mean this was your first time with a man's dick inside you, right?'

'Indeed. Sure, it took some adjusting. He was big after all, but he prepped me well, so it didn't hurt much. The pleasure far outweighed the pain. Although I'm a bit sore this morning. We did it like five times all up.'

Brooke's expression soured, and she slapped Rebecca hard across the face. 'You filthy little slut!'

Shock knocked her back, and tears pooled in her eyes. The verbal barb stung more than the hot palm that had left a red mark on her cheek. 'How is this any different to you sleeping with *your* beard?'

'Am I to infer Troy was the man who fucked you raw?'

A copper tang filled her mouth. Running her tongue along the inside of her mouth, she discovered the split from Brooke's blow.

'Well?' Brooke crossed her arms over her chest and tapped her foot.

'Of course it was Troy. I was hardly going to invite some stranger into my bed.'

'After everything I've done for you, this is how you repay me?' Brooke's voice verged on hysterical. 'I don't sleep with Terry out of some selfish desire. In fact, I derive little pleasure from it.'

Her brow furrowed as she tried to make sense of Brooke's words. 'That's not how it looked the other day.'

'It was all an act, sugar.' Her voice softened, and Brooke traced a delicate finger along Rebecca's jaw. 'I may be bi, but Terry's hardly my type. I pretend to enjoy sex with him to maintain the ruse and get answers.' She sighed. 'We've been over this. You know I'm only seeing him for *your* sake. If I wanted to seek pleasure outside of our relationship, I would have chosen a more attractive beard.'

'I'm sorry. I guess I overreacted. Seeing you with him hurt so much.'

Brooke wrapped a possessive hand around Rebecca's throat. 'Is that why you slept with Troy? To get back at me?'

Their eyes locked together, and she knew there was no hiding the truth. 'Partially, but I was also curious. I wanted to learn what's so great about the thing between a man's legs.'

'Oh sugar, if you want to ride some dick, I'm more than happy to share Terry with you. I didn't think you were into him, though.'

'You're right. I'm not attracted to Terry. He repulses me. Troy, on the other hand, is a true gentleman. He's also the only guy I've ever felt attracted to.'

Brooke's grip around her neck tightened with each word about Troy, to the point where breathing became difficult. 'What you did with Troy was a very selfish act. I know he has feelings for you. I won't stand for it. Keep it platonic or cut him loose. You're mine and mine alone, sugar. If you want to play with men's dicks, you'll do it on my terms. Do you understand?'

She tried to nod, but Brooke's hold restricted her movement so she could only manage a slight tilt. Spots formed in her vision and the room began to spin.

'Good. I'm glad we can see eye to eye.' Brooke released her hand. No sooner had Rebecca inhaled a lungful of air, than Brooke smothered her with a deep kiss.

Sensual lips travelled down her body, nipping and sucking in all the right places. Reaching her core, Brooke flicked her sensitive nub. 'Do you want to come, sugar?' That titillating tongue taunted her tender flesh.

'Yes please,' she begged.

'Then tell me who you belong to,' Brooke demanded.

'You! I belong to you. Oh God!' She shuddered as the teasing amplified.

'And this sweet little pussy?'

'Is yours! All yours.'

'Good girl.' Brooke toppled her over the edge of ecstasy before rising to her feet. 'Now get up. We have gala planning to do.' Brooke waltzed out the room, leaving her a hot, quivering mess.

Chapter Eighteen

Lucinda

Beauty is one of life's biggest deceivers, Lucinda thought as she watched the glitterati pile out of limousines and parade along the red carpet. They were like poisonous flowers. Stunning people with rotten cores, or the majority anyway. Having met every one of the gala's celebrity guests, she was not generalising either. Sure, they were supporting a charity, but most of them were doing it for the PR boost.

Standing at the top of the grey stone steps leading to the town hall entrance, she assembled with the rest of the planning committee, donning fake smiles to welcome the elite and usher them to their seats. The regular guests who had paid good money to rub shoulders with fame screamed and waved from beyond the stanchions. Bouncers and ticket collectors would greet them shortly, but for the time being, they were happy watching the spectacle.

She led Casper and Drew across silver terrazzo tiles into the main hall.

'Tonight's going to be fabulous,' Casper declared. 'I can feel it in my bones.'

'Tickets sold out, so that's a good start.' Bubbles of pride percolated up from her stomach.

Reaching their chairs, Drew glanced around the room. 'Good venue choice, Lucy.'

'Thanks. I love this place.' She followed his gaze, taking in the high, panelled ceiling from which a dozen chandeliers illuminated the elegant space. White linens and silverware covered round tables sitting upon geometric parquetry. 'I'd better get back to it. Enjoy your meal and I'll catch up with you both later.'

Once all the stars had settled, she met Adam outside, saving him from the need to queue. Bypassing the crowd, she spotted a familiar face in the line. 'I didn't know James was coming tonight.'

'Neither did I. Let's go say hi.' Adam tugged at her hand.

She gulped as a lump formed in her throat. Two months had passed since her indiscretion, during which time she had avoided James. Thanks to Nicole's false alibi, Adam had remained in the dark.

A tall, platinum blonde stood beside James, linking arms with him. Lucinda was not short by any means, but this woman towered four inches above her. Although, stiletto heels contributed to at least half of those.

'Hey man, I didn't expect to see you here, with a date no less.' Adam hugged his brother over the rope barrier.

'When I heard Lucy was raising funds for global poverty, I could hardly stay home.'

'Such a gøød cause,' the blonde agreed with a melodic upward inflection.

Lucinda dragged her eyes from the woman back to James. 'Are you going to introduce your friend?'

'Of course. This is Claudia. I met her on a skiing trip in Norway some years back.'

Claudia grinned. 'I vas so happy to see Yames again vhen I bøøked[7] a tour vif him.'

'You're dating a client?' Adam asked with wide eyes.

---

[7] Pronounce the ø by pursing your lips.

James shrugged. 'We dated before she became my client. Claudia, this is my brother, Adam, and his wife Lucy.'

Extending her hand, Claudia offered her a soft smile. 'It is so lovely to meet you. Yames has told me so much about you both.'

'Is that so?' Shaking Claudia's hand, she doubted the woman knew how intimate she had been with James.

Claudia nodded. 'Did you organize all dis?' She waved her hand toward the town hall.

'Not by myself, but yes, I am on the committee that planned this event.' She turned her gaze on James. 'If you told us you were coming, I could have saved you from lining up.'

'And spoil the surprise?' A sly grin tugged at James' lips.

She made a mental note to have a word with their ticketing guy. He should have warned her James was coming so she could prepare herself. Or hide.

Adam unhooked the red rope from the gold bollard. 'Come on then. No point waiting around longer than you have to. I'm sure Mum will be pleased to see you.'

Checking their allocated seats, she groaned. Of course they were at the same table. It would have made sense to stick family together. She showed James and Claudia to where the rest of the Fairfax clan had gathered, along with Brooke and a few folk Lucinda did not recognise. *Brooke's family maybe?*

'Regrettably my beloved Terry couldn't make it tonight,' Brooke announced, prompting a wave of nausea in Lucinda's stomach. 'In his absence, I have invited my cousin Derrick.' She pointed to the dark-haired guy beside her. 'Along with his girlfriend Sofia and her brother Stefano.'

Rising from her seat, Rebecca rounded the table. 'You must be the Pacini twins I've heard so much about. I spoke to your parents at New Year's....'

The conversation faded into the background as Lucinda caught James looking at her. For a moment, she lost herself in his eyes, in the memory of sizzling touches and steamy kisses. His smirk told her he recognised exactly where her depraved thoughts had gone. Knowing James, his mind took up permanent residence in debauchery town. Claudia drew his attention a second later, breaking the spell. But the ache remained deep in her core.

A green haze clouded her vision when she imagined James in bed with the Norwegian model. She had no idea what Claudia did for a living, but somehow her subconscious had decided modelling was the ideal career for the tall blonde with minimal curves. Or she was a local celebrity in her home country. Anything to support the theory that she was hollow with a pretty shell. Ridiculous really, demonising the girl for being with a man Lucinda should *not* be lusting after. Yet it did not stop her plotting all the ways she could separate the couple. *The trick is finding an approach that won't incriminate me.*

A stand-up comedian entertained them during the second course. During the show, her eyes wandered across the table, seeking a taste of her forbidden fruit. In doing so, she glimpsed the way Stefan watched Sofia rather than the performance. A familiar yearning burned in his gaze; one she knew all too well. James often looked at her in the same way, and she imagined her own stolen glances betrayed her taboo desires. *Curious. Does Sofia know how her brother feels about her? Are they —*

Sofia turned to face Stefan and her cheeks flushed as they shared a secret moment. It was like a whole conversation transpired in the silence between them before they returned their attention to the man on the stage. Something was definitely going on between them, to what extent, she had no idea. All she knew was nothing good could come of it, especially if word got out.

The twins' predicament put her in mind of her own. As much as she craved his sensual kisses and all the explosive things James could do to her body, she could not afford the fallout. Yet the moment her eyes landed on him; she felt her resolve slipping.

James shook with carefree laughter, exchanging the occasional smile with his date. He appeared joyous for the first time in years, and she had nothing to do with his happiness. She should have felt pleased for him, but instead the sight stirred the monster in her chest. It sank its fangs deep inside her heart while trying to claw its way out. The atmosphere grew heavy, and her short breaths failed to take in enough oxygen. *Has the monster pierced my lungs?* Pushing back her chair, she sprang to her feet.

Adam's attention shot to her. 'Are you okay my love?'

She nodded. 'I need some air.' When Adam started rising, she put a hand on his shoulder. 'Stay. I know you're enjoying the show. I'll be okay.'

'Are you sure?'

'Yes. Promise.' Turning on her heels, she beelined for the exit before anyone else fussed over her. Making her way out a side door, she sucked in a lungful of the cool night air. She sat on a park bench, bringing relief to her unsteady legs, although her body still trembled. Focussing on her breathing for a few minutes helped release the toxic thoughts from her mind.

Something clicked behind her, and she startled. Peering over her shoulder, she frowned at James. Leaning against a wall, he lit up a cigarette. *When did he start such a nasty habit?* 'You shouldn't have followed me. People might get suspicious.'

Smoke billowed out from his pursed lips. 'They won't. I told them I needed a ciggy and used a different exit.'

Watching the glow of flickering embers, she avoided eye contact. 'So, you didn't come out here to get me alone?'

Smirking, he drew closer, polluting her air with noxious gases. 'Who says I didn't?'

Waving away the offending plume, she glowered. 'Since when do you smoke?'

'Since always. I just don't do it much.' Stubbing it out on a nearby bin, he discarded the cigarette. 'Most women detest the taste of tobacco on my breath.' James sprawled out beside her. His larger-than-life presence filled more than the physical space he occupied. He managed to touch her without laying a single finger on her.

Every hair covering her skin prickled with awareness. 'I gather Claudia doesn't mind.'

He chuckled. 'She goes through a pack a day.'

'Explains why she's so skinny. I can't imagine it does wonders for her complexion though.' She bit her lip. She had not intended to voice the thought.

James turned to face her. 'Not all beautiful women are blessed with your luscious curves, Cindy.'

Deaf to his compliment, she only heard the inference he made. *James thinks Claudia is beautiful.* 'Why did you bring her tonight? Are you trying to make me jealous?'

His gaze smouldered. 'Is it working?'

Shaking her head, she averted her eyes. 'Why would I be? I'm a happily married woman.'

James snorted. 'Right—and I'm the King of England. I know Adam has been working plenty of late nights this month. Why haven't you called me?'

'You know why, James.'

His hand rested on her thigh. Heat emanated from his touch, scorching her through layers of gold chiffon. 'I have certain… needs, Cindy.'

She stared at his hand as it glided toward her apex.

'I'd rather have you in my bed, but I'll settle for the next best thing.' With a gentle nudge, he uncrossed her legs.

'James,' she warned in a breathless plea.

'I can't tell if you want me to stop, or if you're begging me to continue.' Finding the slit in her dress, his fingers brushed against her sensitive flesh.

'You should stop,' she rasped.

'Is that what you *want?*'

Closing her eyes, she thought about all the people she would hurt if she gave in. She pictured the rift she would tear in the Fairfax family. 'Yes. Please stop.'

A low growl escaped him as he jerked his hand back. 'You are the most frustrating woman I know! Stop pretending to be a saint when I know how much you love sinning with me.'

Springing to her feet, she put her hands on her hips and glared at him. 'This isn't about us, James. It's about all the people we'll hurt in our wake.'

James rose, invading her space yet again with a tight grip on her shoulders. 'Assuming they even find out, they'll get over it. We're a resilient lot. I admire your altruism, sweetheart, but there are times you need to look out for number one. I can tell you're hurting. Please let me soothe those aches.'

'That's not your job.' Her voice quavered and tears welled in her eyes. 'Adam—'

'Lucy?' Adam's voice stopped her heart for a split second.

Pulling free of James' grasp, she rushed into her husband's arms. Sobbing against Adam's chest, she knew when James disappeared because he took all the warmth with him. A chill crept down her spine, and she shivered.

'Good God, you're freezing.' Adam wrapped his tuxedo jacket around her shoulders and searched her eyes. 'What's wrong, my love?'

How could she tell him everything plaguing her mind? Her guilt would destroy them both. Instead, she resorted to the one excuse he would not question. 'I-I don't think I'll ever be able to give you a baby.'

He squeezed her tight. 'We'll get there, my love. Please don't worry.'

She huffed to herself. *Easier said than done, I'm afraid.*

UNDENIABLY WRONG

ಇನ್ನ

James

'You know, I don't need a chaperone anymore, Russ.' Tapping a bottle of reserve shiraz against his thigh, James scanned the crowd. Melbourne's elite had turned out in droves to see Casper Van der Berg's new limestone mansion. The television star stood upon the front steps beside his boyfriend, greeting his guests. Most people had come to see him and Drew, but James was there for the real star of the show. *And there she is.* Lucinda wore a sexy-as-sin red dress stopping short of her knees by a few inches. Hot blood rushed through his veins as he imagined bending her over and hiking up the hem.

'Sure ya do, I can tell by how you're looking at her now. If I don't keep an eye on ya, you'll be stealin' her away to christen one of the guest rooms by the end of the night.' Russell twisted his own housewarming gift between his enormous hands. He had brought wine too, although much less expensive than the one James had purchased. Tense and awkward, the man looked like a fish out of water even with the designer tuxedo covering most of his tattoos.

'With any luck….'

'Dude, ya can't risk it.'

'Bit late,' James huffed.

Russel stared at him with a slack jaw. 'No effing way! When did it start?'

'Eight months ago. Not that I've succeeded in getting her back in my bed since then. I know this isn't your scene, so feel free to go home if you want.'

After a slow shake of his head, Russell snorted. 'Nah man, I'm all good. There's plenty of babes about tonight.' His gaze followed Lucinda's friend, Nicole, as she climbed the steps with her fiancé.

'You're barking up the wrong tree with her, Russ. Can't you see she's taken?'

'Never stopped you.' Russell flashed his teeth.

'Touché,' he agreed with a laugh. 'Still, Nicole's happily engaged.'

'Is she though?' Russell smirked. 'I hope I can win her over before she marries the idiot.'

He narrowed his eyes on Russell as they shuffled forward with the sea of bodies. 'What am I missing?'

'From what I gather, Nicole spends a lotta time alone while Michael works late most nights.'

'Sounds familiar.' He stepped forward to offer well wishes and wine to Casper and Drew. Once inside, he joined the rest of his family as they gathered in the atrium. Sweeping an eye over the interior, he whistled his approval. Terracotta pots of boxwood and palms surrounded a shallow pool. A fountain sat within, trickling water over mosaic tiles. 'This place is incredible, Lucy. You've done a fantastic job. It has a real Mediterranean vibe. What style of architecture do you call this?' When he met her eyes, a slight blush coloured her cheeks.

'Thank you, James. I based my design on Tuscan Revival. Casper and Drew wanted something to harmonise with the other Italian style houses along the street. Would you like to see the rest of it? I'm sure the guys won't mind if I take you all on a tour.' Lucinda showed them around the enormous house, pointing out little touches she added at her clients' request. Features like a ground-floor master suite, custom shelving, larger kitchen benches, and cabinet lighting. Taking pride in her work, she appeared happy for the first time in ages, almost glowing. Her smile warmed his heart and he wanted nothing more than to fill her heart with such joy over and over. *I should ask her to design my next home… among other things.*

As the hours flew by, he wondered if he would ever catch Lucinda alone. Between toasts and speeches, canapes and mingling, Casper kept her busy. Even Adam looked desperate to catch a moment with his wife. James glared at his brother from across the patio. *You should make the most of the time you have at home. Or not. By all means, let her fall back into my arms. You don't deserve her, arsehole.* He started at the bitterness of his own head voice, wondering when jealousy gave way to hatred and contempt.

When Lucinda ducked inside, Adam began to follow her, but Troy caught him in conversation.

Seizing the opportunity, James stalked after her. His foot tapped against floorboards as he waited outside the closed bathroom door. Finally, the door opened.

Her eyes widened the second they landed on him. 'James—'

Backing her into the bathroom, he locked the door behind him.

She leaned against a marble vanity and crossed her arms. 'You need to stop ambushing me in bathrooms. It's not very romantic.'

A short laugh slipped out. 'If you chose me instead, I wouldn't need to steal you away like this.' Caging her in his arms, he hovered close to her trembling lips. 'Don't worry,' he whispered. 'I'm not going to pressure you. I wanted to remind you I'm here and I still love you, Cindy.'

Sucking in a breath, she glanced at his mouth a moment before returning his gaze. 'Where's Claudia? I haven't seen her tonight.'

'She went home to Norway.' He toyed with one of the curls hanging loose from Lucinda's updo. 'Claudia never meant anything to me. She was nothing more than a… distraction. You're the only woman who occupies my waking thoughts and vivid dreams.' He gave her a lascivious grin. 'Even the wet ones. Especially those.'

Her cheeks heated and her arms lowered. 'James—'

He silenced her with a finger against her lips. 'Let me finish. I mean it when I say I'm in love with you, Cindy. Nothing makes me happier than seeing joy radiate from your smile. I'm not asking you to leave Adam, but I do think you would be better off with me. I would never leave you alone at night knowing how much it terrifies you.' His fingers trailed along her bare arm, giving rise to goosebumps. 'I'll give you whatever you want and everything you need.' Tears welled in her eyes, and he cussed. 'I didn't mean to upset you, sweetheart. Please don't cry.'

Swallowing, she schooled her expression. 'I can't leave Adam. It would destroy him and… we have a baby on the way.'

Something bitter climbed his throat. 'Shit! Here I thought you were glowing with pride.'

'I am, just—'

'Not for the house alone,' he finished for her.

Lucinda nodded. 'We're through the first twelve weeks now, so I'm feeling positive. Adam and I plan to announce it tonight once Casper's celebrity friends leave.'

'I suppose congratulations are in order.' His voice grew distant, as though he was hearing himself across a field of fog. He wanted to feel happy for her, but his mind conjured up images of her and Adam. Making a baby, holding their child, and being a perfect little family.

'James?' Her hand waved in front of his face.

'Sorry, I lost myself in thought.'

'Clearly. I'm sorry James—'

'Please don't apologise for being happy. I'll be here for you no matter what, okay? Even if you only want me to be Uncle James.' Wrapping his arms around her, he hugged Lucinda tight.

'Lucy?' Adam's voice carried along the hallway.

Lucinda stiffened, her heart hammering against his chest.

'Go. I'll hide in here until the coast is clear,' he assured her.

'Thank you,' she replied before planting a chaste kiss on his lips, although it felt anything but.

The intimate gesture sent a wave of desire straight to his dick. Taking cover behind the door, he considered a cold shower.

Then he heard Casper's booming voice, 'Can I get your attention please? Lucinda and Adam have an announcement to make....'

Shit! I should make an appearance for this. Not that he wanted to rub more salt in the wounds. *But family blah, blah, blah.*

The frivolities continued well into the night. Plastering on a fake smile hurt almost as much as the dawning realisation, *Lucinda will never be mine*. If she had not plucked up the courage to leave Adam during her recent bouts of loneliness, she sure as shit wouldn't do so while raising their kid together. At least he could count on his trusty friends, Jack, Johnny, and Jameson. Staggering up beside Casper, he clapped a hand on the man's shoulder. 'Tank for de well-stocked bar, buddy.'

Casper chuckled. 'Sounds like you've had a bit.'

'Mind if I sleep it off for a bit in one ya spare beds?'

'Go for it. Do you know where they are?'

With a nod, he stumbled across the spacious living room, grabbing hold of furniture where possible. Nearing the grand foyer, he heard a feminine giggle coming from the study, followed by a scuffle. Brooke left the room a second later sporting swollen lips and messy hair.

He knew Terrance had stayed away because of the restraining order, which must have meant.... He scanned the room and spotted Rebecca attaching herself to her fake boyfriend. *Huh, I guess Brooke likes a little action on the side.* Then he tensed. *Does Becky know?* Ironic really, despising the thought of someone cheating on his sister. Then again, he had always felt more protective of her than of Adam.

Stopping behind a pillar, Brooke adjusted the straps of her dress and smoothed a hand over her hair. Heaven forbid she appears less than perfect. Looking up, she froze when her eyes met his.

He glanced at the door she walked through a moment ago, curious to know who had left Brooke so flustered. *Has Terrance snuck in anyway, or is she betraying Rebecca with someone else?* As he edged toward the room, Brooke's eyes widened, revealing a hint of emotion before she turned to ice again. She spun on her heels and stormed off toward her girlfriend.

Interest piqued, he continued toward the door. Reaching for the handle, he was a second away from uncovering the truth when a woman cried out behind him.

'No! No! No! Not again!' Lucinda sobbed as she collapsed to the floor in a pool of blood. *So much blood.*

Never had anything sobered him so promptly. Acting on pure instinct and a shot of adrenaline, he sprinted across the room. Several people crowded around Lucinda by the time he reached her. He pushed his way through, shouting at them to give her space. Sitting beside her, Nicole gathered Lucinda into her arms where she wept against her best friend's chest. *Where the hell is Adam?* Scanning the group of onlookers, he spotted his brother. Staring at Lucinda, he appeared as rigid as one of the columns holding up the ceiling.

'Someone call a damn ambulance,' he spat as he knelt down in front of Lucinda. He didn't know much about pregnancies, but he figured miscarriages beyond the first trimester were dangerous. 'Is there anything I can do for you, Lucy?' he rasped.

'I've got her,' Nicole assured him. 'Go help your brother.' She gestured to Adam who stood frozen in place.

Jesus, the man's in shock. He guided Adam to a nearby sofa and poured him a stiff drink. Lost for words, he sat in silence as they waited for the paramedics to arrive. Better that than verbalise how he felt about the situation. He clenched his fist. *If Lucy dies tonight because of Adam… there will be hell to pay.*

Chapter Nineteen

Lucinda

Staring out the side window, Lucinda slipped into a trance as traffic whizzed by in a blur.

'Are you sure you're up for this?' Adam asked for the zillionth time.

'It's been six weeks. I need to get on with my life. Our life. Besides, I can't miss Becky's birthday.' This was the first social engagement she attended following her monstrous miscarriage. Aside from a few medical appointments, she had spent most of her time either resting in bed or sitting in the garden. The first few weeks had been especially rough both physically and psychologically. Her doctor had given her antidepressants, but it took a while for them to kick in.

'So long as you're sure.' Adam's kid gloves routine was getting old fast.

She missed being intimate with him. Avoiding sex during her recovery was one thing, but he had barely touched her. Nothing more than chaste cheek kisses and feather-light hugs. *At least he has spent more time at home.*

'Becky will be delighted to see you.'

Her lips quirked with a slight smile. *I doubt she'll be the only one.* James had all but confirmed his attendance in his last text. They had maintained constant communication through messages and phone calls. The correspondence had started innocently when he was more concerned for her health and wellbeing. But the sexual tension had ramped up in the last fortnight, filling her with a need her husband no longer satisfied.

Adam's family greeted them in the dining room and Rebecca gave her the first real hug she'd had in ages. 'Gosh I've missed you, Lucy.'

'Same.' Truth. Rebecca had become the sister she had always wanted. 'Oh and Happy birthday.'

'How are you feeling, hun?' Michelle asked as she drew Lucinda into her embrace.

'Good.' A chestnut gaze reeled her in as she replied, and she met his heated stare with equal fervour. 'Much better, thank you.'

James smirked, accepting the sentiment she had directed his way. The medication may have levelled her mood, but he had single-handedly resurrected her happiness.

'I'm surprised to see you here,' Adam admitted as he shook James' hand. 'You don't normally bother with birthdays.'

He shrugged. 'I guess I've come to realise the importance of time with family.'

Adam pulled him in for a bro hug. 'Glad to hear it.'

Conversation flowed during the meal and she smiled as a sense of normality returned.

'We're planning a family camping trip for next month,' Michelle explained. 'It would be great to see you all there.' Her gaze swept across everyone gathered around the table. 'Including you, Troy.'

Choking on his wine, Adam burst into a coughing fit. Once his throat had cleared, he stared at his mother. 'We haven't been camping since I was a kid. What brought this on?'

'James put the idea to me, actually. He suggested it would be a good family bonding activity, and I agree.'

Lucinda bit her lip, wondering what James was playing at. *Surely a private getaway for the two of us would work more in his favour.* 'I've always loved camping. It's a great idea.'

Squealing, Rebecca leaped from her seat, and threw her arms around James. 'You are the best! Where are we going?'

I guess that explains it. I'm not the only girl here he wants to cheer up.

'We haven't decided yet,' Michelle explained. 'We're looking for a campground with some nice cabins available.'

Placing his cutlery to the side of his plate, Adam sighed. 'Hopefully I can get some leave for it. They made me QA Manager at work.'

Rebecca's eyes lit up. 'Oh wow! That's great news.'

As a chorus of congratulations chimed across the crockery, James exchanged a look with Lucinda. They both knew what this meant for her, for them. Pushing his empty plate away, he cleared his throat. 'Well done, brother. I hope you don't mind, but I'm dying for a smoke.'

She gave it a few minutes, counting the seconds as they ticked by in her mind. 'Please excuse me, I need to use the facilities.'

'Of course,' Michelle smiled.

Bypassing the bathroom, she headed straight for the backyard where she found James in a poolside deckchair.

Flicking ash into a crystal dish, he glanced up and grinned. 'I didn't think you liked tobacco smoke.'

'I don't, but I wanted to catch you alone, so....'

Stubbing out the cigarette in the ashtray, James rose from his seat. 'This isn't a great spot for a private chat. Come with me.' Grabbing her hand, he led her into the pool house. With two locked doors between them and certain disaster, he took a deep breath. 'What's up sweetheart?'

She beamed at the endearment. 'I can't stop thinking about you. Dreaming too.'

'Erotic dreams?' He waggled his eyebrows, and she laughed.

'Yes,' she replied in a whisper. 'Adam's too afraid to touch me these days, and I'm so....'

'Horny?'

'That's one way of putting it.' She squirmed, trying to soothe the ache between her thighs. 'It's such a silly sounding word though, don't you think? I'm not sure it does justice to the intense desire simmering deep in my core.'

Grasping her hips, he backed her further into the room until her legs hit a bed. 'All you have to do is ask.'

'I want to, James. God, I want to. But not here. It's too risky.'

A guttural noise escaped him as he pulled her body flush against his. 'The next time Adam leaves you alone at night—'

'I'll call you,' she promised.

One of his hands travelled up her back, cupping the nape of her neck. 'I'm desperate to kiss you, but I haven't had a breath mint since—'

Her mouth crashed against his, swallowing his excuses. The tobacco on his breath was not the most pleasant flavour, but it did not taste terrible. Besides, she soon forgot it, losing herself amidst silken lips and calloused fingers. A dying ember in her soul sparked back to life after weeks of neglect. Every inch of skin sizzled and tingled. To love and feel loved, cherished even. Nothing compared. Was it wrong to kiss another man like this? To let him revive her flame? Undeniably. Yet what could she do? She loved two men—two brothers—and only one of them was giving her what she needed. *So what if he is the wrong one?*

೩೦೮೩

UNDENIABLY WRONG

Rebecca

Breathing in the sweet aroma of fried pastries, Rebecca immersed herself in the carnival atmosphere. She loved the vibrant outfits, the sea of smiling faces, and the majestic music. A boy skipping past in a Venetian jester costume almost barrelled into her. Stepping aside to give him room, she pressed up against Brooke. She took the opportunity to share a heated glance with the woman she loved. 'Quite the parade just now. I've never seen anything like it.'

Brooke grinned. 'I should take you to the Gay and Lesbian Mardi Gras then.' She laughed when Rebecca's eyes widened. 'Relax, sugar. No one can hear us over this din. Besides, it's in Sydney. We could take advantage of anonymity.'

'Have you been before?' she asked in a quavering voice.

'No, but I've seen footage. I'm keen to check it out one day.'

'I don't know....' She resumed browsing the market stalls. 'Wow! These Venetian masks look so authentic,' she remarked as she surveyed the vendor's goods.

'Because they are.' The thick, rich timbre of the voice drew her eye to the man behind the counter. He smiled at her with plump lips and cocoa eyes. A wisp of ebony hair dropped onto his square forehead as he peered down at her. Then he turned his attention to Brooke. '*Ciao Cugina. Chi è la tua bella amica?*' The merchant waggled his eyebrows.

'*Ciao Edoardo. Siete volgare,*' Brooke replied with a chuckle.

Rebecca's gaze pinched at the bridge of her nose as she tried to make sense of the swiftly spoken Italian.

Placing a hand on her arm, Brooke returned to English, 'This is my best friend, Rebecca. We are celebrating her birthday tonight. Edward is my cousin,' she explained. 'He makes these masks himself. Given our heritage, it's fair to say he knows what he's doing.'

'Oh gosh! I didn't know you had such an accomplished artist in the family.' She picked up a delicate turquoise mask with intricate beading. 'Are you any relation to the Vianellos?'

'*Si,*' Edward replied. 'Our mothers—' he gestured between himself and Brooke ' —are Paolo's sisters. That one suits you.' He pointed to the handcrafted masterpiece in her hands.

'Do you like it, Becky?' Brooke asked.

'I love it!' Fitting it in place, she admired her reflection in a small mirror to the side of the van.

'Then it's yours!' Edward beamed. 'Happy birthday, *bella*,' he added with a wink.

She gasped. 'I couldn't possibly take it without paying. You put so much work into these—'

'Please. I insist. You would be doing me service.'

'Um… okay. Thank you, Edward.'

'He likes you,' Brooke murmured in her ear as they strolled away.

Looking away with heated cheeks, some familiar faces caught her attention. She nodded towards them. 'There's your other cousin.'

'I figured I'd see him here tonight. Let's go say hi.' Brooke ushered her over to Derrick's little party of three.

They exchanged a few pleasantries before Rebecca added, 'I believe congratulations are in order. I'm sorry I missed your engagement party.'

Brooke had taken Terrance as her date; not a sight she wanted to witness, so she had spent the evening in Troy's bed instead.

Slipping a hand around his fiancé's waist, Derrick tucked her into his side. 'Thank you, Miss Fairfax. Sofia has made me a very happy man. I look forward to a lifetime of love with my soulmate.' He kissed Sofia's cheek.

Blushing, Sofia wiped away a rogue tear. 'We are both very happy.'

Rebecca's heart melted. 'You guys are so sweet. I hope I can make it to your wedding.'

The young lovebirds excused themselves, dragging Stefan with them.

Brooke studied them walking away. 'Don't you think it's strange how Stefan always tags along to their dates?'

She shrugged. 'Twins are often closer than other siblings.'

'They're too close if you ask me. I should have a word with my uncle about it.'

She giggled. 'Maybe they're a ménage à trois.'

Spinning to face her, Brooke frowned. 'Do you realise how gross that sounds? You're talking about incest, sugar.'

'Oh. I didn't think of it like that. My mind went somewhere else. Like what if the twins shared Derrick? That'd be hot.'

'Unlikely. There's always tension between the guys, and not the sexual kind. And look—,' Brooke pointed toward the trio ' —Sofia is usually in the middle.'

Shuddering, she spotted a gelati van. 'Let's get ice cream.' She was keen to change the subject.

As they stood in line, Brooke leaned in close to whisper, 'Speaking of threesomes, I have another surprise for you at home later.'

She gaped at Brooke. 'Seriously?'

'Quite. I know you've grown more interested in men of late, and since it's your birthday, you get to be the centre of attention.'

'Who?' She prayed to God for Troy.

'You'll have to wait and see.' Brooke winked as they reached the gelati vendor.

After choosing pistachio and baci, she reached for her purse, but Brooke grabbed her hand.

'This is on me. Birthday treat, remember.'

Grinning, she seized her dessert before it melted. 'Thank you. I've thoroughly enjoyed tonight.'

'We haven't even gotten to the best part yet,' Brooke purred in her ear.

The moment they stepped into their apartment, Brooke pushed Rebecca up against the door and kissed her passionately. Clothes flew across the room in a frenzy to get each other naked.

'Now for your surprise.' Brooke held up a blindfold. 'You'll have to wear this the whole time though.'

Her eyes widened. 'W-why?'

'It will help you put all your preconceived notions aside. Not to mention….' Stepping behind her, Brooke bought the blindfold down across her eyes and secured it. 'Losing one sense heightens the others.' She emphasised her point by pressing a finger to Rebecca's sensitive bud. The pressure almost made her explode in Brooke's arms.

'Can you at least tell me who he is first?'

'Nope. I promise you he is sexy though.' Brooke's hands moved up to cup her breasts. 'What's it gonna be, Becky? Threesome with an enigmatic hottie, or a night alone in bed listening to our guest make me come instead?'

'The second option doesn't sound very fun,' she protested.

'Not for you, it doesn't. I'm hoping it will incentivise you to take a walk on the wild side with me tonight. You can stop anytime if things get uncomfortable.'

She gulped. 'Okay. I'll do it.'

'Good girl.' Brooke led her into their bedroom where a sweet fruity scent infused the air.

Apple and vanilla. He smells like Troy. Excitement bubbled in her chest.

The mysterious stranger gasped, his short breaths growing louder as the women approached.

Is he already hard? 'C-can I touch you first?' she squeaked.

Brooke chuckled. 'He nodded, forgetting you can't see him.' She guided Rebecca's hands to the man's shoulders.

He must be sitting on the edge of the bed. She started with his face. Smooth cheeks, full lips, and a hint of stubble. *Like Troy.* Combing her fingers through his hair, she felt a hint of the wax Troy used to achieve his designer scruffy image.

With a moan, his large hands clasped her backside. He collapsed onto the mattress, pulling her down on top of him.

She yelped at the sudden movement. Finding her bearings, she straddled him and explored the landscape of muscle covering his torso. When she reached his nipples, he hissed and prodded her soft flesh with his erection. Her cheeks heated, yet despite her nerves, she felt a sense of power over him. Toying with his on switches, she squeezed and rolled them between her fingers. She enjoyed the mounting pressure at her core. His cock throbbed against her slick entrance.

Brooke came up behind, peppering her back with kisses and stroking her soft folds. 'Mm, you're so wet and ready for him. Do you want him inside you, sugar?'

'Yes,' she rasped.

'Then say it. You have to tell him what you want.'

'F-fuck me w-with your hard dick.'

He slammed into her.

'Oh God!' she cried out as a bright light flashed against the back of her closed lids. Between his relentless thrusting and the force of Brooke's thumb against her clit, she exploded.

But neither of them had finished with her.

'Christ! She's as tight as a damn virgin, Brooke. I'm not sure how much longer I can last here.' His voice sounded familiar, but not in a good way.

Brooke growled. 'Then slow down. My girl deserves way more orgasms.'

Groaning, he eased the pace. 'Are you sure she's slept with other men?'

Her heart shattered. She knew without doubt the man inside her was not Troy. Which meant— 'Wait!'

They all froze.

'What is it, sugar?' Brooke cooed.

'I thought—'

Brooke brushed her fingertips along her spine. 'You shouldn't be thinking about anything right now, just *feeling*.'

She shivered. The mood had shifted in the room, and she wasn't sure she liked it.

The man who was most definitely not Troy snickered. 'She realised I'm not her boyfriend. I guess my voice gave it away.'

'You deceived me? On purpose?' She reached for the blindfold, but Brooke pinned her arms behind her back.

'Don't spoil the moment, Becky,' Brooke warned. 'This isn't a trick, but a gift.'

Rough hands glided along her ribs and groped at her breasts. 'Come on Becky, you climaxed for me once already.' Rolling his hips, he worked to build more momentum. 'Let it go.'

'He could still be Troy if you let your imagination loose again,' Brooke whispered.

'I-I'm not sure I can.'

Brooke sighed and moved over. 'Here, come kiss me, sugar. Forget him for a moment.'

Shuffling across the bed, she climbed onto Brooke. Their lips merged and the heat returned. Before long, she was dripping all over Brooke's deft fingers.

'Now,' Brooke demanded.

Confused, she opened her eyes, only to find the strip of black fabric still covered her vision.

Then Mystery Guy slid inside her from behind.

The sudden invasion startled her. '*Ah!*'

Taking it as an invitation, he pounded into her. Brooke claimed her lips and together, they brought her to the edge again. He held her there a moment before letting her freefall.

Hours later they all collapsed in a heap of sweaty limbs. Brooke lit a cigarette while Mystery Guy wrapped his arms around Rebecca and spooned her.

'Can I see who you are now?' she rasped, tugging at her blindfold. The material slipped away, revealing the glow of Brooke's cigarette in the dim room.

'Are you sure you want to know?' he asked in a gruff voice. 'What if we want to do this again?'

She sought Brooke's gaze for approval.

A puff of smoke billowed out from her mouth as Brooke laughed. 'Go on. I don't mind if you peek now.'

Turning over, she peered into eyes as black as night. Her breath hitched as one corner of his lips twitched. *Terrance.*

'Now you know why I enjoy riding his dick so much,' Brooke announced.

෴

Adam

Stepping off the tennis court, Adam guzzled a gallon of water.

'Good match.' Brooke smiled, offering him an orange wedge.

Accepting her citrus offering, he bit into it to hold his tongue. Ever since discovering the sports club he frequented, she had made a habit of watching him play. Like all the time.

She took his silence as a cue to continue. 'I'm glad you have such a healthy outlet for your grief. You're an inspiration, Adam. That's why I've taken up the hobby too.' She waved her pristine racket in his face.

His gaze slipped to her indecent skirt. The slightest breeze would flash her panties, but he supposed it was the point.

Greg grunted beside him. 'Nice outfit, gorgeous. So many of the chicks around here wear shorts these days. It's like a global conspiracy to rob us blokes of our eye candy.'

'This is a tennis court, not a strip club,' Adam grumbled.

Slapping his back, Greg chuckled. 'I'll see you inside, mate.'

Waving Greg away, he fixed his eyes on Brooke's. 'I can't see you enjoying the sport. You end up rather dirty and sweaty afterwards. Try your hand at golf, like Lucy.'

The left side of her mouth quirked up. 'I happen to enjoy getting dirty and sweaty, especially where hot guys are concerned.'

He rolled his eyes. 'You should go see your *boyfriend* then. Where is Terrance anyway?' He did not care where the creep was, so long as he kept well enough away from Lucinda.

'Yes, I suppose Terry is a hottie. He's in the gym, getting all *sweaty*.' Closing the distance between them, Brooke placed her free hand on his chest. 'I've been meaning to offer my condolences over your loss.'

'I don't need your pity,' he seethed.

Brooke shook her head. 'You know me better, sugar. I can sympathise with losing a baby.

Marriage to a woman who doesn't want kids must be hard.'

'What?' he snapped almost hard enough to dislocate his jaw.

Dropping her racket on a bench, she retrieved a piece of paper from her designer duffle bag. 'I found these blood test results in her desk when I was looking for a pen.' She handed him the pathology report. 'Isn't misoprostol acid a byproduct of the abortion pill?'

He gaped at the sheet of paper showing hard evidence of misoprostol use. 'How? This pill isn't even legal here yet.'

Brooke shrugged. 'I don't know. Maybe she's getting it on the black market. All I know is, Lucy doesn't want those babies you keep putting in her. I'm sorry to bring these awful tidings, but I thought you deserved the truth.'

The paper crinkled in his hand as his fist clenched around it.

Snaking her bony arms around his waist from behind, she propped her chin on his shoulder. 'Terry won't mind if I spend tonight comforting you.'

He shrugged out of Brooke's slimy embrace and stormed into the men's locker room.

Greg emerged from a cloud of steam in nothing but a towel and a lewd grin. 'Please tell me you're tapping that fine piece of Venetian arse.'

He huffed. 'Been there, done that, no thank you sir. Listen man, can I stay at your place for a few days?'

The smile dropped from Greg's expression. 'Yeah, of course. What's wrong?'

He shoved the test results in Greg's face. 'Lucy has been lying to me.'

Chapter Twenty

Lucinda

Unlocking the garage door, Lucinda entered a dim, desolate house. *'Adam?'* Her voice rang out through the twilight. Nothing but her own echo replied as it settled with specks of disturbed dust. *Odd. He is usually back from tennis well before my golf days finish.* Flicking on a light, she put her keys on the hook in the foyer. *Unless he went to bed early?* She mounted the stairs two-at-a-time and dashed into a dark bedroom. 'Adam?' she asked in a hesitant whisper; afraid to wake him if he slept, but anxious to find him all the same. Creeping across the room, she patted both sides of the bed. Empty. 'Maybe he stayed out for drinks with the guys,' she mused to herself.

Tipping the contents of her duffel bag onto the bed, she tossed her dirty clothes into the laundry hamper. When she turned back to the bed, a familiar style of envelope caught her eye, and she froze. Black letters spelled her name, taunting her from the middle of the white parchment. The serifs began to slither from the font like tendrils seeking to strangle something. To choke her. Ice coiled down her spine.

She blinked a couple of times and the name on the envelope returned to normal. Retrieving her phone, she dialled Adam with a trembling hand. It rang several times before—

'Lucy?' Adam greeted her with a cold, distant tone.

'Where are you? I got home and—'

'I'm staying with a friend to cool off. I can't be around you yet; not after what you did.'

'Hang on, wha—' The line disconnected, leaving her to gape at the silent device. Then everything sunk into place, and she let the mobile slip from her grip. *Oh shit! He knows.* Her heart thumped as she tried to suck air into her starving lungs. Terrance had succeeded in getting her alone and vulnerable. *Right where he wants me. Although….* If the creepy notes had formed part of a twisted plan to split her and Adam apart, he had not accounted for the other man who stood waiting in the wings.

She snatched her phone up from where it had fallen onto a throw pillow and tried James. It rang and rang. *Come on, please pick up*. It continued ringing. *Please*. His message service answered. 'Damn it!'

'—Please leave your message after the tone.' The voice recording ended with a *beep*.

'Hey James? Where are you? I need you right now,' she quaked. 'Adam knows… about us. And there's more. I found another letter. I haven't opened it. I'm too afraid to do so alone. Please call me as soon as you get this.' Hanging up, she considered her options. Leaving the house alone would be a bad idea. Her stalker could be out there ready to pounce. Yet staying put grew less appealing as the night wore on. *I'm a sitting duck here by myself.*

With her two main lifelines out of reach, she contacted the security company. 'Has there been a security breach at my house today?' she asked the man who had greeted her with a thick Aussie drawl.

'Nah ma'am. We would've let ya know if any of the alarms went off.'

'Okay thank you.' On the verge of signing off, she paused as an idea sprang to mind. 'I'll be home alone for a while tonight and I'm concerned about my safety. I have a stalker and… there's a man… can you keep an eye on things tonight? If anything suspicious happens… what if I send you his photo? There's a restraining order out on him, so you could notify the police.'

The security guard sighed. 'Such intense surveillance would incur a hefty surcharge ma'am.'

'I don't care. I'll pay whatever it takes to keep Terrance away.'

'Okay, fine. Email through ya pics and I'll watch the place. Buzz me when ya wanna call off the extra surveillance. Might I suggest inviting a friend to stay with ya? If nothin' else, should help ya peace of mind.'

'Will do and thank you so much.' She sprinted across the house to her study and fired up her laptop. It did not take long to send through a photo of Terrance. She wondered how the letter even made it into her bag. She had been around women pretty much all day, well except when Michael met Nicole for a drink after the tournament. The only time she had left her bag unattended was during her shower. *Did Terrance sneak into the women's change room?* A chill crawled across her skin.

Time to summon reinforcements. Scrolling through her directory, she considered ANNETTE. She did not fancy the idea of putting the dear woman at risk, but if she bought her husband too…. *Worth a shot, I guess.* It went straight to voicemail.

Not bothering to leave a message, she continued looking through the list. BECKY popped up next, but she dismissed the idea out of hand. She did not know if Adam had broken the news to her yet, but there was no way in hell she would hear it from Lucinda. The thought alone broke her heart.

Casper's name followed shortly, and she did not hesitate to contact him. Straight to voicemail, *again. Why isn't anyone answering?* Then she remembered Casper and Drew were out of town at a rural location film set.

Working her way down the alphabet, she paused and hovered over MICHAEL. She knew he was out with Nicole. *Surely they would cut their date short for a friend in need?* Alas no. Both phones rang out.

Finally, she reached TROY. There was a remote chance he was the friend putting Adam up, although Greg seemed more likely. *Not to mention the risk of word getting back to Becky.* Swallowing her pride, she took a chance.

'Hi Lucy,' he answered on the third ring, sounding as chipper as ever. 'What's up?'

Well at least he doesn't know about me and Adam yet. 'Um hi. This is going to sound strange but—'

'Hey bunny, who are you talking to?' Rebecca's soft voice chimed in the background.

'Bunny?' she snorted. 'That's got to be the cutest pet name I've heard in a while.'

Troy groaned. 'Please don't tell Adam, I'll never live it down.'

'Don't worry, your secret's safe with me,' she replied with an ache in her chest. Given how things were going, she would likely take it to her grave.

'So, what can I do for you, sister?'

Her handset beeped. 'Hang on a sec.' Glancing at the screen, she read JAMES and breathed a sigh of relief. 'Sorry Troy, I gotta go, there's someone on the other line. Thanks for the chat.'

'Um, sure?'

'Yes, all good. Bye for now.' She accepted the incoming call without further delay. 'Hey James, I'm so glad you got back to me.'

'Ah, hi, this is Hannah,' the woman replied with a timid voice.

'Oh.' Her heart sank. *Is he seriously with one of his... distractions tonight?*

'I didn't know who else to contact. Neither of his parents would pick up and well, your text message history with him looks rather… intimate.'

Dear God! You were supposed to delete those, James. 'What's this about, Hannah?'

'Well, you see… there's been an accident.'

ॐ

James

James turned on the headlights as the sun began dipping beneath the horizon. Pulling up to a red light, he peeked in his rear-view to check Hannah was still following. Sure enough, her glitter speckled face beamed back at him.

He had picked her up at one of the dive bars he frequented. As soon as he'd suggested taking the party somewhere more comfortable, she jumped at the idea. Then she'd insisted on driving her own car because there was 'no way in hell (she) was leaving her baby in some dingy carpark overnight.' He had relented of course. He'd seen merit in allowing her a quick getaway.

As the lights turned green and he eased his foot off the brake, his phone chimed to life with

Bootylicious. He glanced at the handset sitting in the centre console tray, even though he knew whose name lit up the screen. He had only assigned that ringtone to one woman. He grinned as thoughts of a night with Lucinda filled his mind. *Sorry Hannah. Looks like you'll be on your own now.* Scanning the road ahead, he searched for a safe spot to pull over. Unfortunately, there was nothing but yellow lines as far as the eye could see. Lucinda's call went to voicemail before he could find anywhere.

Tyres squeaked behind him and as soon as he looked in the mirror, bright high beams blinded him. 'Impatient wanker,' he scoffed in disgust. Accelerating, he sat at the speed limit for a second, hoping to appease some road rage. The moron swerved into the oncoming lane and gained on him.

He glimpsed the enormous black pickup in the side mirror moments before it nudged him. *'What the fuck?'* he screamed at the road hogging arsehole. Not that there was any chance his voice carried beyond two closed panes of glass. The pickup shoved him harder, and he felt his SUV crunch over gravel. 'Christ! Are you insane dude? Overtake me and be done with it.'

The small truck swung out again before ramming him even harder. With the momentum he had built up and the impact of the collision, he went flying across the soft edge. His car skidded along wet grass and launched itself into a large gum tree.

Something white flashed before his eyes, then nothing.

ℬℭ

Lucinda

Lucinda double-checked the peephole before opening the door to Russell. 'Thank you so much for picking me up.'

'Hey doll, it's no probs. Thanks for lettin' me know 'bout ol' Jimmy.' He gave her space to lock up before helping her into his dusty four-wheel drive. They sat in silence as he reversed out of her driveway and soared along the street. 'Mind tellin' me why your hubby ain't takin' ya to see his brother?'

Sniffling, she dabbed at the tears spilling from her eyes. 'It's kind of personal.'

Russell sighed. 'Jimmy told me 'bout you and him. I swear I ain't blabbed to a soul, nor am I gonna. I hope ya both know what ya doin'.'

'I don't think we do,' she confessed with a sob. 'Adam found out. Hence his absence tonight.'

'Ah man, that sucks.'

They both slipped into contemplation for the duration of the drive. Twenty minutes later he pulled into the multi-level carpark.

She marched up to reception. 'Hi. I'm here to see James Fairfax.'

The nurse scrutinised her through thick-rimmed glasses. 'And you are?'

'Lucinda Fairfax.'

'Oh shoot!' a woman yelped from the waiting area. She jumped up and stumbled over to the desk. 'You're his *wife*? I swear I had no idea he was married.'

She narrowed her eyes at the slightly shorter and much younger blonde. 'You must be Hannah.' Running with the convenient lie, she turned her attention back to the nurse. 'Can I please see my husband? Is he okay?'

Russell coughed behind her.

After clicking away on her computer, the nurse smiled. 'Yes, your husband is fine. He is in recovery. You may see him, but please save the lecture until he is out of hospital.'

Lucinda spun around to face Hannah. 'Thank you for calling me. Russell and I will take it from here. You may go now.'

With a quick nod, the young woman made a mad dash for the exit.

Walking beside her, Russell chuckled. 'Man, you scared that bird half to death.'

She shrugged it off, not having room for any more guilt in her aching heart.

Chestnut eyes lit up the moment she stepped past the curtain. 'Hey sweetheart. It's so good to see you again.' He eased himself up into a sitting position.

She wanted to throw herself at him, to wrap her arms around him and never let go. But she took one look at the machines connected to his arms and froze. 'You could have died,' she rasped.

James huffed. 'It'll take a lot more than some road-raging jerk to strip me from this mortal coil.'

Perching on the bed, she reached out and held his hand. 'What happened?'

His gaze lifted as Russell entered the recovery bay. 'Oh, hey Russ. Not that I'm complaining, but what are you doing here?'

'Lucy got my number from your phone via Hannah and asked me to bring her in.'

James shot her a look.

'Adam wasn't home tonight.' She left it at that, not wanting to send his blood pressure through the roof while he sat on a hospital stretcher. 'Tell us what happened.'

He nodded. 'I was driving home from the pub when some dickhead in a pickup truck ran me off the road. I guess I'm lucky Hannah was following in her own car. She pulled me out of the wreck and phoned for an ambulance. The doctor says I escaped with a few minor bruises and a mild concussion. I should be good to head home soon.'

Closing her eyes, she breathed in deeply. 'Did you see who drove the other vehicle?'

'No. The windows were tinted, and I was too focussed on my own driving.'

Russell grunted. 'Bummer dude. Would 'ave been nice to sue the bastard for every last cent.'

'I think I know who was responsible,' she admitted.

James studied her with wide eyes. 'Who?'

'Someone who wanted me completely alone tonight.'

A fire blazed in his eyes. 'What happened?'

She shook her head. 'I'll tell you later. You need to rest and heal first.'

Tugging her closer, James pressed a kiss to her forehead. 'Thank God you're safe and here with me now.'

'I'll leave you love birds to it. Good to see ya fightin' fit, Jimmy.' Russell bumped fists with James before strolling away.

Shuffling into his side, she snuggled with James as best she could.

'I was driving when you tried ringing earlier. Please tell me that was a booty call.' His gruff voice sent tingles down to her core.

'You wish,' she jibed with a laugh.

Turning his head to face her, he stared into her eyes. 'I'll always wish for nights with you in my bed, Cindy. Well maybe not like this.' His free hand pointed to the drip in his other arm. 'But I'm sure you catch my meaning,' he finished with a yawn.

'Try to get some sleep. I'll be right here,' she assured him.

ഇരു

The instant the door clicked shut behind them, James pushed Lucinda up against his foyer wall. He claimed her lips with deep passion and hunger, feasting on her like the best meal he had had in hours. Knowing hospital food, this was probably true. She did not hold back either, feeding her own lust as much as his. But when he started removing her blouse, she halted his progress. 'I'm not sure this is a good idea.'

James growled in her ear. 'It's a fantastic idea. I promise you I am well enough recovered.'

'Not what I meant. I still don't know where I stand with Adam.' She had filled James in on the whole Adam debacle, along with the stalker scare, as she drove him home from the hospital.

He sighed, tucking strands of hair behind her ear. 'If what you suspect is true, I doubt this will do any *more* damage.' His fingers brushed against her nipples, tugging at the last of her restraint.

Arching her back, she moaned as the pressure increased. 'You raise a good point.'

'I'll raise more than one good point.' James picked her up, eliciting a squeal as he carried her to his room. He lowered her to the bed and stripped away layers of chiffon and lace. 'A goddess stands before me,' he whispered.

Her cheeks flushed. 'I'm not sure I can stand upright much longer with you making me so weak at the knees.'

He smirked. 'I can think of some positions that will get you off your feet.'

Biting her lip, she dropped to the mattress and posed like a fashion model on her side. 'Like this?'

'Hmm. Not exactly what I had in mind.' Flopping beside her, James nudged her onto her back. He straddled her as he plucked his t-shirt over his head.

Her eyes roamed over his bare flesh, taking in the black and blue patches of skin. She traced one of the larger bruises. 'Would you like me to kiss your boo boos better?'

A raspy chuckle slipped out. 'Sweetheart, you can kiss any part of my body you so desire. I'll feel better from having your lips on me.'

She smiled at the sentiment. 'Come here then.' When he drew near, she trailed kisses across his chest, along his shoulders, and up his neck. Their mouths collided and heat surged through her body. Her desire reflected in his eyes. 'I know you've mostly healed, but we should still take it easy.'

He stroked the pad of his thumb along her bottom lip. 'You worry too much, but I'm happy to go slow if you want to make love.'

The thought sent a welcome shiver through her chest. 'Have you ever made love to a woman before?'

'Nope. But there's a first time for everything right?'

She beamed. 'Seems fitting that I get this one since you took my virginity.'

A guttural noise slipped out as though something pained him. 'I wish I had appreciated the gift you gave me more at the time. My biggest regret in life was leaving that room without you.'

'Don't beat yourself up about it. We have each other now, so let's make the most of it.'

He kissed her again and their passion evolved into the most incredible pleasure she had ever experienced.

Warmth surrounded her as she snuggled into James' embrace. Everything was perfect for the moment, then her stomach grumbled. She tried to laugh it off. 'I guess there is still one part of me sex can't satisfy.'

'You're right. We should eat.' James rose, leaving a cool breeze in his wake.

Shuddering, she jumped out of bed and searched the floor for her clothes.

'Here.' James draped a plush dressing gown over her shoulders. 'You can borrow this for now.'

'Thank you.' She slid her arms into the sleeves and turned to watch him don a red silk robe. 'Now who looks like a fricking god?'

His lips quirked. 'I'm glad you approve.' He waltzed out of the room with a little more swagger than usual. Pots and pans clanged together as he rifled through his kitchen cupboards. 'Fancy a steak?'

'Mm, yes please. Medium rare since I'm not currently pregnant.'

His brows arched. 'How is that a thing?'

'There's all sorts of foods pregnant women should avoid for the health and safety of the unborn child. Rare steak is one such example.'

James shook his head as he seasoned a griddle pan with a light coating of oil. 'Sounds like torture to me.'

'Like you wouldn't believe. Is there anything I can do to help? I could make a salad.' She opened the fridge to see what ingredients she could whip together.

'Sure. Go nuts.' He reached past her to retrieve a tray with two large beef fillets.

She gaped at the contents of the refrigerator. 'I'm impressed. This thing is way better stocked than mine. Not what I expected for a long-term bachelor.'

James laughed. 'I'm not twenty anymore, sweetheart. I've learnt how to look after myself over the years. I guess there's something to be said for staying single this long.'

She chose to ignore the bittersweet taste of his words. Rummaging through the fruit and vegetable crispers, she pulled out some gourmet lettuce mix, an avocado, a mango, olives, and a punnet of raspberries. 'Where are your mixing bowls and chopping boards?' Following his directions, she retrieved the crockery she needed and tossed the salad. She raided the pantry, finding extra virgin olive oil, cherry vinegar, and orange blossom water. Using a few of the raspberries she had reserved, she pureed them into a light, fruity dressing.

After setting the table, James poured them both a glass of sparkling shiraz. 'This has been fun.'

She offered him a questioning gaze.

'Cooking together. I never fancied myself the domestic type, but I could get used to more of this with you.'

Her breath hitched at his confession. Raising her glass, she tapped it against his own crystal flute. 'To domestic bliss.'

'Cheers.'

Sinking her teeth into the juicy meat, she moaned as the flavour exploded in her mouth. 'This is so good.'

He smiled, holding a piece of mango on his fork. 'I love your salad too.'

Once they had both finished their meals, she rose to start clearing the dishes.

James held his arm out to stop her. 'Leave them for now. Something has been plaguing the back of my mind and we should get this out of the way sooner rather than later.'

She gulped, fearing what he might say.

'Did you bring the stalker letter with you?'

Her eyes bugged out. *Okay, not what I expected.* 'Um, yes actually. It's in my handbag.'

'Mind if I have a look at it?'

'Be my guest.' She retrieved the white envelope and handed it to him.

His forehead creased as he read the note. 'I don't think Terrance wrote this. Sounds more like someone who wants Adam for herself.' He placed it on the table beside her empty dinner plate.

As her eyes scanned the page, she stifled a gasp with her hand.

You will never have Adam's baby because a sinful harlot like you is unworthy of mothering his child.

Tears formed in her eyes as they peered into his. 'D-do you think someone has been drugging me to bring on my miscarriages?'

A scowl marred his beautiful face. 'I sure as hell hope not, but I wouldn't put it past this psychopath. You should stay here while Adam decides what he wants to do. I don't want you alone in his house anymore.'

She should have declined his offer. People would talk if they found out. Yet, her frayed nerves had worn so thin they became threadbare. 'Okay. I'll stay, but just for a few days.'

ഏരു

A few days turned into the best part of a week. The only word Lucinda had heard from Adam came two days after he had left. A text message, nothing more.

{ADAM} I'M NOT READY TO RETURN HOME, BUT WE NEED TO TALK. I'LL SEE YOU ON THE FAMILY CAMPING TRIP.

The night before said vacation, Casper invited everyone out for drinks.

'Are you sure you want to do this?' James asked as they reached the cocktail bar.

Putting her sporty red car into park, she took a deep breath. 'Yes. I can't keep hiding forever. People will get suspicious.'

'Do you think Adam will be in there?' James drummed his fingers on his thighs; one of the few nervous ticks he had revealed to her during their week of domestic bliss.

'I doubt it. He knows I'm close to Casper and wants to avoid seeing us until the weekend. We'll play it cool tonight. Give the impression my marriage is still hunky dory.'

James nodded. 'As much as I'd love to walk in linking arms, we should enter separately. You can go first, and I'll keep an eye open for trouble.'

She simpered. 'Thank you.' A cursory glance assured her no one loitered in the carpark. She tossed him her keys and headed inside. It did not take long to spot the large booth Casper had booked. Brooke already occupied the space, dazzling the crowd with her glittering black dress and diamond jewellery. Rebecca and Troy sat across from her, and the trio were laughing. All three sets of eyes met hers as she approached.

'Hi Lucy,' Rebecca beamed, embracing her. 'It's great to see you.' As they pulled apart, she glanced over Lucinda's shoulder. 'Where's Adam?'

'He's working late tonight.'

'What a shame.' Brooke pursed her lips together in a smug grin leaving Lucinda questioning how much she knew.

A devastating thought infiltrated her mind. *What if Adam is staying with Brooke?* She tucked it aside, determined to enjoy a night out with friends. 'What's everyone drinking? I'll get the next round?' After taking their orders, she headed to the bar. Nicole and Michael met her there a few minutes later, helping her carry all the cocktails back to the table.

'What are you drinking, sister?' Rebecca asked as she eyed the creamy chocolate treat in Lucinda's glass.

'A Toblerone.'

'It looks delicious.'

She nodded. 'It's my new favourite.'

'Why are you drinking alcohol?' Brooke asked, raising her voice over the thumping electro music. 'I thought you were trying to get pregnant?'

Her cheeks flushed with a mix of shame and anger. 'We're taking a break from the family planning, under doctor's advice. Not that it's any of your business.'

Brooke harrumphed and toyed with the umbrella on her piña colada.

Nicole tapped Lucinda's hand and leaned in to whisper, 'Are you going to tell me why you need an alibi?' She referred to the text message Lucinda had sent her earlier in the week. She had begged Nicole to cover for her, telling Adam how Lucinda had spent the week at her house. If he even bothered to ask.

She shook her head. 'Now's not a good time, but I promise to explain later.'

Nicole nodded. 'Sorry I missed your call the other night, by the way. Michael took me out for a twilight cruise, and we left our phones in the car.'

'Oh wow, that sounds so romantic.'

'It was,' Nicole agreed. 'Is everything okay? I heard you tried to reach Mum too. She only mentioned it today, else I would have rang you earlier.'

She shrugged. 'I was feeling lonely and sorry for myself. Adam's been working lots of late nights again.'

'I can relate,' she huffed, shooting Michael daggers.

'What?' Michael met her glare head on. 'Someone has to bring home the bacon.'

'Hey there, friends and fam!' A deep, familiar voice bellowed across the table, fanning the flames deep in her core.

She met James' grinning face with a smile of her own. She could not wait to get back to his house. After the obligatory hugs and handshakes, James sat opposite her, a convenient yet dangerous spot. She hoped they did not get caught exchanging too many heated glances. At least no one peeked beneath the table to see the game of footsies taking place under their noses.

Charging up to the booth, Casper smacked his hands down on the table. All the glasses jiggled, and the umbrella toppled from Brooke's glass. 'Oh my God! Did you hear? The Pacini twins eloped together. I'm talking like full sibling incest. Can you believe it?' He shuffled in beside Lucinda and gave her a quick peck on the cheek. 'Hello darling.'

'Wait, didn't Sofia already marry Derrick?' She asked with a furrowed brow.

'Yes, but he helped Sofia annul their marriage so she could be with Stefan.' Casper accepted the martini Drew offered him. 'Thank you, cupcake.'

'Oh wow! Poor Derrick. He must be heartbroken,' Nicole mused.

'Ick!' Rebecca screwed up her face. 'That is so gross. I can't imagine sleeping with my brothers.'

Lucinda felt James shiver through their foot connection.

'Oh, I don't know, Becky.' Brooke flicked her rogue umbrella across the table. 'Haven't you ever stopped to think about how much Troy resembles your brothers? You may as well be bumping uglies with James.'

'For the love of God, woman! You are vile!' James spat.

Brooke snickered. 'I'm not the one having sex with my brother's doppelganger.'

'No, you're just dating a damn sex offender!' James seethed.

'What?' several of their friends chimed together.

'Oh, didn't you know? Why do you think Terry keeps his distance from Lucy?'

She paled as all eyes fell on her. Nicole rubbed a comforting hand across her shoulder blades.

'What is he talking about, Lucy darling?' Casper asked with wide eyes.

'I….' Her throat dried out and words failed her.

'You want me to explain?' Nicole offered. She took the silent nod as consent. 'Terrance has a history of sexually assaulting Lucy. In fact, Adam rescued Lucy when Terry was seconds away from

raping her at my mum's Christmas in July party
years ago.'

Several mouths gaped open.

Rebecca's fist pounded the table as she stared
at Brooke. 'Did you know about this?'

'Of course. Terry tells me *everything*.' Brooke
sipped her drink and peered at Lucinda over the
rim of her glass. 'Seriously though, Lucy, what did
you expect after leading him on?'

'*Get out!*' James demanded in a deadly voice.
'Get the hell out of here right now before I drag you
by that ridiculous necklace!'

Rising to her feet, Brooke cackled. 'I love
how you are so quick to defend poor Lucy in her
husband's absence. Makes me wonder if there's more
to this story than either of you are letting on.' After
squeezing past the guys on her side of the booth,
she sauntered out of the bar.

'Well!' Casper exclaimed. 'That was quite a
show. She even put some of my performances to
shame.'

'I'm sorry.' Rebecca reached across the table
to grab her hand. 'I swear I had no idea what he did
to you.'

'Don't sweat it, Becky. It's not like you're the
one sleeping with him.'

Rebecca's gaze lowered for a second before meeting her eyes. While brief, the moment of hesitation was enough to make Troy stiffen beside her. 'No, but I am best friends with Brooke. I don't know what's come over her lately.'

A short, dry laugh escaped James. 'Please tell me you aren't so blind, Becky. Brooke is and always has been a self-serving bitch.'

'You don't know her like I do,' Rebecca complained.

James shuddered. 'Trust me when I say I don't care to. I never envied Adam for garnering her attention back in the day.'

'I know she has a mean streak,' Rebecca went on. 'But she can be kind, and generous—'

'Are you seriously defending the woman right now?' Troy barked. 'After all the shit she flung at Lucy?'

Lucinda's mind whirled with the words as they flew around the group. 'Wait a sec!' Everyone paused to stare at her. 'James, what did you say about Brooke and Adam?'

'Oh that. Brooke used to have a huge crush on Adam when they were teenagers. It was pathetic really, the way she followed him like a lost puppy.'

She brought to mind all the conversations she had shared with Adam about past loves. 'Huh.

He never mentioned it. I assume her feelings went unrequited.' Everything clicked into place, and she shared a silent understanding with James.

'Oh shit!' James sprang to his feet and dashed outside.

'What's going on?' Casper pleaded.

'I'll explain later.' She clambered out of the booth and chased after James. She found him scouring the carpark.

'Damnit! She's already gone.' He spun around and pulled her into his arms. 'Are you okay?'

She nodded the least convincing lie of all time. 'What if Brooke *and* Terry are in this together?'

Chapter Twenty-One

James

When Lucinda started carrying her bags out to her car, James grabbed them and tossed them in the back of his repaired and repainted SUV. 'As cute as it is, there's no way your sportscar will fit all our stuff.'

She gaped at him. 'Since yours is back from the repair shop, I was planning to go in separate cars.'

A growl rumbled through his diaphragm. He closed the distance between them, pinning her up against her red chassis. 'Like hell you are. If your *stalkers* are upping their game, I don't want to leave you alone.'

'Adam won't be happy—'

'Screw Adam! Your safety is my priority right now and it should be yours.' While he loved her in every conceivable way, he wouldn't mind seeing less of her stubborn streak.

She stood there staring at him, her chest rising and falling in short breaths. Her posture deflated with the last of her resolve. 'Fine. But you can explain to him why we came together.'

The left side of his mouth curved up. 'Sure you want me to mention that?'

Her eyes narrowed as she processed his comment. As realisation dawned, she rolled her eyes. 'I meant *travelled* together.'

'I'll tell him the truth.' When her eyes widened, he added, 'I'm protecting you from the bad guys. With any luck he'll thank me for being a hero.'

'In your dreams,' she scoffed in a mirthful tone.

Conversation remained light as they drove through the suburbs. As soon as they hit the freeway, James heaved out a sigh. 'We should devise a plan for how to handle the situation with Adam.'

'How? I don't even know what he wants to do.'

'What do *you* want?' Hardening the walls around his heart, he steeled himself for her inevitable rejection.

'Honestly, I wish I could have you both.'

He snorted. 'This is reality sweetheart, not some French porno.'

She huffed in that cute way she does, her breasts bobbing in his peripheral vision. 'I've heard of real people making it work.'

'You know it'll never happen. Adam is far too conservative.'

Sighing, she turned her gaze out the side window. 'I know. If he wants to make a go of things, to repair the damage to our marriage, then I'm willing to give it a shot. I still love him after all.'

'And if he wants a divorce?'

Her breath hitched at his use of the D word. 'If it's what he *really* wants….'

'Will you consider moving in with me for good?'

Her head jerked back to face him. 'I didn't think you did monogamy?'

He glanced at her with pursed lips. 'First time for everything, right?'

Her jaw dropped, and if he weren't driving, he would've smothered her gaping mouth in kisses. 'You'd do th-that for me?' Her voice cracked halfway through her question.

'Of course I would. Don't get me wrong, I'm still opposed to the whole marriage thing, but I'd love to have you in my bed every night for the rest of our lives.' A tense silence filled the car. Unable to bear a second more, he broke it by adding, 'I know you're worried about my track record, and I guess I would be too. There's every chance I'll slip up along the way, but I don't expect a perfect relationship. Hell, look at where we are right now. You're cheating on your husband with me, and I've done little to discourage you. All I ask is we stay open and honest with each other.'

'I'll think it over. I crave the security that comes with true commitment. Your offer is good, but it still looks like a life raft with a bunch of holes. If I'm going to jump ship, I need to protect my heart in other ways.'

He gritted his teeth. 'Wow okay. I see how things are.' It occurred to him she still hadn't returned his sentiments of love at any point. Opening his heart to her may have been the most reckless stunt he had ever pulled. Riskier even than base jumping.

'James, please don't be like that. You're the one who pushed for me to go ahead with the wedding.'

He drummed his fingers on the steering wheel. 'Because I thought you would be happy together.'

'And we are for the most part.'

'Stop kidding yourself, Lucinda,' he replied with a dry laugh. 'In a perfect marriage, you wouldn't keep returning to my bed.'

She sucked in a sharp breath. 'Can we change the subject please?'

'Okay fine. What are you going to do about Brooke and Terrance?'

'Hmph. Way to kill the mood entirely.'

He let out an exasperated sigh. 'Unless you want to fall prey to a sexual deviant, you need to put a plan in place to protect yourself. I'll help, but I can only do so much from the sidelines.'

'What can I do? Without evidence to put them away....'

'You could hire a private investigator to dig up dirt on them,' he suggested. 'Dad happens to be friends with a couple of good ones.'

'Don't PIs usually spend all their time hunting down people like me?' she scoffed.

'While it's true some specialise in cheating spouses, these guys don't. They're all about helping innocent victims find the evidence they need to build a criminal investigation. Police don't have the resources to act on civilian hunches, but if you have enough money....'

'Not a bad idea actually. I'll talk to your dad this weekend and see what I can do.'

'May I make one other suggestion?' He knew she wouldn't like it, but he had to ask.

'Go on.'

'Hire a full-time security escort until the case resolves.'

She coughed and spluttered at his proposal. 'That'd cost a small fortune. Plus, with the PI fees—'

'I'll pay for the bodyguards.'

'James—' she pleaded.

'I insist.' He cut her off before she could mount an argument. 'If I can't be with you twenty-four seven, let me do this to ensure your safety.'

'Okay, thank you,' she croaked.

෨෬

Lucinda

A golden canopy arched overhead as they drove through the Yarra Valley. Leaves dropped from branches, dancing around in a breeze before joining the vibrant blanket of foliage flanking the road. Lines of vines sat beyond the deciduous trees, drawing the eye for miles.

Lucinda wanted to lose herself in the scenery, to dream of the wine and delicate food the region had to offer. Instead, she found her thoughts drifting to her crumbling marriage. She did not feel ready to part ways with Adam, no matter how strained things had become between them. Losing him meant losing everything and everyone she had come to know since settling in Melbourne. *Everyone except James*, a niggling thought reminded her. How would her own parents react if they found out? *Would they disown me as surely as my new family would?*

After driving through a small, picturesque town, they arrived at the caravan park. A variety of large trees lined the paved driveway, some shedding with the season, while others remained green and lush. As she spotted Adam waiting in the carpark, her heart began to hammer out a death march. James steered into the spot beside him, bringing her door adjacent to Adam's. She met his frown and gulped.

'Let's get this over with,' James prompted in a resigned tone. His door slammed shut, and she startled.

Climbing out of his sedan, Adam leaned against the driver's door with his arms crossed. His glaring eyes flicked over to James before locking on her. His mouth remained shut while he waited for her to alight.

With trembling legs, she clambered out of the SUV.

'Before you ask,' James began, drawing Adam's gaze. 'I offered to drive Lucy here for her own protection. While you were off "cooling down" she received another letter from her stalker. The threat was more overt this time.'

The anger in Adam's eyes faltered as he looked at her again. 'Mum and Dad are already inside. I'll drive you down to the cabin, so they think we came together.'

She replied with a nod and transferred her bags to Adam's car.

Adam crawled along the driveway at the snail's pace speed limit. 'I called into the house to grab a few things last night. I was surprised to find the place empty.'

'I didn't want to spend the week alone after receiving that note, so I stayed with Nicki.' She waited for the incredulous remark.

'Fair enough. What did it say?'

'What?' *Either he doesn't care or —*

'The stalker letter; what did it say?'

'I have it with me, so I can show you later. I'd rather not recite those ugly words.'

Adam answered with brooding silence.

So much for a fun getaway with family. 'I'm surprised you bothered to show up. We could have met anywhere to talk things over.'

'My folks still don't know what's going on,' he deadpanned. 'I'd like to keep it that way for now.'

Rebecca was bouncing around like bubbles in a champagne flute as they reached the campsite. She hurled herself at Adam, then at Lucinda as she chimed affectionate words of welcome. Troy stood back, chuckling at her enthusiasm as he waited for them to approach the cabin. The men hugged like real brothers before disappearing inside.

Lucinda greeted Michelle and Daniel with familial warmth, making the most of what could very well be the last time. She glanced around the spacious cabin with modern furnishings and nodded her approval.

A knock sounded at the door and James entered a second later. 'Thought I'd check out our new HQ before I go settle into my own lodgings.'

Rebecca embraced him in a bear hug. 'Wait? You're not staying in here?'

He shook his head. 'No, I've got my own studio cabin across the way.'

Her brow furrowed. 'Why do you get your own cabin? 'Mum put me and Troy in the bunkbed room, probably because we aren't married yet.'

James ruffled her hair. 'Because I insisted on my privacy. Not my fault you didn't think to do the same.'

Privacy. Is that for my benefit too?

Fidgeting with the handle of his suitcase, Adam glanced at her a moment before turning his attention to Rebecca. 'You guys can swap with us. Lucy and I won't mind separate beds for the weekend.'

Rebecca's eyes widened. 'Really?'

He nodded before ambling over to the bunkbeds room.

Lucinda joined him a moment later, closing the door behind them. 'Well, isn't this convenient for you?'

Adam shrugged. 'Let's talk after dinner when we can get a quiet moment alone.'

With a sigh, she laid claim to a bottom bunk. 'Fine.'

The Fairfax family shared a barbecue dinner, over which Adam played the good, doting husband. His act only prompted James to cast wary glances at Lucinda. Once they had all cleared and washed their dishes, Daniel and James set about starting a fire in their designated pit.

Rebecca tugged at Lucinda's arm. 'Will you help me find some sticks for toasting marshmallows?'

'Of course.' She followed Rebecca into a thicket and surveyed the ground for suitable candidates.

After gathering a few long, thin branches, Rebecca approached her. 'I wanted to apologise again for Brooke's behaviour last night.'

She sighed. 'You don't have to. None of it was your fault, Becky. At least now you know, so you can be careful around the creep. Don't let him catch you alone, okay.'

Rebecca nodded with a mist of tears in her eyes.

Lucinda embraced her. 'Hey, please don't worry about me, okay? It was years ago and there's a restraining order keeping him away from me.' They returned to a roaring campfire. Settling into a comfortable chair, she let the guys soothe her frayed nerves with their light-hearted banter and raucous laughter.

୨୦୯୫

'Please excuse us, but I need to borrow my wife for a bit.' Smiling, Adam offered a hand to help Lucinda rise from her low deckchair.

Taking his hand, she followed him, feeling another pair of chestnut eyes bore into her back as she strode away.

Once inside the cabin, Adam began pacing the living area.

She slumped onto the sofa and waited for him to speak. No way in hell was she starting this conversation.

'I don't know how to proceed with this marriage anymore.'

Tears welled in her eyes and a lump formed in her throat. 'Are you saying you want a divorce?'

'Maybe? I don't know. I still love you, but I don't know how to reconcile the fact you killed our babies.'

What the...? She launched to her feet and placed her hands on her hips. 'Excuse me? What are you talking about?'

'Don't play dumb, Lucinda. I know you aborted all those pregnancies.'

The blood surging through her veins boiled over. 'I would *never* do such a thing,' she seethed.

'Then how do you explain this?' Adam retrieved a crumpled sheet of paper from his pocket and handed it to her.

She read the unfamiliar pathology report with her name on it. None of the results made any sense to her. 'What is this?'

'A tox screen showing the byproduct of an abortion pill.'

'Either this is a fake, or someone took my blood without consent because I never ordered these tests.'

'So you aren't denying you took Misoprostol?'

'I don't even know what that is, Adam. What I do know is I never elected to miscarry our babies. Whoever gave you this—' she waved the page in his face '—wanted to drive a wedge between us. In fact, I have a strong suspicion they drugged me to bring on the miscarriages.'

His eyes narrowed to pin pricks; the fire in them giving way to cold cinders. 'What gives you such an absurd idea?'

She exhaled her exasperation. 'Think about it logically, Adam. You're a damn scientist, after all. Why would I go to the trouble of terminating pregnancies when I could have avoided them in the first place? There are plenty of contraceptives I could have used without you knowing if I had a mind to be deceptive about this. But I hope you know me well enough to trust I would have told you upfront if I didn't want kids. I would never go to such extremes to kill my own babies, especially not during the second trimester when my own life is at risk.'

Adam's expression relaxed as she explained her reasoning. 'You're right. I let rage cloud my judgement.' An unspoken apology hung in the air between them, but he made no moves to comfort her. She could almost see the cogs turning in his brain as he processed the situation.

'There's also the latest stalker letter,' she added in a soft tone. Heaving herself up, she trudged across to the bedroom.

He followed her, hovering in the doorway as she retrieved the note from her handbag. When she handed it over, he hesitated a moment before plucking it from her fingers. A new blaze sparked in his countenance as he inspected the words. Letting the page slip away and float to the floor, he wrapped her in his arms. 'I'm so sorry, Lucy. I never should have doubted you.' His voice crackled as the emotions poured out of him. 'You've been so good to me. Always so loving and loyal.'

A lump formed in her throat as she thought about the times she had betrayed their marriage vows. Adam may have been in the wrong this time, but if he ever discovered what she had done….

'Brooke,' he muttered the bitch's name under his breath.

Lucinda gasped. 'You think she did this?'

Adam nodded, pulling back to look into her eyes. 'Makes sense. She's the one who showed me the pathology report.'

'Doesn't surprise me. I recently heard about the crush she had on you.'

'Why are you talking in the past tense?' he scoffed. 'That woman never stopped trying to sink her claws into me.'

A wave of nausea swept through her stomach. 'Why didn't you tell me Brooke was a suspect?'

He sighed. 'Because up until recently, I thought your stalker wanted *you*, not me.'

'I suspect they want us both.' When Adam blinked at her, she explained, 'Brooke is dating Terrance, right? What if they are scheming against us together?'

Abject horror marred his face as he stared at her with wide eyes. 'I need to go nip this issue in the bud while you are out of harm's way.'

Her heart skipped a beat. 'What? How do you intend to do that?'

'By confronting the Toorak Troublemaker.'

She huffed. 'A fitting nickname. Seriously though, what do you hope to achieve?'

'I'll force a confession from her.'

Placing her palms on his chest, she felt the life thrumming inside him. 'Please be careful. There's a good chance she won't be alone tonight.'

He nodded. 'Then I'll go tomorrow and meet her somewhere public. For now, I'd like to hold you.' Pulling her down to the bottom bunk, he gathered her into his embrace.

৪৩

Rebecca

A couple of hours had passed since Rebecca's siblings had called it a night. The flames of the campfire flickered in their death throes as she poked the embers with a long stick.

Dad rose, stretching his old bones as he addressed Mum, 'We'd best be getting to bed. Big day tomorrow.'

Mum nodded and smiled at Rebecca. 'Night sweetie. Don't stay up too much later.'

'I won't,' she promised. Once her parents had disappeared inside, she snuggled closer to Troy. Listening to the fire crackle, she inhaled the romance in the air as she sat beneath a shimmering blanket of stars. 'I love it out here.'

'I can't stop thinking about last night,' Troy admitted. The ice in his voice sent a shiver down her spine.

She hugged her shawl tighter around her shoulders. 'What do you mean?'

'When the conversation centred around Terrance, and you apologised to Lucy. She told you not to worry because you weren't the one sleeping with him. Do you remember how you lowered your gaze and hesitated?'

Closing her eyes, she recalled the moment in vivid detail. She had hoped her reaction had escaped his attention. 'Yes. I remember.'

'Mind telling me what that was about?'

'I'm sorry, bunny. I thought he was you at first.' Chancing a glance, she observed the way his jaw clenched.

'Go on,' he ground out in a gritty tone.

Unable to bear Troy's frown, she focussed on the dying fire. 'Brooke arranged a surprise threesome, making me think she had invited you to our bed for the night. I don't know how she knew I wanted this, because I'd never told her about my fantasies involving you both.'

Troy's breath caught in his throat.

'When we got home, she insisted on blindfolding me. She said it would "enhance the experience." I played along, already wound up in the heat of the moment. She led me into the bedroom, and the scent of your cologne hit my nose straight away. When I touched him, I thought I was combing my fingers through your hair and running my hands along the ridges of your chest. He resembled you so much, even the way he felt inside me.' She sensed Troy tense beside her. 'Everything was perfect while I thought you and Brooke turned my wildest dreams into reality. Then he spoke, shattering the spell. I couldn't place his voice at first, but I knew he wasn't you.' Inhaling a deep breath, she took his trembling hands into hers. 'I know I should have taken the blindfold off then, but I was afraid to learn the truth while his thing was still inside me. They taunted me, manipulated my fears and desires, and compelled me to continue with the charade. I didn't look upon Terry's face until after the debauchery had ended.'

Squeezing her hands in his vice grip, he almost crushed her bones.

She yelped and stared at his distant eyes. 'You're hurting me.'

Focussing his attention on her, he released her hands. 'Sorry. I'm so fucking furious right now. That woman is bad news, and she is ruining you. Please, I beg you to leave her. You can come live with me.'

She shook her head. 'No! I love her and she isn't a bad person, I swear. It's Terry, he is a dreadful influence. I need to find a way to break his hold on her.'

'You're delusional,' Troy scoffed. 'You need to take off those rose-coloured glasses, sunshine. They are blinding you to the truth. Brooke has always been a conniving cow.'

'Not to me she hasn't,' she protested in a rasp.

'How can you justify her behaviour, Becky? She tricked you into having sex with another man. And not just anyone. The sleaze you slept with assaulted your sister-in-law. Now he's had a taste, do you think he won't try to force himself on *you*?'

Tears streamed down her face. 'Brooke was only trying to make me happy,' she sobbed. 'She knows how much I want you both.'

Hauling her into his lap, Troy hugged her against his pounding heart. 'Shh, sunshine. Please don't cry. I didn't mean to upset you. I'd never want that. I worry about you because I love you so much.' He planted a chaste kiss on her forehead.

'I feel so filthy for letting Terry touch me,' she mumbled against Troy's t-shirt as her tears soaked into the cotton.

'You, my sweet girl, could never be dirty.' His lips ghosted along her cheek. 'But if you're worried, would you like me to wash away the sensation of his touch on your body?'

Hot waves of desire emanated from where his mouth pressed against her skin. 'Yes please,' she squeaked.

He smothered her mouth with his own. As her lips parted, he traced them with delicate strokes of his tongue. A furnace blazed in her core, and she mewled with wanton need.

'I'm going to take you to bed now. As much as I love those pretty little noises you make, your family won't be far away, so you'll have to be *very* quiet,' he cautioned.

A surge of adrenaline rushed through her veins at the prospect of sneaking around with her boyfriend. 'Okay,' she whispered.

Wrapping her legs around his waist, he instructed her to 'Hold on tight.'

She looped her arms around the back of his neck and clenched her thighs against him. Their lips locked together again as he rose and walked them toward the cabin. Her back hit the frigid timber door, providing a contrast to the rising temperature of their writhing bodies.

After retrieving the key from his jacket pocket, Troy fumbled with the lock. When she giggled at his attempt, he clamped a hand over her mouth. Hot breath tickled her ear as he spoke low and gruff, 'Do I need to gag you, Becky? I've already warned you once about making a sound. Do you want your parents to hear how much you enjoy my hands on your body, or my cock buried deep inside you?'

Her head jerked left to right and back again, while lust pooled between her legs.

'Good girl.' His praise almost tipped her over the precipice.

The lock clicked and the door burst open behind her. If she had not clung to Troy like a koala on a gumtree, she would have fallen flat on her backside.

He backed her into their bedroom and sat her down on the mattress. Pressing a finger to his lips, he reminded her one last time to keep the noise down. When she nodded, he stood and began to undress with a calculated slowness, teasing her impatient desire.

Moisture seeped from both sets of lips as she perched on the edge of the bed, watching him saunter forward in his designer Y-fronts. The dark blue fabric did nothing to hide the thick, throbbing bulge between his legs.

Reaching the bed, he placed her hands on the waistband of his underpants and offered her a lop-sided grin.

Tempted to tear the things off him, she settled into the slow, seductive pace he had set. His erection sprang free as she lowered the briefs down his muscular thighs. Feeling adventurous, she licked the tip of his dick and beamed when he hissed and shuddered. Peering into his burning eyes, she licked the salty residue from her lips. His amber orbs glimmered and darkened, filling her with the confidence she needed to proceed. Digging her fingers into his buttocks, she eased his shaft into her mouth. She sucked him deep into her throat, triggering her gag reflex. She pulled back a little and concentrated on the intoxicating mix of control and arousal swirling through her insides. Bobbing her head up and down, she caressed his tangy flesh, feeling him grow harder still.

He shoved her back and pinned her to the bed with quivering arms. 'I won't last long if you keep this up,' he warned in a hushed voice. Sitting back, he slid her jeans and panties down, stopping only when he reached her shoes. He yanked them off and let them drop to the floor with a thud.

The noise startled her, and she glanced at the door, hoping no one else heard.

'Relax, Becky. They won't question the sound of us getting changed for bed. It's the sounds of pleasure we need to put a lid on.' He lifted her blouse over her head and gaped at the turquoise bra covering her breasts. 'This can stay for now.' He tugged the lace down, exposing her hard nipples to the crisp air. Taking them into his mouth, he flicked them with his tongue and nipped them with his teeth.

She arched her back, desperate for more friction. Yet he continued his deliberate pace. Such sweet torture. *How am I supposed to stay silent when I feel like screaming?*

He peppered kisses along her chest before sucking on her other nipple. When she gasped, he shot her a smouldering look. His tongue trailed up her body, and along her neck until he reached her ear. Biting into the lobe sent shockwaves down her spine. 'I'm going to make sweet, delicious love to you, sunshine. I want to savour the feel of you encompassing me in your warmth.' He sank into her, all the way to the hilt, and stayed there for countless seconds.

They held each other's gaze as a thick fog of emotion swirled between them. Then he drew back, completely unsheathing himself before gliding back into her rippling folds. The need to moan overwhelmed her and she bit into her bottom lip.

Smirking at her predicament, he whispered, 'Good girl.'

Their bodies continued to merge, bringing her closer and closer to the brink. She chased the high, but his languid movements kept the climax out of reach.

'Troy, ple—' she begged.

His lips crashed against hers, muffling her plea. The moment his thumb found her clit, she exploded around him. Pulling out of her, he wrapped a large hand around his shaft. After a few strokes, he painted her stomach and chest white.

Gobsmacked, she stared at him with wide eyes, then realisation dawned. They had not used protection. Relief flowed through her lungs, and she silently thanked him for taking evasive measures.

'You're mine,' he growled. His assertion made her freeze.

Did he mark me like some kind of territorial alpha?

He hovered above her. 'No matter what Brooke does to you, or who she makes you fuck, you will always belong to me. You hold a special place in my heart and soul. Do you understand?'

The sentiment melted her heart. 'Yes,' she whispered.

'Good girl.' He ducked into the ensuite bathroom, returning seconds later with a damp cloth. Kneeling beside her, he wiped between her legs and cleaned away the mess he had left on her torso. He climbed into bed and tucked her against his chest. 'I love you, Becky.'

'I love you too,' she admitted as she drifted off into a peaceful slumber.

Chapter Twenty-Two

Adam

Adam excused himself from the day's activities as the rest of his family prepared for their sunrise excursion. He told them something urgent had come up at work, which they all bought hook, line, and sinker. Only Lucinda knew the truth and she almost broke down when they said their goodbyes.

'Promise you'll avoid any conflict with Terrance?' she pleaded in a quavering voice while standing on trembling legs.

'I promise. What if I take Greg with me, will that make you feel better?'

Nodding, she threw her arms around him and squeezed tight.

Returning the embrace, he kissed the crown of her head. 'I love you.'

'I love you too.' Letting go of him with reluctance, she joined Rebecca and Troy in James' SUV.

After watching them drive out of the carpark, he fixed himself a quick breakfast and planned his approach. By about nine o'clock, he had gone over several scenarios and contingencies in his mind, assessing the risks and likely outcomes of each. He was ready to make a move. Using the long drive home, he contacted the relevant players, starting with Brooke.

'Hi Adam. Is everything okay?' she asked in a saccharine voice.

'Not really,' he rasped, laying the emotion on thick. 'I could use some company right now. Will you meet me for a coffee?'

'Of course, sugar. Whatever you need. Why don't you come over to my apartment?'

He had anticipated her suggestion, but he would only go there if she left him no other choice. 'I'm not sure that's a good idea. Is there a café near your place?'

'None making coffee as good as mine. Besides, it will be easier to chat in private.'

Predictable. He sighed. 'Okay, I'll be there in about an hour.' As soon as they hung up, he phoned Greg.

'Hey man, what's up? Did you sort things out with Lucy?'

'Yeah, looks like someone drugged her with the Misoprostol, and I think I know who.'

'See I told you I had my doubts. Lucy's a good girl. Who do ya reckon did it?' Greg asked.

He took a deep breath before replying, 'Brooke. She's the one who showed me the results, plus she's been trying to worm her way back into my bed ever since….'

'Fuck! That's messed up.'

'You're telling me. I'm on my way to confront her now. Can you back me up; in case Terrance is there?'

'No probs. Name the time and place.'

He gave Greg the details. 'She probably thinks this is a booty call, so you'll need to wait outside the apartment door, then bust in if you hear any signs of trouble.'

'Understood. See you there, mate.'

Brooke answered the door in a figure-hugging black dress barely covering her backside. Her seduction attempts were pathetic. She knew little of what he desired in a woman.

'Hi sugar,' she purred, placing a hand on his chest.

He pushed past her and scanned the living area. No sign of another man, but it did not mean Terrance was not hiding in the bedroom. Spinning around to face Brooke, he scowled at her. 'Did you slip the abortion pill into Lucy's drink?'

Brooke covered her gaping mouth with a manicured hand. 'I would never want to kill your babies, Adam.'

He winced. 'Not even if they are with another woman?'

'How would making you hate me help my cause? You know how much I want you back.' Tracing the collar of his polo shirt with a delicate finger, she peered up at him with doe eyes.

It occurred to him she had left her shoes off, emphasising the inch of difference in their height. His brow furrowed as he puzzled things out. 'Then what were you doing in Lucy's office and how did the test result get there? She told me she never went for a tox screen.'

Lowering her gaze, Brooke scrunched his shirt in her fists. 'It was Terry. He forged the pathology report and told me to give it to you.' Her body shivered against him.

He tensed. 'You aren't really dating Terrance, are you?'

She shook her head. 'He promised me if I help him break your marriage apart, he would leave you unharmed. He's still obsessed with Lucy and will do anything to get his hands on her. I'm so sorry, Adam. I never wanted to hurt y—'

His fists clenched at his sides. 'Did you play any part in delivering those letters to Lucy?'

She stared straight into his eyes. 'I have no idea what you're talking about.'

He shoved her back. 'Damn it, Brooke! This is important. You need to tell me the truth, because this might be our only shot at putting Terrance back behind bars. He has clearly spooked you. Did he ever threaten you?'

Brooke wrapped her arms around herself. 'Not me personally. Everything I did was to protect you. Although, if he learns I told you about this….'

Slumping onto the sofa, he hunched over and steepled his hands beneath his chin. 'You need to stay away from him until things blow over. Is there somewhere safe where you can stay?' Glancing up, he saw unshed tears pooling in her eyes.

'I'm always welcome at Uncle Paolo's.' She shrank into the opposite armchair, looking more fragile than he had ever seen her. 'What about Becky? She can't stay alone in this apartment with that psycho on the loose.'

'Good point. I'll get Troy to keep an eye on her once they get back from the camping trip. Don't worry Brooke, I'll take care of this.' He felt sorry for her, but as much as he wanted to comfort Brooke, he could not risk leading her on. 'Can I drop you off at your uncle's?'

She offered him half a smile. 'That would be good. Thank you, Adam. Let me pack a few things.' When she returned from her bedroom with a full suitcase, he ushered her outside. She startled when Greg came in to view from the shadows of the foyer.

'What's going on?' Greg asked.

'Looks like Terrance is behind it all. He threatened Brooke, so I'm taking her somewhere safe. Can you trail behind and make sure no one follows us?'

'Of course,' Greg agreed.

Brooke remained silent for the drive, which suited Adam fine. He needed to collect his thoughts. Her confession had shed more light on the situation, but there was still no hard evidence to pin on Terrance. *Time to hire one of Dad's PI friends.*

౫౧౨

Lucinda

A sunrise balloon flight provided a great start to the day, although it did little to settle Lucinda's anxieties. As she watched the sun-kissed landscape of rolling hills drift by, she tried to push her fears for Adam's safety aside. The strong breeze made her glad she thought to tie her hair up in a ponytail.

Michelle grinned at Troy. 'This would be a great place to propose marriage.'

Rebecca blushed. 'Mum!'

Troy brushed his knuckles across her rose-coloured cheek. 'You know, she's not wrong. I should bring you out here again one day.'

Michelle echoed Rebecca's gasp, and Lucinda felt a flutter of happiness in her chest. Rebecca and Troy were perfect for each other, and she looked forward to seeing them tie the knot. *At least someone will get their happily ever after.*

Rebecca pressed her lips into a simper. 'I'm sorry you didn't get to share this romantic experience with Adam.'

Lucinda shrugged, feeling James' warmth close behind her. 'At least I still get to enjoy the amazing view.'

'As do I,' James admitted softly in her ear while the others turned their attention to the scenery below. His heat seeped into her bones despite their lack of physical contact.

Awareness of his attention rose as millions of tiny goosebumps across her flesh. His proximity reminded her of all the ways he had brought her pleasure. Unable to help herself, she leaned back against him, inhaling his spicy, smoky fragrance. She had fallen hard for James, and she knew that regardless of what happened with her marriage, she would never be able to resist his charms.

He stroked her arms, then let his hands wander down to her hips. 'Will you come to my bed tonight?' he asked gruffly.

'Yes,' she replied before putting a more respectable distance between them.

Stepping into a modern brick building, Lucinda surveyed the bright, airy cellar door. This was the first winery the Fairfaxes had decided to visit on their tour of the region.

Michelle and Daniel browsed the displays, while Rebecca and Troy took in the view through the massive window. Approaching the front counter, she caught the eye of a staff member. The woman smiled and promised to be with her shortly.

James slunk into the spot next to her and whispered, 'How did things go with Adam? The pair of you looked rather cosy when we said goodbye this morning.'

Glancing over her shoulder, she confirmed the rest of the family were still distracted. 'We can't talk about this now,' she hissed.

'Please tell me what I need to know,' he begged. 'Did he leave for a work matter?'

Lucinda sighed. 'The issue he took with me had nothing to do with you, and no, he isn't away for business. I'll explain more later.'

James slumped against the bar. 'I see.'

The woman behind the bar introduced herself as Matilda and talked them through the tasting menu options.

After choosing a sparkling wine flight[8], she followed Matilda into the tasting room. The rest of the group joined her a moment later, and they all settled into the soft booth. The cellar door consultant explained the winery's history as she poured sparkling brut into vintage champagne glasses.

Closing her eyes, she let the dry, zesty bubbles tingle her tastebuds and calm her nerves.

---

[8] Connoisseur's term for wine tasting selection

After several more glasses, she left the winery feeling buoyant on her feet and lighter in her chest.

When they got back to the caravan park, James asked, 'Who's up for another campfire?'

Daniel shook his head and rubbed Michelle's shoulders. 'We're beat after such a big day.'

'Same here,' Troy agreed. 'Becky and I barely slept a wink last night.'

Lucinda caught the colour rising in Rebecca's cheeks.

'I guess that leaves the two of us,' James mused as they watched the others walk away. 'Alone at last.' He grinned at her. 'Shall we skip the fire and head straight to my room?'

'We should talk,' she protested.

His eyes narrowed on her. 'I agree, and my cabin will provide the privacy we need for this conversation.'

'Okay.' She needed little persuasion. His cabin was furnished much like her own. The main difference was the large queen-sized bed taking up one side of the living space. No doors or walls stood between them and the promise of what was to come.

James sauntered over to the kitchen area. 'Can I get you a drink?'

She laughed nervously. 'I've probably had enough today, but sure, why not?'

Opening the tawny port he had purchased on their tour, he poured them each a small glass.

She accepted his offering and got comfortable on the couch. Her brain almost melted when James sat beside her, and their thighs touched.

Snaking an arm around her shoulders, he leaned in to clink his glass with hers. 'I hope you managed to relax and enjoy yourself today.'

'I did,' she assured him. 'Thank you for organising everything.'

He began to coil strands of her hair around his fingers. 'One day, I want to take you on a proper camping trip. Just the two of us sharing a snug little tent in the middle of nowhere.'

'James—'

'Tell me what's going on with Adam,' he interjected.

She gulped down a generous mouthful of her fortified wine. With a little liquid courage warming her belly, she explained the situation and Adam's theory regarding Brooke. Tears trickled down her cheeks as she voiced her fears for his life.

Taking her empty glass, James placed it on the coffee table along with his own. He pulled her onto his lap and embraced her. 'Hush, sweetheart. I'm sure Adam will be fine. He's a smart man, and I doubt he'll put himself in danger. The thing with Brooke makes sense though, right? We already had our suspicions about her.'

She nodded against his chest, letting his essence surround her.

'What happens for us now?' A hint of trepidation laced his gentle tone.

Pivoting in his lap, she straddled him. Her hands traced his hairline and dropped to his broad shoulders. 'Nothing needs to change. I still want you, James.' She kissed his mouth. He hesitated a second, so she coaxed his lips open with her tongue. Their passion intensified and as the heat grew between them, she ground against his growing arousal.

James wrapped his hand around her ponytail and tugged her hair. Exposing the crook of her neck, he grazed her flesh with his teeth. 'I wish I could bite you without leaving a mark for him to find.'

She shuddered, wishing for the same.

He yanked the elastic band out of her hair, letting her long golden locks fall around her shoulders. Gripping the nape of her neck, he pulled her back in for another deep kiss.

Bucking against him, she moaned into his mouth, seeking more friction through her chiffon slacks.

'You already sound close.' He kneaded her breasts through her silk blouse.

'I am,' she rasped.

He made a guttural noise and pinched her nipples. 'Then come for me, Cindy. Right here and now.'

As the pressure on her puckered buds increased, she worked herself up into a frenzy. Feeling James grow hard filled her with an intoxicating mix of desire and control. *He wants* me *as much as I need him*. Pleasure erupted in her core, and she cried out, 'Oh fuuuck!'

'Mm, that's it sweetheart.' Unfastening the top buttons of her blouse, he tugged it over her head and gaped at her red lace bra. His already shallow breaths quickened. 'Did you wear this intentionally? For me?' His low voice reverberated through her belly.

'Yes,' she whispered. The same lingerie set she wore the night he had taken her virginity once again made an appearance.

'Show me the rest,' he demanded in a gruff voice.

Rising from his lap, she unlatched her pants and let them slide down her legs. She stepped out of the pile of chiffon and placed a high heel-covered foot on his thigh.

'Dear God! You're killing me here, Cindy.' His fingers made quick work of the buckle on her shoe-strap. He removed one stiletto, then gestured for the other. 'I had half a mind to make you leave them on, but these heels look deadly.'

Her other shoe dropped to the floor, and she laughed. 'Depending on the position, I suppose they could be.' Resting both feet on the ground, she peered down at him with hooded eyes.

A growl escaped James. 'I'm going to fuck you in *every* damn position I know tonight.' Leaping to his feet, he pulled her against his body. Their lips merged as he backed her toward the bed.

When her calves hit the mattress, she sank until she sat on the edge. Her eyes roamed over his blue linen shirt and brown chinos. Evidence of her recent climax left a dark patch over his crotch. 'You're still wearing too much.'

He smirked. 'What are you going to do about it?'

Clutching his waistband, she drew him closer and unbuckled his belt. Running her hand over the erection straining against his pants, she enjoyed the groan slipping from his lips. She plucked the button out from its loop and eased the zipper down. His dick sprang free, and she grabbed it through a layer of navy satin, squeezing tight.

He sucked a sharp breath through his clenched teeth. Stumbling back, he kicked off his shoes then yanked off his trousers and boxer shorts. Heat blazed in his eyes as he strode toward her. 'Lie back.'

Her nerves tingled and lust pooled in her core as she reclined against the cotton bedspread.

'At least I can bite you here.' Shoving his face between her thighs, James nipped at her clit through damp fabric.

'Oh God!' she screamed. Waves of ecstasy rippled through her.

Hooking a finger through the gusset of her panties, he pulled them all the way down her legs and tossed them aside. His mouth returned to worshipping her. Each flick of his tongue and thrust of his fingers sent more shockwaves through her body. When another orgasm bombarded her, he climbed up the bed and claimed her lips in a savage kiss.

Tasting her own musk on his mouth heightened her excitement.

He nudged her opening and plunged inside her a second later. 'You feel sensational, sweetheart.'

She really did. The way he hit all the right spots deep within sent euphoric bursts of energy cascading throughout her body. 'You're still wearing your shirt,' she complained. 'I want to touch your bare chest.'

His breath tickled her ear as he murmured hoarsely, 'I won't stop you tearing it off me.'

Sucking on her bottom lip, she read the challenge in his dark chestnut eyes. Her mouth quirked into a wide grin as she gripped the front seams of his shirt and wrenched them apart. Several buttons sprayed out across the room. Some chimed against glass while others clicked as they bounced off the walls.

James chuckled. 'I didn't think you would take my invitation so literally. But damn, that was hot.' Thrusting into her, he showed his appreciation.

'I'm not even done yet.' She ripped the rest of the shirt apart, sending the remaining buttons flying. Admiring his taut muscles, she caressed his chest. She slid her palms over his shoulders and down his arms, taking the sleeves with her. 'I hope this wasn't a favourite shirt.'

411

'It wasn't before, but it is now.' The linen garment gathered around his wrists, so he popped the cuff buttons and flung the shirt aside.

When she stroked his abs, his cock pulsed within her, and she mewled.

'This is hardly fair. I'm butt naked, yet you still have your bra,' he teased.

'I thought you liked this one,' she taunted back.

'I fucking adore it, but I love your bare tits even more.' Slipping his hands behind her, he heaved her up into a sitting position, keeping himself immersed inside her. He unhooked her bra and threw it on the floor before taking her right breast into his mouth. James sucked and bit so hard on her nipple that painful bliss flooded her system and she screamed incoherently. 'Better,' he mumbled against her other breast. As his teeth sank into her, the tension exploded in her core.

He moved her across the bed and lowered her onto her back with her head dangling over the edge. 'Brace yourself, sweetheart, because things are about to get rough.'

Clutching the mattress, she welcomed his onslaught. James rammed into her with all his force, fucking her as if his life depended upon it. Her head swam as a giddy high encapsulated her very being. Reaching the peak of rapture, she blacked out.

When she came to, her head rested against a soft pillow and his husky voice rumbled in her ear, 'I hope you're not done, because I'm just getting warmed up, Cindy.'

Smiling, she whispered, 'So am I.'

༺༻

James

Laying on his back, James played with Lucinda's hair as she sprawled out across his chest. He had grown obsessed with the feel of her locks in his fingers. The soft strands felt finer than silk. The post coital haze wore off sooner than he would've liked, and a quiet melancholy settled in the atmosphere. 'You'll never leave him, will you? Not of your own volition.'

Lucinda propped herself on her elbow to study his features. 'It's not a simple matter. There's a lot at stake.' Her eyes misted over, and her hoarse voice broke as she spoke. 'I love your family, James. All of you. I can't bear the thought of a world where any of you hate me, let alone each other.'

He'd feared as much. Only a fool could let himself believe he had a real shot at convincing Lucinda to end her marriage. *Joke's on me, I guess.* She would never be his, not truly.

'What's wrong, James?'

A violent thump at the door startled them both, putting an end to the conversation.

She stared at the door with wide eyes and whispered, 'What if that's Adam, back from his meeting with Brooke?'

The rebellious side of him wanted to yell, *Fuck Adam! Let him see what happens when he neglects his wife!* But he couldn't bring himself to destroy her snug little cocoon of security. 'Hide under the quilt for now.' He clambered out of bed and staggered to the door.

Rebecca gawked at him through the minuscule doorway opening. 'Put some clothes on, for the love of all things holy!'

'Sorry, Becky.' He tucked his junk behind the door. 'I wasn't expecting a late-night visit from my sister. What do you want?'

'I can't find Lucy. She's not in her room. Do you know where she is?'

'Not a clue. Now if you'll excuse me.' He tried to shut the door—

But she pushed it open and barged in, declaring, 'This is urgent. Lucy might be in danger.' She made a point of turning around while he slid into some boxer shorts and a t-shirt.

'I'm sure she's out for a stroll,' he suggested, bringing her attention back to him.

Rebecca crossed her arms and glared at him. 'At this time of night? By herself? Are you insane, because I doubt she would do something so crazy.'

'You raise a good point. Why are you out of bed this late?'

'Adam rang me. He's been trying to get hold of her for hours. He got some dirt on Terrance. Looks like the creep might have caused her miscarriages. He even roped Brooke into his twisted scheme, threatening Adam's life if she didn't help him destroy their marriage.'

Lucinda gasped from her hiding place, and he tried to ignore her reaction.

The sound didn't escape Rebecca though. She jerked her attention toward the lump in his bed and frowned. 'Oh, hell no!' She started stalking toward Lucinda.

He grabbed Rebecca's arm. 'Don't! She's a random chick I hooked up with. Please don't embarrass the poor woman.'

Rebecca pinned him with the most vicious scowl he had ever seen on his sweet sister's face. 'Do you take me for a complete moron? The pair of you have lusted after each other for years. I guess I was a bit naïve to hope you wouldn't act on those desires.'

His grip tightened around her arm. 'That's not Lucy. I don't know where she is, and I'm too busy to help you look,' he seethed in a low, menacing tone as he dragged her toward the door.

'James!' she shrieked. 'You're hurting me. Let go!'

He opened the door, shoved her outside, and slammed it shut.

Her tiny fists hammered against the hollow timber. 'If you don't let me back in, I'll tell Adam all about you and Lucy!'

Lucinda sat up and peeked over the top of the quilt. Her wide eyes darted between him and the door.

'What should I do?' he mouthed at her.

Her shoulders slumped, and she hugged the blanket around her chest. 'Let her in.'

As he turned the handle, Rebecca stormed back inside and marched up to the bed. 'How could you!' she spat. 'You promised you would never act on your desires for James. Adam loves you, and this is how you repay his kind, generous heart?'

'Becky, things got complicated,' he explained.

'And you!' Rebecca spun around and pointed an accusing finger at him. 'How could you betray your own flesh and blood like this?'

'Trust me, I tried to stay away. But I fell in love with Lucy, then when I learned Adam was neglecting her....'

She slapped him hard across the face. 'Don't try to justify your vile behaviour.' Rebecca turned back to Lucinda. 'If you were miserable with Adam, you should have left him rather than cheat on him like this.'

Lucinda lowered her head. 'I'm sorry, Becky. It's not that I don't want to be with Adam. I'm in love with them both.'

He sucked in a breath. What a time to finally hear those words cross her lips.

'Well, you can't have them both. You know Adam will never abide sharing you.' Rebecca gave him a dirty look. 'Even if *you* don't seem to mind. This affair ends now, otherwise I *will* tell Adam where I found Lucy tonight.'

'Fine. I'm leaving Melbourne anyway.' Grabbing his suitcase from the closet, he retrieved a clean pair of jeans and started throwing his dirty clothes in it.

'Wait, what?' Lucinda screeched.

He shimmied into his jeans and stepped into shoes. They felt weird without socks, but whatever. 'I can't do this anymore, Lucy. I'm sick of being nothing more than the crutch you lean on when you feel lonely.' Crouching beside the bed, he retrieved the shirt she had torn off him earlier. The garment would need new buttons, but it had otherwise escaped unscathed. Then he flung her underwear onto the mattress.

'That's not what this is.' Lucinda put her red lacy bra back on.

Why did she have to wear those tonight? There was a cruel symmetry in the way they were the first and last lingerie he had seen her in. 'No? Then why don't you come with me? Leave Adam right now and be mine.'

'I….' Her mouth gaped as words died on her tongue. 'I can't leave him.'

'I didn't think so.' He paused when he picked up his chinos, still wet with Lucinda's pleasure. If it weren't for his sister lurking a few feet away, he would have inhaled Cindy's scent one last time. Instead, he tugged the belt from its loops and tossed the trousers in a laundry bag. After shoving them in his luggage, he threaded the belt through his jeans.

Rushing up to him, Rebecca wrapped her arms around his chest. 'You're overreacting James! You don't have to leave town. Surely your self-control isn't so bad.'

'It is with her.' He shot Lucinda a pained look.

'Stop and think about this,' Rebecca pleaded. 'You've built a life here. Everyone will miss you. Mum, Dad, Adam, *and* me. Not to mention Russell! How will he manage the business without you?'

'What do you want me to do, Becky? If I stay, I'll keep fucking our brother's wife because I'm a twisted masochist.' She winced at his vulgar language, but he was beyond caring about decency. 'At least if I go, their marriage has a good chance of recovering from its latest hurdle.'

Lucinda started bawling her eyes out.

Looking at her broke his heart. He almost caved, wanting nothing more than to pull her into his arms and comfort her. Clenching his fists, he straightened his spine. He needed to stay strong and do the right thing for everyone's sake, his own sanity included.

Ambling over to the table, he pocketed his phone, keys, and wallet. He handed Rebecca the room key. 'Can you check me out of here in the morning?'

She nodded with tears welling in her own eyes.

Kneeling on the bed beside Lucinda, he combed his fingers through her hair one last time.

Gazing up at him, she blinked away her tears. 'Please don't go.'

He shook his head. 'I have to. The offer still stands, but you'll have to make a choice. Me or him. Let me know when you figure out who you love more.' Rising to his feet, he turned on his heel and headed for the door, dragging his suitcase behind him.

'How do I explain your sudden disappearance to Adam and our parents?' Rebecca asked.

He halted at the exit, refusing to look at either of them. 'Tell them an urgent business matter came up. It's not like they aren't used to my vanishing acts.' Treading out into the brisk night air, he took a deep breath. He drummed up the last of his courage to do what he should have done years ago. Then he walked out of Lucinda's life.

Chapter Twenty-Three

Lucinda

Apiece of Lucinda's soul shattered as the door slammed shut, like glass exploding into a million shards and piercing her heart. She half expected her tears to run red with the blood of her anguish. James had never insisted she choose between them. *How could he abandon me at a time like this?* His behaviour seemed out of character, more akin to how Adam might have reacted had he discovered—

She glared at Rebecca—who had collapsed onto one of the dining chairs—and screeched, 'This is your fault! You forced him to leave me. Why couldn't you leave well enough alone?'

Rebecca's brow furrowed. 'Don't you dare pin this on me. You're the one who couldn't stay faithful to your husband. You claim to love Adam, but have you ever stopped to think how this would affect him?'

'My affair with James never once interfered with my marriage. What Adam doesn't know won't hurt him. Do *you* want to be the one to break his heart?'

'Why can't you take responsibility for your own mess?' Rebecca seethed. 'You may think your relationship with James doesn't upset Adam, but how can you give him all the love and emotional support he needs when you divide your time between two men?'

She shook her head. 'You don't understand what it's like. Love isn't a finite resource to ration amongst the people we cherish, but something that flows in abundance for all of them.'

An awkward silence descended like thick fog.

'If that's how you feel,' Rebecca started in a croaky voice. 'Why hide your relationship with James from Adam?'

'Because Adam is too conservative and jealous to accept it.'

Rebecca replied with a silent nod as she stared at the Laminex table.

'What did Adam tell you on the phone?' She asked in a softer tone.

Sitting up, Rebecca returned her attention to Lucinda. 'Brooke confessed to aiding Terry in his plan to break you and Adam apart. She only helped him under duress because he threatened to hurt Adam. Now she is hiding at her uncle's house while Adam is working with a PI to hunt for incriminating evidence against Terry.'

Shivering, she hugged the quilt closer. 'I had my suspicions. I'll ring Adam back in a bit, but first I need a shower. Can you give me some time alone? I'll bring you the key once I'm done.'

'Of course.' Rebecca dropped the cabin key on the table and left her alone.

After cleansing her body and soul under scorching water, she dressed in her rumpled clothes. Retrieving her phone from the clutch purse she had left on the coffee table, she turned it back on and discovered twenty missed calls. Figuring they were all from Adam, she dialled his number.

He picked up after one ring. 'Oh my God! Lucy! Are you okay? Where were you?'

'Yeah. I went for a walk along a nearby trail.'

'At this time of night? Are you insane? What if Terrance had found you?'

She sighed. 'I didn't go alone. James joined me. Becky found us returning to camp. She told me what happened with Brooke and Terrance.'

'Crazy huh? I can't believe the lengths that jerk will go to.'

She shuddered. 'I can. You don't know him like I do.'

Adam's breath hitched. 'I'd rather *he* didn't know *you* quite so well. Do you want me to come back there tonight?'

'Yes please.' She could not bear the thought of spending the rest of the night alone.

'Okay my love. I'll see you in an hour or so.'

හ○ශ

Rebecca

The stench of cigarette smoke seeped into Rebecca's unconscious mind. Pleasure rippled through her body, tugging her back to the waking world. *Am I still dreaming or is Troy giving me the royal treatment?* As her brain fog receded, she became more aware of the titillating sensation between her legs. Then she remembered how Troy had left for work earlier. A wave of panic surged through her as she recalled Adam's warning about staying home alone with Terry at large. She tried to sit up, but a pair of soft, feminine hands clamped down on her thighs, pinning her in place. Glancing down, she breathed a sigh of relief when she recognised the raven locks on the crown of Brooke's head. Relaxing, she focussed on the feel of her girlfriend's velvet tongue inside her.

As the pressure built to the point of imminent climax, Brooke burned her inner thigh with a cigarette. 'You've been a naughty girl again, haven't you Becky baby?'

After screeching through the pain, she shook her head, tears streaming down her cheeks.

Brooke mirrored the burn on her other thigh, releasing another scream. 'Oh, but you have. I know what you've been up to with Troy. I can smell *and* taste him all over you.' She capped off the punishment with a searing spot in the centre of her pubic region.

She wailed as sheer agony emanated from her scalded sensitive flesh. 'Stop! Please,' she sobbed with salty blobs plopping down her cheeks. 'I'm sorry.'

Stubbing out her instrument of torture in a crystal ashtray, Brooke tsked. 'Sorry won't cut it, sugar. Not after I warned you to be a good girl for me.'

Clambering up against the head of the bed, she hugged her knees against her chest. 'I couldn't help myself after being in forced proximity all this time. You could hardly expect me to feel safe alone in this place. Not with a psycho rapist on the loose.'

'You could have come to stay at my uncle's. There are plenty of spare rooms.'

She gaped at Brooke. *Why had the thought never crossed my mind?* Deep down she knew the answer but could not muster the courage to admit it.

'I want you to break off your relationship with Troy and cut all ties with him. You don't need a beard anymore. Not for the short-term. We've put everyone off the scent for now.'

'What if I'd rather be with him than you?' she huffed, wondering where her defiant edge appeared from.

Brooke sniggered. 'Don't be silly. I know how much you love me.'

'I love Troy too,' she confessed. 'And I don't need to hide him from my family.'

A menacing scowl took over Brooke's gorgeous face. 'If you leave me, I'll tell the world about all the filthy things we have done together. Are you ready for your family to know how much you love my pussy? Are you prepared to face the consequences of coming out? We live in an ultra-conservative society, sugar. How do you think your parents will take it? They can't even stand Casper and Drew. If they learn you are a lesbian, they will disown you. You won't. Have. Anyone.'

Prickly heat rose from her chest up to her cheeks. 'Would you really hurt me like that?'

'Hurt *you*?' Brooke scoffed. 'Trust me when I say the pain you will endure would pale in comparison to the heartache *I'd* suffer over losing you.'

Something cracked deep within her soul, and she began to understand Lucinda's predicament. Softening her tone, she asked, 'Do I mean so much to you?'

All the anger vanished from Brooke's visage. 'Of course you do, sugar,' she purred. 'You are *everything* to me, and I couldn't possibly live without you.'

'Okay, I'll dump Troy,' she lied. 'I'm so sorry I hurt you.'

Brooke threw her arms around Rebecca and peered into her eyes. 'All is forgiven.' She claimed Rebecca's lips in a deep, possessive kiss.

೮೧೪

Lucinda

Inspiration eluded Lucinda as she attempted to sketch her next big masterpiece. It was as though her muse had stowed away in James' bandwagon. Cradling her aching head, she grimaced at the scribble on her page. The design may as well have been a first grader's attempt at line art for all the sense it made. Scrunching up the page, she tossed it in the wastepaper bin along with its fifty or so predecessors. A shadow emerged across her desk, and she swivelled around to face her boss.

Lisa smiled at her over a steaming mug with a parody definition of an architect. 'Take a break hun. I find fresh air and sunshine usually help when I'm in a creative slump. Failing that, copious amounts of caffeine.'

Lucinda doubted any of those options would help her current mood, but she liked the idea of a break. 'Thanks. I'll take an early lunch in the courtyard.'

'Good idea,' Lisa agreed.

With coffee and sandwich in hand, Lucinda took a seat beneath the wisteria pergola. At this time of year, the soft sunlight filtered through vibrant gold foliage rather than lilac blooms. Taking advantage of the privacy, she phoned James.

It rang for a while before he answered with a sigh, 'Hi Lucy.'

'I miss you.' She failed to suppress the emotion in her voice.

His breathing grew heavy for a moment, leaving her hanging before he eventually responded. 'Have you made a decision?'

Closing her eyes, she held back the tears, not wanting to explain the puffy racoon look to her colleagues. 'Please don't make me choose. I love you both, and I can't bear the thought of living without either of you.'

Silence filled the airwaves.

'James?'

'Yeah, I'm still here…. How do you think the rest of my family will react if they find out about us? Because with Becky on high alert, I guarantee they will discover our affair. It will be far worse than if you leave Adam and come live with me now.'

'What if you moved somewhere not far from Melbourne? Then we could see each other away from prying eyes. My parents have a spare rental shack in Barwon Heads. I could stay with you under the pretence of visiting them.'

'Damnit, Cindy! You're making it impossible for me to do the right thing.'

Hope sparked like flint and steel in her heart. 'You'll do it?'

Another pregnant pause.

She watched the seconds tick by on her desk clock. One, two, three… ten.

'Yeah, okay. Send me the details for your parents' rental.'

Curtailing the urge to squeal, she grinned like a maniac. 'Thank you, James. I promise we'll make this work.'

'I don't need your broken vows, Cindy. Save those for Adam.'

She winced. 'Ouch. What's wrong, James? Why the sudden change of heart? You were okay about sharing me with Adam before.'

'I can't pretend to be happy about taking a backseat in your love life anymore. I'm sorry I let things get this far. I should have put my foot down earlier, when our affair first started, but I'm a sucker when it comes to you, Cindy. I didn't have the balls to snatch you up before I lost my chance, so I let myself clamber for the crumbs you tossed my way.'

A single tear escaped, trailing mascara down her cheek. 'Please believe me when I say, I don't love you any less than Adam. I'm sorry it took me so long to tell you.'

'I love you too, Cindy, which is why I'm agreeing to this crazy idea of yours. I hope you don't come to regret it.' His own voice had grown thick and gruff.

She shook her head, forgetting he could not see her. 'I could never regret being with you, James.'

By the time she arrived home from a more fruitful afternoon at work, James had claimed the rental shack at Barwon Heads. He followed up the news with a text making her toes curl:

{JAMES} I SHOULD BE MOVED IN BY THE WEEKEND. WHEN CAN YOU HELP ME CHRISTEN MY NEW BED?

Shutting off the engine of her car, she typed out a response with jittery fingers. JUST GOT HOME. I'LL CHECK AND GET BACK TO YOU TONIGHT. Adam's sedan already sat idle in the garage beside her. He had assured her she would not spend any time alone at home until Terrance was back in prison, and he had remained true to his word.

Footsteps barrelled down the stairs and Adam greeted her at the door with a bear hug. 'I'm so glad you made it home safe. How was work?'

Soaking in his warmth, she returned the comfort he offered her. They both needed it. 'Work was fine. Nothing strange happened.'

'Good. James rang today,' Adam started as he released her from his arms. 'He told me he wanted to help fund full-time bodyguards for you.'

'A generous offer.' She tried to sound surprised.

He nodded. 'I'm inclined to accept it. When I ran the idea past Dad, he suggested hiring someone to protect me too. At first, I thought it was overkill, but then I thought about what Brooke told me. In the end, I conceded. If you are okay with the idea, we should be able to organise a team by the weekend.'

She was not keen on having strangers watch her every move, but it beat the alternative, so she nodded. 'Do it. Oh, and speaking of the weekend, I was thinking of visiting my parents.'

'It's a good plan,' Adam agreed. 'It would be best for you to get away in case Terrance retaliates. I'd go with you, but I want to help with the investigation as much as I can.'

She kissed his cheek. 'Thank you for taking this issue so seriously.'

He played with a strand of hair that had escaped her ponytail, then tucked it behind her ear.

'You don't need to remind me how dangerous this man is. You're my whole world, Lucy. There's no way I will let the creep get his hands on you ever again.'

After another tender embrace, she explained how she needed to contact her parents. Once alone in her study, she messaged James. I WILL DRIVE DOWN THERE ON FRIDAY AFTER WORK AND SPEND THE WEEKEND. CAN'T WAIT TO SEE YOU AGAIN. LOVE YOU.

{JAMES} I CAN'T WAIT TO BE INSIDE YOU AGAIN. LOVE YOU TOO, SWEETHEART.

Chapter Twenty-Four

Lucinda

The worst thing about looking forward to the weekend was the way each intervening day had stretched out like being on a torture rack. Lucinda did not dislike her job; she loved it in fact. Work simply held less appeal than her upcoming getaway with James. When the clock finally ticked over to five, she shut down her computer and followed Alex—one of her bodyguards—out to the car. James had hand-picked her security detail, briefing each of them on the need for discretion where her love life was concerned. She suspected he may have paid a little extra for their loyalty to him.

Alex opened the passenger door of his black sedan, ensuring she was safe within its bulletproof interior before taking the driver's seat. The extra measures her guards went to were unnecessary since Terrance wanted her alive, but who was she to tell them how to do their job? The vehicles were probably company standards.

Soft classical music filled the cabin. The gentle, lilting notes combined with the car's rocking motion to lull her to sleep in a matter of minutes. She awoke to the booming sound of a jet. They were passing the airfield about six kilometres from their destination. She wiped the sleep from her eyes and fixed her makeup in the sun visor mirror. 'Will you be staying for the weekend, Alex?'

'Yes ma'am,' he replied in a baritone voice. 'I am under strict orders to stay close to you and Mr. Fairfax.'

Her brow furrowed as she mourned her loss of privacy.

'Don't worry, ma'am. I won't interfere with your personal time.'

Driving through town filled her with memories from her childhood. They passed the quaint little church she had attended every Sunday; the Italian restaurant she had frequented with family and friends; the monstrous mansion where Erin Higgins had hosted countless sleepovers; even the house Lucinda had once called home. She intended to visit her parents the next day, after a full night of loving James.

The car pulled into the driveway of a white weatherboard house. Her parents had recently acquired the investment property, so she had not seen it before. The building stood two stories tall, with a large balcony on the upper floor. Given their proximity to the beach, she hoped for a view of the ocean. When Dad referred to the place as a shack, she had expected something smaller and less luxurious, although she should have known better.

'Please wait in the car, ma'am,' Alex reminded her as she reached for the door handle.

'Oh right, sorry.' In her excitement she had forgotten the protocol: always let her guard check the area before she exited any vehicle.

The locks clicked in place the moment Alex left the car. He surveyed the front yard before carrying her luggage up to the porch. James appeared a few seconds later wearing a grey slim-fit t-shirt over khaki cargo pants. Even his casual clothes hugged his figure like a tailored suit. Her heart began racing at the sight of him, then it skipped a beat when he sent a grin her way. He shook Alex's hand before giving him access to inspect the house. Leaning against the panelled siding with crossed arms, James held her gaze. He exuded pure sex appeal from the ruffled blond hair on his head down to his black skate shoes and every carved muscle in between.

She had thought the past week bad enough. The true torment was feasting her eyes upon James when she could not jump out of the car and run into his arms. The heat rose despite the mild weather, and her breathing quickened the longer they stared at one another.

Alex returned after what felt like hours, although in reality it had only been a few minutes. As he opened her door, she burst from the car and crashed into James. She wrapped her arms around the back of his neck, while his hands cupped her backside. Their lips came together in a scorching hot kiss compounded by the feel of his hard body pressing against her.

'Fuck, Cindy!' he rasped. 'We should take this inside before things escalate. I doubt the neighbours would appreciate the show.'

'You'd be surprised,' she replied with a sly grin. 'Although I know half of the people who live here, so it's not a good idea to broadcast my secret love life in these parts.'

He tugged her by the hand, leading her through a bright, open living space. They strode up a curving staircase and through another lounge area before reaching the master bedroom where she spotted her suitcase beside the walk-in closet.

James pulled her back into his arms. 'We have a dinner reservation in town tonight. Did you want to freshen up first?'

Glancing at the crisp white linen on the king-sized bed, she shook her head. 'I'd rather shower *after* we get dirty.' She yanked her blouse over her head and tossed it aside, revealing her burgundy bra.

His chest rumbled with a primal noise. 'I love the way you think.' Reaching behind her, he unclasped her hooks. He slid the straps down her arms, leaving goosebumps in his wake, and let the lingerie drop to the floor. Her nipples pebbled under his hungry scrutiny.

A phone rang downstairs, and the murmurs of a familiar baritone voice reminded her she was not alone in the house with James. She tensed, feeling self-conscious.

After stripping himself bare, James closed the door and led her closer to his bed. 'Ignore Alex. He won't care, much less make a fuss about us.'

Easier said than done. She kicked off her shoes and let James remove the last of her clothes while she stood as stiff as a board.

'Lie down for me,' he instructed gruffly.

Perching on the edge of the mattress, she shuffled back into the centre. As her head rested against a pillow, James pried her legs apart. Hot breath tickled her delicate folds moments before his tongue slid inside her core. His thumb pressed her clit and she moaned at the rush of pleasure. He eased back before applying more pressure. The sound escaping her throat seemed louder this time. He continued pushing her nub like it was a button: one easing more of her stress and tension with each touch, filling her body with waves of desire.

As soon as she unravelled around his tongue, James straddled her. Beaming down at her, he whispered, 'I love you, Cindy. Thank you for not giving up on me.'

Her heart flooded with warm, fuzzy emotions, and she smiled. 'I love you too, James.'

The sweet moment morphed into raw passion as their bodies merged. Lifting her legs over his shoulders, he struck her deep with his relentless pounding. Closing her eyes, she lost herself in the euphoria. His spicy scent encapsulated her in their own little universe. Nothing and no one else existed in this bubble they had created. His panting and her moaning became the only noises she heard. His minty breath and salty skin became the only flavours she tasted. She felt every single stroke of his hand, graze of his nails, and pinch of his fingers. When they came together, she roared loud enough to wake the dead.

Once he had caught his breath, James snorted. 'There's no hiding what we did from Alex. I bet the neighbours even heard you.'

Her cheeks heated at the thought. 'Oops. I forgot about Alex.'

Smirking, James brushed his thumb along her rosy cheekbone. 'Good thing too because that's exactly what I wanted you to do. There is nothing more erotic than the sight and sound of you letting go.'

A nervous laugh slipped out. 'It's all well and good for you. I'm not sure I'll be able to make eye contact with Alex after blasting his poor eardrums.'

'Don't sweat it. Those guys have seen and heard worse. They're used to it, trust me.' James kissed the tip of her nose before climbing out of bed. Holding out a hand, he helped her to her feet. 'Come shower with me.'

The Italian restaurant in town appeared much the same with its warm timbers and red gingham tablecloths. The smell of wood oven pizzas wafted across the room, making Lucinda's stomach growl.

They sat at a small table in the back corner, hoping to avoid unwanted attention. While reading over the wine list, she heard a familiar woman's voice and froze.

'Lucy?'

Gulping, she peered up at Tiffany Seymour's hazel eyes; the same ones she had given Lucinda. 'Hi Mother.'

Dad waltzed up to their table and grinned. 'Well, hey there buttercup. We weren't expecting to see you until tomorrow.' His gaze shifted to her date. Scratching at his salt and pepper locks, he squinted a moment. 'James Fairfax, right?'

James shook the hand Dad offered. 'That's right. Good to see you again Mr. Seymour.' He did well to hide the nerves that must have been nipping at him like a feisty dog.

'Please, call me Harry. We're family now, after all. Speaking of which, where's Adam?'

She met her father's eyes. 'He is busy working on the Terrance case this weekend.'

Dad spun around and summoned a waiter. 'Would you mind moving us, so we can all sit together?'

'Certainly sir.'

She exchanged a worried look with James before following her parents to a table for four. Her parents always sat next to each other, which left two adjacent chairs for her and the wrong Fairfax brother. Hiding her shame behind the menu, she studied every ingredient before choosing a pasta dish. As the waiter took their orders, she squirmed under her mother's scrutiny.

'What brings you to town, James?' Dad asked, still oblivious to the tension at the table.

James waited until their server had finished pouring his wine. 'I'm looking to expand my travel agency here, maybe even put down some roots.'

She choked on the mouthful of shiraz she had guzzled for her own anxiety.

As if on instinct, James rubbed her back and asked, 'You okay?'

'Yes,' she replied with a croaky voice before sipping some water.

'James is our new tenant,' Tiffany explained. 'The one who requested an extended stay at the new holiday house. Now I understand why he wants to stay so far away from the city.' She directed her comment at Lucinda.

Shit! Nothing escaped Tiffany Seymour's attention, making her one of the most formidable gossip queens in town.

While Dad engaged James in a conversation about business, Tiffany leaned across the table and whispered, 'A word please, Lucy.'

Nodding, she rose. 'We need the facilities.'

The bathroom door slammed shut behind her and she jumped. She stared at her mother who stood tall with arms crossed.

'How long has your affair been going on?'

'On and off since April last year.' Her voice wavered as the confession poured out. 'Although I've harboured feelings for him since I was seventeen, when I first met him at Mt. Hotham.'

Tiffany sighed. 'You need to tread very carefully in this town. Word travels faster than light here. If one of your school friends see you alone with a man who is not your husband—'

'I know, mother,' she snapped. 'You don't need to remind me what those girls are like.'

Tiffany's brow furrowed. 'Why did you send him here, of all places?'

'So I could tell Adam I'm visiting you.'

'Promise me one thing. Don't drag our names through the mud when this all blows up in your face.' Tiffany stormed passed, her heels clicking like castanets against the tiles.

Dinner conversation remained light until dessert. Dad glanced at Lucinda over his steaming cappuccino. 'I wish you had given us more warning about your early arrival. We haven't finished preparing your room. I recently used it for storage while repainting the neighbouring rooms.'

'Oh, I don't think Lucy intends to sleep at our house, dear.' Her mother's voice sent a chill down Lucinda's spine.

'Don't be silly, Tiffany. Where else would she stay? We'll deal with the mess when we get home.'

'It's okay Dad. I can stay at the holiday rental with James.'

Her father frowned at her. 'I thought I raised you with better manners, young woman. Don't you know it's rude to impose on people's hospitality at such short notice?'

'It's no trouble,' James insisted. 'Besides, I already invited her.'

Dad gave her a puzzled look. 'But why would you stay at your brother-in-law's when you could—' His cake fork dropped like the proverbial penny and clattered on his plate. Green eyes darted between the adulterous couple before settling on James.

'Dad, it's not what you think.'

'Oh, I'm quite certain it is.' The muscles in Dad's arms and shoulders stiffened. 'Tell me James:

does Adam know you're fooling around with my daughter?'

Unflinching, James held Dad's hard stare. 'No sir, and I'd like to keep it that way.'

'I have heard all about your womanising ways and lack of respect for the sanctity of marriage. Despite knowing what a cad you are, I never would have thought you capable of betraying your own flesh and blood to scratch an itch.'

'I understand your concern, but my relationship with Lucy is more than a fling. I'm in love with her. I'd rather not sneak around behind my brother's back, but this is her choice. She won't leave him, and I'll do whatever it takes to be with her.'

Dad chuckled. 'You've got balls, I'll give you that much.' His expression turned serious again. 'If Adam divorces Lucy over this, you better make an honest woman of my baby girl. Otherwise, I'll cut those balls of steel right out of their sack and feed them to you.'

'Daddy,' she protested with the same bratty tone that always twisted his arm.

Dad's gaze snapped to hers. 'Image is everything in our world, Lucy. I don't care who you mess around with behind closed doors, so long as you do so discreetly. If any scandal comes to light, it affects us all.' He turned his scowl back to James. 'I will not allow you to hurt my precious buttercup's heart *or* reputation. Is that clear?'

'Perfectly, sir.'

Her phone carved through the cloud of tension. Adam's name lit up the screen and she worried someone else may have spotted her with James. *Could word travel* that *fast?* 'Hi Adam. Is everything okay?'

'Yes actually. How are you and your folks?'

She glanced at her mother. 'We're all good. I'm out having dinner with them.'

'Ah, I won't keep you long. I wanted to let you know we have cracked the case. The PI trailing Terrance followed him to an apartment in the complex next door. While Terrance was there, our man was able to sneak up onto the balcony and peek inside. The place appears to be full of evidence.'

She gasped. 'What sort of evidence?' She sensed James tense beside her.

'Surveillance gear, notebooks, and… photos all over the walls,' Adam answered.

A lump formed in her throat as she asked, 'Photos?'

After a long second of silence, Adam replied, 'I don't know what they depicted, but I could hazard a guess.'

Bile swirled in her gut. 'Was there anything linking the place to Terrance?'

'Yeah, sort of,' Adam explained. 'They ran a property title search and discovered his cousin owns the place. It's in her married name, which almost threw our guy off the scent, but then he looked her up on Facebook and bingo!'

'Well, I'm glad we have something to pin on the creep. Have you spoken to the police yet?'

'Yes. They are organising a search warrant as we speak.'

'That's great. Thanks for letting me know.'

'You're welcome. I figured the news would help you relax more and enjoy your trip. Send your folks my love.'

'Will do. Love you.'

'Love you too.'

Three sets of eyes stared at her with anticipation. She had already explained the latest Terrance situation to her parents. A smile tugged at her lips as she announced, 'I think we've got him.'

೫೦೧

Him

He brought them both to the brink as his phone chimed to life with 'Gangster's Paradise' by Coolio. 'Damnit!' Slumping against His woman's naked body, He took a moment to catch His breath.

'What's that?' she rasped.

'A work call.'

'At this time of night?' she complained.

'Yeah, sorry. I need to take it. They wouldn't ring at this time if it weren't urgent.' Climbing out of bed, He ignored her pout and grabbed His phone. He took it to His study and closed the door before answering. 'This better be important!'

'Hey cuz, love you too,' she snarked.

'Stop testing my patience. What's going on?'

'Thought you'd like to know that someone broke into the apartment. You want me to send the security guys to check it out?'

He sighed. 'No, I'll swing by.' Ending the call, He returned to the bedroom and threw some clothes on. 'I have to go, sorry.'

'Sometimes I feel like you love your job more than me,' she whined.

'Don't start with me right now. Do you honestly think I'd rather put out fires at work than

448

enjoy your sweet little pussy?' Not waiting for her
answer, He strode out the room to finish making
Himself presentable. Driving across the city did not
take long in the middle of the night. The downside
of less traffic meant He would need to be careful
approaching the apartment. Turning the corner
onto what they had dubbed Lucy Street, He winced
at the flashing blue and red. A few patrol cars had
parked outside the tenement block. Cursing under
his breath, He parked a block away and joined the
crowd of nosy neighbours across from the scene.
Tuning out their gossip, He focussed on the police
chatter.

'This guy was a real sicko. Did you see the
photos in there?'

'Yeah man. I feel sorry for the bird he's been
stalking.'

Another spoke into her radio, 'I want an APB
out on one Terrance Bristow, twenty-seven-year-old
male....'

Slipping away from the horde of bystanders,
He returned to His car and dialled Terry. When the
idiot failed to answer he started the ignition and
floored it toward Toorak. Stopping at the gates to
Vianello's mansion, He punched in the code Brooke
had given Him. The staff ignored Him as He

stormed through the house and hammered on Brooke's door.

She greeted Him with dishevelled hair and a full-frontal view. 'Well, hello, sugar. Here to join the fun?'

'Where's Becky?' He growled.

'Down the hall and fast asleep.'

Movement behind her drew His attention and He spotted Terrance—also naked—clambering out of the massive four-poster bed and sauntering toward them. Pushing Brooke aside, He burst into the room and shoved Terry against the wall. 'What the fuck did you do?' He seethed, caging the man between His arms.

'Ooh, I do love watching the guy-on-guy action,' Brooke purred.

'Shut your trap, bitch.'

Sniggering, she pressed herself into His back. 'Sounds like you need some tension relief.'

He met Terry's hooded gaze with a glare. 'Mind telling me why cops busted into our safehouse?'

Terry's eyes widened and his spine straightened. 'What? How?'

'That's what I'm asking you. Did you do something stupid to put the pigs on your trail?'

'Hell no. I stuck with the plan.'

His hands moved to Terry's shoulders. 'It's not safe to stay here anymore. You need to leave the country.'

Terry shook his head. 'Not without Lucy.'

Exhaling a breath of exasperation, He tightened His grip on Terry's shoulders. 'We can't take her yet. Too risky. Brooke and I will stay here and continue trying to break her. She needs to be alone and vulnerable for our plan to work.'

'What am I supposed to do in the meantime?' Terry asked with a scowl marring his gorgeous face.

He brushed His knuckles along the side of Terry's face. 'Live it up in Europe for a bit. Suss out an ideal place for us all to settle down.'

Snatching His hand away, Terry clenched His wrist between long, thick fingers. 'Promise me you won't touch her before I get a chance.'

A dry laugh slipped out. 'Lucy is your obsession, not mine. I'm only doing this for you. You can trust me to deliver her to you in one heartbroken piece. I look forward to watching you defile her.' The thought alone made His dick hard.

The mere suggestion did the same for Terry who thrust his hips to bring attention to his erection.

Pulling Terry's hair in one hand and squeezing his cock in the other, He whispered,

'Don't even think about fighting me tonight. I *will* have your arse before you run away like the little bitch you are.'

Pushing off from the wall, Terry shoved him back. 'Fat chance, my friend. You're the one getting fucked tonight. Think of it as a farewell gift.' Terry charged and tackled Him to the bed.

They grappled, each vying for supremacy while Brooke cooed and gasped from the sidelines. Terry overpowered Him and yanked His pants down, along with a pair of silk boxer shorts. Taking advantage of the situation, He escaped Terry's hold.

The wrestling match continued until He pinned Terry to the mattress. 'Will you yield to me?'

Terry nodded.

He smirked as Brooke handed Him the lube. 'I'm going to miss you and your sexy arse, Terrance Bristow.'

Waking up the next day in His own bed, He grabbed His phone to check for updates. Scrolling past a few legitimate work messages, He found one that made Him smile:

{TERRY} EVASION ATTEMPT SUCCESSFUL. DON'T FUCK THIS PLAN AS HARD AS YOU DID ME. I'M STILL WALKING FUNNY.

Part 3

Something Blue

Chapter Twenty-Five

About 4 Years Later

Lucinda

Lucinda followed James along the trail running from the back of his house down to the beach. Navigating around the tussocks of Spinifex, her bare feet sank into the soft, cool sand. As they descended the dunes, the sea came into view. Silver light shimmered on the surface of the ocean beneath a blanket of twinkling stars. The surf lapped at the shore, and aside from the hum of crickets, nothing else disturbed the tranquillity on the beach. James had purchased his coastal home three-and-a-half years ago, choosing the secluded property because it offered the privacy they needed to continue their affair. Plus, it was still a short drive to her parents' house in Barwon Heads should she need to prove her alibi.

Stopping a short distance from the water's edge, he dropped their towels on the sand. Embracing her, he made quick work of the hooks holding her bikini top in place. His hot, shallow breaths tickled her ear as he slid the straps down her arms. 'I've missed you, Cindy. Quarterly visits aren't enough. You need to find more excuses to see me.'

The fresh sea breeze met her breasts as they sprang free of their fetters, turning her nipples to stiff peaks. 'If I came to Barwon Heads any more often, I'd need to drag Adam with me. That would mean finding ways to sneak away from my folk's house at night. He would get suspicious.'

He tugged at the bows at either side of her bikini briefs and let the fabric fall away. 'What if you came here on nights when he is working late? He knows you don't like staying home alone.'

True. Terrance may have fled the country, but an aspect of him still lingered in Melbourne, filling her with dread whenever she spent a night alone. While the letters had stopped, the miscarriages had not, and she still felt someone sinister lurking in the shadows, watching her. Barwon Heads was the one place she felt free of an oppressive atmosphere. 'I'll think about it later. Right now, I need to feel you inside me.' Kneeling in the sand, she pulled James' boardshorts down, and licked her lips at the sight of his engorged dick. Due to the nature of Terrance's sexual abuse all those years ago, she rarely felt the desire to pleasure a man with her mouth. The Fairfax brothers understood, so they never pressured her, and she loved them all the more. Yet in this moment, nothing aroused her more than the thought of tasting James, of taking him deep into her throat.

James hissed as she swallowed him. 'I don't know what's turning me on more: the feel of your soft lips around my cock or knowing you love and trust me enough to do this.'

Smiling, she cupped his balls in her palms and licked his shaft. After sucking on him for a few minutes, she grabbed the foil packet from his shorts. She slid the latex over his dick and lathered on more lube. They would need it where they were going. Taking his hand, she rose to her feet and kissed him.

Keeping their lips locked, James hoisted her up, and she wrapped her legs around his waist. He carried her into the water, submerging them enough to defy gravity. Gripping her hips, he sank deep inside her.

She held on to his shoulders, mooring herself to his hot, pulsing body. The contrast to the frigid sea went to her head like a shot of whiskey. They had become addicted to making love in the ocean. James knew it was something he could give her that Adam never would, so he took every opportunity to bring her out to their favourite spot.

Cresting the tidal wave of euphoria, she threw her head back and cried out, a bright light filling her vision. She collapsed against his solid chest and mewled. 'Christ! I came so hard my eyes flashed.'

'Wasn't just you, sweetheart,' James replied gruffly.

'Mm, you felt it too?'

He kissed her forehead. 'No, I mean the flash was real. We should head back inside.'

'It was probably lightning further out to sea. I'm sure it's fine.'

'Maybe, but I don't want to take any chances.' He pecked her lips, and she grumbled as he withdrew.

She missed the warmth of him inside her. Holding hands, they trudged back to shore. Seizing her towel, she draped it around her shivering body.

With his own towel in place, James hugged her close. 'Let's warm up in the shower while I run us a spa bath[9].'

'God, I love you, James.'

Nuzzling into the crook of her neck, he whispered, 'I love you too, Cindy.'

ॐ

Arriving home late Sunday afternoon, Lucinda found a dark, silent house. 'Adam?' Her voice echoed in the emptiness. 'Great,' she huffed. 'Alone again.' Storming up the stairs, she dropped her luggage beside the closet. At times like this, she regretted calling off the security detail, even if the apparent risk had long since traversed oceans. As far as she knew, Interpol were keeping close tabs on Terrance, and they had not reported any of his movements since they last spotted him in Russia. Needing to chase away the chill creeping down her spine, she stripped out of her clothes and strode into the bathroom. She adjusted the shower faucet, watching clouds of steam billow out of the cubicle

---

[9] Spa baths— like small hot tub—have jets and room for one to three people. They are generally designed for indoor use.

until the temperature reached something shy of scorching.

Standing beneath the warm deluge, her thoughts turned to James. She already missed his comforting arms, sensual hands, and filthy lips. Yearning for every part of him and all the amazing things he could do to her, a devastating realisation shook her to the core. *I love James more than Adam.* Reaching for the shampoo, her hand trembled as she poured a generous blob into her palm. The difference in her love for the two men felt significant too. Somewhere along the way, she had grown emotionally distant from Adam. *Is it because of the miscarriages, or have I subconsciously driven a wedge between us with my affair?* Scrubbing her scalp, she tried to shake the nagging itch in the back of her mind. But as the suds washed down the drain, she acknowledged a divorce would be the fairest option.

As soon as she had recognised the truth, doubts seeped in. *Would life with James be any better with how much he travels?* If anything, she would likely end up home alone more often. *I need to pay my husband more attention. To rekindle the old spark.*

౬౦౪౩

Brooke

Nestling into His side, Brooke lit up and took a deep drag of nicotine. 'Not that I'm complaining, but why have you been seeking me out more often of late?'

'I'm eager to execute the final stages of our plan which requires frequent communication.' He bummed her cigarette, smirking at her exasperation.

She watched the coils of smoke drifting out the corners of His mouth as He sprawled out across the motel bed. The erotic display sent a rush of blood to her core. 'Sure, but how does fucking me fit with the plan?'

He shrugged. 'You're much kinkier than my other woman and without Terry here… you fill a void.'

She beamed. She prided herself in offering more than her vanilla counterparts and she hoped Adam would appreciate this quality one day. *Soon*.

'How are things progressing with Becky?' He asked, returning her cigarette.

Closing her eyes, she inhaled the smoke, letting it soothe her nerves. 'Becky has been slipping away from me ever since I forced her to leave Troy.'

'So much for keeping her under your thumb,' He huffed.

'She'll still play her part, I'm sure of it.' She understood Rebecca's moral compass better than anyone.

'See that she does. I was visiting family recently, and you'll never guess who I saw.' He shifted on the mattress and reached for an envelope on the nightstand.

'Lucy?' she guessed, knowing it was hardly a long shot.

'Indeed. I copped quite an eyeful too, mind you. Good thing my cousin had her camera on hand.' He handed her the cropped photos.

She gaped at the series of pictures. A few of them were of Lucy alone, likely for Terry's sake, but most depicted her in the throes of passion with one James Fairfax. *The wrong brother.* She squealed with delight. 'These are perfect! Do you have some copies for me?'

'Not yet, but I will. We need to approach this matter delicately. No more letters because as far as Lucy knows, they came from Terry. And if you take the evidence straight to Adam, he'll grow suspicious of your role in all this. It's time to whisper in Becky's ear.'

ॐ

Rebecca

Troy's amber eyes stared down at Rebecca with such longing she drowned in their depths. She could not even recall the last time Brooke looked at her with such emotion. 'I love you Troy, more than anything in this world.'

He grinned at her confession as he slid between her wet folds. 'I love you too, sunshine.'

Pleasure stretched through her core like a lazy cat waking up from a nap, his slow, ardent strokes teasing and titillating by holding her climax at bay. She usually enjoyed the way he made love to her, gently building to a volcanic finish. But too much time had elapsed since their last tryst. Absence did not just make the heart grow fonder; it turned her into a writhing, wanton mess of a woman. 'I need more!' she demanded in a gruff voice.

Troy cursed under his breath. 'Don't tell me your girlfriend hasn't been taking care of you.'

She pulled back as he withdrew, hoping to increase the friction. 'She has but… not like you can.' Not that they had ever tried much out of the ordinary. No, Brooke claimed responsibility for most of her sexual exploration, including the many threesomes and orgies they had indulged in over the last four years. 'Please,' she begged.

'What do you want me to do?'

'Bring my legs up over your shoulders and *fuck* me.'

Obliging, he sank deeper than ever before, his eyes bulging from their sockets as she groaned. 'Do I want to know how you discovered this position?'

'Unlikely,' she warned. 'Don't think about it. Focus on how amazing this feels.' She bucked against him, spurring him on.

He increased the pace, but not enough.

'*Harder damnit!*' She winced at her own licentiousness.

'Jesus, Becky! I don't want to break you.'

'I'm not a fragile virgin anymore, babe. We can do slow and gentle later. Right now, I need you to be brutal. Fuck me like your life depends on it.' Because her sex-crazed nerves did depend on it.

His hips began working like pistons, giving her everything she desired, everything she needed from the only man she had ever loved. The ferocity of his passion catapulted her into a euphoric bliss.

It took her several minutes to recover her senses. 'Wow!' Her voice still sounded hoarse after straining her vocal cords.

'My thoughts exactly.' Pulling her into the crook of his arm, he kissed her forehead. 'Mind telling me what aroused your voracious appetite?'

'Is it wrong to want my sexy boyfriend?' she asked, feigning the coy tone.

A deep, erotic laugh rumbled in his belly. 'Quite aside from the fact you are cheating on your other lover, no, it isn't wrong to enjoy intimacy with someone you love. That's not what I was implying though. You have become more… sensual and adventurous. I'm curious to know why.'

Clambering onto his sweaty body, she straddled his hips. 'Brooke has been… showing me things. I guess she unleashed a new side of my sexuality.'

He frowned. 'Like coercing you into sex with strange men.'

Averting her gaze, she bit her lip to stop the extent of her sordid life spilling out. The sex was one thing, the blackmail another.

Troy's hand caressed her sides on their way to her shoulders. With a firm grip, he drew her closer. Their eyes locked and he softened his expression. 'Hey, I'm not blaming you. I wish there was something I could do to free you from that vicious woman. Is it so bad for your parents to know about your relationship with her once it is over? Does it matter if you are with me?'

With a sigh, she rolled back onto the mattress and snuggled into his side. 'It's not so simple. Brooke won't just out me as a lesbian, or bisexual. She'll show the world what a deviant I am. She has tonnes of video footage to prove it too.'

Jack-knifing, Troy balled his hands into tight fists. He glared at the hotel wallpaper with lethal intent. As if nothing offended him more than the blue geometric designs. 'You can't let her get away with this, Becky.'

Swallowing against a lump in her throat, she almost choked on her words, 'What else am I supposed to do? If I leave her, she will bury me and my family in shame and ruinous scandal.'

Fast as lightning, he pulled her into his lap and hugged her tight. 'Not going to happen. Let me help you, to find a way to deal with her first. Because the way things are going, it's only a matter of time before she destroys you one way or another.'

'Thank you, bunny,' she sobbed against his hammering heart.

Chapter Twenty-Six

Rebecca

Sandalwood and honey base notes greeted Rebecca as Brooke wafted into the apartment wearing her latest perfume acquisition. She glanced up from where she was reading on the couch. 'You were out late. Or should I call it early now?' She nodded toward the window where Venetian blinds filtered rays of dawning sunshine.

Brooke smiled. 'I told you not to wait up for me. I knew my meeting would take a while, so I booked a room at the hotel.'

'I didn't wait up. Sleeping in proves difficult when I don't have someone to snuggle with in bed. I figured I should get up and read.' She waved her copy of *The Scarlet Letter*[10] in the air for Brooke to see.

---

[10] Novel by Nathaniel Hawthorne

Ignoring the paperback, Brooke strode into the kitchen. Her lack of reaction to the book should not have surprised Rebecca. Brooke had never shown an inkling of interest in literature. 'Have you eaten breakfast?' she called out from across the island bench.

'No. I'm not hungry. I'd love a coffee though.'

'Why don't you fix us a brew while I cook myself some eggs?' Brooke demanded.

Huffing, she rose from her warm, comfy spot to comply with Brooke's wishes. *So much for expecting Brooke to do me a small favour out of the goodness of her heart.* She laughed at herself. *What heart?*

They sat together at the dining table a while before Brooke spoke again, 'I have some news concerning your brothers.'

'Oh?' She gazed at Brooke over her steaming cup.

'A friend of mine saw Lucinda in Barwon Heads on the weekend.' Brooke paused for effect as she bit into her toast.

'So? I knew Lucy was visiting her parents. How is this news and what does it have to do with my brothers?'

Brooke grinned. 'Lucy went skinny dipping in the ocean, and she wasn't alone.'

She gaped. 'I wouldn't put it past Lucy, but I couldn't imagine Adam doing something so bold. He's not exactly the adventurous type. Plus, he hates the beach.'

'He wasn't the brother getting down and dirty with Lucinda.'

Her jaw dropped a further inch as Brooke's revelation sank in. 'Are you saying someone witnessed her having sex?' She gulped. 'With James?'

'Exactly,' Brooke beamed. 'Your hunch was right all along, sugar. Now you can tell Adam how much of a cheating whore his wife is.'

Wincing at the harsh language, she hunched over her espresso. She did not need this news to confirm her suspicions, not after walking in on the adulterous couple four years ago. Hearing how they had not ended the affair broke her heart because she knew it was only a matter of time before word reached Adam. Not that she intended to tell him. Lucinda's personal business was her own and Rebecca was in no position to judge another woman for seeking comfort outside a flawed relationship. Not wanting to betray her inner conflict, she sighed. 'You don't have to look so happy about it.'

Brooke's expression sobered. 'You're right. I'm sorry, sugar. This will devastate Adam. I let my dislike for Lucinda outshine the true tragedy. You should invite Adam to stay here when you break the news. He is going to need you close at hand to comfort him.'

'I'll let him know he is welcome here, but I imagine he will stay with Greg when shit hits the fan.' She had a strong feeling that when the time came, Adam would need a break from female company.

༻❀༺

Lucinda

Lucinda sipped her pinot gris as Adam cleared the dinner dishes. He had made more of an effort to get home from work at a reasonable hour for the last few nights. Plus chatting with her over dinner and cuddling on the couch while they each read. *Is it a coincidence, or did he realise how alone and afraid I was when he got home on Sunday?*

'Let's watch a movie,' he suggested when he returned.

'Good idea.' She refilled their glasses and followed him into their media room. 'What did you have in mind?'

Adam shrugged. 'Whatever you want. Maybe something upbeat.'

Running her fingers along the spines of the DVD cases, she picked *Mamma Mia*. After putting the disk in the player, she snuggled in beside Adam. When Sophie and Sky started singing 'Lay All Your Love on Me' Lucy turned to Adam and coiled a strand of his hair between her fingers. 'You never did tell me the real reason why you dislike the beach.'

'I haven't always,' he admitted. 'I used to love sailing and swimming in the ocean. Brooke went and ruined it all for me.'

'How?' she asked tenderly.

Grabbing the remote, he paused the film and pulled her into his lap. 'During the summer between high school and university, I spent a lot of time socialising at the St. Kilda marina. The Aquilla family hosted lots of parties on land and at sea. New Year's Eve was one such occasion:

> *Brooke eyed him across the*
> *clubroom as she sipped a bright red*
> *cocktail from a martini glass. Enjoying*

471

the buzz from several beers, he lifted his glass and saluted her with a lascivious grin.

That was all the encouragement she needed to sashay over. The teal silk of her slip dress hugged every curve as she approached, and his libido took notice. 'Dance with me?' she pleaded, batting her lashes as she extended a manicured hand.

Rising from his seat at the bar, he took her hand and led her to the dancefloor. They jived, waltzed, and swayed to the music for hours. The more time they spent in each other's arms, the more his body wanted her.

'I need some fresh air. Will you join me for a walk along the beach?' Her question sounded so innocent at the time. In hindsight, he was too naïve to detect the innuendo in her tone.

As soon as their feet hit the sand, she kicked off her designer stilettos. 'Race you to the pier?' Brooke took off before he could respond, laughing as she ran.

Sitting on a large boulder, he yanked off his own shoes and socks. He tossed them beside the discarded heels and chased after her. A strong breeze whipped through his hair as sand blasted his face. Dress pants hindered his movement a little, but he still sprinted fast enough to catch her a second before she reached the finish line. Wrapping his arms around her, they stumbled together beneath the jetty and collapsed in a giggling mess.

Merriment faded as they gasped and wheezed. Next thing he knew, Brooke was straddling him. Desire replaced the humour in her gaze. 'I've wanted you for so long,' she confessed.

He had seen that hungry look in her eyes before, so he knew she meant it. Her feminine charms had often caught his attention before, but then she would open her snarky mouth and turn him right off. Besides, she had been his sister's best friend for as long as he could remember, so he had dismissed her as an option years prior. Until that fateful night. When she brought her lips to his, he returned the kiss, not having the willpower to resist. Driven by lust, he escalated the make out session. She consented to everything, and they both enjoyed the unbridled passion.

'Yet whenever I recall the night, it's not the sexual pleasure I remember, but the chafing sand and stinging brine.'

She stared at him with a furrowed brow. Her gut coiled at the thought of Adam sleeping with Brooke, but she could not fault him for enjoying the company of an acquiescent woman. 'Why?'

'The aftermath soured everything,' he explained. 'Brooke wanted to date, but I wasn't interested. Then she approached me six weeks later with a positive pregnancy test.'

She gasped. 'Yours?'

He nodded. 'We were too drunk and stupid to think of protection.'

'What happened?' she asked in a hushed voice.

'Brooke wanted to keep the baby. She begged me to help her raise our child. I hated the thought of spending my life with her. Her bitchy and shallow personality had always rubbed me the wrong way. With uni on the horizon, I wasn't ready to be a father either. To be honest, the thought of parenting at such a young age terrified me. I told her to terminate the pregnancy. She wasn't happy with my suggestion, but she complied after much persuasion.'

The room fell silent for several excruciating minutes. She did not know how to respond to such a heartbreaking story. Had she been in Brooke's shoes, Adam's actions would have destroyed her. Yet, she could also appreciate where he was coming from.

'Sometimes,' Adam whispered, 'I believe God is punishing me for murdering my first baby. It's why he won't let us conceive.'

Tears trickled down her cheeks as she shook her head. 'You were young and scared, Adam. I don't think God would punish you for that. Brooke would, however. Are you sure she wasn't behind my miscarriages?'

'She swore that was all Terrance.'

Icicles formed along her spine. 'I don't think we should take her word for it. The letters may have stopped since he fled the country, but my miscarriages haven't. I know we ordered tox screens to rule out Misoprostol, but is it possible Brooke drugged me with something else?'

Closing his eyes, Adam pinched the bridge of his nose. He dropped his hand and looked at her with a weary expression 'You raise a good point. Without knowing what to test for, we can't rely on pathology results. How is the culprit even slipping this stuff into your food or drink? The security on this place is like Fort Knox.'

'She probably strikes when we are out socialising. Brooke runs in the same circles as us, so she would find plenty of opportunities.'

Adam nodded. 'I'll keep a close eye on her in future. Let's finish watching this movie.' He hit play and held her tight for the rest of the night.

Lucinda entered the cinema complex holding Adam's hand. 'Casper asked us to meet him in the bar.' The mouth-watering scent of popcorn filled the air as they crossed the foyer.

'Did he tell you what his movie is about?' asked Adam.

'He mentioned something about a psychological thriller.'

A security guard greeted them at the entrance to the bar to check their names off the guest list. Stepping into the room, she spotted the stars of the show amidst a buzzing group of fans, friends, and family.

Casper's eyes lit up, and he waved her over. 'Hello gorgeous!' He pulled her into his arms and kissed both of her cheeks. 'You look radiant, so this husband of yours must be doing something right.' Releasing her with a wink, he shook Adam's hand.

A faint blush heated her cheeks when she thought back to the way Adam had ravished her the moment he got home. Not to mention all the other sex they had enjoyed over the last twenty-four hours. A little romance and seduction could do wonders for a relationship. 'Congratulations on the new release. I'm looking forward to seeing the movie.'

'Cheers, darling.' Casper introduced her to the filmmakers and a few other cast members.

As more guests arrived, she left Casper to his meet and greet. After ordering a sparkling brut, she squished into a booth next to Nicole. 'Hey hun, how are you?'

'Fine,' she shrugged and forced a smile bordering on a grimace.

Lucinda frowned at the false bravado. 'What's wrong?'

'Nothing,' insisted Nicole.

Draping an arm across his wife's shoulders, Michael grinned. 'Of course there's nothing wrong. We're living our happily ever after. Like you and Adam, right?'

'Right.' Lucinda eyed him sceptically. *Does Michael know about my marital problems? Or is he deflecting from his own?* She decided to check in with Nicole when they could afford some privacy.

'Hey Lucy!' Brooke barked across the table. 'How was your recent stay at Barwon Heads?'

She narrowed her eyes at the bitch, wondering where this train of conversation was headed. 'It was good, thanks.'

'How lovely. I heard you caught up with James there. I haven't seen that man in years. How has he been?'

Adam shot her a look. 'You never mentioned seeing him.'

Turns out they had hopped on the express to interrogation station. Chancing a glance at Rebecca, she hoped this news would not arouse any suspicions. Her sister-in-law gave nothing away, so she wiped her sweaty palms on her skirt and shrugged. 'Must've slipped my mind. We didn't see much of each other.'

A scornful snort slipped from Brooke's throat. 'Don't tell me Adam doesn't even know James is living near your parents. You shouldn't keep so many secrets from your husband, Lucy. It's not good for a healthy relationship.'

'What would you know about a healthy relationship?' Rebecca snapped. 'Why don't you leave well enough alone? Are you so incapable of withdrawing your sticky beak from other people's business?'

Brooke gaped at her. 'Since when did you grow a spine?'

'Since I got sick of your bullshit!' Rebecca rose and stomped off toward the screening room.

Everyone at the table stared at her retreating form. *Now there's the epiphany I've been waiting to see for at least nine years.*

Chapter Twenty-Seven

Rebecca

In a bid to avoid Brooke, Rebecca joined Adam and Lucinda as they left the movie theatre. 'What an unexpected twist. There's no way I would have picked Casper's character for the stalker.'

Lucinda shuddered. 'It was all a little too close to home for me.'

Thanks to all her own turmoil and trauma, Rebecca had almost forgotten Lucinda's ordeal. 'I'm sorry. That must have been hard to sit through. What was Casper thinking, inviting you to such a film without warning?'

'I guess the clue was in the name. What else would you expect from something titled *Always Watching*? To be fair, it's not like he knew much of what went down with Terrance.'

They reconvened in the bar where waiters handed out complimentary glasses of bubbly to toast a successful launch. During the speeches, Brooke pulled her aside. No one paid attention as they slipped through a door marked STAFF ONLY, or if they did, none of them cared.

She scanned her dimly lit surroundings: shelves of cleaning chemicals and boxes filled the claustrophobic space. Crossing her arms over her chest she turned her attention back to Brooke. 'What?'

Brooke approached, steering her into the depths of the closet. 'Why are you behaving like this?'

Like a feral cat backed into a corner, she lashed out, 'Why are you always such a bitch?'

'Excuse me?' Brooke huffed as she advanced further.

She stumbled and tripped on a steel bucket before righting herself against a wall. 'I'm sick of the horrid way you treat people.'

'Is this because of Lucy? You're the one who wanted me to investigate the possibility of her having an affair with James. We have proof now, so why haven't you told Adam?'

She glanced at the mop hanging beside her, wondering if she could use it as a weapon should the need arise. 'Because it's none of my damn business, or yours for that matter.'

Brooke smirked as if reading her mind and grabbed the cleaning tool. Dropping the mop head to the floor, she twirled the wooden handle between her fingers. 'It is our business when it hurts the people we care about.'

'You only care because you want to get in Adam's pants.'

A dry shrieking laugh escaped Brooke. 'Don't be ridiculous. Adam made his distaste for me clear on countless occasions. That ship left the harbour years ago.'

'So you do still have feelings for him?'

'Oh sugar, this is rich. You're jealous of your brother even though you're the one I make love to most nights of the week. My concern for Adam has nothing to do with a silly old crush. I want him to be happy and respected.'

'How altruistic of you,' she spat the words like venom.

Plunging the mop into its bucket, Brooke sent the pair sailing across the floor until they crashed into a shelf. 'He has a right to know about his wife's affair. Wouldn't you want to know if I were cheating on you?'

She gave the issue some serious thought. Her situation differed to Adam's immensely. *But if I were in his shoes?* 'Only if there was a risk of you bringing home a nasty STI. They say ignorance is bliss, right? Adam looks happy enough to me, but if someone tells him about Lucy and James, his world will come crashing down.'

When a styled curl dropped in front of Rebecca's eye, Brooke leaned in and tucked it behind her ear. 'Perhaps. The spiteful things you said about me tonight stung, you know? Your outburst felt like a dagger to my heart.'

Melting at the sight of tears in Brooke's eyes, she bowed her head. 'I'm sorry.'

'I'm still madly in love with you, sugar, but lately I feel as though you are slipping away from me.' Grabbing her, Brooke lifted Rebecca's chin, bringing them eye to eye. 'Do you still love me?'

'Of course I do,' she lied, hating the taste of deception on her tongue.

ഇരു

Adam

Adam waited for one of the bartenders rushing about behind the blue tiled counter. He surveyed the range of single-malt whiskeys sitting high on a glass shelf.

'We need to talk,' announced Brooke as she sidled up to him. Her bronze complexion glowed beneath the warm orange lighting. She waved at one of the male bartenders, catching his attention. There was no denying she was an attractive woman, on the outside at least. 'Two glasses of your finest scotch on the rocks. One for me and one for my friend here.' Retrieving a one-hundred-dollar bill from her purse, she slid it across the bar. 'Keep him topped up for as long as this lasts.'

'Brooke,' he protested. 'I'm driving. One will be enough.'

'Then catch a cab home. Trust me sugar, with the bombshell I'm about to drop, you'll need a few stiff drinks.'

Accepting his whiskey with thanks, he gulped down a large mouthful. 'Does this have anything to do with James taking up residence in Barwon Heads?' Hearing this intel second-hand disturbed him almost as much as knowing Lucinda had seen James without letting him know. *Why would she omit such news? Unless….* His eyes widened, letting the doubts creep in.

484

'You always were a smart cookie. A tasty one too, if memory serves,' purred Brooke.

With how tight he clenched his glass, he feared it would shatter in his hand. 'Give me the facts.'

'Lucy and I have mutual friends in her hometown. One of them recently informed me James went skinny-dipping with your wife. He fucked her in the ocean before taking her back to the house he owns there; a secluded beachside manor.'

The glass slipped from his vice grip, slid along the bar, and smashed on the floor. Witnesses sniggered and shouted 'Taxi' but the cacophony washed over him. 'How reliable is your source?'

'Very,' she assured him. 'I can see why you would doubt my word, but I promise I wouldn't make this shit up.'

'Do you have proof?'

'Not on hand, but I can get it.'

Slumping forward, he closed his eyes and nodded. Prying his lids open again, he stared blankly at the man who poured him another dram, this one neat.

'Here you go buddy. Looks like you could use another.' The bartender placed the glass on a cardboard coaster in front of Adam.

Has he been listening to my conversation? He threw the whiskey down his throat, letting the burn distract him from the real pain. Then another, and another.

Bartender chuckled and refilled the glass a third time. 'Try and savour this one, yeah? It isn't a cheap label.'

'Would you like me to get anyone for you? Rebecca maybe?' Brooke's voice squeaked, sounding uncertain and a little concerned. Both qualities sounded foreign coming from her.

'Get me the evidence so I can be done with this already.' If what she said was true, James was a dead man. And Lucy…? Well, he did not plan on sticking around to find out what she did with the rest of her wretched life. He finished his drink and stormed across the room.

Lucinda engaged Casper and his sycophants in an animated discussion, all of them laughing. Her eyes met Adam's as he approached, bright and cheerful at first, but they dimmed when she observed his furious scowl. 'What's wrong?'

'We're going home.'

'Okay, give me a few minutes.'

'*Now!*'

She startled at his abrupt demand.

'Jesus, buddy! How much have you had to drink?' Drew asked. His gaze darted from Adam to Lucinda and back again. 'You should go cool off. We'll take care of Lucy.'

Invading Drew's personal space, Adam tried to intimidate him with an extra half inch of height. 'Don't you dare insinuate I would *ever* hurt my wife.'

The older man refused to back down, however. 'I never said you would, but something is upsetting you and I think it best you calm down before hashing things out with Lucy. Nothing gets resolved in heated arguments. Can I call you a taxi?'

'I can sort myself out,' he huffed. Retrieving his phone, he made a show of dialling one of those cab companies who used jingles to hardwire their numbers in your memory banks. He even mumbled the sequence aloud as he punched it into his keypad. 'There, done,' he declared as he hung up. Focussing his attention on Lucinda, he tossed her the car keys. 'Don't stay out too late. We need to talk when you get home.' Spinning on his heels, he marched out of the cinema complex.

ာၢ

Lucinda

Two hours after Adam's spectacle at the afterparty, Lucinda returned home, chest aflutter. *Is he that angry about me keeping James' new home a secret?* She gulped. *Or does he suspect the reason for my silence?* Whatever the cause, she had never seen him so furious with her. He tended toward quiet brooding when there was a problem, even when he had thought she aborted their babies. Dragging her trembling legs into the loungeroom, she found Adam sitting on the couch with his laptop.

He lifted his gaze, a sinister inferno blazing in the depths of his soul. 'Take a seat.' He waved to the armchair facing the sofa rather than inviting her to sit beside him.

She dropped into the plush suede and waited for him to start.

Leaning forward, he steepled his fingers beneath his chin. 'All these years I thought you were a dutiful daughter visiting your parents as often as you did. I never questioned why you would pick weekends when I was busy with work.' He laughed drily.

'You think I would lie about visiting my parents? I can show you photos from all my visits if you need proof.'

'I don't doubt you saw Harry and Tiffany. But did you spend all your time with them? You have to admit, the timing of each trip is rather suspicious in hindsight. At first, I figured you weren't keen to stay home alone after… you know.'

Perspiration dripped from her brow despite the climate-controlled air. 'You know I'm afraid of being alone. Terrance saw to that early in my life.'

'Is that why you strayed from our marriage?' he deadpanned.

'Excuse me?' Her voice quavered. 'What are you talking about?'

'Enough lies, Lucy. It's time you came clean. Are you having an affair with James?'

Her eyes popped from their sockets. 'What?' she screeched, fighting to conceal the lump in her throat. 'Why would you even think such a thing?'

'Answer the question.'

'Did Brooke whisper in your ear? You know how that bitch loves to twist the truth. I'm sorry I didn't tell you about James moving down to Barwon Heads, but I figured if he wanted to tell you, he would've. Seriously though, this is hardly grounds to jump to such outrageous conclusions.' She needed to know if there was any substance to the allegations, or if he was going off hearsay. In case of the latter, she might be able to talk her way out of a messy divorce.

Springing to his feet, Adam marched up to her. Using the armrests for support, he caged her between his muscular limbs. 'Someone saw you with him, Lucy, so *cut the crap!*'

'Yeah, we caught up for a chat. So what?'

'Is that what the kids are calling it these days?' he huffed. 'Rumour has it you had sex with James at the beach behind his house. I looked into the deed for the property, by the way. James has owned the place for three years now, which begs the question—how long have you been sleeping with him? Since he bought the place, did it start during our week of separation four years ago, or'—he swallowed—'have you been fooling around with him since he returned to Melbourne?'

Oh shoot! This was more than a rumour. Lost for words, she gaped at him. Then again, he was still basing his accusation on word of mouth.

Adam straightened, towering over her with arms crossing his chest. 'Brooke told me there is photographic evidence.'

'And you believe her,' she scoffed. 'You yourself admitted she is trying to sink her claws into you again. You can't let her poison our marriage, Adam.'

'This has *nothing* to do with Brooke! She is the messenger, nothing more. You are the one destroying our marriage, Lucy. Not Brooke, *You!*'

She narrowed her eyes. 'Like you've been the perfect fucking husband!' she spat.

He recoiled, taking two steps back. 'What the heck does that mean?'

Rising to her feet, she closed the distance between them. 'It means you're the one who neglected me all these years, pouring all those long hours into your stupid job. If I didn't know better, I'd think you were the adulterer banging some floozie in your office. Who knows, maybe you have been.'

Rage rippled from his taut muscles and the creases in his forehead. 'How. Dare. You! I have invested *everything* into this relationship, and I don't just mean financially.'

'Really?' she sobbed as the tears began to flow. 'Because it hasn't felt that way. I've spent way more nights alone than I care to remember. And it seems like you're only ever intimate with me when you want to make a baby.'

Something flickered in his eyes, then he schooled his expression. 'This conversation is going nowhere. Seek me out when you're ready to come clean. I'll be sleeping in the spare room.' He turned and strode toward the stairs.

She collapsed back into the chair and bawled her heart out. *If there* are *photos, this could mean the end for me and Adam.*

Chapter Twenty-Eight

Lucinda

After a restless night through which Lucinda awoke several times in a crying fit, she called in sick to work. Taking one look in the mirror assured her she had done the right thing, about work at any rate. No amount of makeup would conceal how red and puffy her eyes looked. Not to mention the fatigue. Stepping into a warm shower, she tried to clear her head. *Should I tell Adam the truth before he sees those photos? Should I warn James first? Is it even worth salvaging this marriage?* Thoughts swirled round and round in her head like the steam encircling her. By the time she wrenched off the faucet and wrapped herself in Egyptian cotton, her brain fog had grown thicker. 'I need advice from a good friend,' she told herself as she unplugged her phone from the charger.

Nicole picked up on the third dialtone. 'Hi Lucy. Is everything okay with Adam?'

'No,' she rasped, choking on the emotion swelling in her throat. 'Can we go somewhere private to talk?'

'Sure. I'm meeting a client in the afternoon, but I can take the morning off. My parents aren't home, so we could use their place. See you there in half an hour?'

'Okay. Thank you.' She finished getting dressed and slopped on some basic makeup for what good it did. When she reached the Parkers' Toorak mansion, she spotted Nicole climbing out of her BMW. They embraced briefly before heading inside. Nicole led her upstairs to a sitting room she would rather forget. She froze at the threshold. 'No. I can't. Not in here.'

Nicole glanced at her with a puckered brow until comprehension dawned. 'Oh shoot! I'm sorry hun. I'd forgotten this was where....' Her voice trailed off, and Lucinda appreciated her hesitation.

She could not bear to hear his name while staring into the room where he had almost defiled her. The empty fireplace triggered another memory, one distressing her even more given her current situation. *This is where I met Adam.* A more superstitious person might have pinned her marital problems on the inauspicious nature of their first encounter. They were not the ideal conditions for chancing upon a future spouse. The events of that night replayed in her mind with more clarity than ever before. *The monster's approach, their struggle, the moment when he disappeared only to be replaced by....* She gasped as the image of those beautiful chestnut eyes peered back at her. At the time she had mistaken him for Ski Resort Guy, the man she came to know as James. Yet her subconscious had fallen for the memory of her first lover, not the brother who had rescued her.

'*Lucy!*' Nicole shook her out of her reverie. 'You're scaring me.'

Blinking, she focussed on her best friend. 'Sorry, I got lost in thought.'

Nicole nodded. 'Come on, let's use my old room.'

Lucinda followed her into a large bedroom with mahogany furniture matching the colour of Nicole's hair. An assortment of cream-coloured cushions and blankets sat atop a queen-sized bed. Kicking off her heels, she climbed onto the mattress and cuddled one of the fluffy pillows.

Perching next to her, Nicole gave her shoulder a light squeeze. 'What's going on, hun?'

Tears brimmed her eyes as she sought the right words. 'I messed up, Nicki. Real bad. I don't know what to do, or if we can even come back from this.'

Sighing, Nicole wrapped an arm around her shoulder. 'I'm guessing this has something to do with all the times you asked me to be an alibi. I never asked because I figured you'd tell me when you were ready. Is it James?'

Nodding, she wept against Nicole's chest.

'Are you in love with him?'

'Who?' she croaked.

'Either really, although I meant James.'

Reaching for the nightstand, she plucked a few tissues from a carved wood dispenser. She dabbed at her eyes and took a few deep breaths. 'I'm in love with them both. I know things aren't perfect with Adam and that's partly why I sought comfort from James. But I built a life with him, and I can't imagine a world where we aren't together.'

'And James?' prompted Nicole.

'The love we share is deep and passionate. And the sex? Dear God, that man is talented in the bedroom. I need James in my life as much, if not more than Adam, yet I can't see a way forward for the two of us. He is a commitment-phobe who travels a lot for work. I'd end up spending more time alone than I already do.'

Nicole fell silent, apparently mesmerised by an intarsia marquetry landscape on the wall.

'Do you think I'm a terrible person for cheating on my husband?' she asked in a hesitant whisper.

Turning back to face her, Nicole shook her head. Tears had begun to spill from her own eyes. 'No hun, your heart is torn between two wonderful men. I can't fault you for that. It's just… all this talk of adultery….' She grabbed a few tissues of her own to wipe away the emotion and blow her nose. 'I think Michael is having an affair.'

She gasped. 'I'm so sorry, Nicki. I suspected something was up last night and I wanted to follow up, but then Adam found out about me and James.'

Nicole's eyes widened. 'He knows?'

'Kind of yeah. Brooke told him about what I got up to with James when I was there last. I don't know how she knows exactly, but I'm guessing one of my old school friends saw us and blabbed about it. Adam doesn't haven't proof yet, but he strongly suggested he would soon. Why do you think Michael is doing the d—' She swallowed her words before spitting out something derogatory. *Glass houses,* she reminded herself. 'Why do you think he is seeing someone else?'

'Michael works a lot of absurd hours. At first, I thought nothing of it, but then I started noticing things like the way he would get secretive about his phone calls and text messages. Whenever I looked at his internet history, I found he would wipe it clean after every use. Recently, he has been coming home smelling of feminine perfumes. Not one, but an assortment. I don't know if this means he has been employing prostitutes or hooking up with random women each time.'

'How horrid! I know I have little room to criticise, but—'

'But you do,' Nicole countered. 'Your relationship with James is one borne of love and a deep connection you forged long before you knew Adam. If I'm right about Michael, then he is just using other women to get his dick wet. I might have been able to forgive him if the situation was like yours.' She broke down and Lucinda embraced her. Together they purged their sorrows.

As their grief eased, she asked, 'Have you challenged Michael about this?'

'Yeah, I did. Earlier in the week, hence the tension you picked up on last night. He denied it of course, claiming I was overreacting. This escalated into a full-blown argument where I threatened to leave him if he didn't fess up.'

'Wow! How did he respond?'

A dry laugh escaped Nicole. 'Not well, as you might imagine. After a bunch more heated words, he begged me not to leave him, claiming he loved only me. This morning he suggested we get away this weekend to work on repairing our relationship. Maybe you and Adam should join us. We could make it a couples' retreat. What do you say?'

'I don't know, Nicki. Adam isn't exactly talking to me right now, and I wouldn't want to interfere with what you and Michael need to work through.'

'It's fine, really,' Nicole assured her. 'After seeing the state Adam left in last night, Michael figured the pair of you could use some quality time to patch things up. He was the one who suggested I invite you. I think this could be a good way to clear the air, and if everything goes to hell, at least we'll have each other.'

'Where are you planning to go?'

'Michael has a gorgeous beach house down south along The Great Ocean Road. The views are amazing, and the fresh sea air will do us all wonders. We leave this evening, straight after work.'

'Adam hates the beach,' Lucy huffed.

'Staying in a beach house is not the same as being on the beach,' Nicole pointed out.

'True. I'll talk to Adam, if he'll even let me.'

ഛാരു

Lucinda gaped in awe of the postmodern masterpiece sprawling before her eyes. All the contrasting angles and colours of the rooms jutting out juxtaposed one another. Following her host inside, she walked beside Adam, marvelling at his willingness to work things out, especially this close to the coast.

After a brief tour of the living quarters, she stepped out onto the deck overlooking Bass Strait. Michael's beach house, nestled among the bushland, offered a stunning view of the water. Yet its own beauty had captivated her the most. Turning back towards the mansion, she admired the shimmering reflections of land and sea on the floor to ceiling windows.

Warm hands clamped onto her shoulders from behind and Michael whispered in her ear, 'I knew you'd love this place. When I bought it, I thought of you and how this is exactly the sort of building you would design here.'

She shivered despite the heat radiating from the summer sun. Something was off about Michael, and his proximity made her feel uncomfortable. Shrugging out of his grip, she spun to face him. 'Yes, the house is impressive. Why did you invite us here, Michael?'

His lips quirked. 'I didn't. That was up to Nicki. I merely suggested she might want a friend here this weekend and pointed out how you and Adam were clearly having problems of your own.'

Fixing her glare on his smug mug, she demanded, 'What do you know about my altercation with Adam?'

'Nothing really. I saw what went down at the movies last night. He looked *pissed*.' Michael chuckled. 'Pun intended.'

'Are you cheating on Nicki?'

'Woah!' He threw his arms up in surrender. 'Put those claws away, sweetheart. This weekend is all about mending bridges, not burning them.'

'It's a simple question, Mike. Are. You. Cheating. On my best friend?'

Closing the distance between them, he breathed in her face, a hint of tobacco on his breath.

'A simple question doesn't always have a simple answer. You ought to worry about your own issues and let me deal with mine.' His visage brightened a second later. 'You hungry? I'm going to cook us a barbecue for dinner.'

She helped by setting the glass table before sitting in one of the aluminium chairs. Nicole served an assortment of salads and took the seat beside her. The scent of sizzling meat drew Adam outside too, and he chose the place opposite Nicole. They all maintained a tense silence while Michael grilled their sausages, skewers, and steaks.

Once the food was ready, she busied herself by filling her plate. She wanted to occupy her mouth with anything but talking.

'So…,' Michael began as he poured everyone a glass of sparkling shiraz. 'I was thinking we should all voice our grievances to help clear the air. Let's try to avoid pinning blame though, yeah?'

There goes that plan.

'Fine, I'll start,' Nicole announced. 'I'm upset because Michael spends too much time away from home and every time I see him, he smells like a different woman. The only conclusion I can draw from this is that he is sleeping around.'

Dropping his fork, Adam let it clatter on his plate. 'My condolences, Nicole. I know how you feel because I also suspect my wife is cheating on me. Although as far as I know, she only has one lover outside our marriage. The thought of Lucy in bed with James is like a dagger in the back, one that pierces my heart.'

She ached for him, wishing she could soothe the pain even though she had caused it.

After sipping his wine, Michael wiped his mouth with a linen napkin. 'Well, I feel hurt and offended by Nicki's accusations. There's a perfectly good explanation for the various fragrances lingering on my clothes when I come home, and it does not involve sex with an assortment of women.'

'What is it then?' Nicole demanded.

'Tsk, tsk. We'll get to that. Now it's Lucy's turn.' Michael grinned at her.

She considered her words carefully. 'For the last eight years I have often felt neglected by my husband. I know he has been working hard, but given my fear of being alone, I had hoped he would have made more of an effort to balance work and home life. I also miss the level of intimacy we used to share before getting married.'

Biting into a chunk of smoky chicken, Michael nodded. He washed his mouthful down with more shiraz. 'I have a hypothetical question for Adam and Nicki. If your partner confessed to fucking someone else, would there be any hope of reconciliation?'

Nicole sucked in a sharp breath. 'What are you implying here?'

'You do know the meaning of the word hypothetical, right?' Michael asked.

She frowned at him. 'Of course I do! Seriously though, if you are seeing someone else, I might give you a second chance depending upon your reasons for cheating.'

'Fair enough,' Michael agreed. 'Adam?'

Adam peered deep into her eyes. 'Sorry Lucy, but if you are sleeping with James, there is nothing you could do or say to stop me divorcing you. This isn't some random guy you made a mistake with. I know how much James desires you. I've seen it in the way he looks at you, and I'd be willing to bet you're as hot for him. You could promise to end things with him until you're blue in the face, but you'd be wasting your breath. Your word would mean nothing.'

Focusing on her meal, she fought the grief threatening to pour from her eyes. Showing such emotion would give her away and spell the end of her marriage. She knew there was no point admitting her guilt. All she could do was pray Brooke had lied about there being evidence.

'This has been an enlightening meal, don't you think?' Michael rose to clear his plate. 'How about a game of Monopoly?'

ജ

Lucinda rinsed the plates and handed them to Nicole who was loading the dishwasher. 'Did you mean it? What you said about giving Mike another chance?'

'Yes, although I'm not sure how I'd cope if it turns out he's in love with someone else. I know I said I'd forgive him if his situation was more like yours, but that doesn't mean I would feel comfortable continuing our relationship.' With the last of the crockery in place, Nicole added detergent and powered up the machine.

'Speaking of uncomfortable, how do you fancy this boardgame idea of Mike's?'

Nicole shrugged. 'Can't fault him for trying. I'm going to change into something more comfortable first.'

'Good point,' she agreed. 'I'll go do the same.'

'Nice. Meet you in the games room.'

Once in her room, she stripped out of her shorts. The summer heat had faded over the horizon, giving way to an Antarctic chill leaving goosebumps on her bare legs. She slipped into a pair of lounge pants and pulled on a hoodie. Not knowing where the games room was, she checked the upper floor first. Each door revealed another guest suite, so she jogged downstairs and continued her search. When the first and ground floors yielded no results, she descended into the basement. Warm downlights illuminated a spacious area with floating timber floors. A pool table stood front and centre; its surface unmarked by use. She spotted a wet bar to her left, while shelves of books, DVDs, and games lined the opposite wall.

Beyond it all, Michael sat at a long oval table with a green felt top. It looked like something out of a casino. The Monopoly game remained in its box to his right.

'Oh, hey.' She scanned the room. 'Where are the others?' She had thought for sure she would be the last one there.

A sly grin crept across Michael's face. 'Adam left.'

Her brows took the opposite trajectory to her heart. 'W-why?' she spluttered.

'Because I gave him the evidence he needed. If the look in his eyes was anything to go by, he is probably en route to murder James as we speak.'

'What evidence?'

'Copies of these.' Michael dropped a handful of cropped photos on the table.

Drawing closer, she gasped. 'You took those?'

'No. You have Erin's photography skills to thank here. Don't you think she did a superb job of capturing your expression in the heat of the moment? Like she did all those years ago when you first fucked him.'

'It was you all along! You're the one who sent me the letters with the photos.' She began to back away, but Michael sprang to his feet and pounced like a puma.

He caught her in a headlock, and she screamed. 'Make all the noise you want, Lucy. No one will help you, not even Nicki.'

Her eyes stung as she asked, 'What have you done with her?'

'I gave her a little something to help her sleep. She'll be fine when she wakes up. Just like you.'

Something pricked her arm and she yelped. 'What was that?' Kicking and thrashing about, she tried to free herself to no avail. The room began to swim, and her movements became sluggish.

Michael's voice grew deep and distant as he replied, '*Clinical Ketamine.*'

She slumped in his grip, her eyelids drooping under their own weight.

'*Don't worry it's perfectly —*'

Chapter Twenty-Nine

Rebecca

Glancing up from her book, Rebecca watched Brooke sashay across the room, dressed to the nines in one of her glitzy black gowns.

'Why aren't you ready yet?' Brooke demanded.

'Because I'm not going. You're not whoring me out to sleazy tycoons anymore.' The thought of sleeping with another one of those slimy dirtbags churned the bile in her gut. Ever since Terry had left, Brooke had made it her mission to seduce Melbourne's elite into sordid threesomes, secretly filming the whole thing to use as blackmail material. She never asked what Brooke got out of the shady deals because she did not want to know.

'Don't flatter yourself, Becky,' Brooke scoffed. 'Whores get paid for what they do. You're nothing but a filthy skank to those people, and I have the evidence to show how much you love debasing yourself for their pleasure.'

She hated the way her body betrayed her soul, giving into primal desires that had left her feeling broken and ashamed. Yet it was the only way she survived all those nights of debauchery. 'I guess that makes *you* the prostitute then, and I'm still not going. You don't even need me anyway.'

'Oh, but I do.' Brooke perched beside her on the couch. 'I need you to distract them while I set the camera to record.'

'Forget it. I want no part of this anymore,' she insisted.

Brooke sprang to her feet and glared down at her. 'Shall I leak the latest footage all over the internet?'

She shrugged. 'Go ahead and waste your blackmail material on me. See if I care.' She impressed herself with the level of confidence in her voice while in truth, she trembled on the inside. Those videos could ruin her and the Fairfax name.

'Damn it, Becky! I need you tonight. Imagine the power of holding one of Melbourne's most influential judges in our pocket.' Brooke began pacing like a caged animal.

'Not happening.'

Brooke stopped by the kitchen counter and batted her lids. 'Come on, sugar. If you truly loved me, you would do this for me.'

'No, Brooke. If you truly loved *me*, you wouldn't keep doing this.'

Gasping, Brooke grabbed one of the glass tumblers off the bench and hurled it at the wall mere inches from her head. '*Enough!* You will do as I fucking say!'

Jumping off the sofa, she whirled around to inspect the damage. Shards of glass lay scattered on the floor behind her seat. 'Are you nuts?' she asked as she turned back to face Brooke. 'You could have hit me!'

'Trust me, Becky. If I wanted to mess up your pretty face, I wouldn't have missed.'

'That's it. We are done. I've had enough of your abuse. Go find some other sucker to use in your twisted games.' Plucking up her handbag, she threw it over her shoulder and started toward the door.

Brooke cut her off, readying a wine glass as a projectile. 'Approach the door, and I will cut you. Besides, I have plenty of footage that won't give away the identities of my *other* blackmail victims.'

She whipped her phone out of her bag. 'Touch me, and I ring the police.'

Fast as lightning, Brooke charged and seized the phone. She chucked it across the room where it smashed against the guestroom door. 'Try making a call now, you insolent little turd.'

She made a dash for the door, but Brooke caught her bag and yanked her back. Stumbling, she considered relinquishing the handbag, but someone could do a lot of damage with the credit cards and identification in her purse. Plus, she needed her car keys for a quick getaway.

Using this hesitation to her advantage, Brooke tackled her to the ground right beside the discarded wine glass. Brooke picked up the drinking vessel and cracked it against the floor. Still holding it by the stem, she pressed the sharp edge to Rebecca's throat. 'You will *never* leave me!'

Slapping Brooke's hand aside, she knocked the improvised weapon out of her grip. 'Get off me!' she screamed with the full force of her diaphragm.

Ignoring her request, Brooke wrapped her hands around Rebecca's neck and started squeezing.

Rebecca flapped about like a fish on a hook, but she could not budge the muscular woman pinning her down. When her vision began to blur, the front door slammed open.

'Get off her now!' Adam's voice bellowed as heavy footfalls thudded across the floor. He lifted Brooke from her position of power and tossed her aside like a bag of rubbish. 'What the hell do you think you're doing?' He growled at Brooke.

'Just a little foreplay,' Brooke purred while fluttering her lashes. 'Becky's my lesbian lover, didn't you know?'

Adam stared aghast at Rebecca. 'Is this true?'

'Yes,' she croaked, rubbing her sore throat. 'The lesbian bit anyway. The rest was downright assault.' The adrenaline that had pumped through her veins abandoned her, and she shattered into a million pieces. 'Please get me out of here,' she sobbed. As he scooped up all her broken fragments, she whispered, 'My handbag.'

Nodding, he snatched the designer tote and carried her outside amidst Brooke's cries of revenge. Once he had strapped her into the passenger seat of his car, he sat behind the wheel and asked, 'Where to?'

'Home,' she rasped. She knew he didn't need clarification because the apartment they drove away from would never be home again.

'Mind telling me what I walked in on back there?' Adam asked after manoeuvring out of his roadside park. 'Aside from attempted murder that is.'

'Fed up with Brooke's abuse, I tried to end our relationship. She didn't take it well.'

'You think? How long have the two of you... been a thing?'

'Almost nine years.'

He swerved on the road, narrowly avoiding a head-on collision. 'What about Troy?'

'He knows all about me and Brooke. At first, he agreed to be a fake boyfriend to cover up my sexuality, but then we fell for each other, and the relationship became real. Brooke didn't like it, so she forced me to break up with him, although I've continued seeing him on the side ever since.'

'Talk about convoluted. I assume Terrance played Brooke's beard?'

'Yeah, although they did sleep together too.' She sighed. Her throat still ached and talking made it worse, but she needed to clear the air. 'I've wanted to leave Brooke for years now, but she waves threats of outing me in my face and hangs scandal over my head. I'm going to need a whole lot of legal help to deal with her.'

'Sounds like I dodged a bullet there.'

'What do you mean?'

'I guess Brooke never told you about the time I had sex with her. Small mercy I suppose.'

She spun around to face his profile. 'What? When did this happen?'

'The summer between high school and uni, for me anyway. You and Brooke were embarking on your senior year. Point is, she wanted a relationship, and I didn't. She's been trying to win me over ever since. I hate to think she is taking my rejection out on you.'

'I wouldn't put it past her vindictive nature,' she huffed. 'God, I am such an idiot to have been blind to her true nature all this time.'

His hands clenched the steering wheel. 'I know how you feel. I learned Lucy is having an affair with James.'

'Ah heck! Did Brooke tell you that? Please don't trust a word out of her deceitful mouth.'

'She mentioned it a couple of days ago,' Adam explained. 'Earlier tonight, Michael showed me the proof. He had photos of them together.'

'I'm surprised you came to me about this,' she admitted. 'Don't get me wrong, I'm beyond thankful for your intervention. Still, don't you usually sulk at Greg's when you're having girl trouble?'

ℰꙅ

Adam

'I don't sulk. I quietly reflect,' Adam retorted with a dry laugh. If not for Rebecca's fragile state, he might have ribbed her about the way she used to mope around the house.

'Tomayto, tomahto. Why did you come to… the apartment?' she asked with a quavering voice. 'Please tell me it was to see *me*, and you weren't about to do something stupid with Brooke.'

He snorted, hating the way he sounded like James when doing so. 'Don't worry, Becky, I won't make that mistake again. I wanted a word with our brother, so I was hoping you or Brooke had his address.'

'I know where he lives.' Rebecca paused before adding, 'I understand how you're hurting right now and I'm sure you want to punch his lights out, but violence won't solve anything. Take some time to cool down first. Talk things out with James when you've got a clear head.'

'Fine. If it makes you feel better, I'll sleep on it.' After all the driving, he could use the rest anyway. Another long trip this late at night would likely prove fatal.

Rebecca stared out her side window for several minutes before turning back to him. 'Does the fact I'm bi freak you out?' she asked meekly.

'No more than the thought of my sister having sex with anyone. I was a little shocked by the revelation at first, but only because you and Brooke blindsided me. Is this why you kept it from me all these years? You thought I wouldn't accept you?'

Tears welled in her eyes as she nodded.

Stopping at a red light, he playfully punched her arm. 'You can be so dense sometimes, sis. I love you no matter what.'

'Really? What if I'd been the one having an affair with Lucy?'

He jerked the wheel to the left and the tyres scraped along the wakeup lines. 'I did *not* need that image in my head. Still, I get your point and yes, I'm a hypocrite. I doubt I'll ever forgive James, yet I would overlook a queer fling so long as Lucy still wanted me. Hell, if the other woman was anyone but you, I'd ask to join in.'

'Hmph. Do you realise how sexist you sound right now?'

'At least you can't fault me for being dishonest.'

'How am I going to break this to Mum and Dad?' Rebecca mused.

'I'll help,' he promised. 'For one thing, I intend to tell them about Lucy's infidelity, which ought to soften the blow for you.'

'You can't tell them about James! Give him a chance to fight his own battles with our parents.'

His chest cinched with some uncomfortable emotions. 'How can you be so quick to defend James after what he's done to me and our family?'

'Sorry Adam, but I'm not taking sides on this one. I love you both and while his betrayal sucks, that's between you guys.'

The truth rubbed salt into the wounds when he would rather hear the salves of solace. *That's what mates are for*, he reminded himself.

'Can I please borrow your phone to ring Troy?' Rebecca asked once he had parked in his parents' garage. 'Brooke broke mine.'

Rebecca's predicament brought him back out of his head. He could not feel vexed with her at a time like this. 'Here.' He handed her his phone and listened to her end of the conversation.

'I broke things off with Brooke. … No, she didn't take it well. She even tried to kill me.'

Troy's muffled voice came through louder this time and Adam caught a hint of words, 'With me there....'

'It's not like I planned to end things tonight. I got so tired of her exploitation. She wanted to use me in another blackmail scheme tonight. ... Yes, I'm with Adam. He arrived in the nick of time. ... We're at my parents' house now. Can you meet me here? ... Thanks Bunny, love you too.' She handed the phone back to him.

His ears had pricked up at her mention of blackmail. It would be hard to prove Brooke's assault and the attempt on Rebecca's life, but blackmail often involved incriminating evidence. It could be enough to put the bitch away for a decent amount of time. 'What were those blackmail schemes you referred to?'

Rebecca sighed. 'She seduced rich and powerful people into threesomes with us, then filmed me having sex with them. Men and women alike and all against my will. Some of this footage may go public soon. That's what I meant by scandal.'

Every muscle in his body tensed at the thought of anyone using his baby sister for such depraved acts. If Brooke had been a guy, he would have unleashed the full force of his fury. As it stood, a costly lawsuit would prove their best course of action.

Stepping into the house, he heard laughter and chatter coming from the backyard. A small group gathered under the patio with his parents as they all sipped from crystal wine glasses. He wrapped a supportive arm around Rebecca's shivering shoulders. 'Mum, Dad? Can we speak in private please?'

Taking one look at her daughter, Michelle's expression deflated.

'Oh gosh, look at the time!' exclaimed one of the ladies. 'We ought to get going.'

A man followed her inside, catching a leering glimpse of Rebecca on his way past.

Balling his hands in fists, Adam wondered if the pervert had been one of the men Brooke had forced her to sleep with.

The rest of the guests announced their agreement. With the space to themselves, Michelle asked, 'What's wrong sweetheart?' She directed the question at Rebecca who looked like a derelict in her rumpled tracksuit, ruffled hair, puffy eyes, and tear-streaked cheeks.

'I....' Rebecca choked on her confession.

'I pulled her out of a domestic violence situation,' he explained. 'Can we go inside to talk?'

Mum's brow furrowed as she nodded. 'I didn't know you had a boyfriend,' she stated as they settled into the lounge room.

'Actually, I'm still seeing Troy, but he didn't hurt me.'

He rubbed her back as she began to sob. 'I found Brooke strangling her. I know this will be hard for you both to digest, but Becky and Brooke were more than flatmates. They were lovers until Becky ended things tonight.'

Mum gasped while Dad held his tongue and schooled his expression.

'I implore you to put your opinions of homosexuality aside and see things for what they are. Brooke is a wicked woman who has abused your daughter for years. I don't know the full story, but I have learned she pressured Becky into compromising situations without consent.'

Tears leaked from Mum's eyes. 'What sort of situations?'

'There's video footage of….' He swallowed the bile climbing his oesophagus. 'Footage of her having sex with various men and women.'

'Damnit!' Dad cursed, the closest he had ever come to swearing. 'How could you be so stupid?'

Rebecca crumpled into Adam's side.

'Dad!' he spat. 'Becky's in a fragile place right now, and it's not like she had much choice in the matter. Brooke is a master manipulator. I would know because she sank her claws into me once and I fear Becky is paying the price for me pushing her away. If we don't nip this problem in the bud, our whole family will suffer for it.'

The doorbell rang and Rebecca's head turned toward the sound. 'That must be Troy,' she whispered. She ran into his arms when he appeared a minute later.

Troy's astute eyes scanned the room. 'Judging by the sombre mood in here, I take it you all know about Brooke?'

Dad huffed and Mum nodded.

'Becky?' Adam prompted. 'Where does Brooke keep the blackmail videos?'

'She emails them to someone before deleting the files from her laptop and camera.'

'Dad, you should get in touch with your PI friend, the one who helped us with the Terrance case,' he suggested. 'He should be able to recover those deleted files and turn them over to the police as evidence of Brooke's blackmail. He might even be able to track the IP address of her email recipient. Becky can give him her keys.'

'Good idea.' Dad retrieved a phone from his pocket and left the room.

Mum rose to her feet and placed a hand on Rebecca's shoulder. 'I'm sorry, sweetie.'

Rebecca swivelled in Troy's arms and hugged Mum.

'Mind if I stay here tonight?' Adam asked. He decided not to add to the current drama with his own news. There would be time enough to tell his parents about Lucinda's affair.

Returning Rebecca to Troy's arms, Mum glanced at him. 'Of course you can. The three of you are always welcome here.'

⁗⁗⁗

Lucinda

After slipping in and out of sleep, and spending her waking hours delirious, Lucinda finally gained a sense of lucidity. She awoke with a crick in her neck and a chill deep in her bones. The wall she sat against felt smooth and cold, much like the slate tiles beneath her. As the brain fog faded, she assessed her situation. She still wore her bra and underpants, but the rest of her clothes had gone.

Police regulation handcuffs bound her wrists and a thick leather strap almost choked her throat. Attempting to shuffle forward, she realised a chain shackled her collar to the stone wall. In the dim light, she glimpsed rows upon rows of wine racks lining the opposite wall, most of them full of assorted bottles. *Is this still Michael's beach house?* Her stomach churned when she recalled her last conversation with him.

Feeling the urgent call of nature, she wriggled about, testing the length of her tether. It was not long enough to stand, but she managed to kneel. 'Hello?' she cried out, her voice echoing off the high ceiling. 'I need to use the bathroom.'

The click of a lock answered her call and Michael appeared with a bucket in one hand and a roll of toilet paper in the other. His six-foot stature loomed over her as he dropped them beside her. Retrieving a switchblade from a back pocket, he crouched before her and placed the tip of the blade near her jugular. 'Don't try anything stupid,' he warned. Removing a lanyard laden with keys from around his neck, he unlocked her handcuffs. 'Do your business.' Rising to his feet, he stepped back an inch and glared at her.

'Please don't look at me,' she pleaded. 'I have a shy bladder.'

Michael sniggered. 'I've seen the things you do with men in the bedroom, Lucy. There's nothing shy about you. Now get on with it or I'll leave you to stew in your own piss.'

She removed her knickers under the weight of his lecherous stare and squatted over the bucket. Closing her eyes, she tried to forget his piercing gaze and relieved herself. Once finished, she returned to her seat on the icy floor and redressed in her last scrap of dignity.

After cuffing her hands again, Michael put the bucket aside and upended an empty milk crate. Perching on the plastic seat, he twirled the switchblade between his fingers. 'It's time we had a little chat.'

'If you sent those letters, did you also cause my miscarriages?'

'I obtained the drugs, but I never administered them. Someone else has a vendetta against you and it has more to do with her feelings for Adam.'

'I knew it!' she hissed. 'And the letters? Did Brooke help you with those too?'

He laughed. 'This isn't a movie where the villain incriminates himself by explaining all the evil shit he did.' Leaning forward, he slid the knife along her arm.

Wincing as the steel stung her flesh, she tried to ignore the blood seeping from her shallow cut. 'What do you want from me, Michael?'

He grinned. 'Now we are getting somewhere.' The tip of his blade tickled her throat. 'You will renounce all claims made against Terry and ensure the cops drop all charges against him.'

'Wait, so Terrance did have a hand in all this too?'

He shook his head. 'I thought we had moved past the blame game. I haven't even finished my list of demands yet.'

She sighed. 'What else do you want?'

'You will leave Australia with me so we can go join Terry. After a year of separation, you will divorce Adam, who I'm sure will oblige. Once that's finalised, marry Terry *and* me in a commitment ceremony and live out the rest of your days with us.'

She gaped at him. 'You intend to share me with *that* creep?'

'No, Lucy. *I* intend to share *Terry* with you, although I'm sure I'll have some fun with you too. I tried to convince the lovesick puppy to get over you, but he is like a pit bull who won't let go. I'd sooner see you rot to death down here and believe me I will leave you to die if you don't give us what we want.'

After a pregnant pause in which she digested Michael's bombshell, she schooled her expression. 'What about Nicki?'

'I thought you'd never ask. As an added incentive, if you agree to all our terms, I will bring Nicki with us. I figure you'll want some female company around. If not, she will… disappear.'

Risking her own life was one thing, but leaving Nicole at the mercy of three psychopaths? She needed to escape. 'Can I think about it?' she asked, hoping to buy enough time to hatch a plan.

'Of course.' Michael's lip curled up, showing a glint of his pearlescent teeth. 'Take all the time you need, just don't expect anything to eat or drink in the meantime. Holler when you've reached a decision.' Striding across the room, he left her trapped and alone in the dark.

Chapter Thirty

James

Sitting at his kitchen table, James was sorting through a backlog of work emails when the doorbell rang. Unaccustomed to visitors, the sing-song chime sounded foreign to him. Few people knew where he lived, and a thicket of trees hid his house from the view of anyone passing by. *Could that be Cindy?* His heart thumped with anticipation. As soon as he threw the door open, his chest deflated.

Adam scowled at him. 'Why did you do it?'

'You're going to have to be a little more specific here, bro. What have I done?' He had a pretty good idea what Adam referred to, but he wouldn't give the man a morsel of guilt to chew on.

'Why did you betray me? You have your pick of women. Why did you stick your filthy dick in *my* wife? I know you don't believe in the sanctity of marriage, but I would have thought you'd at least respect mine. I'm your brother for crying out loud! Your own flesh and blood! Is nothing sacred in your eyes?'

Recoiling at Adam's verbal assault, he stepped aside to let him in the house.

Adam shoulder checked him as he stormed down the hallway. Leaning against a bench in the renovated kitchen, he crossed his arms and glared. 'Well? What's your excuse? And don't even try to deny it. I've seen the evidence.'

'Does Lucy know?'

'That I found out about your affair? Yeah, she knows I'll be serving her divorce papers as soon as possible.'

The selfish part of his soul launched itself over the moon. Pushing aside thoughts of finally having Lucy to himself, he sobered his expression by imagining the grief she must be feeling. *Why didn't she call me?* 'To answer your first question: I sleep with Lucy because I'm in love with her. And no, I don't give a crap about your marriage vows, not when you always neglected her. I give her what you fail to provide.'

'Love? You don't even know the meaning of the word!' Adam scoffed.

'Believe me, I was as shocked when I discovered my loss of appetite and sleepless nights were due to my intense feelings for her. I couldn't get her out of my head. For years I tried to suppress my love and desire because I didn't want to hurt you. That's why I left after your wedding. You grew complacent, Adam, leaving her alone and vulnerable.'

'So, you swept in and took advantage of her?'

'I took advantage of the opportunity, but never of her. Lucy has always wanted me. She admitted as much when she told me about the guys she slept with during her uni years. Once the truth about me popping her cherry was out, didn't you ever wonder why all the others looked like me?'

'Enough already. I get it.'

'Did you ever consider how she dated you because of our family resemblance?'

'I said enough!' Adam clenched his fists.

'Go on and hit me. I'll give you one free shot.' He chuckled darkly. 'I guess I owe you that much for all the times I fucked your wife.'

Adam's hands remained glued to his sides.

'A woman never forgets her first time, not if it was good, and I guarantee Lucy enjoyed every minute of our night together in Hotham. Why else would she obsess about it ever since?' He didn't like taunting Adam, but he knew the man needed to blow off some steam before having an aneurysm, a likely outcome considering his crimson complexion. Plus, James knew he deserved the reckoning.

With nostrils flaring, Adam advanced. 'I promised Becky I wouldn't get violent.'

Explains how Adam tracked me down. 'It's one punch, dude. Come on, it'll be cathartic.'

Adam stood frozen in place.

'Should I tell you about the night our affair started? Lucy came to me, begging for a re-enactment of our first time together. You've seen the photo, so you know how much she enjoyed me bending her over and—'

Crunch! Adam's fist slammed into his jaw.

He stumbled back and braced himself against the wall. After spitting out blood, he rubbed his swollen lip. 'Feel better now?'

'Hardly,' Adam huffed, examining his bruised knuckles. 'But at least the pain in my hand distracts from the agony of a broken heart.'

'Indulge my curiosity here. Who the fuck told you about me and Lucy, and what sort of evidence did they have?'

'Brooke told me, then Michael showed me these.' Adam plucked a bundle of cropped photos from his jacket pocket and dropped them on the counter.

Studying the four-by-four square pictures filled him with a sense of déjà vu. Then the penny dropped. 'Oh shit!' Dashing across the room, he grabbed his phone and dialled Lucy. Straight to voicemail. 'Damnit Lucy! Why won't you pick up?'

'She doesn't have very good coverage at the beach house,' Adam explained.

'What beach house?'

'Michael's beach house. A secluded place in the middle of scrubland south of Lorne. The four of us were staying there when he showed me these.' Adam waved a hand above the photos.

'And you *left her there?*'

'Well yeah, I was hardly in the mood for a long drive home with her—'

'Jesus Christ! For the smartest kid in our family, you sure can be an idiot sometimes, Adam. How did it not occur to you that Michael is the one behind all those threatening letters and creepy stalker shit? You left her in the damn dragon's den.'

Adam's jaw dropped. 'What makes you think Michael did all that?'

'These pics for one. I'll explain my theories in the car. Right now, my priority is getting there to save Lucy, and I hope for your sake, as well as hers, she is okay.'

Adam gulped. 'Why do I have to go with you?'

'Because, dickhead, if the place is as secluded as you say, I'll need your help to find it. Backup wouldn't hurt either.' Once they had settled into his SUV, he tossed his phone in Adam's lap. 'Call Russell and put him on speaker.'

Russell greeted them with a cheery voice, 'Hey man, what's up?'

'Hi Russ. I've got you on speaker and Adam's with me.'

'Good ta know. What's goin' on?'

'Lucy is in danger. She's trapped in a secluded beach house with Michael who I'm pretty sure is working with Terrance. Can you help us get her out of there?'

'Shit man, that blows. Yeah, I'll come kick some arse for ya. Where we headed?'

'Meet me in Lorne as soon as possible. I'll text an address once I've found a good meeting spot.' He signed off and focussed on overtaking a road train.

'So why do you think Michael is behind those stalker notes?' Adam asked.

Checking his blind spot, he slipped back into the left lane. 'During my time in Barwon Heads I learned something interesting. Did you know Michael and Terrance share a cousin?' He wished he had known about this earlier, then again it took seeing those photos for the pieces to slot together.

'Those guys are related?'

'Not directly. Terrance's father is the brother of Michael's aunt by marriage. The blood relation being Michael's uncle who married Terrance's aunt. Their common cousin is Erin Paxton, nee Higgins.'

'I remember meeting her at Lucy's twenty-first. She was like a red-headed version of Brooke.'

'Indeed. Turns out Erin dared Lucy to hook up with someone during their stay at Hotham all those years ago. She was the reason I ended up… you know.' He didn't fancy poking the angry bear by spelling it out for him; not while they were driving. 'Anyway, when I saw her in Barwon Heads, I recognised her from that fateful ski trip. Then I recalled seeing her exit the room next to mine on the morning I ghosted Lucy. I didn't think much of it at the time, but an SLR camera hung around Erin's neck.'

'Could be a coincidence. Those cameras aren't exactly rare,' Adam pointed out.

'True, but don't you recognise the style of those photos Michael gave you? They were cropped to the same size as those of me and Lucy from Hotham. Even the candid style through which the photographer captured Lucy's expression. And why did Michael wait until he had isolated Lucy before showing you the pics? There's also the fact someone had to be working for Terrance on the outside while he was in prison. According to Lucy's parents, Michael and Terrance used to be best mates. Probably still are.'

'You've been getting cosy with her parents huh? Do they know you've been sleeping with *my* wife?' Adam spat.

'Yeah, they know,' he conceded in a resigned tone. 'Look, I'm going to need you to put your animosity aside until we've rescued Lucy. You're a good man at heart, so I doubt you want to see her suffer anymore at the hands of those creeps, despite how you otherwise feel about her at the moment. Am I right?'

'Yes, whatever.' Adam fell quiet for the remainder of their drive to Lorne.

He didn't mind. The silence helped him devise a plan.

੪ාৎ

Lucinda

Whatever way she looked at it, Lucinda's only hope of escape involved going along with Michael and Terrance's wishes. At least until an opportunity presented itself. She had no idea where Michael was keeping Nicole, let alone how much her best friend knew. A heart-breaking thought crossed her mind. *What if Nicki is helping them?* Her stomach somersaulted. *Then again, would Michael need to threaten Nicki's life if she were?* She worried how far things would progress before she found her chance. *Is it worth risking my sanity, my very soul? Not for my own life, but for Nicki's?* Her stomach growled, boosting her resolution. Flat out refusal would result in a slow, painful death. 'I've made a decision!'

Michael returned with a bottle of water, which he waved in front of her face. 'What's it going to be?'

'I'll concede to your requests.'

A malevolent grin stretched across his face. 'I am so pleased. I'm sure Terry will be ecstatic.' Opening the water bottle, he guzzled a few mouthfuls before replacing the cap. 'I'll need a show of good faith first. Let's video call with Terry and see what he wants you to do.' Michael set up a laptop on the milk crate in front of her.

The face of her nightmares appeared on screen. His gaze perused her half-naked body. 'Well, isn't this a pleasant surprise? Evening Lucy. Although I believe it's daytime there in Australia.'

Stifling the urge to vomit, she forced a smile. 'Terry.'

'Lucy has agreed to our conditions,' Michael explained. 'Given her initial reluctance, I thought you might want Lucy to demonstrate her sincerity before I unchain her.'

Terry beamed up at Michael. 'Good thinking.' He shifted his hooded eyes back to her. 'Do you understand that by agreeing to a relationship with us, you give us both consent to fuck you every which way whenever the hell we want?'

Lucy gulped. 'I understand.'

'Do you still agree to our terms, Lucy?' Terrance asked.

'Y-yes,' she stammered. 'Yes, I agree.'

'Prove it,' Terrane insisted. 'Strip for me, princess. Let me see all your delicious body.'

Michael produced his switchblade as he released her handcuffs.

A few tears trickled down her cheeks as she unhooked her bra.

Terrance's breath hitched as her breasts bounded free. 'Play with your nipples for me, Lucy. Make them as hard as my cock is right now.'

Closing her eyes, she shut out the ordeal and thought of James. She imagined her fingers were his tongue toying with her nipples; his teeth biting into them.

'Good girl,' came the gruff voice that sounded nothing like James. 'Now lose the panties and make yourself orgasm for me.'

The salty stream flowing from her eyes increased. She kept them shut as she obeyed his command, continuing her visualisation of James. The possibility of seeing him again kept her crumbling pieces together like glue.

'Look at me!' Terrance snapped.

When her eyes fluttered open, she almost puked at the sight of him jerking off.

'I want to hear you cry out my name when you come,' he demanded.

No way in hell would she reach a real climax, so she prayed her acting skills were up to par. 'Tell me when you're close, Terry, so I can come with you.'

'Fuck, princess. I can't wait to be inside you!' Terrance's hand worked faster, each sickening slap of skin against skin breaking another fragment of her soul away. 'Now!'

Arching her back, she pressed her palm against her clit and cried, 'Oh Terry! Fuck yes!' She even added a slight body spasm for effect.

'God you're amazing, Lucy,' Terrance rasped. He glanced at Michael and grinned. 'Looks like Mike enjoyed the show too.'

Turning to face Michael, she spotted the massive bulge in his pants.

Terrance's tone turned serious. 'Remember our deal, lover boy. You don't get to touch Lucy until after I've had my way with her. In the meantime, you can get your sexy wife to relieve the ache in your balls.'

Knowing the guys would not defile her for a while yet gave her a sense of relief. *I still have time in my favour.*

Once Michael had disconnected the video call, he handed her a fresh bottle of water. 'Impressive performance. You'd do well as a porn star. I bet Terry will beat off to the recording every night until he can fuck you for real.' Kneeling before her, he leaned in close. His t-shirt grazed her sensitive flesh as he spoke in her ear, 'You may have fooled Terry, but I'm still not convinced. Do anything stupid and not only is Nicole's life forfeit, but your debut will also hit every porn site across the globe. Is that clear?'

'Perfectly,' she deadpanned.

'Excellent. Here's what we're going to do. You'll have a shower and a bite to eat, then I'm taking you to see my friend on the police force. That's where you will go on record and amend your official statement regarding Terry. This is what I want you to say.' He retrieved a folded piece of paper from his breast pocket and handed it to her.

Her eyes bugged out as she read the false statement. 'You want to throw James under the bus? Why can't I tell them I lied?'

'Because then you'll be charged with perjury and risk gaol time. We can't afford the hassle. Terry is desperate to get his hands on you. Besides, this ties our last loose end in a nice little bow; one made with police tape. James can't come after you if he's in prison. Remember, if you stray from the script—'

'I know. You'll kill Nicki and turn me into an overnight sensation.'

'Oh, and if anyone asks—Nicki included—you now hate James for destroying your marriage and you've decided to travel the world with us to get away for a while. Now, let's get you cleaned up and ready for a meal with Nicki and me.'

❧❧

James

Leaving his SUV parked on the roadside, James marched alongside Russell and Adam as a united front. Gravel crunched under their feet as they followed the winding driveway. 'Do you remember the plan?' he asked in a hushed voice.

'Make sure the girls are safe,' Adam recited at the same volume level.

'And get Michael alone,' Russell finished, only partially louder.

Rounding an anti-clockwise hairpin bend that would have been a bitch to drive along, the house came into view. Although it was more like a sculpture made of coloured glass and steel. *Cindy would've loved this place before she discovered it was nothing more than a gilded cage designed to trap her*. His stomach turned as he considered the twisted scheme Michael and Terrance had concocted to lure her there. Surveying the wide frontage of the structure, he spotted a manicured clearing to his right with a couple of garden benches, and a carport to his left. A familiar black sportscar with the pretentious numberplate GAN6STA caught his eye. *Michael doesn't go anywhere without his shiny piece of compensation.* 'What's the best way in?'

Adam shrugged. 'I've only been here once before and it's not like I cased the joint.'

Stepping under the shade of the upper levels, he tried his luck with the glass doors. *Locked.* If he'd had a sledgehammer, he might have been able to smash through the glass. Then again, it's not wise to alert the arsehole to our presence yet.

'Let's try the back,' Russell suggested.

'Someone should stay here,' James insisted. 'In case they make a move.'

'I will,' offered Russell. 'I can make a bird call if I see 'em.'

'Or you could just prank our phones. I've got mine on silent, but it will still vibrate.' He glanced at the device to make sure he had enough bars of coverage. Good thing he switched providers for their business phones recently.

'Course,' Russell agreed as he ducked behind a gnarled tree with a thick trunk that provided a clear view of the front door.

'You take the left side and I'll take the right,' he whispered to Adam. 'And make sure your mobile is on silent like mine.'

With a nod, Adam adjusted his phone settings before creeping across to the opposite side of the building. They exchanged glances before he disappeared through the carport.

A twig snapped under his boot as he fought the foliage to find a path. Judging by the dense scrub, he doubted anyone approached the rear of the property this way. Still, he wouldn't put it past Michael to attempt an escape through the rugged terrain if he felt cornered. Half a minute later—still surrounded by bushland—his phone jerked to life, tickling his backside. Grabbing it, he took one look at Russell's name and dashed back the way he came. Bushes and tree limbs scratched his face and arms, but he didn't care. Nothing mattered more than Lucinda's safety.

When he reached the clearing out front, he spied the love of his life walking a foot ahead of Michael, who had his left arm around Nicole's waist. The group headed toward the carport, halting as soon as Adam appeared around the corner.

Lucinda gasped. 'I thought you left.'

'I did, but then I came back,' Adam replied. 'And I brought company.' He gestured to where James stood behind them.

She spun around and startled, yelling as he edged forward, 'Stop! Don't come any closer!!'

He froze and stared at her. 'What's wrong?'

'You are.' A scowl crept across her sweet face. 'I can't stand the sight of you anymore. You ruined my marriage!'

'What?' His heart shattered, its broken shards like daggers piercing his chest. 'I thought—'

'It's not true,' Adam interrupted. He had managed to gain a few paces, putting him in arm's reach of Lucinda. 'I'd like to give us another shot, Lucy. I'm sorry for running off like I did.'

James gaped at his brother wondering what changed his mind.

'Too little too late, Adam,' she hissed over her shoulder. 'You should have been there more all along. I stopped loving you years ago. Hence, I kept screwing James behind your back.'

What the hell? The buxom blonde standing before him looked like Lucinda, but she sure as heck didn't sound like the same woman.

'Nicole, you need to get away from Michael,' Adam warned. 'Your husband is not the man you think he is.'

544

Nicole's brow furrowed as Michael's grip tightened around her waist. 'What are you talking about?'

'Michael has been stalking Lucy, sending her threatening letters and explicit photos,' Adam explained.

Pushing Michael away, Nicole screeched, 'Is this true?'

'I have been getting letters from a stalker,' Lucinda confessed. 'But not from Michael.'

Nicole's shoulders relaxed and she let Michael snake an arm around her again. 'I can't believe you would keep something like that from me.'

'It's okay, Lucy,' Michael assured her. 'Why don't you tell them about your recent discovery?'

Lucida gulped and directed her gaze at Adam. 'The last time I visited James, I was using his laptop and… I found the original stalker letter files, plus digital copies of *all* the photos.'

'What? This is bull, Lucy. You know I'd never pull such shit! The jerk's trying to frame me.' James pointed an accusing finger at Michael. 'I don't know what you have over her, but this ends now!' He inched forward.

'Don't you dare come any closer!' Lucinda shouted.

Pulling a switchblade from his pocket, Michael held the steel blade against Nicole's throat. His hostage froze, the colour draining from her face.

Shit! This monster is savage.

'What the hell, Mike?' Nicole rasped with tears streaming down her face.

'You were only ever a means to an end, wifey poos. I have one true love and you ain't it. But if everyone plays nice, you get to live and hang out with your best friend. You can even watch Terry and me fuck her.'

James ran forward, his blood boiling at the thought of those two perverts touching his Cindy.

'Easy there tiger!' Michael shouted, pressing the switchblade into Nicole's flesh. 'You wouldn't want this chick's blood on your hands, would you?'

He stared desperately at Lucinda who shook her head. Torn between saving his woman and complying with her wishes, he halted. *Fuck!* He felt like such an idiot for believing Lucinda's hurtful words. She was doing it to protect her best friend.

'Geez, Lucy,' Nicole sobbed. 'Why does everyone want *you*?'

'Not everyone.' Russell emerged from his hiding spot behind the old tree.

Nicole's eyes lit up. 'You came back for me.' Twisting in Michael's hold, she tried to escape. She sprang free of his grip for a second and James held his breath, praying for her escape. But Michael seized her in a grapple. Both their arms flailed for several excruciating seconds, his knife nicking her a few times, until he punched her in the side of the head, and she crumpled to the ground.

'Oops.' Michael stared at his wife's unconscious form.

Russell charged at Michael, swinging a fist, and clocking him in the temple. The concussive blow knocked him out. Then Russell ripped his shirt off and dropped to his knees. Scooping Nicole into his arms, he applied pressure to her bleeding armpit with the balled-up shirt.

'Nicki!' screamed Lucinda as she flew toward her fallen friend.

James watched the scene unfold like a horror movie. There was so much blood.

'Snap out of it, you idiot!' Adam boomed in his ear. 'Deal with Michael while I call an ambulance.'

As he lifted Michael's unconscious body, and dragged him across the yard, a pair of handcuffs fell out of the man's pocket. Upon closer inspection, he realised they were the real deal, not just a sex toy. *Convenient. Saves me going back to the car for rope.* Propping his captive up on a garden bench, he threaded the cuffs through a support beam in the backrest. After binding Michael's wrists behind his back, he confiscated the creep's keys and returned to the others. He hovered beside Lucinda, who sat sobbing at Nicole's feet. 'Lucy?' he asked in a hesitant voice.

Springing to her feet, she launched herself into his embrace. 'I didn't mean any of it.'

He rubbed her back and kissed the crown of her head. 'I understand now. I'm sorry for doubting you, and for misunderstanding the situation. I love you, Cindy.'

'I love you too,' she mumbled into his chest, soaking his t-shirt with tears.

Adam glanced at them as he slid his phone back in his pocket. Something dark flickered in his eyes, hinting at a world of pain and hatred. Then his expression went blank, and he turned his focus back to Nicole. 'I'll help apply compression,' he offered, crouching beside Russell.

James wished he knew first-aid for broken hearts and damaged souls. He wanted to bandage the rift between him and his siblings, to heal the trauma Lucinda had suffered at the hands of so many monsters. Without a psychology degree, he felt next to useless. Instead, he did the one thing he knew he could, he did the one thing he had never truly done, speaking words no other woman had ever inspired in him. 'I promise to be here for you, Cindy. Always.'

Chapter Thirty-One

Lucinda

From her seat in the car, Lucinda stared at the Parkers' mansion behind its tall columns. The sun's final hoorah lent a golden hue to the white stucco siding. Only a week had passed since the incident with Michael, yet it felt like a lifetime ago.

Reaching across the centre console, James squeezed one of her trembling hands. 'Sure you're ready for this?'

'No,' she admitted. 'But I can't leave it much longer.'

When Annette greeted her in the grand foyer, she broke down. 'I'm so sorry,' she sobbed.

Wrapping her up in a hug, Annette hushed her. 'It's not your fault, darling.'

'C-can I see her?' she stammered.

'Of course.' Annette led her and James up the sweeping staircase and down a long hallway lined with cityscape photos from around the world. Stopping at the door beside *Melbourne at Dawn,* she knocked twice and opened it. Laughter trickled out of the open room as two cheerful faces turned to them. 'I have a couple of visitors for you.' She gave Lucinda a smile before leaving her to it.

Her eyes dropped to the sling around Nicole's right arm and everything else faded from view. 'Does it hurt?'

'Sometimes.' Nicole rose from her bed and shuffled forward. 'Most of the time I feel tingling and numbness.'

Her gaze snapped up to meet Nicole's. 'Numbness?'

Nicole nodded. 'The blade severed my axillary nerve. There's a good chance I'll recover from most of the damage with the right physio.'

The unspoken odds nagged at the back of her mind. *She might not be able to use her dominant arm ever again.* A lump formed in her throat as the tears escaped. 'I'm sorry, Nicki. For this and… for not coming to see you sooner.'

Nicole had spent most of the week in hospital, arriving home earlier that day. 'None of this is your fault, Lucy. As for visiting, well… it's not like I've lacked company.' She nodded toward Russell, alerting Lucinda to the burly man's presence. 'Russ hasn't left my side.'

Chuckling, James stepped out of the corner he hovered in. 'Wasting no time there, my friend.'

Nicole's face turned a lovely shade of magenta as Russell harrumphed. 'Don't know what ya talkin' 'bout, mate. I've been keepin' Nicki company while takin' my guard duties seriously. Can't be too careful if ya know what I mean?'

They all knew too well. Michael had ended up in a remand centre without bail because the justice had deemed him a flight risk. But Brooke and Terrance had both slipped through the cracks, which was one of the reasons Lucinda and James had spent the last week in hiding.

'It's good to see some colour in your cheeks,' James teased Nicole with a wink and the blush intensified. 'Especially after all the blood you lost.'

'They gave me a transfusion.' Focussing on Lucinda, Nicole added, 'I worried though, when you didn't visit. I thought you hated me.'

Her jaw gaped as a 'Why' came tumbling out.

'I knew something was up with Mi—' Nicole gulped, unable to complete the monster's name. 'I should have looked into it more.'

She shook her head. 'No, hun. I could never blame you for what those arseholes did to us.' She pulled Nicole into a sideways embrace, taking care to avoid disturbing her injured arm. 'I needed time to process things.' Registering the understanding in her best friend's eyes, she startled when her phone started buzzing inside her handbag. She glimpsed the unknown caller ID and rejected it. It rang again.

'See who it is,' James suggested. 'Then hang up if they're anyone suspicious.'

'Hello?' she asked warily.

'Mrs. Fairfax? This is Police Sergeant Wilkins.'

'Oh hi.' She breathed a sigh. 'What can I do for you, Sergeant?'

'This is a courtesy call. I thought you'd like to know Interpol picked up Terrance Bristow and they are extraditing him as we speak. Our plan to flush him out with word of Mr. Higgins' incarceration worked a treat.'

'That's a huge relief. Thank you.' Once the call disconnected, she found a text message from her doctor's clinic that made her heart race:

YOUR RECENT PATHOLOGY TESTS HAVE RETURNED. PLEASE MAKE AN APPOINTMENT TO DISCUSS THE RESULTS.

This could only mean one thing. Her doctor would not call her in if the results were negative. Tucking her phone back into her bag, she found everyone staring at her.

'What was that about?' James asked.

Her mind flooded with a million worst case scenarios. 'Huh?'

'What did the sergeant say?' he clarified.

'Oh right. They caught Terrance. He scurried out from under his rock to help his partner in crime. Sounds like things didn't work in his favour.'

Nicole grinned. 'Awesome! Two down, one to go.' She settled back down in her bed, letting Russell tuck her under the covers. 'What's the latest with Adam?'

Peering out the window, she admired the illuminated topiary in the manicured garden. 'He wants nothing more to do with either of us. Same goes for Michelle and Daniel.'

James tensed beside her at the mention of his parents. 'Dad even disinherited me.'

'Man, that sucks!' grumbled Russell who had returned to his armchair beside Nicole's bed. 'At least you have each other, right?'

Exchanging a glance with her, James smirked. 'Yeah, we do. No way in hell am I fucking up *this* chance with my Cindy.'

She lowered her gaze, fearing her news might change his mind and send him running for the slopes.

A loud yawn escaped Nicole. 'Sorry guys, but I need to call it a night. The pain meds make me super drowsy.'

They said their goodbyes with promises to catch up soon.

'Why do you seem distracted?' James asked as he closed Nicole's door.

'There's something... personal I need to discuss with you.'

He studied her a moment, his own expression sobering to match hers. 'You want to head back to the hotel?'

'Yes.' She followed him along the hallway, halting outside *the* room. 'Wait a sec.' The unassuming door loomed before her as though it hid every horror imaginable behind an inch of timber.

James circled his arms around her from behind. 'What's in there?'

'A bad memory,' she replied.

'Wha—' He stiffened. 'Oh. Is this where....'

'It is.'

'Come on, let's get out of here.'

As James tugged at her hand, she resisted. 'No. I need to do this.'

He stopped trying to drag her away but kept a hold of her hand.

'I haven't been able to enter this room since….' She swallowed. 'Since Terrance attacked me.' Taking a deep breath, she turned the knob and pushed the door open. Flicking on the light chased away the nightmares hiding in the shadows. The sitting room looked untouched by time. The same leather lounge set surrounded the empty fireplace. 'Let's talk in here.'

He gaped at her. 'Are you sure about this?'

Nodding, she led him inside. The closer she got to *that* spot, the faster her heart hammered against her ribs.

'Where?' James whispered.

She pointed to the floorboards in front of fireplace.

His strong, comforting arms enveloped her. 'You're safe now, sweetheart. Terrance and Michael are both behind bars.'

'Brooke's still loose,' she reminded him.

'So? What's she going to do? Assuming her goal was to get you away from Adam, she got what she wanted.'

Turning within James' embrace, she looked up into his eyes. 'I'm pregnant.'

His eyes widened, while his mouth clamped shut.

'Given the timing of our last tryst, I doubt the baby is yours, which means—'

'You'll make me an uncle rather than a father,' James finished. 'How far along?'

She shrugged. 'I did a home test kit five days ago, then went to see my doctor to confirm the positive result. I need to go back to review the details with her.'

'That's what your "routine check-up" was about?'

A pang of guilt cinched her heart. 'Sorry I didn't tell you earlier, but I wanted to be certain.'

'You don't seem happy about it. I thought you've wanted kids as much as your next breath.'

'I do, but I'm also scared. Like, what does this mean for us?'

James held her close. 'I promised to stick by you, Cindy, and I meant it. You don't need to worry about my work. Wherever my travels take me, I want you to come with me. As for your baby, I will help you raise this child whether I'm his daddy or not.' He laughed drily. 'Adam will blow a fuse when you tell him.'

'I can't,' she replied with a quavering voice. 'If the baby is his, there's a chance Brooke will come after us again.' She explained what she had learnt about Adam's history with Brooke and her motives for killing all the babies he had conceived ever since.

'Fuck! I had no idea he knocked her up.' James peered down at her with a frown. 'You're right though. The vindictive bitch would target the baby if it were Adam's.'

'What if we tell the world you're the father?'

'If that's what it takes to keep the kid safe.' His lips curled into a sly grin. 'We've already practiced lying to my brother for the last four years, so why not continue?'

She smacked his arm. 'You're such a scoundrel!'

'True, but you love me all the same.'

'I really do love you.' Pushing up on her tippy toes, she planted a soppy kiss on his lips.

James crushed her against his hard chest and deepened the kiss, leaving them both panting for breath. Mischief glimmered in his eyes as he asked, 'Want to overwrite your bad memories of this room with good ones?'

Her jaw dropped while heat pooled in her core. 'What if Annette catches us?'

'She won't if you keep quiet, or is that too *hard* for you?' He waggled his brows.

Unfastening his belt, she grinned up at him. 'Challenge accepted.' They sank to the floor and replaced the traumatic mental images of Terrance with ones of James making love to her.

ဆၢ

9 Months Later

Rebecca

Collapsing onto the sofa in her parents' front sitting room, Rebecca stared at the glossy card in shock:

> *It is with great joy that James and Lucinda*
> *Fairfax announce the arrival of*
> *Jackson Zachary Fairfax….*

Not a word from either of them had prepared her for the news. *I guess this explains why Lucy spent months hiding from the world.* She studied the photo of the chubby boy with a head of blond locks and chestnut eyes like James. Like Adam too.

There was no doubting the kid was a Fairfax. *But is James really his father?*

Adam waltzed into the room. 'Hey Becky, what have you got there?'

'I'm not sure you want to know.'

'Come on, how bad can it be?' He snatched the card from her hand and his smile vanished. 'What the heck? Why didn't you tell me she was pregnant?'

'I didn't know.'

'Yeah right,' he scoffed. 'You expect me to believe that? Didn't you visit them two months ago?'

'Lucy was staying with her parents. I haven't seen her since your split. I thought she was avoiding me because of… well you… and her guilt.'

Adam tossed the card aside, letting it flutter to the seat beside her. 'Next you'll be telling me they're married.'

'Won't happen,' she assured him. 'For one thing, you guys aren't officially divorced yet; secondly, James still doesn't believe in marriage.'

Sitting in one of the armchairs facing her, Adam sighed. 'Lucy must hate that.'

She shrugged. 'I can't say for sure, but James seems to think she is happy living in a de facto relationship.' Her heart ached for the crestfallen expression on Adam's face. 'You miss her, don't you?'

'Who are we missing?' Troy asked upon his return from the bathroom.

She handed him the mail she had opened in his absence.

'Ah hell! I'm sorry man. I know how much you wanted a kid of your own with her.' Returning the card, Troy perched beside Rebecca and draped an arm over her shoulders.

'Where are Mum and Dad?' Adam asked, deflecting the topic of his estranged wife and her new baby.

'They're changing for dinner,' she replied.

As if hearing their names, Michelle and Daniel appeared a second later, summoning them to the dining room.

'Let's start with Champagne,' Troy declared. 'Rebecca has an announcement to make.'

'Have we not heard enough of those already?' Adam huffed.

She offered him a sympathetic simper. 'This is good news I promise.' With all their glasses charged, she rose, holding her champagne flute. 'I have finally decided what I want to do with my life. Attending this support group for survivors of domestic abuse has opened my eyes to some

561

terrible truths. I want to help other people like myself, so I am going to be studying law at the University of Melbourne.'

'That's fantastic!' Mum sprang from her seat, rounded the table, and pulled her into a hug. 'Congratulations, honey. You will be a brilliant lawyer.'

'Thanks Mum. I couldn't have done it without the support you and Dad have given me. Thank you both for shifting your paradigms and accepting me for who I am.'

Adam stifled a snort, reminding her their father had not changed his views much. Her relationship with Troy was the only reason he had not kicked her to the curb along with James. That and the fact Brooke never got a chance to release her blackmail material before she went into hiding.

Crystalware chimed as they all toasted to her current and future success.

'I'd like to say a few words, if I may.' Troy stood, squeezing her shoulder. 'I have grown to love this extraordinary woman in every conceivable way, and not a day goes by when I don't thank God for her presence in my life.' Reaching for something in his pocket, he dropped to his knee.

She gasped at the enormous round diamond, easily three carats.

Troy peered deep into her eyes. 'Rebecca Michelle Fairfax, would you do me the honour of becoming my wife?'

Her beaming face must have put the sun to shame. 'Absolutely!' she squealed.

He slid the ring onto her finger and leaped into her arms. Their lips melded together in a kiss, sending tingles through her body until someone cleared his throat.

'Save it for the bedroom, kids,' Adam teased, prompting Troy to chuckle.

Mum tapped a spoon against her glass. 'This deserves another toast!'

Floating on cloud nine, she basked in her spotlight. She even smiled for Lucinda, both in anticipation of meeting her nephew, and because she knew how much her sister-in-law had wanted children. *Now I need to find a way to pull Adam out of his funk.*

Epilogue

*Warning: The following scenes contain **Crystal's Crucible** spoilers. I suggest reading that book before continuing with the last of this story.*

Brooke

The familiar *blat-blat-blat* of an exhaust brake woke Brooke from her afternoon nap. She hopped up from the couch and ran to the front of her alpine cottage. A frosty chill blasted her in the face as she opened the door, so she hugged her jacket tighter and raised the hood. Not willing to brave the last of the season's snow, she waited on the threshold for the courier to bring her supplies to the door. An older man hopped down from the driver's seat.

Looking in her direction, he flashed his teeth in a grin, and her stomach knotted.

No! Her first instinct was to flee, but where would she go? The only option was to fight, which meant she needed a weapon. She began backing away, keeping her eyes glued to the gun in his holster.

'Relax, pussy cat. I ain't gonna hurt you. I'm here to help.' His voice betrayed the hint of a foreign accent, although she could not quite place it.

'You expect me to believe you?' she scoffed. 'You're Adam's friend.'

He snickered. 'That's what he thinks. To me, he ain't nothing more than a means to an end. You, however, could be much more.'

A nervous laugh burst from her. 'Forget it. You're not my type.'

He cast an appreciative eye over her figure. 'Really? From what I've heard, you love fucking wealthy men in positions of power. But don't worry, I'm too faithful to my wife to have my way with you. When I say you could be more, I mean to suggest you and I become allies.'

'No thanks. I don't need your help.'

Inching forward, he smirked at her. 'Oh, but you do. If I was able to find you, it's only a matter of time before the police do. I can help you get out of Australia and escape to an extradition-free country; a place where you'll be free to walk around in public and live amongst society.'

Her heart skipped a beat at the very thought. Isolation had been a bitch, and she yearned for that sort of lifestyle again. 'What's in it for you?'

'I'm looking to strengthen my ties with the Russian mob. I want you to befriend the powerful families, marry into one if it takes ya fancy. Build yourself a whole new identity, then when the time is right, return home and claim the throne right alongside mine.'

She gaped at him. 'You're Russian?'

'No, pussy cat. My family hails from elsewhere. So, what do ya say?'

Genuine hope fluttered in her chest for the first time in months. 'Where do I sign?'

೮ಌ

12 years later

Jackson

Yanking his tie free, Jackson undid the top three buttons of his school shirt and tugged it over his head. The clothes joined the mess on the floor, and he flopped onto his bed. His phone chimed with a notification a few seconds later. Retrieving it from his pocket, he read the message from Mitchell:

HEY MY DUDE! CAN YOU UPLOAD THOSE PHOTOS FOR OUR HISTORY PROJECT? I'M AT DAD'S THIS WEEKEND AND FORGOT TO PACK MY LAPTOP.

Rolling his eyes, he typed out a reply: CAN DO. YOU STILL COMING TO THE GAME TOMORROW?

{MITCHELL} OF COURSE I AM. THANKS BRO.

He clambered out of the single bed that was almost too small for him, making a mental note to ask his parents for an upgrade. *I am in high school now, after all.* The scent of Mum cooking Tex Mex wafted down the hall while Amelia—his two-year-old sister—turned the pots and pans into a drum kit. With his mouth watering, and stomach growling, he ambled into the study. He couldn't be bothered setting up his own laptop, so he switched on the main PC and logged in to LUCINDA's profile. He'd figured out her password months ago. It wasn't hard. 'Jax10Ames20' wasn't exactly original material.

As he sifted through the OLD FAMILY PHOTOS folder, one directory caught his attention: ADAM AND LUCINDA'S WEDDING. *What the hell?* When he opened it, hundreds of smiling faces stared back at him. Sure enough, there they were: Mum and Uncle

Adam holding hands, exchanging rings, and—*Ick!* He skipped past the one of them kissing. No wonder Uncle Adam doesn't talk to Dad anymore.

When did they divorce? He searched through files until he found one titled DIVORCE CERTIFICATE. A double-click later and he stared at the date beneath his mother's name. Sixteenth of March 2011. *I would have been... five months old.*

'Dinner's ready!' Mum hollered.

'Dinah's reby,' Amelia echoed as she went to town on her makeshift snare drum.

Closing all the files, he shut down the computer and joined his family in the open plan living area.

Dad scooped Amelia up from the floor and carried her to the table. 'Come on my little rascal, it's time to eat.'

'I'm a wahskool!' she beamed, wriggling on her chair.

Snatching up a bowl of nachos, he claimed his usual spot across from his sister. He tuned out the noise and began connecting the rest of the dots: *I visit Uncle Adam almost as often as Mitchell sees his dad; Aunt Becky's kids don't visit him anywhere near as often; he was still married to Mum when I was born. Does that mean—*

'How was school today, Jax?' asked Mum, breaking his train of thought.

He shrugged. 'Okay I guess.'

Dad followed up the interrogation with, 'Looking forward to your softball match tomorrow?'

'Yeah.' He poked and prodded at his food.

Mum frowned at him. 'What's wrong, sweetie?'

Taking a deep breath, he blurted out, 'Why didn't you tell me Uncle Adam is actually my father?'

Her fork dropped and clattered against her bowl. 'How?'

'So, it's true?'

'Yes, it's true,' Dad confessed.

Or should I call him Uncle James now?

'We didn't even tell Adam,' Mum explained. 'He found out by… other means.'

He knew? And he didn't tell me! A sharp pain formed in his chest.

Mum shuffled her chair closer and placed a hand over his. 'Please don't get upset with Adam over this. It was my decision. I hid the truth to keep you safe.'

His eyes widened. 'Safe from what?'

'More like from whom,' she replied. 'I lied about your true parentage because someone mean and jealous was hurting all the babies I tried to have with Adam.'

He glanced at Amelia who smashed a piece of avocado against her mouth.

'Don't worry about Ames,' James assured him. 'I'm her bio dad. Brooke—the woman your mum refers to—wanted Adam for herself, to have her own kids with him.'

'Is that why you broke up?' he asked with a slight tremble in his voice.

Mum shook her head. 'No. Adam—your bio dad—and I separated because I fell in love with James. Adam never liked Brooke.'

A terrifying thought occurred to him. 'If this Brooke woman wants to hurt Adam's kids, is Crystal's baby at risk?'

'Huh. I didn't think of that.' Mum directed her gaze at James as if expecting him to know the answer.

James forced a smile more like a grimace. 'No one has seen Brooke around for years. She probably fled the country. I'm sure your little brother will be fine.' His words sounded hollow; his promise empty.

UNDENIABLY WRONG

If that nutjob tries anything on my brother and sister, I swear to God, I'll destroy her.

To be continued....

What's Next?

Thank you for reading *Undeniably Wrong*. Reviews are the lifeblood of authors, and they make a huge difference to the success of a book. Could you please post a review to one or more of the following sites?

- Goodreads
- BookBub
- Amazon
- Other Bookstores

The Phoebe Braddock Books continue with Jackson's story. I do not have a release date for this novel yet because I have not started writing it, but please stay tuned for updates.

Acknowledgements

Writing this book just about killed me! Quite aside from the serious case of writer's block I suffered half-way through the first draft, I struggled with the emotional rollercoaster it took me on. Thank you so much to everyone who waited patiently for me to finish the book. This was a very raw, personal journey for me as I explored aspects of my past and injected a huge dose of myself into the pages. I am so glad I did it though because I found the process therapeutic overall. There's nothing quite like writing a book to work through one's trauma.

I have a few brilliant beta readers I am grateful for. These guys did a marvellous job of pointing out errors and plausibility issues. Thank you so much Deborah Apodaca, Elli Morgan, and Felix Staica.

Let's not forget my amazing street team who are leaving shining reviews and sharing this book with the world.

The Phoebe Braddock Books
(Taboo Romance & Forbidden Love)

The Phoebe Braddock Books started as a budding idea while L. Starla drafted **I Heart Mr. Collins**. The protagonist of this story published a novel of her own, inspiring Starla to write the book that Phoebe wrote. The series has since grown into a rich universe of taboo romance, forbidden love stories, and reflections on difficult issues. While each book can be read as a standalone, existing characters will return in fourth title of the series and beyond.

I Heart Mr. Collins: Phoebe Braddock's Love Story

From Prying Eyes: A Phoebe Braddock Romance

Crystal's Crucible: A Phoebe Braddock Romance

Undeniably Wrong: A Phoebe Braddock Fiction

I Heart Mr. Collins

Phoebe Braddock's Love Story

Is it possible to find love without boundaries?

I might have described myself as innocent a few months ago, but that was before my schoolgirl crush turned into something real and passionate beyond my wildest imagination. Now my lustful appetite has awoken and there is no going back.

The problem is, no one else can know what I do when alone with Mr. Collins because it would jeopardise his career. Other people wouldn't understand what we have.

At least graduation is just around the corner, and I will strike off lying and deception from my current list of sins. That is my hope, but will I find the courage to be completely honest with everyone?

From Prying Eyes

A Phoebe Braddock Romance

Is the true expression of love really a sin?

Haunted by visions of a mysterious stranger making love to her in the dark, Sophie is torn between affections for the guy she's had a crush on for years and strong yearnings for the man of her dreams. And she can't shake the feeling that there is something familiar about her fantasy lover.

Then one fateful night, her dreams come to life at the debutante ball where Sophie is swept off her feet for several blissful minutes. But when the masks come off, she is forced to accept the shocking truth: her enigmatic lover is no stranger.

Does she deny her deepest desires or pursue a forbidden passion?

Crystal's Crucible

A Phoebe Braddock Romance

The laws of attraction are quite beyond science.

Crystal loved rules. A set of principles governed her life. That is why the physical sciences appealed to her. Logic and reasoning kept her afloat amidst the sea of family drama. Intimacy was not part of her equation; she had excluded that variable years ago after a string of disastrous relationships with men who wanted nothing more than sex.

The day she walked through the doors of Aludel Pharma, locking eyes with Adam Fairfax, everything changed. The chemistry between them brought her carefully constructed system crashing down around her. He was her boss, completely off limits. Crystal thought he was safe to admire from a distance. She was wrong. With the magnetism pulling them together, Crystal needed to choose which opposing rules she would break.

And she needed to act fast because a conspiracy was brewing in her department, threatening to bring her down or take her out.

Also By L. Starla

Winter's Magic Series
(Magical Realism / Paranormal Romance)

Winter's Maiden 1
Winter's Maiden 2
Winter's Thrall
Winter's Mother 1 (November 2022)
Winter's Mother 2 (May 2023)
Winter's Bride (November 2023)
Winter's Crone 1 (May 2024)
Winter's Crone 2 (November 2024)

Serial Fiction Boxsets
(Exclusive to Amazon and available on Kindle Unlimited)

Well I'll Be Damned Season 1
The Dark Matter Between Our Hearts Season 1

About the Author

L. Starla is an Australian author who often raided her mother's shelves for any form of fiction she could get her hands on. Her first love was the horror genre, but she owes her love affair with the romance novel to her high-school English teacher, who started her on the classics. Given her earlier reading, magical realism and paranormal romance were a natural progression. Along with steamy romance, these are the genres she writes.

Starla also loves spending her spare time playing tabletop and video games, paper crafting, singing, dancing, and watching anime.

Access Exclusive Content

Join my newsletter to access free stuff like short stories, deleted scenes, fan art, and invitations to future launch events.

Newsletter: www.starlaarts.com>freebies
Facebook Group: groups/l.starlareadersgroup

Follow me Online:
Website & Blog: www.starlaarts.com
Goodreads: L. Starla
BookBub: www.bookbub.com/profile/l-starla
Amazon Author Profile: author/l.starla
Instagram: L. Starla Author
Facebook: L.Starla
Twitter: @LStarla2019

www.ingramcontent.com/pod-product-compliance
Lightning Source LLC
Chambersburg PA
CBHW070148120726
47909CB00001B/25